Playing
the
Game

by

Graysen Morgen

2019

Playing the Game © 2019 Graysen Morgen
Triplicity Publishing, LLC

ISBN-13: 978-1-970042-05-4
ISBN-10: 1-970042-05-2

This is a work of fiction. Names, characters, places, and
incidents are the product of the author's imagination and
are used fictitiously. Any resemblance to actual persons,
living or dead, business establishments, events of any
kind, or locales is entirely coincidental.

Printed in the United States of America
First Edition – 2019
Cover Design: Triplicity Publishing, LLC
Interior Design: Triplicity Publishing, LLC
Editor: Megan Brady - Triplicity Publishing, LLC

Also by Graysen Morgen

Special thanks to my editor, Megan Brady, for her expertise with the story and with my mistakes! *Muchas gracias!*

For my wife.
Tu sei il mio mondo. Ti amo.

1

The bell jingled on the door of The Grind, a small locally owned coffee shop, when it opened. "Morning, Berkley," said Paul, the owner/operator. He waved in her direction and went to work making her an iced cinnamon and unsweetened almond milk latte.

"How's your week going?" she asked.

"Not bad. How are the streets?" he replied.

"Same shit, different day," she said, walking over to the newspaper lying on a nearby table.

Berkley perused the local news section, then turned back towards the counter, nearly dropping the paper from her hand as her eyes landed on a woman walking from the bathroom. Flip flops slapped the ground as she walked, and a nice pair of fit legs moved under a worn pair of cutoff jean shorts with the white pockets hanging down. Her heart rate increased as her eyes traveled over the tight black t-shirt that hugged a lithe torso and small round breasts. Long and wavy, dirty blonde hair cascaded over one shoulder. She could've easily been a model, as she looked like someone who had just stepped off the beach. They were in south Texas right outside of Austin, in a small city called Richey.

The stranger reached for a coffee cup sitting on the end of the counter and took a long swallow, before unceremoniously spitting it out...all over Berkley's white Nike t-shirt. "Ewww! This isn't mine," she grimaced.

"That's because it's mine," Berkley said as coffee dripped down the front of her shirt.

"You can have it," the woman said, handing her the cup.

Berkley's fingers tingled where they'd grazed the woman's as she took the cup.

"Randi, your iced double shot mocha is over here," Paul said, pointing to the other cup on the counter.

"Can I buy you another of whatever that is since I contaminated it?" Randi asked, feeling bad for spewing coffee all over her.

"Do you have any diseases or STDs I should know about?" Berkley questioned, looking directly at her pale green eyes.

"Why? I took a sip of your drink. It's not like we're going to have sex," she laughed.

"Well...we might," Berkley replied with a teasing grin that revealed a small dimple in her cheek.

Randi raised a brow and gave her the once over. She'd never seen this Berkley person before and was sure she would've remembered her if she had. Berkley was an inch, maybe two taller, but jacked and ripped like a Crossfit Pro or some other weightlifting athlete. The large muscles in her biceps and shoulders bulged under the form-fitting t-shirt and were covered in half-sleeve tattoos. The wet material hugged her torso like a second skin, revealing her chiseled chest, small breasts, and abs. A large black Nike check was spread across her front. A pair of black jogger pants hung off her hips, and a black snapback was turned backwards on her head, covering a tuft of short dark hair that was trimmed close on the sides and back, and cut into a faux hawk on top. Dark blue eyes stared back at Randi. She swallowed the lump in her throat and laughed.

"I'm sure your drink is fine…but I'm afraid your shirt is toast."

Berkley shrugged without breaking eye contact.

"I can make you another latte," Paul said, feeling slightly uncomfortable.

"I'm good," Berkley called. "I'm running late anyway." She watched Randi's eyes as she placed her lips on the straw where Randi's had been and took a long sip.

Randi watched her lick her lips as she pulled them from the straw.

Berkley smiled, flashing two rows of straight white teeth, before turning and walking out the door.

Randi's eyes followed her all the way out. "Who was that?" she mumbled to herself as she grabbed her own coffee. "Does she come here often?" she asked, looking back at Paul.

"Yeah, I see her a few times every other week." He shrugged. "About as much as I see you, probably." He smiled.

"Thanks." She grabbed her own coffee and walked away.

When she stepped outside, Berkley was gone, and so was the custom, flat-black-painted, Ducati Monster sport bike that had been parked right up front. The sound of a motorcycle roaring in the distance was all the proof Randi needed. She shook the woman from her head and walked to her car.

2

"What happened to you, Ward?" a guy chuckled as Berkley walked by. "You're late."

"Keep it up, Tomato, and I'll make sure you drop that weight you're trying to lift," she chided with a grin.

"At least tell me she was hot."

"Aren't they always?" she called over her shoulder as she turned on her headphones, blaring an intense rock song in her ears. She took a few deep breaths and began her rigorous workout routine. She alternated between circuits of lifting heavy weights and Crossfit routines to keep her body in amazing shape. She was as strong or stronger than most of the men she knew, and several of her peers envied her workout discipline.

"You ever going to stop playing the game?" the guy asked, spotting her when she moved to the weight bench after her warmup.

Berkley looked up into his eyes as she raised the bar over her chest and back down again. Garrett Tamayo, mostly known as GT or Tomato, was her best male friend. She literally trusted him with her life. He knew her well…almost too well. Ignoring his question, she continued with her reps until her arms shook. He spotted the bar as she placed it back in the rack.

Berkley sat up and turned around, facing him. He had two inches of height on her and his body was stacked like hers from the hours and hours they spent in that gym.

"If you're asking if I want to stop dating and get serious with someone…the answer is yes. Isn't that the goal…to find the woman you can't live without?"

"Before I met Dena, I was a man-whore. So, I know what you mean. I'm just busting your balls." He grinned.

"Grab that bar again before this gets anymore mushy, and keep your balls away from my forehead, got it?"

"What…no teabags for you?" he laughed, moving into position near her head to grab the bar.

Berkley glared up at him and rolled her eyes as she began bench pressing the heavy weights once more.

*

Randi had finished her small coffee by the time she pulled her white BMW into her driveway. She pressed the button for the garage and watched it rise, revealing a black Audi crossover SUV. She drove in, parking next to it. She sighed as sat she in her car with the engine off. She needed to get the stranger *Berkley* off her mind. Chances were, she'd never see her again.

"You're back early," Randi called, as she walked into the house, placing her keys and small purse on the counter.

"It doesn't take long to do a physical," another woman said, as she entered the room from the hallway. The three-bedroom house had an open floor plan, with the kitchen looking out over the living area. "I thought we were meeting at the practice field?"

"We were, but I had to run back by the house," Randi said, as she pecked her on the lips. "Did you get cleared?"

"Yep."

"Fully?"

"Uh huh. I'm good to go. The ankle is back to normal."

"That's great, babe." Randi looked at her girlfriend of five years and smiled. Olivia Zeller, better known as Liv, was a few inches taller with an athletic body like her own. Her messy brown hair was trimmed short around her neckline and ears, but was long enough on top to wear it in different ways depending on her mood, and she had big brown eyes that looked like balls of milk chocolate. She was tan from countless hours in the sun, but her skin wasn't naturally golden like Randi's.

"I already talked to MJ," she said, referring to Mitch Johnson, their coach. "I'll probably be back in goal this weekend."

"Really? You're just coming back from an injury."

"I've been training for three weeks. I'll be fine," Olivia said.

Randi shook her head as she walked down the hall to grab her cleat bag. Olivia was waiting in her vehicle when she stepped outside.

*

The fifteen-minute ride to the field gave Randi time to think as she listened to the music playing on the radio. Olivia was a grown woman. If she wanted to be hardheaded and push herself too far, there was nothing Randi could do about it. She loved her, she always had, and if she got hurt again, Randi would be there for her. They had five years together, in what had started out as friendship and quickly turned into a relationship. It was comfortable, and it fit. The people close to them knew about them, but they'd never really made any kind of announcement, and had never really planned on it either. They were in the spotlight enough as it was with both of them being professional soccer players for the same women's pro team, Richey FC. Social media hadn't helped matters, but at the same time, neither woman had ever denied the claims. And posting pictures together had certainly fueled the rumors over the years.

3

Berkley stepped out of the shower feeling refreshed after the hot spray not only woke her up, but soothed her sore muscles. She tied the towel around her waist and put on her black sports bra before squirting some gel in her hands and running it through her dark hair, styling the perfect faux hawk. The deep blue eyes staring back at her looked tired. She silently wished for another cup of coffee, and that brought on thoughts from earlier that morning at The Grind. She was still surprised at the stranger...*Randi*. She pushed the woman from her mind, knowing she'd probably never see her again as she hung up the towel and pulled on a pair of gray underwear, followed by a pair of black polyester pants. Sitting on the ottoman at the foot of her bed, she leaned over, putting on a pair of long black socks. A platinum Saint Michael pendant dangled on a chain around her neck as she slipped her feet into a pair of shiny black tactical boots that zipped along the inside. Then, she pulled on a black, dri-fit undershirt with the Richey PD logo over the left breast, tucking it into her pants as she stood up. She walked over to the chair in the corner and grabbed her black, tactical-style bullet proof vest. She put her head through the hole in the middle and pulled it down to her shoulders with the vest covering most of her upper torso in the front and back. Once she had it in a comfortable position, she closed the large Velcro straps on her sides. She finished her work ensemble with the uniform shirt that matched her pants. It had a starched high collar, a square pocket over each breast, a pen slip, and buttons down the front, which were actually fake and hiding a zipper. She tucked the tails of the shirt into her pants and slipped her black, web style belt through the loops, fastening it in the front.

Berkley paused in front of the floor to ceiling mirror. A silver badge was sewn on her shirt above the left breast pocket. The State of Texas symbol was in a circle in the center of the badge patch. The words Officer and Richey were above the circle, with Police Department under it. Another patch with City of Richey Police Department was on the outside center of both of her short sleeves. B. Ward was stitched in silver above her right breast pocket. A small red, white and blue emergency star of life symbol patch, about the size of a quarter, was sewn above her name. Satisfied with her uniform, Berkley reached for her tactical utility belt and eased it around her waist, settling the weight of the heavy belt onto her hips before fastening the heavy Velcro closure across the front. She felt around, checking each compartment. Two fully loaded 9MM magazines were in the front. A pair of gunmetal gray handcuffs were in a case at the center of the back. A flashlight was on the front right side beside the magazines. She grabbed her walkie talkie radio and slipped it in place in the center of her right side, opposite the empty gun holster on the left. Then, she brought the microphone cord up under her arm, clipping it to the strap on the top of her right shoulder board. She stretched a little, making sure everything was in place and she could move freely, before walking to her nightstand to retrieve her Glock 9MM handgun. She slipped it into the holster on her left side and snapped the enclosure strap over the grip of the handle.

"Be safe," she said to herself in the mirror, then she placed a kiss on her pendant, tucking it behind her undershirt as she left the room.

*

A shiny black Dodge Charger with Richey Police written in large, bright blue letters along both sides, was backed up in the wide driveway next to a black truck. The red and blue emergency lights were inside of the police car at the top of the windshield and back window, and the windows were tinted very dark, giving it the look of an unmarked car from the front and back.

Berkley hit the button to unlock the door, then she slid down into the seat and started the engine, blasting the AC to cool off the inside of the car. She tossed a blue soft-sided cooler containing her lunch, snacks, and three bottles of water, onto the passenger seat before turning her car's laptop computer on. She quickly signed on when the screen came up and drove off as it came to life with the latest calls for her district of the Richey Police Department. Her shift had officially started, but she still needed to go to the station for the shift change, roll call, and shift assignments.

4

"So, funny story," Randi said as she pulled her left cleat on. She was sitting in the locker room with most of the team. Everyone was in various stages of dress as they prepared for their practice session. "I spewed coffee all over a stranger," she finished.

"No shit?" said Carrie Nipper, a midfielder for the team and Randi's best friend.

"No shit," Randi replied, shaking her head. "I pretty much ruined her white Nike shirt."

"Oh, my God," several players said in unison as they laughed.

"Was she hot?" asked Sasha Wright, the best defender on the team.

Randi shrugged.

"You didn't tell me about this," Olivia added.

"You were too busy telling me you got cleared to play." Randi smiled.

"Yeah!" the team cheered, as this was their first time hearing the news.

"I'm back, bitches!" Olivia yelled.

"On the field in two," the assistant coach called.

Most of the girls walked out together while the stragglers finished dressing.

Olivia and Randi had always made it a point to treat each other as teammates on the field. As soon as they hit the bright green grass of the practice pitch, they went in opposite directions. Olivia's three hours were spent with the goalkeeping staff doing everything from weight training, to shuffling sprints while catching an incoming ball.

The rest of the team was gathered around the other end of the training area. They always started with an easy warm up that increased in speed and control as they moved through the motions. Once their leg muscles were heated and their heart rates were up, they moved onto passing drills, followed by mini sprints, and then more passing.

Randi always wore her hair up in a ponytail, but occasionally when her wild mane was bothering her, she'd fashion it into a messy bun that always seemed to stay together. This was one of those days. It was only May, but the Texas heat was in full swing…even at ten a.m. She wiped the sweat from her brow as she ran to trap a pass and sent it over to Sasha, who quickly passed it to Carrie.

After several minutes, MJ grouped them into small teams for a four versus four small-sided game. One team had their practice jerseys which were baby blue with the club logo in yellow above the left breast and their numbers in yellow on their backs. The other four teams had different color pennies over their jerseys to indicate a different team. One group had white, and the other three had purple, pink, and yellow.

"White versus blue. Let's go!" Mitch yelled.

Carrie, Randi, and Sasha were paired together, along with another midfield player named Jorja. The four women ran around the quarter-sized field, working the ball in and out of traffic. Carrie crossed the ball from the outside. Randi cut between two players and met the ball, scoring easily.

"Purple and pink," Mitch called. Two new sets of teams took the field while the others stepped aside for water before moving to the passing drills that the assistant coach was running.

Once all the groups had played one small-sided game, Mitch brought the two fastest scoring teams back to play each other while everyone else ran through more passing, defending, and shooting drills. Randi's group was up again. This time, Carrie scored after only two passes. Thus, ending the small-sided game drill.

*

An hour and a half later, the women rushed through their showers and cleaned up their locker areas, before moving on with the rest of their day. Randi was thankful the coach had canceled the team meeting. Otherwise, they would've had a team lunch and then sat around for another two plus hours looking at film and discussing their next opponent.

"How did the ankle hold up?" she asked, sliding into the passenger side of Olivia's SUV.

"Fine," Olivia said, smiling at her. "I wasn't as rusty as I probably should've been because I started training weeks ago."

"That's good. Did you have an idea about lunch? I'm starving."

Olivia shrugged. "I thought Carrie invited us to join her and Anna at that new Mexican place."

"That's dinner tomorrow night," Randi corrected. "I think most of the team is going, actually."

"Cool. How about that soup and sandwich place on Golden Trail, for lunch?" Olivia said, changing lanes.

"Fine with me."

"You never finished your story from this morning."

"What story?"

"The Grind?"

"Oh," Randi laughed. "There were two cups on the counter apparently. I only saw one, which I grabbed and took a long sip. I don't know what it was, but it certainly wasn't what I'd ordered. I spit it out as fast as I'd sipped it. I also happened to spit it all over the woman who had ordered it." She shook her head, thinking about the debacle.

"Ohhhhh. I bet she was pissed," Olivia chuckled.

"Surprisingly, no. She even kept the drink. The owner tried to give her a new one. Hell, I tried to buy her a new one, but she was fine with it. I know I ruined her shirt."

"Maybe she was a fan and was trying to get your cooties," Olivia teased.

"She had no idea who I was, so it wasn't that. I've never seen her before."

"It was probably one of those cosmic fluke things."

"Cosmic?" Randi raised a brow. "You mean karmic? Like karma related?"

"Whatever the hell it's called."

"Who knows. I'll probably never see her again. I'm over it."

"I hope this place isn't busy," Olivia said, changing the subject as she turned into the parking lot.

5

"That old fucker puts me to sleep," Garrett said, referring to Lieutenant Lawrence Cooper as he bumped shoulders with Berkley on the way out of the roll call room.

"Coop's a good guy. He's just biding his time until he retires. But, I agree, his lame jokes need some work," Berkley replied.

The hot sun was still high in the sky at the start of their 6 p.m. to 6 a.m. shift. Beads of sweat bubbled on her forehead as she walked across the parking lot to her squad car. She climbed in and started the engine, turning the AC dial to full blast, before getting out and checking her trunk to make sure her rifle was loaded, and her emergency bag was stocked.

"Watch your six," Garrett said through his open window as he pulled up behind her car.

"You too," she said, bumping fists with him before walking back to the driver's side of her car. He drove away as she climbed in.

*

Garrett and Berkley worked in the South 5 District and patrolled two adjoining sections, so they were often each other's backup, as well as backup to the rest of the officers in their district if there was a serious situation.

The start of their shift was usually light, with most people getting home from work. Once the sun went down around 8:30 p.m. the calls picked up and remained heavy until around four in the morning. Weeknights were hit and miss with major calls, but the weekends kept them on their toes. Richey, Texas had a lower crime rate than the surrounding, larger cities, but they had their share of the drug trade, as well as the usual domestic calls, traffic accidents, disturbances, and so on. The police department worked in twelve hour shifts with three days on and four days off, then four days on and three days off.

Berkley pulled off a main road and drove through a predominantly Hispanic neighborhood area called the Valley. The distinct beat of salsa music could be heard in the background and children played in the streets. She rolled her window down, waving at the little ones, as well as a few parents who were sitting out on their porches. She made it a point to make her presence known, hoping it would deter bad situations in certain areas and make the children comfortable seeing the police.

Her computer beeped with a new call for her district. Anytime dispatch had a new call, it was automatically input into the system making it pop up on all the patrol car computers. If the call was in an officer's district or if an officer needed back up, their computer alarm would sound, alerting them to the call, and it would come across their radio.

The new line on the screen read: 10-21 Domestic Assault - 7768 High Ridge Rd.

Berkley grabbed the radio mic attached to the side of the computer stand and squeezed the button with her thumb. "327—responding to High Ridge Road. I'm two blocks out." She'd already flipped the switch for her lights and sirens and was heading to the other side of the Valley by the time she clipped the mic back in its holder.

"414—327, you want company?" Garrett called over the radio.

"Standby—414," she answered back as she pulled up in front of the house. No one was outside. "327—on scene," Berkley radioed, using the mic clipped to the shoulder strap on her uniform as she got out of her car.

"He's gone," a Hispanic woman said as she opened the door.

Berkley was still walking up the driveway. "Where did he go?"

"I don't know. The titty bar probably," the woman huffed, crossing her arms.

Berkley nodded. "Did he hit you?"

"No. He just yells."

"We got a call about an assault. Are you sure he didn't hit you?"

"Yes. I would know if he hit me. I'm fine."

"Want to tell me what happened?"

"Nothing. I don't want to press charges or anything. My nosy neighbor is who called you. You can go. He's not here."

There was nothing more she could do, so Berkley told her to call back if things became heated when he got home. Then, she headed back to her car. "Cancel the 10-21 on High Ridge," she radioed before getting into her car.

"Copy—327," the dispatcher radioed back.

Berkley pulled out of the Valley just before her computer alarm sounded again. This time, an accident with injuries was reported. She grabbed the mic and flipped the switch for the lights and sirens. "327—responding to the MVA on Crescent," she said, as she sped around two cars.

A third car didn't seem to care that her lights were flashing and the sirens were wailing. "Move, asshole!" she growled before checking her mirror and screeching down the turning lane past him.

By the time she made it to the scene, Garrett was there assessing the two vehicles. The ambulance pulled up right behind her. Berkley maneuvered her car to block traffic, routing them to the outside lane around the wreckage. Then, she climbed out and walked over to him.

"Whatcha got, GT?"

"Witness says this red car turned in front of the blue SUV. Driver of the car is complaining of back pain. Guy in the SUV is fine," he said. "How'd it go with the DA?"

"I honestly have no idea. She and her husband had an argument, I guess. He hauled ass to the titty bar, and the nosy old lady next door called us because they were yelling at each other outside."

Garrett raised a brow, then laughed. "I knew I should've responded with you."

"Yeah, well, now you have this mess to straighten out."

A pretty, Hispanic woman with long dark hair wrapped up in a tight bun, walked over to them. She was wearing a paramedic uniform and had a stethoscope around her neck. D. Hernandez was stenciled on her nametag. "We're going to transport the lady in the red car," she said.

Garrett nodded.

"You left dishes in the sink, by the way," she said to him.

Berkley laughed.

"Oh, you don't get off easy either. Why didn't you tell me about this mysterious coffee incident this morning?

Who is she? And what does she look like?" the woman chided, looking directly at Berkley.

"Seriously? Do you tell her when you piss, too?" Berkley shook her head.

Garrett shrugged and rubbed his hand over his closely shaved head. "She's my girlfriend. I tell her everything."

"And I'm *your* best friend, at least the last time I checked," the woman said, waiting with her arms crossed. "I need to get my patient to the hospital, so you have about thirty seconds."

Berkley laughed, knowing she was right. "Dena, it wasn't anything. I don't know who she is. She grabbed the wrong coffee and proceeded to spit it out when she took a sip…all over me, of course. We didn't exchange information. I'll probably never see her again."

"Uh huh," Dena mumbled, checking her watch.

"We're ready when you are," the other medic called from the side door of their rig.

"I gotta go. You two be safe. I love you both," she said before hurrying off to drive the ambulance.

"She's a piece of work," Berkley chuckled.

"She's *your* best friend."

"So are you. But, she's *your* girlfriend."

"You introduced me to her!" he laughed. "It's your fault."

"Well, I'd suggest you wash your dishes before I have to make a domestic call to your house because she kicked your ass!" she teased.

"Get out of here. I have work to do."

"Yep. Glad it's you and not me." She grinned and headed back over to her car to check the computer and see where she was headed to next.

Garrett and Dena were right, they were her best friends, and they were perfect for each other. The best thing she could've ever done was set them up three years earlier.

6

"I hate road games," Randi mumbled to herself as she pulled into a parking space in front of The Grind. Most of the team, including Olivia, was still packing for the two-day trip up to Chicago, and their flight was scheduled to leave in less than three hours.

The door jingled as she walked in and made her way over to the counter. It was mid-morning, her favorite time to go because the early rush had come and gone.

"Good morning," Paul said with a big smile. "The usual?"

"Yeah, add a chocolate chip muffin, too," she replied. "Wait, make that two muffins."

"Sure thing."

While she waited, Randi turned around, noticing the mysterious woman from two days earlier. She was sitting at one of the small round tables, reading the newspaper.

"Who reads the physical newspaper anymore?" Randi said, taking the seat across from her.

Berkley folded the paper and laid it down. "I do. There's news in here you won't find on your phone," she replied, grabbing her coffee cup. "Here, let me move this so that I'm not wearing it in a minute."

"Funny," Randi said with a sarcastic grin.

"Randi, you want both of the muffins chocolate chip? We have banana nut and blueberry," Paul called as he set her coffee on the counter.

"Chocolate is fine," she answered as she walked over to get her coffee and the muffins, which Paul had put into a small container.

"I don't think I've ever met another female named Randi," Berkley said as she walked back over, stopping next to the table.

"I could say the same for Berkley."

"My parents were in school there when they got pregnant with me," Berkley said with a shrug.

"Randi is short for Miranda, but I've been called Randi my entire life."

Berkley nodded as a grin spread across her face, revealing her dimples. Her playful blue eyes perused Randi's body before landing on her eyes.

"What?" Randi asked with a raise brow.

"You still owe me a shirt."

"What? No, I don't," Randi guffawed.

"How about lunch instead?"

Randi laughed and shook her head. "I can't. I have to catch a flight."

"Dinner when you get back?"

"I'm with someone," she said solemnly.

"I didn't ask you to have sex," Berkley teased. "Go on. Have a safe flight."

"Maybe I'll see you again...sometime," Randi said before walking away. As soon as she got into her car, she looked back at the door, hoping Berkley would've followed her out. *Damn it. What are you doing?* she chastised herself as she started the engine and drove away.

*

Olivia's head lulled to the side, landing on Randi's shoulder as the plane shuddered with a bit of turbulence.

"I don't know how she does it," Carrie said, from the opposite side of the aisle. The team and coaching staff were scattered around the coach section of the commercial airliner. Olivia, Randi and Carrie were lucky to be in the same row.

"She can sleep anywhere," Randi said, flipping through the pages of the magazine she'd purchased in the airport. She was quite used to her girlfriend falling asleep next to her. It didn't matter if they were traveling around the world or watching TV on the couch. Olivia had no problem taking a nap.

"I know. I'm pretty sure she'd pass out on the back of a camel crossing the desert," Carrie laughed.

Randi nodded in agreement.

"Have you seen your coffee shop friend again?"

"As a matter of fact, I have," Randi replied nonchalantly as she sniffed the perfume sample on one of the pages and wrinkled her nose in dislike.

"And…"

"And what? She was there this morning. I said hi. It's not like we've become best friends or are going on a date. I don't see the big deal." Randi closed the magazine and leaned forward to stow it in the seat pocket in front of her, forgetting about Olivia lying against her until her head slumped off her shoulder, instantly waking her.

"Are we almost there?" Olivia asked, stretching as much as she could in the small seat.

"Sorry, babe." Randi smiled at her.

"Ladies and gentlemen, we will begin our descent into Chicago momentarily. Please return your seatbacks and tray tables to their proper position," the flight attendant said across the speaker.

"I guess so," Olivia mumbled, answering her own question. She reached for her phone and took a quick selfie of her and Randi and posted it on her Instagram account with the caption: *Chicago here we come!* They had never publicly announced that they were together, but it was a known fact that they lived together. Most of their fans assumed they were in a relationship and had dubbed them with the hashtag #RanOli, which both women hated. Neither woman had posted or announced anything to prove otherwise in the beginning. The posted pictures of them together on and off the field, and vacationing in the off-season had only added fuel to the fire. They both had thousands of fans around the world and all over Texas who followed their social media accounts religiously. After a while, they no longer cared, and sharing their life became second nature.

As the plane taxied to its gate, the players all took turns making silly faces or posing their fingers in a peace sign as Olivia held her phone up, making a video for her Instagram.

Randi pushed her hair back from her left shoulder, and twisted it into a loose bun, held together with a hair tie. Then, she stuck her magazine into the front pocket of her carry-on bag and got in line to get off the plane.

The team was halfway through the season and looking for wins in their next two road games after having won the last two at home. They were sitting in third place in points, but it was anywhere but comfortable when the three teams below them were all tied for fourth.

"Let's get to the hotel and rest up. We'll have a short training session before dinner, then spend tomorrow morning energizing and prepping for the game at three. We have a nine o'clock return flight," Mitch said, gathering his players near the baggage claim area, although no one had checked a bag. "The bus should be outside waiting," he added, looking at his watch before leading the way outside.

A group of about thirty fans were near the bus, wearing the signature baby blue and yellow of Richey FC and cheering for their favorite players. They were diehard members of the fan club who traveled to every away game and led the drum line at the home games. The players always made time for their biggest supporters.

The team wasn't allowed to sign autographs anywhere except the field, but they always walked over to give high fives and take selfie photos, especially Randi and Olivia, whom all the lesbian fans swooned over.

7

Randi walked into her room, flopping down on the bed nearest the window. None of the clubs allowed players who were in a relationship to room together, so Randi and Carrie were roommates, and Olivia roomed with either Jorja or Sasha. She spread the heavy drapes. The late afternoon sunlight was trying to peek through the remainder of the dark clouds as they floated away.

"I feel like a drowned rat," Carrie called as she went into the bathroom. A large rainstorm had dumped water like a mini monsoon during their practice session. With no lightning in the area, they were able to continue. "I'm pretty sure we would've needed paddles if we'd stayed any longer," she added.

Randi laughed and got up to answer the knocking at the door as the shower began running. Olivia was leaning against the wall on the opposite side of the hall, looking freshly showered. She was wearing jeans, a white blouse with a round collar and three-quarter sleeves rolled back to her elbows, and Birkenstock sandals. The top four buttons of her shirt were open, showing off an expanse of tanned, smooth skin. Her damp hair was styled slightly messy, with the longer pieces tucked behind an ear.

"You look like Victoria Beckam." Randi smiled.

"Wish I had her money," Olivia laughed.

"Right," Randi agreed. She checked to see if anyone else was out and about before crossing the hall. She leaned on her toes to kiss her lips briefly. "Carrie called the shower first...so, I'll be a while."

"Jorja was almost finished. You can use ours if you want."

"I'm good. I'll see you at dinner. Save me a seat."

Olivia nodded.

Randi watched her walk towards the elevator. As soon as the door closed, making Olivia disappear, a door down the hall opened. Jorja stepped out wearing jeans, a stylish tank top, and strappy sandals. Her copper-colored hair was pulled back in a ponytail.

"She just got into the elevator," Randi said.

"Let me guess, you're waiting on Carrie?"

"Is that anything new?" Randi laughed.

"I heard that!" Carrie said, pulling their door open. She was wrapped in a towel. "You can have the shower now, princess," she teased.

Randi rolled her eyes.

Jorja laughed as she headed down the hallway.

"I shower first because it takes me longer to do my hair," Carrie added when Randi stepped into the room.

"I know that. I'm just messing with you. How long have we had this arrangement?"

"Since college...and you're still an ass," Carrie called as Randi ignored her, shutting the door.

*

Randi stood next to Olivia, with the rest of the starters to her left as the national anthem played to a packed stadium. As the captain and co-captain of the team, the two of them walked over for the coin toss after their pictures were taken.

"Ladies, we didn't come here to lose. We didn't come here to tie. No. We came here to leave with three points!" Olivia shouted from the center of the team circle. "Play hard. Play tough. Play for that group of Richey fans who drove all the way up here! Win on three!"

Randi held her hand with the group and shouted, "Win!" She fist-bumped Olivia's gloved hand before running out to her place at the midfield line. They had the ball first, and as a forward and co-captain, she always started play. She quickly kicked the ball over to Carrie. The game had begun.

*

Chicago came at them hard scoring on Olivia after a bad pass was collected, leaving her in a one on one situation and off her angle, but Richey fought back when Carrie sent in a beautiful cross that Randi put in the back of the net. Both teams raced up and down the field, losing and winning the ball over and over again. Richey took three more shots, two of which the Chicago goalkeeper stopped, and one that was wide. Chicago only had one other significant shot on Olivia, which she stopped. The rest of their six shots were either wide or too high.

After halftime, the stadium became roaring loud. The score was tied at one all, but Chicago's fans were resilient, just like their team. The Richey players fought hard. Randi had two defenders on her, making it difficult to get a shot off. Jorja set her up twice with great crosses, but she couldn't get on them. They also missed a corner kick opportunity when a bad referee call led to a penalty kick in the ninetieth minute, allowing Chicago to score.

With one minute of overtime to go, Sasha played the ball from the back, dribbling up the left sideline. She sent the ball inside to Carrie, who passed it out wide to Randi before making a run up the center of the field. Randi dribbled around her defender and crossed the ball in front of Carrie, but a tackle from behind sent her tumbling. The referee blew his whistle…ending the game.

The Richey players gathered in front of their bench, shaking their heads and talking about the horrible calls by the referee.

"Where the hell was the penalty when I got bulldozed in the box just now?" Carrie growled.

"That asshole controlled the entire game, but there's nothing we can do now…except stomp them when they come to our house!" Randi said.

"We have better things to do. We can beat this dead horse when we get home," Olivia said, ushering the team towards the small group of people wearing the baby blue and yellow colors of Richey FC, who stood out like a sore thumb in the sea of white.

Randi posed for selfie pictures with whoever yelled for her and even signed a few Chicago jerseys. Olivia signed her gloves and gave them as a thank you to two of the diehard fans who had made the long trip. Then, she caught up with Randi, posing briefly as phones clicked away. Anytime they were talking to each other or even standing near one another, their fans went nuts.

"I thought for sure he was going to bust me," a Chicago player said, catching up to Carrie and Randi in the middle of the field. They were old friends from their college days playing together at Texas. "I came in way too hot," she laughed.

"Yeah, no shit. You damn near flattened me." Carrie smiled and shook her head as she hugged her friend.

"You guys played good, but you had a little help," Randi teased, also hugging her.

"I know," the other girl laughed. "A bunch of us are going to dinner at Peppo's. They have the best Italian food in town. Come with us. We'll pick you up."

"We can't. We're flying back tonight."

"Oh, that sucks. Don't you usually stay over?"

"Yeah," Randi said, adding, "we have a mid-week game on Wednesday, so tomorrow is our only day off."

The girl nodded. "That makes sense. I love you both. I'll see you soon."

"Yep," Carrie called as they separated. "One month, to be exact."

The girl laughed and waved.

"Come on. If we don't hurry up, we'll be eating fast food for dinner," Randi muttered as they walked towards the exit area of the field.

"The airport has an Irish pub. I wouldn't mind going there," Carrie replied.

"Sasha heard we were going to some pizza joint," Olivia said, catching up and throwing her arms over their shoulders as she squeezed between them. "But I'd vote for McDonald's over airport food."

"Gross," Randi cringed.

"You go have your McHeartAttack. I'll take my chances with the airport," Carrie added.

"I'm with you. An Irish Pub sounds wonderful," Randi said.

"Traitor!" Olivia laughed.

"Ugh. How do you put up with her?" Carrie teased.

"Wouldn't you like to know," Olivia replied slyly, wiggling her eyebrows.

"You both drive me crazy," Randi chuckled, shaking her head as she pulled away from them and entered the locker room.

*

"How is your ankle?" Randi asked as the plane leveled out at 27,000 feet.

"It's fine. Back to normal," Olivia sighed, staring out the window at the darkness.

Randi squeezed her hand. "It was tough today. We'll bounce back."

"I still hate losing. Especially to them." Olivia kept a hold of her hand as she closed her eyes.

Randi nodded in agreement. She knew all too well how much Olivia Zeller hated losing, especially to Chicago because of their coach. He'd drafted her out of college with a different team, then put her on the bench behind another keeper, before trading her the next season. Randi thought back to the full-blown temper tantrum Olivia had thrown three years earlier during her second season with Richey, causing her to be suspended by the league for two games, and get a stern talking to from their club owner. Randi was sure they were going to fire her, but once everything cooled down, the team hired a new goalkeeping coach. He grew close to Olivia and helped her learn to channel her anger, putting it all into the game and leaving it on the field. Doing so had made her a better player all around, and a leader on the team.

8

"327—responding," Berkley said into the mic for her car radio. She flipped the lights and sirens switch and quickly cut a u-turn in the middle of an intersection before heading off in the opposite direction towards a call of an elderly man who had stolen a golf cart and was trying to run people over with it.

"414—responding," her radio buzzed with Garrett's voice.

Berkley saw the white cart racing around as soon as she turned the corner. "This guy's nuts," she mumbled, watching him zoom around as people jumped out of the way. She threw her car into park and got out. "Has he hit anyone?"

"No," a lady said. "But he's tried. He almost ran over a kid."

"What the hell?" Garrett said. He'd pulled up right behind her.

"I'm thinking if we come at him from opposite sides he can't go after both of us. Whoever he doesn't go after, jump in and try to stop him," Berkley said.

"Are you nuts?" Garrett laughed.

"How else do you suppose we stop him? Shoot out the tires?"

Garrett shrugged. "That's not a bad idea. Or maybe taser him as he rides by."

Berkley shook her head. "327—dispatch EMS to my location."

"Copy—327. EMS is en route."

"Come on, here he comes. I'll take the right, you go left," Berkley said, taking off running.

Several bystanders watched as the two officers chased down the golf cart ripping through the neighborhood. The driver saw Garrett first and swerved towards him, nearly going up on two wheels. As soon as the cart turned, Berkley dove into the passenger side, grabbing the wheel. The old man fought back, and the cart hit a curb. Garrett dove out of the way as the golf cart went airborne before rolling down into a ditch.

"Oh, my God!" one lady screamed.

Garrett got to his feet and quickly ran to the overturned cart. "Ward? Can you hear me?" Garrett called.

"Yes."

"Are you hurt?" he asked, lying on his belly to look under the cart. He could tell it had dug into the sides of the ditch, which stopped it from crushing them. Berkley was face down with the man under her.

Two men who had been standing by watching the scene unfold, rushed over to help him lift the cart off Berkley and the elderly man as the fire truck and rescue pulled up with their lights and sirens.

Once the cart was out of the way the old man growled, "Get off me!"

"Shut up!" Berkley snapped, slowly standing on shaky legs. A trickle of bright red blood ran down the left side of her face, coming from her eyebrow area, and a dark bruise was starting to form on her cheek bone.

"This nut crashed my cart!" the man yelled.

"Yeah, well you're under arrest, Pal!" Garret said. "Give me your damn hands."

The old man fought back, resisting arrest.

"Don't make me throw you on the ground and do this the hard way!" he said, grabbing his arms. "Ward, you need EMS."

"I'm fine," she said, helping him with the man.

"No, you're not. You're bleeding."

"What?" She reached up, touching her face. Her left hand had a smear of blood when she looked at it.

"Officer Ward, let's take a look at you," the EMT said, ushering her towards the back of the ambulance.

"Dad! Dad! Oh, my God!" a lady yelled out the window of her car as she screeched to a stop and jumped out. "Wait! He's my father!" she called, running over to Garrett's police cruiser. He was busy stuffing the agitated old man inside the back of the car.

"Don't put him in there!" she said, grabbing Garrett's arm.

"Lady, if you don't remove your arm, I'll arrest you for assault, too!" Garrett snapped.

"He has dementia. He doesn't know what he's doing. Please…"

"He knew what was happening when he was trying to mow down all of these people with that damn golf cart. Go take a look at Officer Ward's face. He could've killed her! He is under arrest. You can go down to the jail and bail him out after he has gone in front of the judge."

She turned, seeing the other officer sitting in the ambulance. Tears rolled down her cheeks. "Damn it, Dad. Why won't you just listen to me? You're going to a home now. This is it," Garrett heard her mumble as she walked over to some of her neighbors. He felt bad for the situation, but he had to do his job.

"Ward…you okay?" Garrett asked, walking over to the open doors of the ambulance.

"I'm fine," she said.

"She needs a few stitches above her eye," the EMT added.

"I'll make sure she gets them," Garrett replied, grabbing his radio mic. "414—one in custody, awaiting transport. Advise, 327 has an injury requiring non-emergency medical assistance. I'm going to accompany her to Richey General."

"Copy. Transport en route."

"601—327. Status update," Lieutenant Cooper's voice came over the radio.

Berkley looked at Garrett and shook her head. He shrugged and walked away as another patrol car pulled up to take the old man to jail. She grabbed the radio mic clipped to her shoulder as she climbed out of the ambulance. "327—601. I'm 10-99. Just need a couple of stitches."

"Copy," Lieutenant Cooper radioed. "327—you're 10-10 for the rest of the shift," he said, telling her to take the rest of the shift off.

"Damn it," she growled. "Copy—601," she radioed as she got into her car.

*

The ride across town to the hospital took a little less than twenty minutes. Berkley wasn't happy about her shift ending, but there was nothing she could about it. She parked outside of the emergency room and turned the car off. Garrett pulled up behind her as she got out.

"I'm pretty sure I can get my eyebrow sewn without you," she said.

"I know you can," he replied, walking inside with her. "I still don't know what happened. I dove out of the way and the next thing I know, the cart was barrel rolling down into the ditch."

"I jumped in and he jerked the damn wheel. The front left tire hit the curb, sending it airborne. I think I hit my face when it rolled the first time. We both flew out. I landed on him and the cart landed above us."

"Officer Ward, we were awaiting your arrival. Right this way," the nurse said, showing her through the double doors and into the triage area. She waved to room number five, then walked in behind Berkley and pulled the curtain closed.

"I'll be out here, unless you need me to hold your hand," Garrett teased.

Berkley shook her head. "He's staying out there because he's squeamish."

The nurse laughed. "So, what happened?" she asked, looking at Berkley's face.

"I was a daredevil on a golf cart and the golf cart won."

"Nice," the nurse laughed as she took her blood pressure. "The doctor will be right in," she added when she'd finished.

Berkley nodded and looked around the room. She didn't belong there amongst all that lifesaving equipment. She had a simple cut.

"Officer Daredevil, I presume. Although, I do hope you're not blind as well," the doctor joked as he walked in with his hand out.

Berkley smiled and shook his hand. "No."

"Great. That's a nasty gash you got there. What the heck happened?"

"It's really not a big deal. We had a guy driving a golf cart erratically, and when I jumped in to stop him, he drove us over the curb and we flipped into a ditch," she answered as he palpated her left eyebrow, eye socket, and cheek bone.

"Wow! Well, the good news is nothing is broken. However, you're going to need three, maybe four stitches, and you're going to have one hell of a black eye. How is your vision?"

"It's fine. I didn't lose consciousness or anything."

"What's your pain level?"

"My cheek is a little sore, but I'm fine."

"Alright, tough girl. Do you want me to stitch it or call for plastics? It's in the hairline of your brow."

"You can do it."

"Okay. When you get home, take a couple of ibuprofen tablets for pain and swelling every four hours for two to three days. You can see your primary or come back in here in five days to get the stitches removed."

"Got it," she said.

The doctor stuck a syringe needle in two different places above her eye to numb the area with a local anesthetic, then he sewed the cut closed.

"All done."

"Great. Thanks."

"The nurse will be in with your discharge papers in a few minutes."

"GT, you can come in now, you big baby," Berkley called out.

Garrett walked with his middle finger raised up at her. "Ohhh, you're going to look pretty tomorrow. Good thing you're off for the next three days."

"No kidding."

"Are we still on for the trails tomorrow?" he asked.

"Yeah, I'm not dying. I have a cut and a bruise," she replied as the nurse came back in with her paperwork.

"Here you go, Officer Ward," she said, handing Berkley a white plastic bag with the hospitals named and logo on the side. "I put a compress in there, too. It'll help with the swelling."

"Thanks," Berkley replied.

"She's kinda cute," Garrett said as the nurse left the room.

"You have a girlfriend."

"Not for me."

"I'm not interested," she replied, walking out of the hospital.

"I'm pretty sure she likes you."

"Well, I'm pretty sure I don't want to go out with her."

He rolled his eyes and shook his head.

"Get back to work…and watch your six. I'll see you tomorrow," she said, bumping fists with him.

9

After a grueling week of practice, Randi was looking forward to flying to Salt Lake City for their next game. The loss to Chicago had lit a fire under everyone, especially Olivia, but she'd learned long ago not to bring the game home with her. That was one thing that had caused a rift in their relationship early on. However, Randi knew how much the loss was weighing on Olivia's mind. She'd been in her own world most of the week, training twice a day, once with the goalkeeping staff, and later with the full team for scrimmages.

Olivia finished zipping her suitcase closed. "I'm going to hop in the shower. Are you still going to The Grind?"

"Yeah. I won't be long. Do you want anything?"

"A mocha would be good. Maybe a cheese pastry. Do they still have those?"

Yes," Randi laughed. "Anything else?"

"No," Olivia said, placing a quick kiss on her lips.

Randi watched her walk away, stripping her shirt over her head. She moved to follow her, but stopped herself. Sighing, she turned and left the room.

*

Celebrity Skin by Hole blared on the radio as the white, two door BMW raced down the road with the tinted windows rolled down. Randi was singing at the top of her lungs when she pulled into a parking space next to a Ducati Monster motorcycle that was backed in. Her jaw dropped when she saw the rider grinning at her.

"Hi," she said, turning off the radio.

"Hi." Berkley smirked.

Randi rolled her windows up and stepped out of the car. She was dressed in Capri jeans, Vans, a white, v-neck t-shirt, and a black snapback. Her dirty blonde hair was pulled forward over her right shoulder.

"This is yours?" she asked, checking out the completely black, sport bike.

"Yeah." Berkley nodded towards the tiny pad behind her. "Get on."

"I can't," Randi sighed. "I'm about to catch a flight."

"You travel a lot."

"Comes with the job." Randi shrugged. She couldn't remember wanting something as bad as she'd wanted to climb on the back of that bike and feel the wind on her face. She made a move to walk away, but stepped closer when she noticed the dark bruise below Berkley's sunglasses. Her leg rubbed against Berkley's as she reached up, pulling her shades off. "Oh, my God. What happened to you?" she shrieked, seeing the darkness surrounding her left eye and cheek. Four black stitches made a line just above her brow.

"Got into a fight with a golf cart," Berkley replied, looking at her eyes. Warmth spread up her thigh from where Randi's leg leaned against hers. If she reached out just a little, she'd be able to brush her hand against Randi's body. Feeling the heat spread further, she cleared her throat. "I won though," she added with a big smile, showing off her straight, white teeth.

Randi laughed and rolled her eyes as her head shook. "Be careful on this thing," she said, handing Berkley her sunglasses.

"Always." Berkley turned the key to ignition and paused before pressing the button to start the bike. "Maybe we can go for a ride when you get back. There's no harm in that…is there?"

"Maybe." Randi grinned before walking away. She looked back over her shoulder as the loud bike roared down the road. *You're going to be trouble for me.*

*

The flight to Salt Lake City was uneventful. The plane touched down and taxied to the gate. The players were in no hurry to get off since they had to wait for the entire team and coaching staff. Randi stepped into the aisle with Olivia behind her in line. Slowly, they made their way off the plane and into the terminal. Once everyone was gathered, they headed towards the exit where the charter bus was waiting to take them to the hotel.

"Do you ever get sick of traveling?" Randi said, sitting down next to Carrie, with Olivia across the aisle from her.

"Yes and no. I don't mind traveling, but being away from Anna sucks," Carrie replied, referring to her girlfriend of just over a year.

"Yeah." Randi nodded. "How's law school coming?"

Carrie sighed. "I'll be glad when it's over."

"I bet."

"Have you seen your coffee buddy lately?" Carrie asked, changing the subject.

41

Randi nodded. "As a matter of fact, I saw her this morning. She looked like she got her ass kicked. She has a black eye and stitches above her brow."

"Wow. What did she say?"

"She fought a golf cart and won."

Carrie laughed. "Maybe she fell out."

"That's what I'm thinking."

"Does she work at the golf course?"

Randi shrugged. "We've never talked about work."

"Wait. She doesn't know who you are?"

"Nope."

"She lives in Richey?"

"Yep."

Carrie nodded in disbelief.

"I guess she's not a soccer fan," Randi said.

"Hmm. Maybe she's some kind of vigilante."

"What?" Randi laughed. "I doubt it," she said as the bus pulled up to the hotel. "Come on, we have work to do. You can sort out my mysterious coffee acquaintance later."

As they exited the bus, Olivia put a live video of the team on her social media. "We made it," she said.

Randi walked alongside her, smiling and waving at the camera.

"Hello from Salt Lake City!" Sasha said, squeezing in between them to get on camera. Carrie walked by, waving and smiling.

Olivia turned the video off before she entered the hotel.

"Here are your room keys," the Coach said, passing out the cards. "You already know your roommate assignments. Go get settled in. I'll see all of you in one hour in conference room 3B."

Carrie snatched the set of key cards before Randi could and headed towards the elevator.

"I'll see you at the meeting," Olivia said, squeezing Randi's hand.

Randi nodded and smiled before walking away to catch up with Carrie. Olivia hung back, trying to find Jorja since she'd already gotten their room keys, and Olivia had no idea what the room number was.

*

As soon as they tossed their suitcases on the beds, Carrie called home to talk to her girlfriend, while Randi called her parents. It was their anniversary and she wanted to send her love. She tried not to overhear Carrie's conversation as she waited for someone to pick up on the other end, but it was hard not to. It seemed like all Carrie ever did anymore was try to please Anna. She shook her head and quickly switched to Spanish when she heard a female voice on the line.

"Hola Mamá, cómo estás?"

"Bien, bien. Gracias por las flores," her mother said, thanking her for the flowers she'd sent.

"You're welcome, Mamá."

"Papá says hello. He is mowing the grass."

Randi laughed. "On your anniversary? Couldn't it wait?"

"No. You know how he is," her mother said. "We are going to dinner and a movie tonight."

"Sounds fun. I miss you both."

"We miss you too, Miranda. Is everything okay?"

"Si, Mamá."

"Your game is tomorrow, yes?"

"Si. We arrived in Utah a little bit ago. Anyway, I was just calling to say happy anniversary."

"Gracias. Te queremos tanto."

"I love you, too!" Randi replied before hanging up. She missed her parents, but she loved her life. Miguel and Pilar Rojas were from Santiago, Chile in South America. After having been born and raised there, they decided to move to the United States to pursue the American dream. They packed what they could into a few suitcases and moved to Texas to go to college after both got into the University of Texas on the exchange program. They worked hard to get their degrees, while also taking the test to become citizens. Their oldest daughter, Elisa, was born not long after they graduated. Then, their second daughter, Miranda, was born two years later, right before they left the city of Houston and moved to Galveston, where their children grew up.

"Was that Mama Rojas?" Carrie said, after her call ended.

"Yeah."

"Aw, I miss your parents."

Randi laughed. "Why? because they kept you fed in college?"

"Pretty much," Carrie chuckled.

"How was Anna?"

"Good. Busy. She says hi. She likes your idea of a get together when she finishes the semester. I'm pretty sure she needs a break."

"I would too if I was crazy enough to go to law school," Randi replied as they walked out of the room, heading to the team meeting.

*

The weather in Salt Lake City was cooler than Richey by almost twenty degrees. Randi basked in the afternoon sunlight as she waited for play to reset after a direct kick penalty against her team. So far, it had been a fairly even match and a mostly defensive game for eighty-eight minutes, with neither side scoring. Salt Lake missed their shot on goal with the direct kick thirty yards out. Richey needed to find the back of the net quickly if they were going to leave there with three points.

"Push up!" Olivia shouted to the defensive line.

"Corner!" Randi yelled when Jorja slide tackled a Salt Lake player to steal the ball.

Jorja quickly avoided another opposing player in the midfield, then sent the ball to the far corner. A Salt Lake defender chased Randi down, but she was able to send a cross directly in front of Carrie, who leapt into the air, connecting her forehead to the ball in perfect unison. The goalkeeper dove with her arms stretched out. The ball grazed the very tips of her fingers as it passed by, landing in the top corner of the back of the net.

"Yes!" Randi shouted, racing towards her.

Jorja and another Richey player crashed into Carrie, tumbling to the ground with excitement, and Randi fell on top of them.

"We got this! Come on!" Carrie shouted as the pile got off her.

By the time everyone lined back up to restart play, they were into the one minute of overtime. Sasha stopped a Salt Lake forward, causing the ball to go out of bounds. Once the player for Salt Lake threw it back in, the referee blew the whistle three times, indicating the game had ended.

"Hell yeah!" Randi yelled, jumping up and down as the team ran towards the middle of the field to celebrate together.

Once they finished hugging each other, the players hurried over to the small group of fans who had made the trip. They were much of the same people they'd seen in Chicago, but that didn't matter. The entire team took selfie photos, signed autographs, and made small talk with them until they were called away by the coaching staff to go through their cool down stretches.

"We needed this one," Randi said, shaking her head as she walked with Carrie and Sasha. Olivia and Jorja were walking a few feet behind them.

"Yeah, especially going into a run of four home games. This is great motivation," Carrie added.

"Do you think we'll move up?" Sasha questioned.

Randi shrugged. She hadn't been keeping up with the point standings. All she knew was, the season was halfway over and they needed to keep their foot on the gas if they wanted to make the playoffs and have a chance at the championship.

"Winning is such a great feeling," Olivia said, throwing her arm over Randi's shoulders as they walked down the hallway towards the visitor locker room. "It's like a natural high," she added.

"I've never been high, so I can't compare it, but it definitely feels good," Carrie said.

"It's better than sex!" Jorja announced behind them as they entered the locker room.

"What's better than sex?" another player asked.

"Winning," Jorja said.

"I wouldn't go that far," Randi laughed.

"Yeah, me either," Sasha chuckled.

Carrie and Olivia also shook their heads.

"Honey, you need to find a different man," another player said.

"Or maybe a woman!" someone else shouted.

Everyone was laughing and carrying on as the coach walked in to give his after game speech. He heard the word sex and quickly walked back out shaking his head. He'd give his talk once they were back at the hotel.

10

Berkley backed her patrol cruiser into her driveway next to her truck and killed the engine. She keyed the mic clipped to her shoulder strap. "327—10-10 Alpha," she radioed, letting dispatch know she was off duty and home.

"Copy—327."

Yawning, she reached down with her right hand to the radio attached to her utility belt and turned it off as she climbed out of the car. Another shift was completed, and she'd made it home safely. The rising sun had chased away the darkness of the night, painting everything in its path bright orange.

She pressed the button on her key ring, locking the doors. This marked the start of a much needed four days off. She'd be back on shift Thursday night for a three-day rotation. She enjoyed the rotating three days on, four days off, four days on, three days off schedule. It made the twelve-hour days bearable.

"Morning!"

Berkley turned her head, seeing her neighbor across the street waving as he got into his truck to start his workday. She waved back before heading into her house.

*

After a hot shower to wash away the night, Berkley stood in front of the mirror in her bathroom. The shiny necklace and pendant around her neck contrasted against her skin. She quickly toweled off, put some gel in her hair, and sprayed a hint of lightly scented body spray that smelled fresh and clean. Then, she walked into her bedroom to get dressed in a pair of jeans and a black t-shirt that hugged her muscled upper body, but wasn't skin tight. She slipped her feet into a pair of black Nike shoes and put a black snapback on her head backward.

The sun was high in the sky, already heating the day as she opened the garage and backed her sportbike out. She pulled her cell phone from her pocket and sent a quick text to Garrett. *On the way.* They were going to an escape room with Dena for her birthday. A few people from her fire station were going as well.

Berkley shoved her phone into her back pocket. Then, pulled her sunglasses down over her eyes and thundered down the road. She loved the feel of the wind on her skin and the thrill of the powerful bike between her legs and under her control. She only had to go five miles, but she took a detour that went past The Grind. She slowed, looking for a white BMW, then sped off when she didn't see one. It wasn't like Randi, the mystery girl she kept running into, was going to actually take her up on an offer for a ride. She laughed to herself thinking of the look on Dena's face if she'd shown up with Randi on the back of her bike.

Garrett, Dena, and a few other people were waiting out front of the shopping center when Berkley pulled in. She backed her bike into a parking space, killed the engine, and climbed off.

"You always have to make an entrance?" Dena smiled, shaking her head as she pulled her best friend in for a hug.

Berkley gave a lazy grin and shrugged. Then, she fist-bumped Garrett and shook hands with a few other people who had joined them. "What's up, Mags?" she said to Maggie, Dena's ride along partner at the fire station.

"If I'd known you were riding that thing, I would've said swing by and get me," Maggie said.

Berkley laughed and gave her a half hug. They'd gone out a couple of times, but realized quickly that they were better off as friends. However, that didn't stop Maggie from flirting with Berkley every chance she got.

"Come on. Who's ready to get locked in a room?!" Dena cheered, leading the group inside.

*

"Welcome to Escaping Fame," a young man said. "I'm Leo, and I'll be your escape guide today. Our escape room is based on all things Hollywood and is actually three different rooms that take you on a journey through motion pictures, fame and fortune, and scandal. You will be given riddles and clues that have to do with the theme in each room to help you solve the puzzles in order to make it out of Hollywood and escape fame. Do you have any questions?"

"Can we use our cell phones?" Garrett asked.

"Good question. No. As a matter of fact, now that you've all signed your releases, I'll be taking those from you," Leo said, walking around and collecting their phones. "I'll lock them in a locker over here and give the birthday girl the key. You'll get your phones back, if you make it out of Hollywood...alive."

"This ought to be fun," Berkley chuckled. "We have two cops and four firefighter/EMTs. If it's one thing we *can* do, it's finding our way out of a locked room."

"We've got this," Garrett agreed, fist-bumping her.

"Without further ado...welcome to Hollywood," Leo said, opening up the door to the escape room.

Berkley walked into the small room first, spinning in a slow circle as she took everything in. Garrett moved in the same manner, checking out his surroundings. The space was set up like an old movie set. Three of the walls were painted like 3D backdrops, depicting a large foyer room inside of an old mansion. One had a floor to ceiling window looking out over a rolling field with large drapes on each side. Family portraits from the 1800s were on another wall near two candle sconces. The back wall was made to look like a library wall full of books with a staircase to one side. The opposite wall was solid black. A director's chair with a paper script lying on the seat was next to an old movie camera. Various pieces of antique furniture were in the room, including a roll-top desk over by the fake book shelving.

"This is neat," Dena said.

"What do we do now?" Garrett asked. "You're the only one of us who has done one of these."

"We start searching for clues to help us solve the puzzle; I'm assuming to the movie set we are on. Open drawers, look behind pictures...that sort of thing."

Berkley walked over to the roll top desk and began opening drawers. She found a small skeleton style key in one of them and quickly matched it to the lock on the roll-top. "Hey, I got something!" she called, seeing a piece of parchment style paper sitting in the middle next to a quill and ink jar. "It looks like a letter."

Everyone rushed over to where she was. The words were written in calligraphy.

I'm going to dance and dance! Tonight, I wouldn't mind dancing with Abe Lincoln himself!

"That's a clue!" Dena yelled, snatching it up. "Dance…hmm?" She looked around. Nothing resembled dancing at all. "Everyone, keep looking!" she said, reading over it again.

"Let me see it." Berkley looked over her shoulder. "What about Abe Lincoln? He fits with this era." Her eyes made a slow pass over the room, stopping on the pictures on the opposite wall. She walked away from Dena who was still trying to figure out the movie the quote came from. Just as she'd suspected, one of the pictures was of Abe Lincoln. Berkley pulled it off the wall and flipped it around. Another parchment paper was attached to the back of it. "I have another one!"

The group rushed over to read it.

Now isn't this better than sitting at a table? A girl hasn't got but two sides to her at the table.

"I have one, too!" Maggie shouted, holding up the paper she'd found in the drawer of the side table.

"Obviously, this one led to the table," Berkley said, putting the picture back on the wall. "What does that one say?"

"I've always thought a good lashing with a buggy whip would benefit you immensely," Maggie said, reading the paper. "What the hell does that mean?"

"Gone With the Wind!" Dena cheered. 'The movie is Gone With the Wind!"

"Oh man, how did we not get that?" one of the other EMTs laughed, shaking her head.

"Now what?" Berkley questioned.

"We look for anything that pertains to Gone With the Wind. That's where we will find the puzzle."

It took a couple more minutes, but the group finally found a book titled Tara on the fake backdrop of a bookcase. Looking closely, they found the numbers: 12, 15, 39. Dena rushed over to the door leading to the next room and quickly put the combination into the lock. It clicked open.

"Come on!" she called, pulling the door open and hurrying into the next room.

*

The next room was Fame and Fortune. One side of the room was a red carpet scene complete with a carpet and stanchions. A mural of photographers was painted on the wall. A large movie poster was on an easel nearby, indicating a movie premiere. However, the only word written on it was Rebel. The opposite side of the room had a mural of the California coast on a bright sunny day, along with a two-lane road and a checkered flag off in the distance in what looked to be the end of the winding road. Large fake rocks were placed around the edge of the road.

"I have no idea what the hell this one is, and we already wasted twenty minutes in the first room!" Dena huffed.

Garrett walked over to the mural of the photographers. One of them had a Porsche hat on, which he pointed out to Berkley.

"Hey, there is a road sign along the highway," Maggie said. "Take it easy driving. The life you save may be mine," she read aloud.

"James Dean!" Berkley yelled.

"Sweet!" Garrett high-fived her.

"What about the clues?"

"We've already solved them! We know the actor! We need the puzzle pieces," Dena said, frantically trying to figure out where to look. She knew nothing about James Dean.

"How many numbers do we need?" Berkley asked.

"This one has a keyboard with a pass code," one of the EMTs said.

"How many letters?" Maggie asked.

"I don't know. It says you only get three tries."

"Spyder," Berkley said. "Try that."

He put the letters in as she spelled them. A red x flashed. "Nope. It looks like more letters than that.

"Little Bastard!" she exclaimed, typing in the nickname of James dean's car herself. A green checkmark flashed, and the lock clicked open.

Everyone rushed into the final room. They had exactly thirty minutes left. The entire room looked like the presidential oval office decorated for a birthday party, except one wall that was a black and white mural of a street in New York City.

"Go through the desk; turn everything over!" Dena yelled, scrambling to the first thing she saw.

"I have no clue about this one," Maggie said.

"It's the Scandal Room. What do the president and New York City have in common?" Garrett said. "That could be a hundred things!"

"No kidding," Berkley muttered, looking closer at the president's desk. A birthday card was turned over, having already been looked at by someone else. She opened it, reading the inscription in her head. *I am good, but not an angel. I do sin, but I am not the devil. I am just a small girl in a big world trying to find someone to love.*

"Dena, did you see this card?"

"Yeah. It's obviously the first clue. Does it make any sense to you?"

"President's birthday and a sinning woman looking for love…it could be a few different people," Berkley replied.

"My thoughts exactly," Dena mumbled.

Maggie walked along the New York City mural, looking at all the signs. Madison Square Garden stood out with its name across the top of the building. "Do you see a year anywhere?" she asked Berkley, who had joined her.

"No, but it looks maybe like the sixties."

"Who knows anything about New York in the sixties? Maybe involving Madison Square"

"Marilyn Monroe!" Dena and Berkley said at the same time.

"Huh?" Garrett mumbled.

"Look for anything related to Marilyn Monroe. The white dress, blonde bombshell…anything like that. Think sex appeal," Dena said as she glanced around.

"Wait! I saw something like a bombshell on that side!" Garrett rushed over to the president's desk. A statue of a bomber plane was sitting on the back table behind the desk. He'd looked under it earlier, but had found nothing.

55

Picking it up again, he looked all over it and flipped it upside down once more. Finding nothing, he moved to place it back on the table and the fuselage twisted in his hand. Everyone watched as he pulled the two pieces apart. A yellow key fell out, making a clinking sound as it hit the concrete floor.

Dena snatch it up and ran over to the exit door. The lock clicked and the door swung open.

Leo was standing a few feet away as they shuffled out of the room.

"Forty-one minutes. Not bad," he said. "Welcome out of Hollywood."

"What's the fastest time?" Maggie asked.

"Thirty-five minutes. You guys got a little held up in the first room, but flew through the next two."

"Wow," Berkley said, shaking her head.

"You guys did great. Congratulations. If you step over here, we'll take a group photo for you."

"The whole birthday thing threw me off. I thought maybe they'd decorated because it was your birthday," Berkley said, standing next to Dena as their picture was taken.

"I thought the same thing!" Garrett said.

"I did too, until I read the inscription on the card," Dena replied. "A sinner woman; happy birthday president; New York City; Madison Square Garden. It all pointed to Marilyn and JFK."

"Yeah, makes sense," Maggie said.

"Where to now?" one of the other EMTs asked.

"Anybody hungry?" Dena asked, looking at the Ihop Restaurant next door.

"Pancakes," Garrett said, grinning at Berkley.

She laughed and shook her head.

"What?" Dena asked. "I know it's not exactly healthy, but it's my birthday, so…"

"No, it's not that. GT and I decided to go out for pancakes not long after we were out of the academy. He challenged me to an eating contest—"

"Who won?"

"We have no idea. We lost count, then puked them all up!" Garrett laughed.

"Oh, my God," Maggie giggled. "Who does that?"

"We did," Garrett laughed. "Big mistake."

"So, do you still eat pancakes, or no?" one of the EMTs asked.

"Sure," he said.

Berkley nodded.

"Onward," Dena called, ushering them across the parking lot.

11

Randi ran her hands through her hair, shaking out her long wavy locks before slipping on a backward snapback. Olivia wrapped her arms loosely around Randi's waist, pulling her close.

"What's gotten into you?" Randi questioned, liking the attention.

"Nothing." Olivia shrugged, kissing her quickly before letting go. "We should probably get going."

Randi thought back to the times they were late to the field because of last-minute sex that had rocked both of their worlds. She wrapped her arms around Olivia's neck before she could walk away. "Do you remember when it used to be fun being casually late?" she questioned with a sly grin and raised brow.

"Yeah," Olivia laughed. "I remember getting my ass chewed out and being tired because all of my energy was spent."

"We have time," Randi said, looking at the stove clock.

"It's game day," Olivia replied, reaching back to unclasp Randi's hands so she could back away.

Randy sighed inwardly. She was tired. She knew she hadn't slept well, but that wasn't the only reason. She grabbed her phone off the counter and followed Olivia into the garage where her SUV was waiting to take them to the field.

*

It was the first home game for Richey FC in nearly a month and the fans were overly excited. Two hours before the game they'd already filled the parking lots to pre-party and hang out in the fan zone. Olivia turned the corner, flashing her player ID to the guard at the gate. Fans lined the fenced area, cheering and yelling. The electric gate swung open and Olivia drove inside, parking next to Carrie's blue car.

Fans yelled their names as Randi and Olivia exited the vehicle. Randi smiled brightly and waved as she strutted like a boss towards the black metal fencing wearing a tight white tank top, skinny jeans that hung off her hips, and flip flops. She still had the snapback on over her dirty blonde hair, and a pair of dark sunglasses covering her eyes. Olivia hit the button to lock the doors, then followed her. The security guard kept a watchful eye on the two players as people shoved jerseys, pictures, hats, shirts, posters, and more through the bars, hoping one or both of the women would give them an autograph.

"Sweet win last week!" one fan said as Randi signed her jersey.

"Thanks. Hopefully, we do it again today!" she replied with a smile, signing her signature loopy double R with the number four.

"You're beautiful. Will you marry me?" another fan said as Randi signed her poster.

"Aww…thanks, but I'm afraid I'm not available," Randi replied with a pouty smile.

A few fans wanted pictures, but with the fence bars separating them, that was impossible. The two women signed a few more autographs before going inside the stadium to prepare for the game.

"Did you see the mob outside?" Carrie asked. She was sitting in the locker room, putting on her cleats.

"It looks like a sold-out crowd," Randi said, sitting next to her.

Olivia walked to the other end of the room where her locker was located.

"All happy on the home front?" Carrie asked.

"Yeah. Why?"

"I don't know," Carrie shrugged. "I just got an odd vibe, I guess. Have you seen your coffee friend lately?"

"No, actually. I haven't seen her since before we left for Chicago." She stripped off her shirt and pants and began putting on her warm-up uniform. "It's probably a good thing," she muttered.

Carrie raised a brow. "Something else you want to talk about?"

Randi shook her head.

Carrie sensed Randi was holding back, but figured she'd talk to her when she was ready. She only hoped her best friend hadn't done something stupid. She and Olivia were good together and had been in a relationship for what seemed like forever.

"We're on the field in fifteen for warm-ups," the assistant coach called, popping his head in.

The women came together in the middle of the room, forming a circle.

"This is our house, and we run this mother! Let's go!" Olivia yelled, pumping up the team.

Their coach didn't use her same motivation techniques, but he entrusted her with pushing them to their limits, leading them on and off the field as their captain.

12

Berkley rested her hands on her utility belt. Cool air blew on the back of her neck from the vent above as she stood in the back of the roll call room for shift change. Garrett stood next to her, mimicking her position while the lieutenant went over new assignments, ongoing issues, and anything else they needed to know for the start of their shift.

"Joe Crawford broke his leg playing with his kids on their trampoline last night, so he's riding a desk for the next six to eight weeks. Patrick Moody and Tracy Mann will be cross-covering his riding zone, and Berkley Ward will cover his security shift at the Richey Sport's Stadium for the Richey FC soccer games. The three officers I just named, see me after," he said, finishing with, "that's all I have. Stay safe."

"What did he just say?" Berkley mumbled, looking at Garrett, who simply shrugged.

"Looks like you're pulling security duty for the next six weeks."

"The hell I am," she growled, walking around the exiting officers, towards the lieutenant.

"LT, what is this security detail? I have a riding zone," she said.

Lieutenant Cooper pursed his lips together like a cartoon before he spoke. "The next game is tonight at

61

seven-thirty, so you'll need to head right over. It'll last about three hours by the time the game is over, and the stadium clears out."

"Why not put a duty officer over there?"

"I assigned you because they recently had some security issues. While the soccer team was away, there was a concert and a football game, both of which resulted in numerous arrests, including a felony arrest for someone who had made it through their security with a weapon. I had Crawford over there as the senior officer with two other patrol officers with him. You're my only other senior field officer at the moment, so you're covering for him. All you need to do is keep an eye on the fans and help the stadium security guards keep the teams safe and the fans from getting out of control. Here is the schedule. I highlighted the games you will be at. Watch your six. There are 5,000 fans and only three police officers. I'm not sure how large their security team is."

"What about my zone?"

"Garrett Tamayo will double cover. It's only for three hours, but we'll have other officers riding near the area in case he needs backup before you get over there."

"Roger," she said. This wasn't the first time she'd been pulled from her patrol zone. As a senior field officer, she was often assigned to additional duties.

As soon as she got into her car, she saw a message from Garrett on her computer. *Call me when you can.* She dialed his number and put her cell phone on speaker before pulling out of her parking space, heading towards the stadium downtown.

"Hey, what's up?" Garrett answered.

"There's been some security issues over there, which was why Crawford was assigned to the games. He's out, so I'm the only SFO available. I don't know anything about soccer or whatever the Richey FC is, so this should be interesting. It's only for three hours, then I'll be back in my zone."

"Watch your six. Those stadium drunks can get nasty."

"That's what Coop said. I'll be fine. You watch yours. Tomlinson will be riding nearby if you need backup."

"Roger," he said before hanging up.

*

When she arrived, Berkley parked her patrol car near the main gate and walked inside. The other two officers showed her around. The stadium was already packed with a sold-out crowd.

"Officer Crawford always stayed near the teams. He was at the entrance to the tunnel and once they took the field, he stood outside of the tunnel along the wall with a 300-degree view of the stadium," Officer Sanchez said.

"That's fine. I'll mimic what he did."

"We'll be on channel three. I'm at the north end, and Officer Lowe will be on the west side."

"Roger," she replied, switching her radio channel as she walked over to the tunnel area.

"The teams are already on the field for warm-ups. They'll be coming off in about ten more minutes, then they head back out in fifteen for the start of the game," an older black man said. He was wearing a yellow volunteer security polo shirt and black slacks.

"Thanks."

Berkley heard laughing and light conversation as the opposing team wearing orange shorts and white shirts began walking off the field and into the tunnel. She watched them go by two at a time. Two minutes later, Richey's players came off much in the same manner. They were wearing light blue warm-up jerseys and matching shorts. She smiled or nodded at those who looked her way until a familiar face passed by quickly and turned back around.

"What the hell?" the player mumbled, walking up to her.

"Randi?" Berkley questioned, knowing it was her.

They stared at each for a second, waiting for the shock to wear off.

"You look a lot better," Randi said, eyeing her face where the bruising and stitches had been. There was a faint scar line above her brow.

Berkley nodded.

"Let me guess, it wasn't a golf cart accident and had more to do with this," she said, gesturing to the uniform. "I had no idea you were a cop."

"Yes, it really was a golf cart accident. I was trying to stop a deranged old man who was trying to run people down, and who knew you were a soccer player?"

"Pretty much the whole state," Randi laughed.

Berkley smiled and shrugged. "I guess I've been out of the loop," she replied as her eyes moved past Randi to the couple of players standing nearby, watching their exchange.

"I gotta go, but hopefully I'll see you after."

"I'll be here until the place clears out, for the next six games anyway."

Randi smiled before trotting off to catch up to her team.

*

"Um…who's the hot cop?" Sasha questioned as Randi walked into the locker room.

"I know her from the coffee shop," Randi replied.

"Is she single?" Sasha asked. "Hell, who cares." She grinned.

"What?" Carrie mumbled, confused.

"Randi *happens* to know the sexy ass cop in the tunnel," Sasha said as she stripped out of her training shirt. "Apparently I need to start going with you to get coffee."

"Wait…that's your coffee friend?" Carrie raised a brow. She too had noticed the attractive officer and the fact that Randi had never mentioned what she looked like.

Randi nodded as she changed into her jersey. "I didn't know she was a cop until I saw her just now."

"Looks like a vigilante to me," Carrie mumbled under her breath, bumping shoulders with Randi.

"You have to introduce me so I can peel that uniform off one layer at a time," Sasha said with a catcall whistle.

Randi shook her head and rolled her eyes.

"Shall I go invite her in here, or are we going to go play our game?" Olivia growled with annoyance. She'd been late coming into the locker room and heard the girls talking about the hot police officer. The fact that Randi knew her wasn't a big deal. She was more angered by the fact that they had a game to play and no one was focused. When she finally had everyone's attention, she went into her captain's speech, lifting the team up and refocusing their energy.

After that, the players who weren't starting made their way out to the bench, and the starters lined up in the tunnel with the Houston players, each holding a child's hand as they prepared to walk out.

Randi smiled quickly at Berkley, who was standing outside of the tunnel near the sideline wall.

*

The players lined up as the starter's names were announced. The crowd cheered for each home player, but got twice as loud for their favorites, including number four, Randi Rojas. The national anthem played, then the players dispersed to their sidelines for last-minute talks. Berkley still couldn't believe that the person on the field was the same Randi. She looked nothing like the girl in the coffee shop. Gone were the jeans and snapback she was used to seeing. Instead, Randi's hair was up in a ponytail, and she was wearing a baby blue jersey and shorts, with knee-high white socks and neon yellow and orange cleats. *Randi Rojas*. The name bounced around inside her head.

As the teams took the field, Berkley found it hard to concentrate on the crowd. Her eyes kept searching the grass for number four. She didn't have to look hard. Five minutes into the game the crowd went wild as Randi worked her way past two defenders to score a goal.

"Damn," she mumbled, taken aback. She'd never been interested in going to a women's pro soccer game, but from the game going on in front of her, she definitely saw the appeal. Both teams played hard, hip checking each other, slide tackling, and blatantly fouling. The loud cheering of the fans never seemed to lull.

*

When Richey returned to the field after halftime they were up two to zero with both Randi and Jorja having scored. Sasha took a long hard look at Berkley as she walked by, causing Randi to shake her head and laugh. The players quickly took the field and the ref blew the whistle, starting the second half.

Houston started the ball with a drive through the middle of the field before making a wide pass outside to a player who took it down to the corner. A Richey defender was all over her, trying to get to the ball. The Houston player kicked a hard pass that soared through the air. Sasha body checked the receiving player when they both went up for the header. The ref blew the whistle for the foul and immediately pulled the yellow card from her pocket, showing it to Sasha, who quickly complained but laughed it off as she ran over to her position. The Houston player started the ball again from the spot where she was fouled, quickly kicking it into the box. Olivia leapt into the air, catching the ball easily. Then, she drop-kicked it, sending it forward to Jorja, who crossed it to Carrie.

A Houston defender pushed Carrie deep into the corner, but she was able to outmaneuver her and get a cross off in front of the box. Randi nearly did a split in midair, stretching as far as she could to connect her foot to the ball and send it into the back corner of the net for another goal.

The crowd went wild once more, banging drums, popping smoke sticks that sent light blue smoke billowing from the end of the stadium in the section behind the goal, and waving giant flags back and forth. Berkley was surprised at how involved the fans were. It was like watching the twelfth man at an NFL game as the stadium buzzed with energy.

*

The game eventually came to an end after two minutes of overtime. The Richey players gathered in the middle of the field to do a quick stretch before going over to the section near the tunnel to sign autographs. The Houston players walked around signing jerseys for their fans before retreating to the locker room.

A few minutes later, most of the Richey players made their way towards the tunnel, including Randi, who stopped in front of Berkley.

"Will you be here for a little bit?" she asked.

"Central 6—EMS Code 3 inside Richey Stadium. Requesting assistance. 327—what is your 10-20?" the dispatcher radioed.

Berkley quickly grabbed her shoulder mic and pressed the button as her eyes scanned the stands. "327—copy. On scene, responding code 3," she said as she took off running towards the people waving their arms in the next section. She scaled the three-foot wall easily and moved up the stairs to a woman who was lying unconscious. "Everyone, get back," she said, moving into full EMT mode and kneeling down next to her to check for a pulse. She pressed her hands together under the woman's breasts and began compressions.

One, two, three, four, five, six seven, eight, nine, ten, breathe. She counted over and over in her head as she performed CPR. "What happened? Does she have any medical conditions?" she asked as she compressed the stranger's chest.

"No...not that I know of. She grabbed her chest and fell over," another woman said. She stood nearby with a stone-cold stare on her face that Berkley knew well. She was in shock.

It took almost two minutes for one of the EMTs to get to that side of the stadium. The other had gone to bring the ambulance around to the closest gate. Berkley had restored the woman's pulse, but it was weak and her breaths were labored. She went to work helping the EMT until the other medic showed up.

*

Randi's heart pounded out of her chest as she watched the scene in the stands from her position near the tunnel entrance. She had no idea what was going on, but she could tell Berkley was down on her knees helping someone.

"Randi, you're needed in the locker room," one of the assistant coaches said, walking up to her from inside the tunnel.

"Someone in the stands is hurt," she replied.

"Emergency services will take care of it."

"I'm not going back there right now," she growled, watching in amazement as Berkley continued assisting once the EMTs arrived.

The assistant coach waited nearby but didn't say anything.

As soon as the person was wheeled away on a gurney, Berkley walked back down the stairs and hopped over the wall to enter the field. She was surprised to see

Randi walking towards her. The stadium was completely empty.

"What happened?"

"Looks like a heart attack, but they won't know until they get her to the hospital."

"Did you just save her life?" Randi asked.

"Probably." Berkley nodded. "I was an EMT before I became a police officer. I ride with the fire station a couple times a year to keep my certification up to date."

"Seriously?" Randi mumbled, completely awestruck.

"You can pick your jaw up. It's not like I said I used to be the president," Berkley laughed.

Randi smiled. "I've never met anyone like you."

"I can say the same for you."

"Randi, you have to get moving. You've already missed the team meeting," the assistant coach urged.

"Go on." Berkley winked. "Great game by the way."

"Thanks," Randi said, still smiling as she walked away.

*

"Where have you been?" Olivia asked, coming out of the shower area and into the locker room, toweling her hair.

"A fan had a heart attack and nearly died in the stands. I watched the cop save her life," she said, sitting down and removing her cleats.

"Oh my God! Are you serious?" Carrie gasped.

"Wait. Cop? *The* cop?" Sasha questioned in the middle of dressing.

"The one I know, yes."

"Get out. She saved someone?"

Randi nodded. "Apparently, she used to be an EMT."

"A jack of all trades and she's smoking hot," Sasha said, sounding completely smitten.

Randy laughed and shook her head. "I'm ready when you are. I'll shower at home," she said to Olivia, watching her toss her wet towel into the bin and slick her hair back with a brush.

They quickly said goodbye and headed out of the stadium. Berkley was long gone, but Randi glanced around for the police car anyway.

"I need to eat."

"Me too," Randi replied. She wanted nothing more than to go take a long hot shower, but her stomach was growling.

"Chinese delivery?" Olivia suggested as they got into her SUV.

"Fine with me."

"So, how well do you know this cop?"

"I didn't know she was a cop…at least not until I saw her tonight. She's the chic I spit coffee all over a month ago."

Olivia laughed. "I remember that."

"I see her at The Grind from time to time. We always say hi and chit chat a little. I honestly barely know her other than her name is Berkley and she has a sportbike."

"Like the college or city?"

"Both, I think. Her parents met there while going to school."

"Mine didn't meet in college, but they went to Brock and Carleton, so I would've been screwed either way," Olivia laughed.

"I could've been Houston," Randi chuckled.

"Go ahead and call in the order for dinner. That place takes forever."

Agreeing, Randi searched Google for the number to Peking Duck while Olivia navigated the light traffic. They lived across town, so what was a twenty-minute drive could easily turn into forty-five if traffic was heavy.

13

Berkley's riding zone had been quiet most of the evening, so when she met up with Garrett around midnight for what was considered their lunch, she'd only had three calls. Their cars were facing opposite directions and parked so that the driver's sides were a little over a foot apart with the windows rolled down.

"How was duty at the soccer game?" he asked with a mouthful of food.

"Not bad," she replied. "You'll never believe this. Do you remember the girl from the coffee shop?"

"Yeah."

"She's on the team."

"No shit?"

"No shit."

"Wait, you didn't already know this?"

"Nope. I don't even know her. We've talked here and there, but nothing concrete." She grabbed her phone and Googled Randi's name. Several pictures came up, including a ton of them with another player from the team who was a little taller, with shorter, dark hair. Berkley raised a brow at some of the social media tags attached to the photos. She'd always thought Randi was with a guy, but maybe she wasn't. She'd have to investigate further when she had time. "This is her," she said, clicking on one of the pictures of Randi alone.

"Wow. She's beautiful," he said, leaning closer to get a better look. "Is she Latina?"

"I don't know. Her last name is Rojas, so maybe."

Garrett pursed his lips. "She looks exotic, like Brazilian or something."

"Either way, she's in a relationship, so we're just friends, and honestly, we're not even that. We're more like acquaintances."

"Uh-huh." He grinned.

"Smartass," she muttered as their computers beeped simultaneously with a new active call.

"Shit!" he said, seeing code 211 for an armed robbery in progress.

"327—responding to the active 211," she radioed, then heard Garrett do the same as she threw her car in drive and took off down the street.

At that time of night, there weren't many cars on the road. Berkley pushed her car past eighty MPH. They were only going four miles away, but Garrett stayed right behind her.

"327-414. Code 2," she radioed to Garrett before slowing and turning off her lights and sirens.

"Copy," he said, turning off his lights and sirens. "414—South 5. Do we have a description on the suspect?"

"Advise—327, 414; there are two reported male suspects in the unoccupied home. Owners are out of town. Neighbor is on the line with 911. One suspect was seen carrying an unidentified weapon."

"Copy," they both radioed back.

Berkley turned down the street for the address and parked a few houses down. Garrett pulled up behind her.

"327—on scene with 414. Clear channel and roll another unit to our location," she radioed into the mic attached to her shoulder. "You go to the front. I'm going to go around back," she said to Garrett.

"Roger," he replied, pulling his gun from the holster. The street was dark with minimal lighting, and there were no lights on in the house.

Berkley held her gun out in front of her with the attached flashlight scanning the ground in front of her as she made her way around the side of the single-story home. Her chest tightened with adrenaline when she saw the broken window which was obviously their point of entrance.

"327—found the POE. Bedroom window on the west side of the house is broken," she radioed, adding, "I'm at the back door. Garrett call them out on my count of three. One, two, three!" Then she yelled, "Police! Come out with your hands up!"

The sound of smashing glass came from the other side of the house. Garrett tried to get the front door open while Berkley moved quickly around the house. A man in jeans and a black t-shirt jumped out of the window and took off running. She holstered her gun as she took off after him.

"327—South 5. One suspect fled from the side window. Foot pursuit heading east towards Loop Street," she radioed breathless as she sprinted towards the chain link fence she saw him climb over. She grabbed the top bar and whisked herself over the fence in one swift motion. He was halfway over the second section of the fence when she grabbed him. The man fell back to the ground and immediately jumped up, tackling her. The two of them rolled around scuffling in the dirt as he fought to get her gun from the holster on her side. Berkley was every bit as strong as the man and wound up on top of him, fighting to keep his arm away from her gun with her right hand while her left-hand reared back and clocked him across the jaw. His head snapped to the side, but he kept fighting. She kneed him in the ribs, then punched him again. They rolled once more like two locked up wrestlers. He swung at her face, but missed, hitting her shoulder.

"Stop fighting me, you piece of shit!" she yelled, hitting him a third time when she wound up back on top.

The final hit must've hurt enough because the arm he was using to go for the gun went limp. Berkley was able to wrestle him to his stomach. "Give me your goddamn hands!" she yelled, grabbing his arms to cuff him.

Suddenly, Garrett showed up and dove on the ground with his knee on the guy's head. He helped her twist the man's arms around so that she could cuff him. Then, Berkley rolled to the side while Garrett went through his pockets.

"Punta!" he screamed in Berkley's direction, squirming like a worm and still trying to fight.

She ignored him as she caught her breath and stood up.

"327—suspect in custody," she radioed.

Garrett read him his rights, then pulled a handful of jewelry out of one pocket and a switchblade knife out of the other.

A police cruiser sped down the road with the lights going and came to a stop in front of the house they were located at. Hearing the commotion in their backyard, the homeowners rushed outside.

"Go back inside. We'll let you know when it's safe to come out," Berkeley said, ushering them back in.

The newest officer on scene, Rod Bowman, tossed the suspect into the back of his car. "You okay, Ward? You look like you went through a war zone."

"I'm good," she said not realizing she was covered in dirt and grass. "Did you get the second suspect?" she asked, looking at Garrett.

"Yeah. He came out with his hands up after the other guy fled. Another unit arrived just as I was cuffing him, so I handed him off and went looking for you."

"What a mess," she sighed, shaking her head.

"No kidding," Garrett said.

"I need to go talk to these people," she added, nodding towards the house.

"I'm going to ride back around to our cars with Bowman. I'll come get you."

The patrol car drove away, and Berkley knocked on the front door of the home.

"What's going on?" the man asked.

"Our suspect broke into a home a couple of streets over and fled on foot. I was able to catch up to him in your backyard after he hopped your fence. When I tried to arrest him, it turned into a scuffle."

"Oh my! Are you okay?" his wife asked. "You look like you rolled around in a pigsty."

"Yeah, there's not much grass in your backyard."

"No," the man laughed. "We can't get grass to grow over in that area."

"Anyway, I wanted to let you all know that everything is safe, and I apologize for us being in your backyard."

"No problem. We're glad you got him," the wife said.

Garrett pulled up just then in his cruiser. Berkley nodded and waved at the two people before walking over to the car. Garrett rolled the window halfway down as she grabbed the front passenger doorknob.

"You're not riding upfront," he said.

"I sure as hell am not riding in the back. You unlock this door or you'll be the next one I'm scuffling with," she growled, not liking his humor. The locked clicked and she snatched the door open. "You're an ass," she spat as she got in.

He laughed.

"Thanks for having my six. I was about to break his damn arms to get his hands into the cuffs."

"I got you. Always," he replied seriously.

*

When six a.m. finally rolled around, Berkley was happy to end her shift. She headed home for a hot shower to wash off the massive amount of dirt all over her arms, in her hair, and deep inside her uniform. She had time before meeting Garrett at the gym at nine for a two-hour workout. Her thoughts drifted back to the soccer game. She was still mind-boggled by seeing Randi on the field. She'd seemed just as surprised at seeing her there in a police uniform. Sitting down on the couch, she grabbed her phone and began scrolling the internet. She wasn't a social media person, but it didn't take long for her to see that Randi was in fact in a relationship with that other player she'd seen her with in all the pictures, a Canadian named Olivia Zeller. She noticed in her team bio that Randi was 27, so six years younger than her, and she had a degree in journalism from UT. The main thing that stood out however, was the thousands of fan posts about Randi and Olivia. It seemed like their huge fan base was obsessed with both of them and their relationship.

"I feel like a stalker," she mumbled, clearing her phone from the Google search screen before going to get ready to meet Garrett. Her phone rang before she got into her bedroom, lighting up with Dena's smiling face. "Hey you," she said, answering.

"Rough night I heard."

"Yeah, something like that."

"So...do you have anything you want to tell me?"

"I'm going to murder your boyfriend," Berkley muttered.

"Ah-ha! I knew there was something. I just had this odd feeling to call you."

"Garrett didn't tell you?"

"No. I spoke to him briefly when he called to tell me he was home. I'm on rotation, so I won't see him until tomorrow. What's up? He just said you tussled with a guy and came out looking like you'd been trying to wrestle a pig."

"Pretty much."

"Something tells me that's not everything."

"You should be a psychic or something," Berkeley said. "You could make money reading palms."

"Nope, just reading my best friend. Besides, I told you my *abuela* had special gifts. I guess she passed them to me."

Berkley laughed. She knew better than to hide things from her best friend. "Long story short, I am doing security duty for the women's soccer games at Richey Stadium for the next month or so. I work the first three to four hours of my shifts there when they have home games, then head over to my zone."

"Why do they have you doing that?"

79

"The senior officer on duty broke his leg. I'm covering while he's out. I'm the only other senior officer on our shift."

"That sucks."

"There's more," Berkeley sighed. "So, apparently my coffee acquaintance is a pro soccer player."

"What? Are you serious?"

"Yes. She plays for Richey; she's really fucking good, too."

"Wow."

"Oh, and she's dating another girl on the team…so there's that as well."

"That stinks."

"I wasn't trying to date her to begin with, and she's really young."

"Uh-huh," Dena chuckled.

"Anyway, I have to go meet your boy toy and show him how to lift weights. Let's do breakfast later this week."

"I'm down. Just let me know what day."

"Alright," Berkeley said before ending the call. She quickly drank her supplement shake and headed out the door. Working out was the highlight of her day. She always felt strong and energized afterward.

*

The distinct clinking sound of metal weight plates smacking together echoed in the large open space. The gym Berkley and Garrett belonged to was set up for Crossfit workouts, as well as regular lifting. They always started with lifting heavy weights to warm up, then moved into Crossfit style routines, before finishing with the weight machines.

"Are we going to talk about your Latina soccer star friend?" Garret asked, spotting her as she pushed the bar up for another bench press.

"Nope," she said, concentrating on moving the heavy weight.

"Did you tell Dena about her?"

"Yes." She pushed the bar back into the rack and sat up. "Can we move onto something else? I met a girl...I meet them all the time. It's not like I'm dating her or plan on ever dating her," she stated. "We're barely even friends," she added, trying not to sound harsh, but she'd honestly had enough of it.

14

Randi flopped down on the couch with the TV remote in her hand. They usually had two days off per week, meaning two days away from the athletic trainers and coaches, but they still had to keep active and recover their bodies from the stress of being a pro athlete. She'd spent the morning at the team's training facility, lifting light weights and doing yoga with a couple of her teammates, before going to her sports physical therapist office for recovery treatment in the new cryogenic tank. Olivia hadn't been with her because they had very different routines. Their training and recovery programs were unique and customized, so they rarely saw each other at practice or training sessions.

She was in the middle of catching up on one of her favorite shows when her sister Elisa called. Randi quickly answered.

"Hola. Como estas?"

"Bien y tú?" her sister answered.

"Bien, supongo," Randi said, sounding less enthusiastic.

"What's up? I saw the game, great goals by the way."

"Yeah, thanks."

"Where's Olivia?"

"Still at training."

"Is everything okay with you guys?"

"Yeah."

"Spill it, Miranda Francisca," her sister chided. "We're Latina women. We never talk in one-word sentences," she added, accentuating the word never.

"It's nothing really."

"Does it have to do with this stranger you've been hanging around?"

"She's not a stranger, Elisa. I've run into her a few times at the coffee shop."

"Ah! So, it does have to do with her!"

"Yes and no. She was at my game…working, actually. She's a cop."

"Why does this have you bothered? I thought you weren't into her?"

"I'm not," Randi sighed. "I don't know. She intrigues me. I'm beginning to wonder if it's just because I've been in a relationship for forever."

"Stay away from her," Elisa said, sounding like a stern big sister.

"We're only friends, and hell, we're not even that. I barely know anything about her."

"Does Olivia know?"

"That I know her? Yes."

"What did she say?"

"Nothing. I just told you, I barely know the woman."

"Well, don't do anything stupid."

"You sound like Papá," Randi mumbled.

Elisa sighed. "I don't want to see you make a huge mistake. I know you live life on the edge of your seat."

"Have you ever wondered what your life would be like if things were different? Maybe a different career, or a different…I don't know."

"Lover?"

"Maybe. Yeah, I guess. That's all it is. She made me wonder. It's no big deal."

"You seem to be wondering a lot…and at the hands of this stranger friend whom you barely know. Just be careful."

"I'm a big girl. I'll be fine."

At that moment, Olivia walked in. Randi quickly got off the phone. "How was your morning?" she asked, setting her phone down.

"Not bad. Yours?"

"That cryo tank is super cold. I froze my ass off."

"I told you," Olivia laughed. "But, it works miracles," she added, kissing her softly. "What are you watching?"

Randi glanced back at the TV, which was frozen on two girls in a heated make-out session with their clothes halfway off.

"Orange is the New Black."

"Looks like porn," Olivia called over her shoulder as she headed across the house.

"What if it was?" Randi said.

"To each his own," Olivia yelled as she entered their bedroom.

Randi shook her head and turned the show back on. "Elisa says hi, by the way!"

"Tell her hello," Olivia said, walking back into the living room. "So, how well do you know that cop?"

"I didn't know she was a cop, if that gives you any clue."

"Really?"

"Yep."

"Haven't you talked to her a few times?"

"Yeah, but it was about coffee or her motorcycle. I honestly know nothing about her."

"Well, I'm pretty sure Sasha is in lust with her," Olivia laughed.

Randi rolled her eyes. "She's in lust with anything that has muscles and a pulse."

"That's true." Olivia plopped down next to her and said, "We should get a dog."

Randi's brow creased. "Excuse me?" she said, watching Olivia toss an M&M into her mouth. She held her hand out, wiggling her fingers for Olivia to give her one.

"You don't think so?" Olivia replied, pouring half a dozen colorful candies into her hand.

"Liv, we're barely here as it is. We don't have time for a dog. No," Randi said, tossing the whole handful into her mouth at one time.

Olivia shrugged and turned her eyes to the TV. "I haven't watched this since the first season. Piper and Alex are the only reason I did so to begin with. Then, they broke them up."

"They're back together. You have to keep watching."

"I'll take your word for it," Olivia said, ignoring the TV as she scrolled through social media on her phone.

Randi thought back to her conversation with her sister. Elisa was right. She was in a relationship and didn't need to be having wondering thoughts. At the same time, she was only human. Yes, Berkeley was flirty and very attractive, which she couldn't deny enjoying their playful banter, but there was something more to it. Elisa had no idea the kind of charisma that oozed from Berkeley without her even knowing it. A distant friendship or acquaintanceship was enough. Any more than that and Randi would be in trouble.

15

Berkeley walked out of the roll call room with a little pep in her step.

"Excited to go watch soccer?" Garrett said, bumping shoulders with her.

"Not exactly, but it's not so bad."

"Uh-huh, you mean she's not so bad," he teased.

"Bite me," she growled.

"Hey, are we still on for tomorrow?" he called as they parted ways to go to their cars.

"Yeah. I need a day in the woods." *I need to clear my head.*

"Watch your six!"

"You too!" she yelled, getting into her car.

*

The stadium was already packed with fans by the time Berkeley arrived. She grabbed the radio mic on her shoulder. "327—10-20 Richey Stadium. Moving to channel three," she said before changing the channel and radioing the other two officers as she walked inside. Fans and paid security personnel nodded in her direction as she made her way through the crowd.

Before she could get to her post, she was stopped by a parent who had lost her child. She quickly grabbed her radio. "327—10-57 minor in progress; 10-20 south gate.

Richey Security seal the exits immediately. We have a missing child in the stadium. No one in or out until I give the all-clear."

The other officers radioed quickly and began rushing to her location.

"Subject is a seven-year-old, Caucasian male with brown hair and brown eyes. Last seen wearing a blue Richey jersey, black shorts, and black Nike shoes. Goes by the name Leo," Berkley radioed to them as she tried to calm his mother. "Did he go to the bathroom? Or maybe get in line for a snack?"

"No. He was right beside me. We were looking at merchandise right over there. I turned around and he was gone," she said frantically, trying not to cry. Her jaw shook and her voice cracked when she spoke.

Officers Sanchez and Lowe made their way through the fans who were trying to get to their seats to watch the team warm-ups, which had already begun.

"What can we do to help?" the head of stadium security asked. He'd also received the radio call.

"I saw at least thirty kids with that description coming this way from my location," Sanchez stated. "This is a needle in a haystack."

"I agree, but I honestly doubt he went very far. Sanchez, you check the men's bathrooms along this corridor. Lowe, you check all the food vendors in the area. I'm going to go check their seats. Go up to any child in this vicinity that fits his description and ask if his name is Leo." She turned to the security manager. "Alert all of your personnel on this side of the stadium. Have them start doing the same thing I'm doing. I want you to stay here with the mother. Her name is Patty."

"Got it," he said and began radioing his workers.

"We are going to find Leo," Berkeley said before rushing away. She shook her head as she entered the stands. There were several small male children wearing jerseys in every single row. "Damn it," she sighed in frustration when she reached their empty seats. With nothing left to do, she began questioning all the children in that section who fit the description. Several parents offered to help, but she told them they had it under control.

*

"Where's your hot cop?" Sasha asked Randi as they walked off the field after warm-ups.

"She's not *my* anything," Randi replied, shaking her head. "I have no idea where she is. I haven't seen her since the last game." She was telling the truth. She'd been to The Grind twice during the week, but Berkeley hadn't been there. The owner figured out she was looking for Berkeley when she sat at her usual table and waited…alone, while looking out the window the entire time she drank her coffee. Just before she left on the second day, he told her she doesn't come in every week, but when she does, it's always around eighty-thirty. Randi kept that in mind but didn't return the rest of the week.

"Maybe you should set her up with Sasha," Carrie said once they entered the locker room.

"Why? All she wants to do is have sex with her," Randi muttered as she changed into her uniform.

"And you don't?" Carrie questioned.

Randi looked at her best friend, who stood with her brows raised and her arms crossed like a scolding mother. "I never said I did."

"You didn't have to. I saw your eyes searching the stands while we warmed up. You were looking for her as much as Sasha was."

Randi sighed. "That doesn't mean I want to sleep with her," she whispered, thankful Sasha and Olivia were on the other end of the locker room and no one around them was paying attention to their hushed conversation. "Come on. We have a game to play." Randi finished tying her cleats and walked over to the team huddle.

*

Berkeley was about out of options when she spotted two young boys walking with a man, both carrying snow cones. One kept looking around, scanning the seats. She rushed in front of the people seated in the first row as they rose for the national anthem, then sidestepped over to the next section where they were coming down the stairs.

"Leo!" she yelled. The searching boy looked up in her direction as they stopped for the anthem. "Leo?" she said again, rushing up to him on the steps.

"That's my name," the boy said.

She held out her hand, pulling him behind her. "Sir, are you his father?"

"What? No. He knows my son. What's going on?"

Berkeley grabbed her radio mic. "I have the boy. Section 29, Row F."

"What's going on?" the man demanded.

"What's your name?"

"John. John Larson. This is my son Jacob. That's his friend from school," he said, pointing to the kid behind Berkeley.

"This child has been reported missing."

"What?! I didn't take him!"

"Calm down. We can do this nicely, or I can put you in handcuffs in front of your kid until we straighten this out," she said sternly.

"I don't even know what the hell is going on," he sighed.

The two other cops finally made their way to her location, rushing down the stairs to meet them.

"Mr. Larson, please walk up the stairs to the breezeway with these two officers. I'll escort the children," Berkeley said.

"I didn't do anything wrong," the guy huffed as he began walking back up. Sanchez stayed on his left, with Lowe on his right.

Berkeley waited for them to get all the way up before she walked with the boys. "Both of you stay right here with me," she said, walking between them.

When they reached the breezeway, Leo's mother saw him and rushed over, tears streaming down her cheeks as she threw her arms around him. A security guard stood with Jacob, who looked visibly shaken, while the security manager stood with Leo and his mother.

"Mr. Larson, start at the beginning," Berkeley said.

"My son Jacob and that boy are in the same school class. We were walking by the snack stand down there and he ran up to my son to say hi. He said his mother was getting a drink. Jacob told him we were going to get snow cones. I asked if he wanted one. He said sure. I thought he told his mother. We literally walked around the corner and came right back. The snow cone line had about ten people in it in front of us. I didn't take that boy. I was just trying to get my son and his friend a snow cone."

Leo's mother walked over, holding his hand. "Are you Jacob's dad?"

"Yes. John Larson," he said, holding out his hand. "I'm sorry. I thought you knew we were getting snow cones."

She shook her head. "Leo said he saw Jacob and said he was getting a snow cone. I thought he meant Jacob was getting one. The next thing I know, the line I was in moved and I realized he was gone. I never put two and two together."

"I'm so sorry. I can imagine what you must've went through. I thought he told you. We came right back here, and you were gone. We tried to find your seats, but the anthem started, and everyone stood up. I really am sorry."

"It's okay. It just scared me to death. Thank you, Officer. Even though it was a misunderstanding, you still found my son."

"It's fine. I'm glad we were able to find him and straighten this out. Enjoy the game," Berkeley said, leaving the two families to sort things out. "What a mess," she said to the other officers as they walked away.

"You'd be surprised at how often that happens," the security manager said, shaking his head.

"Thanks for all of your help. The rapid response helped us comb through this crowd to find him."

"No problem," he said before walking away.

"Everyone back to your posts," she said. "Hopefully, this is the end of our excitement." As the other two officers walked away, she mumbled, "This is becoming a weekly thing."

*

The first half of the game was nearly over by the time Berkeley walked out onto the field to stand by the tunnel entrance. Richey was up one to zero. She had no idea who had scored, but that didn't matter. She scanned the grass, looking through the sea of players; the Washington half in red and white, and the Richey half in their signature blue. Her eyes landed on the one she was looking for just as Randi dribbled between two players and took a shot a few yards outside of the box. The ball sailed wide, narrowly missing the goal. Everyone ran back the other direction as the goalkeeper punted the ball to midfield.

Washington tried to make a play by kicking a long ball forward, but Olivia ran out of the box, easily catching it. The ref blew the whistle, ending the first half as she put the ball back into play. All the players trotted towards the sideline, then slowed to a walk as they made their way into the tunnel.

"Hey you!" Randi said, stopping in front of Berkeley. "I didn't think you were here."

"Yep. Been here, actually."

"Let me guess, you were off saving lives?" Randi teased.

"Something like that." Berkeley grinned.

Randi laughed and shook her head.

"Looks like you're winning."

"For now. I'll see you after," she replied, rushing off to catch up to her teammates before the coaches came looking for her.

*

Berkeley watched the fans jump to their feet each time Richey brought the ball down the field, and then sit down in disappointment when they didn't score. They came close, getting three great shots at goal, but Washington's keeper flew through the air like Superwoman to catch them all.

By the time the ref blew the whistle, ending the game, Berkeley's attention was fully on the crowd. There were only a dozen or so fans wearing red, Washington jerseys, making the rest of the stadium look like a sea of blue.

"Not our best performance," Randi said, breaking her concentration.

"You won, right?"

"Of course." Randi smiled.

"Introduce us to your friend," Sasha called, grabbing Carrie and ushering her over.

Randi shook her head. "Sasha and Carrie, this is Berkeley—"

"Wait, don't forget Olivia!" Sasha pulled her over as she walked by.

Berkeley smiled. "It's nice to meet all of you. Great game tonight."

"Be honest, it was a shitty game. At least we won," Sasha said as Olivia walked away to sign autographs.

"True," Carrie stated with a nod. "It was nice meeting you," she added, pulling Sasha with her to go sign with Olivia.

"Hey, I'm going four-wheeling tomorrow. My friends and I usually go on one of our days off every couple of weeks. We own a piece of property not far from here. We ride four-wheelers and ATVs and swim in the creek. Do you want to go and bring some friends?"

Randi thought about it for a second, then smiled and nodded. "Yeah, that sounds like fun. I'll see who wants to go."

Berkeley reached into the front breast pocket of her shirt and pulled out a Richey Police Department card with her name and the station phone number on it. Then, she pulled a pen out of the holder next to the pocket and wrote her cell number on the back. "We usually go around eight or nine and stay until noon or one. Text me how many want to go, and I'll text you my address. It's easier if you come to my house and follow me."

"Sounds good. Tomorrow is our recovery day, so basically our day off."

"Great." Berkeley grinned and watched her walk away. She waved when Carrie and Sasha looked back at her before going into the tunnel.

With the stadium seats cleared out, Berkeley walked into the tunnel and turned to come out in the corridor where fans were still exiting, instead of continuing towards the locker room at the end. She was looking forward to a day of four-wheeling. She hadn't been in close to a month, and it was always fun showing new friends around what she and Garrett referred to as their play area.

*

"Well…what did she say about me?" Sasha gushed when Randi sat down to remove her cleats.

"Nothing," Randi laughed. "She did invite me to bring a few people to go four-wheeling tomorrow. Apparently, she and some friends own property and go ride four-wheelers and stuff on their days off."

"Oh, I'm totally down to go," Sasha said.

"I figured," Randi shook her head and chuckled. "What about you, Carrie?"

"I can't. I have plans with Anna."

"I'll go," Jorja said.

"Sweet!" Sasha cheered, giving her a high five.

"I'd go, that sounds like a lot of fun, but I have head to Vancouver," Olivia said.

"I know," Randi sighed. "I hate that Canada is pulling you guys in a day early for national team duties."

Olivia was on the Canadian National Team, and Randi and Carrie were on the U.S. National Team. Whenever something came up involving the national teams, players had to go fulfill those duties. Most of the time, they were called away from their NWSL teams to go into pregame camps before games or tournaments, then came back once they'd finished. It always threw a wrench in the NWSL team when they had national team players away, but it also gave them a chance to use their full bench. Olivia and Randi were used to shuffling their schedules around for national team duties. They'd both been doing it for the last five years.

16

"414—clear channel. This car isn't pulling over," Garrett said over the radio.

"Copy—414."

Randi had just finished her lunch and returned to her cruiser from using the restroom at the cleanest gas station she could find, when the call came in. She started the car and quickly keyed the mic next to her computer as she pulled out of the parking lot. "327—414. What's your 10-20?"

"Uh…passing Fairview, heading south on Comanche Trail. Speed varying over 50."

Berkeley slammed the gas pedal down and flipped the switch for her lights and sirens. "Copy, I'm four blocks away on Riviera," she radioed.

"10-4," he replied.

Berkeley raced through a red light, looking in both directions, but at twelve-thirty in the morning there was no traffic on the road.

"414—he's stopping. Put me out at Comanche Trail and Delta Point," Garrett radioed.

Berkeley saw the lights up ahead and pressed the pedal down even further. She skidded to a stop behind Garrett's car and threw it in park. Then, she swung her door open and got out with her gun drawn.

"Driver, turn off the car and put both of your hands outside of the window!" Garrett said on the PA system.

"I'm going for the passenger," Berkeley said, closing her door and moving between the two patrol cars to the passenger side of Garrett's car. She kept her gun drawn and pointed towards the late model, red Chevy Malibu. "I see movement."

"Come on, asshole," Garrett mumbled. "Driver, turn off the car and put your hands outside of the window!" he repeated from his position standing behind his open patrol car door.

Berkeley moved away from Garrett's car to get a better view inside the vehicle when all of a sudden, the driver floored the gas pedal and sped away.

"Son of a bitch!" Berkeley yelled, running back to her car.

Garrett slid into the driver's seat of his car and easily sped away. Berkeley peeled out in the dirt and gravel as she stomped the gas pedal to the floor and raced down the road behind Garrett.

"414—clear channel. Suspect fled in his vehicle," Garrett radioed.

"327—heading south on Comanche Trail, passing Havilland. Speeds over 70. Requesting spike strips across Comanche before Fowler," Berkeley radioed.

"359—copy. En route to Comanche from east Fowler. ETA one minute."

"GT, you copy?" she asked.

"10-4. Scrubbing speed. Passing Gardener."

Berkeley slowed, putting at least four car lengths between herself and Garrett as he began backing off from the car they were pursuing.

"359—spikes in position."

Garrett slowed way down as the red car blasted past the patrol car parked on the side of the road, and over the metal spikes. All four tires blew out causing the car to skid around recklessly. The driver overcorrected, making the car completely lose control and spin around in circles. It finally came to a stop when it crashed into a fence.

The other officer quickly pulled the spikes away before Garrett and Berkeley raced past, positioning their cars so that the crashed vehicle would not be able to flee again.

"414—11-83. The suspect vehicle has stopped."

"Copy—11-40," dispatch radioed, asking if they needed an ambulance.

"327—on scene. Standby," Berkeley radioed as she got out of her car. She and Garrett both had their guns drawn and pointed at the red car.

The passenger door swung open first.

"Get out with your hands on your head!" Berkeley yelled.

"A young, skinny white male practically fell out of the car. Blood trickled down his right cheek from a cut on his forehead.

"Drop to your knees!" she yelled, moving to put him in handcuffs.

The similar-looking driver stumbled out as well.

"What the hell were you thinking?" Garrett snapped as he rushed up, putting the man in handcuffs.

Both Berkeley and Garrett got the men to their feet and began searching their pockets. The smell of marijuana coming off them was strong.

"Are you kidding me?" Garrett growled. "You caused all of this because of weed!" He pulled the bag of marijuana out of his pocket and tossed it onto the hood of his patrol car.

"I want my lawyer," the guy said.

Berkeley shook her head as she searched the passenger. He also had a small bag of weed on him.

"Sit down," she said.

"Where?"

"Right here."

"Bitch, you sit on the ground," he mumbled.

"Sit your ass down, or I'll sit you down!" she growled.

"What are you, some kind of wrestler or something? You're all like WWE and shit," he joked as he plopped down in the grass.

"You're lucky you sat, or you would've seen WWE and shit," she muttered. "Do you need EMS?"

"What's that?"

Garrett shook his head.

"Do either of you need an ambulance? Are you hurt or dying?"

"I'm fine," the driver said.

"Shit, man. You're bleeding everywhere," the passenger said.

"So are you."

"327—request EMS."

"Copy—327."

A fourth officer arrived on scene to help out as Garrett and Berkeley searched the vehicle. It wreaked of marijuana, and they found a pipe in the console with marijuana residue. Bud crumbs and seeds were all around, but no other drugs or paraphernalia were found.

"They really ran because they were smoking pot," Garrett muttered, shaking his head. "That's a first."

"Yep. Idiots," she agreed. "Go call the tow service. I'm going to check on Cheech and Chong."

Garrett walked away laughing.

"So, what's the verdict? Can they head to central?" Berkeley asked, stepping up to where the two men were sitting on the bumper of the ambulance.

"They'll be fine. I put some skin glue and a couple of bandages on their cuts. They don't require stitches," Dena said.

"Great," Berkeley replied, waving for the two assisting officers to come over. "Each of you haul one of them to central booking. I don't want them in the same car. Oh, and roll the windows down or you'll be smelling pot for days."

"10-4," they both replied before walking away with the two men.

"Advanced Towing will be here in fifteen," Garrett said, walking up to the ambulance.

Berkeley nodded. "Hey, so I invited a few people to come with me to the woods."

Garrett stared at her.

"Oh, really? Do any of these people happen to play soccer?" Dena questioned with a grin.

"Yes. They all do, as a matter of fact. It's no big deal. I told you, she has a girlfriend, which she will probably bring with her anyway. It's not like that."

"Fine with me," Garrett said. "I'll bring my extra helmets. Any idea how many of them?"

Berkeley thought back to the text she'd seen while eating lunch. "Just three of them. I'm bringing my ATV and my quad, just in case."

"Sounds good," Dena said as a call came in for a sobriety test a couple miles away.

"327—responding, code 98. Two minutes out," Berkeley radioed. "Gotta go. Watch your six," she said to Garrett, fist-bumping with him.

"I'll bring coffee and donuts!" Dena called.

"I love you!" Berkeley called back, laughing.

*

Randi plopped down on the couch next to Olivia, who was flipping through TV channels. "Are you all packed?"

"Yep. My flight leaves at eight a.m.," Olivia said with a smile.

"Do you want me to cancel hanging out with Berkeley? Maybe we can do it another time when you can go, too."

"No, go on. Have a good time. Just don't get hurt."

"Right," Randi laughed.

"Is it just you, Sasha, and Jorja?"

"Yeah. Carrie is spending time with Anna before we leave on Monday."

Olivia nodded.

Randi thought about snuggling closer, but Olivia got up.

"I'm going to bed. Are you staying up?"

Randi looked at the clock on the wall. It was ten-thirty. "Do you want me to come to bed?"

Olivia bent down, kissing her softly. "Of course, but I'm exhausted from the game. What time are you leaving in the morning?"

"I'm picking Sasha and Jorja up at seven."

Olivia nodded and turned towards their bedroom.

Randi watched her walk away. Then, she grabbed her phone and sent a quick text message. *We're on for 7:30 a.m. There are 3 of us. Can't wait!*

17

Berkeley was outside, strapping the tie-downs to the quad and ATV on the trailer hitched to her truck when a white BMW pulled up in front of her house. She smiled and waved as three women got out.

"I called to see if we needed to bring anything, but you didn't answer," Randi said, walking up the drive between the police cruiser and truck.

"My phone's in the house. It's fine. I have a cooler with water, and my friends are bringing donuts and coffee," Berkeley said, hopping out of the trailer. "We're about ready to go."

"Have you met Jorja?" Randi asked.

Berkeley wiped her hand on her jeans and held it out. "Not officially. It's nice to meet you."

"You too. Thanks for inviting us. I haven't done this in years!" Jorja said.

"No problem. We're a bunch of adrenaline junkies, so this is what we do in our downtime." Berkeley grinned. "Let me lock up the house, and we'll be on our way. You probably want to ride with me, unless that beamer has four-wheel-drive," she teased.

"Oh, she has jokes," Randi replied sarcastically, smiling at her friends.

*

The ride out to Berkeley's property took about thirty minutes. Randi was glad she'd left her car behind when they pulled off the main road in front of an old metal cattle gate that led to a dirt road. Berkeley got out and unlocked the gate, then she pulled the truck through and relocked it. The truck bounced and weaved as Berkeley drove slowly.

"Your beamer would've never made it," Jorja laughed.

"No kidding," Randi agreed.

"It's not all like this. The trails are just dirt and mud. We put the gravel in to make somewhat of a road that won't get washed out in a rainstorm," Berkeley said as the road came to an end in a small clearing that looked like a campsite. There was a 10 by 12 concrete slab with a large picnic table in the middle and a park-style metal grill attached to a pole stuck in the ground nearby. Four large wooden posts held a wooden roof over the slab to offer some shelter from rain or the sun. Another truck with a trailer was parked close by. Berkeley pulled up alongside it and shut her truck off.

"We have coffee and donuts!" Garrett exclaimed as the women got out of the truck.

"Come on, let me introduce you to my best friends," Berkeley said, walking over to the picnic table where Dena was pouring boxed coffee into metal travel mugs.

"Help yourself. Everything is hot and fresh. There are several types of donuts, so have at it," she said.

Berkeley reached into the box, retrieving a blueberry pastry. "Dena, this is Randi, Jorja, and Sasha. Ladies, these are my best friends, Dena, a paramedic for Richey Fire Department, and GT, an officer with Richey Police Department."

"GT?" Sasha questioned.

"His name is Garrett Tamayo, but she either calls him GT or Tomato. He calls her Ward. I think I've heard them use their first names maybe three times, and I've known them a while," Dena said with a smile.

Randi, Sasha, and Jorja helped themselves to coffee and a donut while Berkeley and Garrett unloaded the quad and the ATV, parking them beside the other two ATVs. As soon as they'd finished, Dena walked over, handing Berkeley one of the filled mugs.

"She hasn't taken her eyes off you," she whispered.

"Which one?" Garrett laughed.

Berkeley rolled her eyes. "Who's ready to ride?" she asked, walking back over.

"Ready when you are," Sasha replied, grinning from ear to ear. "I'll ride with you."

"I'll take one of you with me, and Dena can take the other," Garrett said, handing them the two extra helmets he'd brought to Sasha and Jorja. Berkeley had two helmets with her, so she handed her extra one to Randi.

"Come on, Randi. You can ride with me," Dena said, walking towards her red ATV.

"Sweet!"

"Sasha, you ready?" Berkeley asked, nodding towards her yellow machine.

"Uh, yeah," she replied sarcastically.

Garrett and Jorja had already gotten into his blue ATV and were waiting for the others.

"I won't be able to hear anything, so if you need something, just tap my arm," Berkeley said as she settled into the seat and pulled the shoulder straps of the seatbelt harness together to secure them.

"Sounds good. This is awesome," Sasha squealed.

Berkeley laughed and started the engine. "GT, you copy?" she said into her helmet.

"Loud and clear. Babe, you hear us?"

"Got you both," Dena answered.

One thing they'd invested in was helmets with radio systems for the three of them in case anyone ever got lost or needed help.

"Let's take them over Wolf Pass and down to the gulch," Berkeley said.

"Got it," Dena replied.

"You lead. I'll bring up the rear," Garrett said.

"Roger," Berkeley said, stomping the gas pedal. The two-seater machine took off at breakneck speed, throwing a small rooster tail from the thick, knobby tires.

The other two sped off behind her as they raced up a trail that would around, climbing up over a thousand feet to a flat cliff, before dropping down the other side into a v-shaped clearing.

Sasha threw her hands up in the air like she was on a rollercoaster ride, then quickly grabbed the handle in front of her as they whipped around a turn. She had no idea how fast they were going, but the feeling rushing through her body was like nothing she'd ever felt before.

*

Randi wanted to be riding with Berkeley, but she was better off away from her. She had no doubt Sasha was eating up every minute of the wild ride next to Berkeley, but she was getting the same thrill. She even screamed a few times, more from excitement than being scared, but the ride was a little hair-raising. Dena handled the ATV like a boss, whipping around corners and jumping over hills as they sped around the rugged terrain full of pine trees, rolling valleys, and steep canyons.

Once they entered a wide valley between two cliffs, the machines came to a stop. Everyone took off their helmets.

"Holy shit!" Sasha said, still trying to catch her breath.

Berkeley laughed. "Everyone make it okay?"

"That was insane!" Jorja yelled.

"Yeah, I'm pretty sure this voids our contracts with the team," Randi chuckled.

"This is Pine Gulch. Early in the morning, we sometimes see mountain lions up on the cliffs. I wanted to get out here early enough to see if we could see anything," Berkeley said.

"Wow. That's crazy," one of the girls muttered in amazement.

"We'll sit quiet and wait around here for a few minutes. If we don't see anything, we'll move on and slow things down a bit, show you some of our beautiful land."

*

After an hour of riding around, the ATV drivers headed back to 'camp' as they called it. Everyone was ready for more coffee and donuts, and the machines needed to be refueled. While Garrett went to work topping off the tanks, Dena poured the coffee.

"Would you like to see more of the property?" Berkeley asked, stepping up next to Randi. "I need to go check the water level in the creek."

"Sure," she replied.

"We have to take the quad. The ATVs are too wide. We're working on cutting a new trail, but it's taking longer than we planned."

Randi nodded and followed her over to the yellow quad.

"Are you going to check the water?" Garrett asked.

"Yeah."

"Check the new trail, too. With storm season coming, we need to make sure it won't wash out."

"Alright. We'll be back in a little while. If you go back out mark the time you left," Berkeley said.

"Don't we need helmets?"

"We won't be going balls to the wall, but yes," Berkeley replied, handing her the helmet she'd worn on the ATV.

"I trust you," Randi murmured, looking into her blue eyes.

Berkeley winked and got onto the quad, starting the engine as Randi climbed up behind her, leaving six inches of space between them.

"You have to hold on or you'll fall off the back," Berkeley called over the roar of the motor.

Randi slid up closer and placed her hands up on Berkeley's shoulders, feeling the hard, contoured muscles through her thin t-shirt. *You can do this. It's nothing sexual,* she said to herself, but that didn't stop the butterflies in her stomach.

Berkeley laughed and shook her head before pressing the throttle button with her thumb. The quad raced off at half the speed they'd gone in the ATVs. Nonetheless, Randi's body lurched back. She quickly wrapped her arms around Berkeley's slim waist, holding on for dear life. Thoughts of Berkeley's warm, chiseled body slid down her spine like melted butter. She knew she should pull away, put a little space between them, and truth be told, Berkeley wasn't driving like a maniac, but she couldn't move. Her chest was nearly glued to Berkeley's back and her hands were spread out over the ripples of her abs. She inhaled the fresh, clean scent of Berkeley's cologne and shampoo. It contrasted nicely with the smell of pine wafting by as they cut through a section of dense forest.

They rolled to a stop at the top of a cliff and the engine went quiet. Randi felt Berkeley take a deep breath before she let go of her and slid back enough to allow cool air to tingle the heated flesh where their bodies had been pressed together.

Berkeley removed her helmet, holding it in her lap. "This is Eagle Point, and down there," Berkeley pointed, "is Ancestors Canyon. Supposedly, the Indians who once owned this land, went there to hear the voices of their ancestors in the wind blowing through the canyon."

"Wow," Randi muttered, looking over the edge of the cliff.

Berkeley moved to the side a little so she could see Randi's face. "We're about 1,000 feet up right here. We have to take several switchbacks to get down to the canyon. The creek coming off the river is on the other side of it."

"This place is so beautiful."

"Thank you."

"We have thirty-five acres that back up to a wilderness area outside of the state park. There are miles of trails all through here that we've cut ourselves over the past four and a half years," Berkeley said, giving her a bit of history on the property.

"What made you buy something like this?" Randi asked.

"GT's brother is a big wig for the manufacturer of all of our machines. He was talking about buying a quad and asked if I'd be interested in getting one because of the great deal. We practically got them at cost. Anyway, we started looking for a place to ride and realized there wasn't one unless you wanted to travel a couple of hours to this huge, overrun recreational park. When we found this property, the only trails were some old horse paths, so we couldn't see much of it, but we had to have it. We went in 50/50 and purchased twenty-five acres. Then, a few of our close friends wanted in after we brought them here, so we bought ten more and split the cost between the four of them."

"That's really cool. Do you all work in emergency services?"

"Yes. We're cops, firefighters, EMTs, or paramedics. Dena and I worked together as EMTs, and then I left to become a police officer. I met GT in the academy. I actually introduced them. Anyway, that's how everyone knows each other. Emergency services is kind of like a brotherhood."

"That's really cool. Our team is a lot like a sisterhood, I guess you would call it. So is the national team for that matter. We would all do anything for each other and always have each other's back, win or lose,"

Berkeley nodded.

"Speaking of my team…" Randi paused. "Sasha has a thing for you, if you haven't already noticed."

"I kind of picked up on that," Berkeley laughed. "Let's go check the creek," she said, ending their conversation as she moved back into position and started the quad.

Randi wrapped her arms around her torso, inhaling her tantalizing scent as they roared away, heading towards a narrow trail on the other side of the cliff. She couldn't hear anything but the purr of the engine, but she imagined Berkeley describing everything they passed by. Her genuine love for nature was something Randi hadn't expected, although she seemed to intrigue her more and more as she got to know her.

The ride down into the valley where the creek was located only took about five minutes, but they had to go through several switchbacks that had extremely narrow paths. Randi saw the flowing stream of water nearby when Berkeley killed the engine.

She slowly removed her helmet, hanging it on the handlebars before turning her head and holding her finger to her mouth, signaling for Randi to be quiet.

Randi nodded and took her helmet off, placing it on the fender rack.

"There's a mountain lion perched up on the rocks just on the other side of the creek," Berkeley whispered.

Randi peered over her shoulder, their faces only inches apart as she tried to follow Berkeley's line of sight. Not seeing anything, she scanned the large rock formation. Her body went rigid and she held her breath when the most beautiful creature she'd ever seen came into view. It looked like a giant, tan cat, lying on the rock with its neck stretched out. Its head slowly searching back and forth for any signs of prey. "Oh my God," she whispered.

"Isn't it gorgeous?"

"Its…I've never seen anything like it. Wow," she mumbled breathlessly.

They sat there for a few minutes, watching the majestic creature in its natural habitat as the large cat-like animal laid its head down, evidently bored that there was nothing for it to hunt at the moment.

"We should head back. The creek looks nice and high. There's no need to go any closer."

"Would it try to attack if we went down to the water?"

"No. The noise would probably make it scurry off, but why disturb him or her when there's really no need?" Berkeley said, turning to look at her. "We swim in the creek and camp out here. We've never been bothered by any of the animals."

Randi was already on edge after seeing the ferocious creature. Her heart felt like it was going to leap out of her chest. She wasn't sure if it was fear or adrenaline or fascination, but it felt like a combination of all three until her eyes locked onto Berkeley's. She knew in that split second it wasn't the dangerous animal a mere twenty yards away heightening her senses. Her eyes moved down to Berkeley's slightly parted lips, then back up again. Lost in the dark blue pools, Randi leaned forward, closing the gap between them. Fire burned in her belly as their lips touched.

Berkeley held her breath, reveling in the sensation of Randi's soft lips. Her mouth opened, allowing Randi's warm, wet tongue to ease inside, sliding against her own like a long-lost lover. *How could something so wrong feel so damn right?* she thought, backing away and breaking their connection. She sucked in a breath of hot, muggy air that tasted like pine sap. "Aren't you dating someone?" she said softly, meeting beautiful green eyes that were a shade darker than normal.

"Yes," Randi replied, hanging her head. "Isn't this why we came out here away from everyone?"

Berkeley reached up, grazing her knuckles along Randi's cheek as her thumb moved over her lips. "You're beautiful," she whispered, smiling softly. "I tripped all over myself the day I met you, which isn't something that happens to me," she sighed, "but I abandoned the idea of pursuing you the day I found out you were with someone." She dropped her hand to her own lap.

"I admit I brought you with me to check the water so we could be alone, but I wasn't going to make a move on you. I don't do that to someone who is in a relationship...at least not anymore. I've been down that road, and neither side is pretty," she sighed. "I like getting to know you. I thought you might like a change of scenery, so I invited you to come today. You could've brought your girlfriend with you."

"How do you know I have a girlfriend?"

"Well, you told me you were dating someone. Anyone on social media could figure out right away that it's your teammate...Olivia, if I remember correctly. Besides, you kissed me, so you're obviously into girls."

"You follow me on social media?" Randi questioned with a grin.

"No. I'm not even on social media. However, I was curious about you after I found out you were a soccer player. I stumbled onto your Instagram."

"I see."

"Anyway, I'm sorry if I gave you the wrong impression by bringing you out here. If things were different..." She trailed off, looking back at the giant cat still lounging on the rock. "Let's just leave it at that." Clearing her throat, she added, "We should probably get back."

Randi stared up at the mountain lion one last time, wishing she had her cell phone with her to snap a picture, but she'd left it in Berkeley's truck, so she didn't lose it or smash it.

*

"That's crazy!" Sasha said when Randi told her about the mountain lion. "I want to go see one!"

"You go on. I'll stay right here," Jorja added.

Berkeley overheard the conversation while she was eating another donut. "Let me gas up the quad, and we can go for a ride," she said.

"Sweet!" Sasha fist-pumped the air and gave Randi a knowing grin.

Randi laughed and walked over to Dena, wanting to know if she and Garrett could take her and Jorja for another ride. She needed something to clear her head, and speed-fueled adrenaline was sure to do that.

"We're going to take them to over to Timber Valley," Garrett said.

"Oh, they'll either like the rolling hills or puke," Berkeley laughed. "We won't be gone long. Let's head out when we get back," she added, looking at the time on her watch.

Randi sighed watching Berkeley and Sasha ride away as she put on her helmet and climbed into Garrett's ATV.

*

Sasha loved every minute of holding onto Berkeley's strong body as they rode along the same path she'd taken with Randi. However, this time Berkeley hadn't stopped to chat about the land. Instead, she kept going, finding the narrow trail that led to the creek. Once they arrived, she pulled to a stop and looked out at the rocks. The mountain lion was gone.

"It was right there on those rocks," she yelled over the noise of the motor. "I don't see it anywhere. We should probably get out of here," she added.

Feeling a little scared of the fact that no one knew where the creature was, Sasha quickly nodded in agreement. She'd wanted to see it, but wasn't interested in getting eaten by it. Besides, her enjoyment was mostly in being able to put her hands on Berkeley.

The quad roared back along the trail, but Berkeley had kept it at a safe speed as they rode around, taking a different route back to camp. It wasn't that she wasn't interested in Sasha or hadn't found her attractive, she simply hadn't taken the time to find out, and right now wasn't the best time either. Her mind and body were still reeling from everything that had happened with Randi. Her senses were heightened, which only made it worse when Sasha held on tightly. The fact that she knew it wasn't Randi's hands, was the only thing that kept her from stopping the machine.

18

"What does the rest of your day look like?" Randi asked as Berkeley backed the trailer into her driveway.

"I have to wash these," she said, referring to the ATV and four-wheeler, "then I'll probably eat something, take a shower, and go to bed."

"Do you keep the same schedule on your days off? Staying up all night, I mean."

"I work four days on shift with three days off. Then, three days on shift with four days off. I usually adjust a little on my days off, but yeah, I try to keep it close. Otherwise, it's a jumbled mess. We usually switch every other month between days and nights, but I prefer nights, so I have no problem switching shifts," Berkeley answered as she got out of the truck. "What about you? Do you all train every day or do you get days off?"

"We are doing something every day. We have training with the team four days a week and the other days are our days off and game day. Although, we do recovery on our days off and light activity every day to stay moving. When we are traveling it's a little different. We sometimes only get one day off that week. Our workdays start on the field early in the morning to beat the heat. Then we have lunch and usually do gym workouts or other indoor training in the afternoon. I'm actually leaving for LA in the morning for national team camp."

Berkeley nodded.

"By the way, we're staying to help clean up," Randi said.

"You really don't have to. Don't you need to pack and stuff?"

"It's fine," Randi said. "I have plenty of time. My flight leaves tomorrow morning."

"We want to help," Jorja added. "Thanks again for taking us. I had a blast."

"No problem. I enjoyed it. You guys don't have to stay. It's really not a big deal. I just hose them off, then put them back on the trailer."

"I don't mind," Sasha said. A big smile plastered on her face.

"Okay then. There's a bucket with soap and a brush on a stick inside the garage. If one of you will get it, I'll get them off the trailer."

*

With the trailer neatly tucked away in the garage, Berkeley stood in her driveway, waving as the white BMW drove away, unsure when she would see Randi again. It was already noon. She was starving and should've been in bed an hour ago. She went inside and quickly ordered a pizza, then she hopped in the shower to wash the dirt and sweat from her body while she waited for her food to arrive.

As the hot spray washed over her, she thought about the kiss with Randi. It wasn't exactly a mistake. Randi kissed *her*, she just allowed it for a brief minute before pulling away. She hated that Randi had felt like she'd invited her to go to their property purposely to get her alone, but at the same time, she wondered why she'd even let it happen in the first place if she was with someone else.

Either way, Randi *was* with someone else. Berkeley knew the game; she'd played it many times. However, mostly with straight women. She enjoyed flirting with Randi, but she wasn't sure she wanted to go down that road with her. She had a strong feeling she'd find heartbreak at the end of it. "Why'd you have to kiss me? Damn it!" she growled at the showerhead. "Fuck!" she yelled, hearing the doorbell. She'd obviously stood under the water, lost in thought, a lot longer than she realized. She quickly turned the knob and got out, towel-drying her body as she searched for a pair of shorts and a shirt.

The young pizza delivery guy had turned around to walk back to his car when the door opened.

"I'm sorry. I didn't hear the bell," Berkeley said apologetically. Her stomach growled when she inhaled the scent of fresh pizza.

"No worries. Sign right here," he said. "Are you a cop?" he asked.

"Yep. Are you a hoodlum?" she questioned.

"Nope," he replied, shaking his head.

"Good. Hopefully, when I see you again, it's because you're bringing me dinner." She smiled.

He nodded and quickly walked away.

"I'm going to pay for you at the gym tonight," Berkeley said to the box as she tossed it on the bar in the kitchen. "It'll be so worth it though," she added, sitting on a stool as she swung the lid open. Her cell phone rang, lighting up with Dena's picture before she could swallow the first bite. She knew why she was calling and contemplated pretending she was sleeping, but she answered anyway, chewing a mouthful of cheesy goodness.

"Hello?" Dena said.

"Hold…on," Berkeley mumbled as she devoured the rest of the piece.

"You sound like you're in a tunnel or something," Dena laughed. "What are you doing?"

"Eating pizza."

"Oh…I'm telling Garrett!"

"Big deal. He ate a cheeseburger the other day."

"Oh my God! You're both cheating. You already had donuts earlier!"

"No one is cheating. I'm still going to the gym tonight to work it off. It's not like I eat like this every day. It's once a month at most. And, why are you busting my balls? Don't you have better things to do?" Berkeley huffed, snatching another piece from the box.

"First of all, you don't have balls. I've seen you naked. Second, I'd love to be *doing* something else, but he is sleeping at the moment."

"That's…where I…should be," she replied between bites.

"Having sex?"

"What? No! Sleeping," Berkeley grumbled.

"So…you want to talk about today?"

"Not much to talk about?"

"Really? Care to explain why you were gone over half an hour with Randi…alone?"

Berkeley sighed. "She has a girlfriend. I already told you, I'm not going there."

"By the way she looks at you, I'm pretty sure she's been there and back in her head."

"Good for her."

"Why are you so snappy?" Dena questioned. "Is there more to it than that?"

"No. We sat there watching that mountain lion for a while. I also gave her some history on the land. I lost track of time, and I'm snappy because I'm tired. I've been up for twenty hours."

"Alright. I'll let you eat and go to bed. Call me tomorrow. Let's do something."

"Like what?"

"I don't know…go shopping."

"I hate…shopping," Berkeley muttered as she started on another piece of pizza.

"Or something else. Hell, I don't know."

"I'll think about it. I'm meeting GT at the gym around ten-thirty tonight. Why don't you come with him?"

"The gym is your guys' thing, not mine. I do what I need to do to stay in shape. That's it."

Berkeley laughed. "Fine. I'll call you tomorrow."

*

Randi maneuvered through the afternoon traffic as *Pony*, a throwback tune by Ginuwine, played on the radio. Sasha reached over, turning the volume up as they all sang, "Jump on it, let's do it. Ride it. My pony!"

"We're gonna get nasty, baby!" Jorja sang.

As the song ended Sasha said, "I'd like to ride Berkeley's pony. She's so damn hot!"

Randi shook her head.

"You couldn't handle that," Jorja laughed.

"Oh, please. She couldn't handle this," Sasha replied, sticking her tongue out as a new song started. "Apple bottom jeans…boots with the fur!" she sang, bobbing her head.

"What about you?" Jorja asked, looking at Randi in the rearview mirror from the backseat.

"Me? What about me?" Randi said. "I think they'd probably kill each other," she laughed, checking her side mirror as she changed lanes.

"I'm so jealous of you," Sasha said.

"Me? Why?"

"You and Berkeley…" She trailed off, singing more of the song.

"What about me and Berkeley?" Randi's chest began to tighten. Had Berkeley said something to her?

"You guys saw the mountain lion!" Sasha pouted. "That's okay, she'll just have to take me back out there."

Randi nodded without saying anything.

"I love this station," Jorja said.

"Me too! Love me some throwback tunes!" Sasha cheered.

Randi pulled into the apartment complex where a lot of the team members lived, including Sasha and Jorja, who were also roommates. She rolled to a stop in front of building two.

"I had a blast, and can't wait to do it again," Jorja said, getting out of the car. "Thanks for inviting us."

"No problem. I'm glad you guys went. I wish Olivia and Carrie could've come along," Randi replied, hugging her bye.

"I know. They would've had fun," Sasha added, also hugging her.

"You girls don't have too much fun without me. I'll see you in four days," Randi said, getting back into her car.

The song on the radio changed as soon as she drove away. She quickly changed Usher's *U Got It Bad*. She wasn't in the mood for slow jams that made her think.

"Keith Sweat…seriously?" she muttered, changing the radio to a different genre. When another love song started playing, she switched the radio off. "What the hell was I thinking?" she whispered, replaying the kiss with Berkeley in her head as she drove home. *That's just it. You weren't.* She answered herself as she turned into the driveway and hit the button for the garage. The space was empty as she pulled inside. For a split second, she felt a bit of relief wash over her knowing Olivia wasn't home and she wouldn't see her for at least four days. It wasn't like she'd slept with someone else, and flirting was harmless, but she'd taken things too far by kissing Berkeley.

Her phone beeped with a text message from Carrie as she walked into the house.

How did it go? Call me when you get home.

Randi knew her best friend would scold her if she told her how it *really* went, so she opted to keep it to herself as she pressed the call button.

19

The plane ride over to Houston was less than an hour long, but it beat the three-hour drive. Randi had felt like as soon as the plane was in the air, they were beginning the descent. She and Carrie had just received their drink and package of cookies when the pilot had alerted the crew to prepare for landing.

*

"Home sweet home…or at least close to it," Randi said as she drove along the busy streets.

Carrie laughed. She wasn't from Texas, but had attended University of Texas along with Randi.

"I'm so glad you got a rental. I hate when the coaches shuttle us around," Briana said from the backseat. She was another national player who'd flown in around the same time, so Randi said she'd bring her to the hotel with them.

"I got it so I can go see my family, but also to get away from the hotel when I want." Randi smiled. As a senior member of the team, she had a little more pull with the coaches than the newcomers who were being called up as the coaches began preparation for the next World Cup. She didn't need the GPS on, telling her turn by turn directions. She knew her way around the area like the back of her hand. Growing up in Galveston, she was only an hour from Houston and ventured all around the area in between every chance she got until she actually went to college in Austin.

"Well, that didn't take long," Carrie said, referring to the time from the airport to the stop and go traffic Houston was known for.

Randi often missed the laidback beach life in Galveston, but she hated the traffic in the big cities. "We only have to go about two miles, but it'll take about thirty minutes," she sighed in frustration, thankful their little car had cold A/C.

"Great. We'll arrive in time for lunch," Briana said.

Carrie laughed. She hadn't paid much attention to their surroundings because she'd been texting with Anna.

"Text my mother and tell her we landed safely and are on the way to meet up with the team. And, I'll call her tomorrow," Randi said, handing Carrie her phone while she watched the traffic pattern, hoping to pick the correct lane.

"You have a message from Olivia. *Miss u. Have a safe flight,*" Carrie said.

"Tell her the same thing as my mom, except miss her too and I'll call tonight," Randi replied, quickly cutting someone off, who blew their horn. She laughed as she turned down a side road.

Carrie chuckled and Briana quietly buckled her seatbelt.

"Is all of Texas like this?" Briana questioned. She played for North Carolina and was fresh out of college.

"Every big city has bumper to bumper traffic at rush hour, some just have it all day long…like Houston," Randi said.

"Yep." Carrie nodded.

The side road took them to another road that ran parallel to their destination, but they were moving much faster now that they were out of the main traffic through the center of town. Instead of nearly forty minutes on the road, they arrived at the hotel in twenty.

"Welcome to your home for the next few days, ladies." Randi smiled, pulling into the hotel parking lot.

*

After an afternoon of team meetings, followed by a rubber chicken dinner, Randi and Carrie made their way back to their shared room. Carrie flipped on the TV, while Randi stepped out onto the balcony with her cell phone.

"Hey, babe," Olivia answered on the first ring.

Randi closed her eyes, breathing in the thick night air. "Hey," she said softly.

"You okay?"

"Yeah, just tired," Randi lied. How could she tell her the truth? She was feeling like shit for kissing another woman, while wondering why she even did it in the first place. What had driven her that far? She talked with Olivia about everything...until now.

"Me too. I think I've been tested more in the last twenty-four hours than I have all season with Richey. Our new goalkeeper coach has us doing all kinds of crazy things. Today, we were catching tennis balls while standing on one foot."

Randi laughed. "That sounds crazy. All we've done is had meetings about meetings. I'm ready to pull my hair out. We start in the weight room at sunrise tomorrow and go from there. I can only imagine what we'll be doing."

"How's the weather down there?"

"Hot and muggy," Randi sighed.

"It's nice up here. Mom says hi, by the way. I saw her this evening."

"I love Vancouver...and your mom. I'm going to see my family tomorrow when we're finished for the day."

"Wish I was going. I love her cooking."

Randi laughed. "Carrie can't wait, especially after the meal they served us tonight. I'm pretty sure a blind person could've cooked better chicken and vegetables."

"We've had a buffet every night. It hasn't been too bad."

"I miss you," Randi said.

"Miss you, too. How was the four-wheeling trip yesterday?"

"We had a fantastic time. You would've loved it. I'm pretty sure all Emergency workers have some kind of adrenaline habit," she chuckled. "But, they kept us safe. Their land is gorgeous. I even saw a mountain lion!"

"Are you serious?"

"Yes. We were I don't know, maybe thirty yards away. It was just lounging up on a rock like a huge cat."

"Wow. Now, I'm jealous!" Olivia said.

"Hopefully, we'll get to do it again. It really was a lot of fun."

"I bet Sasha was in heat the entire time. I'm pretty sure she has it bad for your cop."

"My cop?"

"Your friend...what's her name?"

"Berkeley."

"Right. Sasha trips all over herself around her at the stadium."

"She pretty much did yesterday, too. You know Sasha. I don't think she actually wants to date Berkeley. I think it's a conquest to sleep with her."

"Of course, it is. That's how Sasha operates," Olivia laughed.

Hearing enough of Sasha and Berkeley, Randi quickly called it a night and said goodbye. She set her phone on the table next to her chair and picked her feet up onto the rail.

"Whatever it is…I'm here if you want to talk," Carrie said, stepping outside and taking the seat next to her.

"Can I say it's complicated…and we leave it at that?" Randi muttered, lulling her head to the side to see her best friend's eyes.

"I just want you to know I'm here."

"I know. And, I love you for that." Randi reached out, grabbing her hand.

*

A popular Spanish tune played on the Bluetooth speaker in the kitchen, sending thumping sounds through the house. The smell of spices wafted through the air, tickling Randi's senses as she opened the front door. *Home.*

"Mamá y papá, estoy en casa!" Randi called, telling her parents they had arrived.

"My stomach is growling already," Carrie laughed.

"Miguel, ella está aquí!" her mother, Pilar, yelled, rushing out of the kitchen, still holding a spoon. She looked like an older version of Randi with darker hair and a little more weight around her mid-section. "Mi pequeña niña," she said, pulling Randi into her arms.

"Hola mamá," Randi said, kissing her cheek.

Her father sounded like a herd of elephants coming down the stairs. He adjusted the waistband of his trousers before reaching the bottom. "Mi superestrella," he said, throwing his arms around his youngest daughter.

"Hola Papá," she said, returning his hug and kissing his cheek.

"Come in. Come in," Pilar said. "Is good to see you, Carrie," she added, hugging her.

Miguel hugged her too before Randi and Carrie followed Pilar into the kitchen.

"Where is Elisa?" Randi asked, taking a seat at the counter.

"I was upstairs looking at Papás paint job on my old room," Elisa said, rolling her hips to the beat of the music as she walked up, hugging her little sister from behind. She quickly kissed her cheek. "Carrie, good to see you."

"You too." Carrie smiled. "I have no idea what it is, but it smells wonderful, Mrs. Rojas," she said.

"Mamá Rojas," Pilar corrected with a smile. "Empanadas de mariscos y cazeula de vecuno," she said, checking the oven with one hand while checking a fryer with the other.

Randi leaned over and whispered, "Seafood patties and beef casserole."

Carrie's mouth watered. She honestly didn't care what was cooking. She'd never had a bad meal in all the numerous times she'd eaten with the Rojas family over the years. They were always kind and treated her like one of their own.

"How's life in the fast lane little sis?" Elisa said, leaning against the counter.

"Same as always, I guess."

Elisa bobbed to the beat as the song changed to a popular Spanish hit by Ricky Martin. "Why are all the hot ones, gay?" she sighed.

Randi laughed. Growing up, her sister had been enthralled with Ricky Martin. She had to admit he *was* good looking, but she knew early on that she preferred girls. "Funny, I picture you more with someone like Pitbull."

"Funny is right." Elisa rolled her eyes.

"Mamá Rojas, may I help?" Carrie asked.

Pilar turned from the stove and shrugged. "Sí," she said with a smile, waving her over.

"Mamá ella no habla español," Randi said.

"I can speak English, Miranda," her mother chided. "Here, Carrie. I will teach you to make leche asada for dessert." Pilar looked back at Randi. "I wish my daughter would let me teach her to cook. Poor Olivia must starve to death."

Randi laughed and shook her head.

"Come upstairs. Let me show you what Papá did to my room," Elisa said, nudging her sister's shoulder.

Randi gave her an odd look.

Elisa tilted her head sharply.

Randi rolled her eyes and got up. "I'll be right back," she said to Carrie.

"I'm fine," she replied, enjoying her time in the kitchen.

*

"What's going on with you?" Elisa said, shutting the door to the newly painted and decorated room.

"Nothing," Randi said, looking around. "What the hell is this?"

"He made Mamá a yoga room."

Randi laughed. "I didn't think she was that serious about it. I knew she was going with a few friends."

"Yeah, well, she got certified as an instructor, and now they come here. She's even trying to get Papá to do it."

"Now that, I want to see," Randi laughed.

"How are things with your coffee friend?" Elisa asked, changing the subject.

"Huh?"

"The cop? You know, the person who has you wondering…"

Randi bit the corner of her lip and sighed.

"What happened?"

On the way to her parent's house, Randi told herself she wasn't going to say anything, but she and her sister shared a keen sense. One always knew when the other needed to talk. She grabbed one of the yoga mats from the corner, unrolled it in the middle of the room, and flopped down on it. "I kissed her," she whispered, hanging her head.

"Oh no," Elisa said, shaking her head as she sat down beside her.

"It wasn't planned. I didn't even mean to do it…it just…happened."

"What did she do?"

"Kissed me back at first, but pulled away. She knows I'm with Olivia."

"Have you talked to her?"

"It just happened two days ago. I came straight here for camp."

"What are you going to do?"

"Not kiss her again, that's for damn sure."

"Randi, you need to think about why it happened in the first place. Are you and Olivia having problems?"

"No. I honestly think I just got caught up in a moment. We were out on her four-wheeler, watching a mountain lion. It was so majestic…I think I got lost for a minute."

"Ay dios mio! A mountain lion? Where the hell were you?"

"She and some friends own a bunch of land. They go out and ride ATVs and stuff. I took a couple of girls from the team with me. I never expected to be alone with her."

"Did she plan it that way?"

"No. She's not like that. We have a connection, but she's not going to go there. She made it pretty clear about me dating someone."

"Well, that's good. At least she's not trying to steal you away." Elisa looked at her sister's eyes. "Unless…you want to be stolen away," she said softly.

Randi shook her head and sighed. "I think I've made a big deal into nothing. I need to quit beating myself up about it and move on. It was a simple kiss. It's not like I had sex with her."

Elisa nodded. "Yes, but not too long ago, you told me she made you wonder. Now, you've kissed her."

"It doesn't matter. It's not happening again."

"Okay."

We should probably get back down there before Mamá starts teaching Carrie yoga," Randi said, standing up. She held her hand out to her sister and pulled her to her feet.

*

The next two days of training camp went off without a hitch. Carrie and Randi were both worn out from doing drill after drill and playing at least a dozen scrimmage games with various numbers of players. They both yawned as they boarded the flight to go back to Richey.

Randi pulled one of her wireless ear pods out and shoved it in Carrie's ear. An old Milli Vanilli song was playing on her iPhone as she danced down the aisle, looking for their seats. "Girl, you know it's true!" she sang, "Oh, oh, oh I love you!"

Carrie bobbed her head.

"Get on my level!" Randi said as they sat down.

"I'm tired," Carrie laughed.

"Me too!"

"No, I think you're more like delirious," she teased.

"I'll get on your level," a female voice said.

Randi and Carrie looked around before the girl in front of them popped her head up over the seatback.

"You scared the shit out of me," Carrie mumbled.

"Would you mind taking a selfie with me? My girlfriend and I are huge Richey fans."

"Sure," Randi said, leaning over to Carrie.

The girl held her phone out, snapping a quick photo that included the three of them. "Sweet! She's going to die when I send this to her! Thank you!"

"No problem," Randi replied, looking over at Carrie with a smug grin. "My level."

Carrie shook her head and laughed.

20

Berkeley checked her watch as she turned onto one of the central streets of Richey. It was four a.m. No one else was around except for another vehicle a couple hundred yards in front of her. She watched as the truck crossed slightly over the left side lines of the lane. The driver corrected too far, pushing the vehicle over the right side, before bringing it back to the center. Giving them the benefit of the doubt, Berkeley didn't make a move. She simply kept riding along. Less than a half-mile down the road, the truck veered over the lines again. Then, the brake lights lit up.

"Something's not right," she mumbled, hitting the switch for the lights and sirens in her car.

The truck kept riding along as if the driver hadn't noticed the lights illuminating everything in red and blue behind him.

"Come on, dude. Stop," Berkeley said, pulling within two lengths behind him. "She grabbed the radio. "327—11-95; Texas: Zebra, Boy, Two, Nine, Nine, Alpha. Be advised, driver has not stopped. Possible 502," she said, asking for a license plate check and warning of a possible DUI stop.

"Copy—327."

The tinted windows were too dark for Berkeley to see how many occupants the truck had, making the situation a little more heated than it already was. "Come on, asshole," she grumbled, still following one and half to two car lengths behind.

"Vehicle is clean," the dispatcher said over the radio.

"327—copy. He's stopping. 10-20 Henderson and Wickham," she radioed back as the truck finally pulled off the road and came to a stop. She threw her car in park and got out. "Stick both hands out of the window," she yelled, stepping to the side as she cautiously approached the vehicle. The smell of rancid alcohol permeated the air as she grew closer. "Turn your truck off," she growled, stepping up to the open window and shining her flashlight all around the cab.

A middle-aged white male with scruffy facial hair was the only person she saw.

"Why are you bothering me?" he mumbled, then added a few more words she couldn't comprehend.

"I'm Officer Ward with Richey Police Department. I need your license and registration."

"I don't have to give you anything. I have rights."

"Sir, have you been drinking this morning?"

"Have you?" he asked.

"327—request assistance to my location," she radioed. "Come on out of the truck," she said, pulling the door open.

"What? Why? I didn't do anything."

"Come on. Let's have a talk back here," she said, ushering him towards the back of the truck in front of her patrol car. Then, she patted him down and found his license, which she called in, before going through a battery of drunk driver field tests, all of which he failed.

A few minutes later, another patrol car pulled up behind hers. The officer walking up was brown-skinned and bald, with a mustache and goatee. The muscles in his biceps bulged against his uniform, which looked similar to Berkeley's, except he had the silver chevron strips indicating he was a sergeant.

"Whatcha got, Ward?"

"Failed sobriety check," she said.

He nodded and stepped over to the man. "I'm Sergeant Jones with Richey PD," he said, shining his light up to see the man's pupils.

"She just did the same thing with me. I'm not touching my nose or walking in a line again. I told her my balance was bad," the man spat, crossing his arms. "She wouldn't listen to me."

"I'm going to grab my breathalyzer unit," Sergeant Jones, said, walking away.

Berkeley caught the man before he tumbled down into the ditch when he took a wobbly step back.

"Your balance doesn't matter when you blow into this," Sergeant Jones said, returning and handing him the tube. "Put your mouth on the end and blow out nice and easy."

"If this will get you two to leave me the hell alone…fine!"

Berkeley watched the numbers climb until it beeped at .14.

"Sir, you blew nearly twice the legal limit. How much have you had to drink this morning?"

"It's not morning. It's still dark out, dumbass." The man shook his head. "Me and the old lady got into it and I went for a drive."

"How much have you drank?" he asked again.

"Hell, I don't know. Three, maybe six." He shook his head.

Sergeant Jones nodded for Berkeley to proceed.

"Turn around and put your hands behind your back," she said as she began cuffing him. "You're under arrest for Driving Under the Influence of Alcohol," she continued as she read him his rights, then helped him sit on the ground so he didn't hurt himself.

"You don't have a cage in your car, do you?"

"No," she replied, grabbing the radio attached to her shoulder strap. "327—10-15. Requesting 10-16."

"Copy—327. Transport unit is en route."

Sergeant Jones checked his watch. Their shift was almost over. "When are you going to come over to the dark side?" he asked, referring to the SWAT Team, where he was a team leader.

"I don't know. Maybe one day." She grinned.

"When you're ready. I'll put in a good word."

"Thanks," she said, waving as he walked back towards his car when the transfer car arrived to take the drunk man to jail.

*

Traffic was much heavier at eight a.m. as Berkeley maneuvered through the back streets on her motorcycle. She rolled to a stop in front of The Grind and backed into a parking spot, unaware of the white BMW parked a few spaces away. It had been a long night and she needed something to pick her up before she met Garrett for a lifting session at the gym.

"I was wondering when I'd see you again," a familiar voice said as Berkley killed the engine.

She turned her head and grinned. "Hey, you," she said as she climbed off the machine and slid her hat on backward.

Randi got out of the car. A smile lit up her face as Berkley walked over to her. Fire burned in her belly as Randi gave her a light hello hug.

"How was...uh, the thing you went to?" Berkley asked, trying to clear the fog from her brain. She hadn't expected Randi to hug her, and it took her a second to recover.

Randi laughed. "National team training camp."

"That's it. How did it go?" Berkley asked.

"Fine. The same as usual, I guess. It's a bunch of training drills and meetings. It's actually quite boring," she chuckled. "I did get you something though," she added, reaching into the backseat of her car. "I had to guess the size, but hopefully it's good enough to replace the one I ruined," she said, handing Berkley a new white Nike shirt.

Berkley checked the size and held it up. Randi had guessed right. "Wow. Thank you. You didn't have to do that, you know."

Randi shrugged. "Nike sponsors the national team, so it wasn't a big deal for me to get it. Besides, I felt horrible, and it's the least I could do after you took us out riding with your friends."

"Thank you," Berkley said with a smile as she tossed it over her shoulder.

"You know, Sasha hasn't stopped talking about that day...or you for that matter."

Berkley nodded. "She's cute. Maybe I should ask her out sometime," she said, holding the door open for Randi. "She *is* single, right?"

"Yeah, go for it," Randi mumbled, shrugging and walking past her. She wasn't thrilled about the idea, but there was nothing she could do. She had no claim to Berkley and no say in who she dated.

*

"I needed this," Berkley said, taking a long swig of her iced coffee.

"Long night?" Randi asked.

"Something like that. I'm pretty sure my last shift caused a few grey hairs to come in."

Randi shrugged. "I don't see any."

"One chocolate chip muffin," Paul said, handing Randi a small brown bag.

"I better go feed the beast or practice will be Hell today," she said with a grin.

"Why doesn't she ever come here with you?" Berkley asked.

"She's not a coffee drinker," Randi said with a shrug.

Berkley nodded, smiling as she watched her leave. *I'm right where I want to be, and in the wrong place at the same time.* She shook her head.

*

"Trouble in paradise?" Garrett said, breaking through the clouds filling Berkley's head.

Huh?" she muttered.

"You look lost in thought."

"I'm fine. Just tired, I guess."

"Uh, huh. Are you sure that soccer player doesn't have you all twisted up?"

"What?" She shook her head and tossed her sweat towel at him. "No," she sighed. "I ran into Jones this morning. He hinted that I should put in for SWAT."

"Really?"

She straddled the bench and sat down. "Yeah."

"Wow. I know how bad you want SWAT."

"I know."

"What's holding you back?"

"Honestly...nothing, I guess." She shrugged. "Women don't exactly get invited to join SWAT."

"You're not *women*. You're a badass, and anyone in this department would give their life for you and vice versa." He put his hand on her shoulder. "Don't get caught up in that female/male bullshit. You've never been like that before. Why start now?"

"You're right."

"Good. Is it too early for a cold beer?"

"Nope," she said with a grin. "My house or yours?"

"Dena's asleep. She just got off shift, so yours...unless you want to face the wrath of a sleepy Mexican."

"Nope. Been there, done that." She shook her head.

Garrett laughed and smacked her on the back. "Come on, let's get the hell out of here."

*

Randi wiped sweat from her brow as she dribbled the ball at her feet, looking for a clear shot on goal. It was a small-side practice game, but she still gave it her all when she cleared Jorja, who was defending her. The inside of her foot caught the sweet spot on the ball, sending it sailing through the air. Olivia had anticipated the shot and dove to her right side, but the ball curled at the last second, narrowly missing her hands as it flew into the back of the net. Randi jumped up and down yelling and fist-pumping the air. Olivia shook her head in Randi's direction and threw the ball over to the assistant coach, who was running the practice game.

"Let's call it a day. It's hot as hell out here. MJ wants to go over game film before we leave today, so hit the showers," he said.

"That was a killer shot!" Jorja exclaimed. "I thought I had you, but you slipped past me."

"She has the best footwork on the team," Sasha said. "She's crossed me up several times. You have to watch the ball, not her feet."

"No kidding," Jorja laughed.

"So, who has the winning score between the two of you?" Sasha asked, knowing how competitive they were when facing each other.

"Who?" Randi asked.

"You and Olivia."

"I don't know, actually."

"Me," Olivia said, tossing her gloves on the bench before removing her wrist tape. "You sneak one by me every now and then, but I stop most of them," she added, smirking in Randi's direction. "And, I still get pissed every time, but that was a sweet ball."

Randi laughed.

"Let's go, ladies. MJ's waiting. We all know how much he loves game film," Olivia said, referring to their coach.

21

It had been ten days since Berkley put in her request to join SWAT. She knew they were looking to replace a person who had stepped down when he'd decided to join VICE as a detective recently. Still, she figured she'd know something by now.

"Ride or die," Garrett said, fist-bumping her as they left the roll call room to head out on their shifts.

"Ride or die," she replied.

"Ward, stop in my office before you hit the street," the captain said, catching her in the hallway.

"Yes, sir," she replied, adjusting the utility belt around her waist before walking in behind him. Garrett had already left.

"I see you want to join SWAT," he stated, folding his hands into a triangle with his elbows on the desk. She stared at him for a second. He'd always reminded her of Richard Gere with the thick grey hair, dimpled smile, and wireframe glasses. He was laidback as far as captains went, but that was because he'd been around a long time and had a very strong support staff under him.

"Correct," she answered.

"We've never had a woman on SWAT."

"First time for everything…sir."

"I said the same thing when I spoke to Lieutenant Sullivan earlier today," he said. "You'll have to take the exam and go through a psych evaluation, and a PT evaluation. If you pass all of those, you'll come out of the field for a week-long course at the state academy."

"Uh…" Berkley cleared her throat. "Great. When do I take the exam?"

"You have to study first. It's a pretty intense exam."

"Actually, I've been studying for over a year. This is something I've wanted for a while."

"I see." He typed a few keys on the computer. "The next exam session is Wednesday. How does that sound?"

"I'll be off for three after tomorrow, so that works out fine."

"Alright. You're on the schedule. Be at the testing center at nine in the morning. You'll have two hours to complete the hundred questions, plus the written portion." He stood and held his hand out. "Good luck."

"Thank you, sir," she replied, shaking his hand.

*

Stepping outside of the building, Berkley pulled dark sunglasses down over her eyes. She was still in shock. SWAT was her goal from the beginning. They were the bad boys, and she wanted to be one of them. It was part of the reason she was built like a brick house. She'd mentally and physically trained herself to the point there was nothing left to do, except put in for the promotion. She was ready, and she knew it.

"Well?" Garrett said, answering his phone when he saw her name.

"I'm in."

"Hell yeah!" he yelled.

"I take the exam on Wednesday and go from there."

"Sweet. You're ready for this."

"Thanks."

*

Richey's biggest rival, Houston, was on the field for warm-ups first, but they quickly followed. Each player went through the monotonous dynamic warm-up, stretching their muscles, before getting their feet on a ball. At the same time, the goalkeepers went through a completely different warm-up. Then, the goalkeeping staff shot balls on them over and over, working top to bottom and side to side in front of the goal.

"I hope we stomp them," Carrie said as they made their way across the field to go into the locker room and get ready for the game.

"Me too," Randi replied.

"What are we discussing?" Jorja asked.

"Kicking Houston's ass," they said in unison as they neared the tunnel.

Randi immediately noticed Berkley standing off to the side in her uniform. She couldn't help the tingle that ran down her spine. *Why does she have to be so good-looking?* "Hey, you," she said with a smile.

"Hey," Berkley replied with a grin.

"Do you ever take those off?" Sasha asked, pointing to her sunglasses. "I want to see your eyes."

Berkley laughed and pulled them down, revealing her gorgeous blue eyes in a move that seemed way more seductive than it really was. She grinned and slid them back up as Randi shook her head.

"That uniform, the tattoos down her arms, the deep blue eyes…she's one sexy beast," Sasha muttered as she entered the locker room.

"Uh-huh," Randi mumbled as she started changing her shirt.

"Hey, I saw your cop outside. You should invite her to the island tomorrow," Olivia said, passing by her. "It looked like she was into Sasha."

Carrie watched Randi bite her lower lip. "Sure. She probably has to work or something, but yeah, I'll ask her after the game," she said as Olivia continued past them to her end of the locker room.

"Are you sure you want to do that?" Carrie whispered.

"Why wouldn't I?"

Carrie shrugged.

*

Richey took the field for the start of the game. Randi started play by passing the ball back to Carrie who dribbled over the midfield line but lost it to a Houston player. Jorja was there to win it back. She quickly sent it over to Sasha to switch the field.

"Let's go! Press up!" Olivia shouted.

Randi saw Sasha on a breakaway run and quickly separated from the defender who was marking her. Sasha passed the ball up to another player who sent it right through the middle of the field. Randi trapped the pass and dribbled towards the box. The defender whom she'd gotten away from came back, tackling her hard. Randi flew through the air and landed on her back.

The referee blew her whistle and held a yellow card up to the Houston player, before signaling a penalty kick. The foul had happened just inside of the box.

"How's your head?" Jason, the team's athletic trainer asked as he looked over her ankle.

"I'm fine," she growled, standing up.

"That bitch has it coming to her!" Carrie snapped. "Let's go! You've got this!" She clapped her hands and ran over to the rest of the team on the line while Randi readied herself to take the kick.

Go left...go left...go left, she thought over and over. As soon as the ref blew the whistle, she wasted no time. It took three short steps before she launched the ball into the air. The keeper had gone left, as had the ball, but she'd dove for a low ball. It sailed way above her head and into the top corner of the net.

"Yes!" the team cheered and rushed over, hugging Randi.

*

Berkley had to force herself not to watch the game. She was there to keep everyone safe, which meant her eyes needed to be trained on the fans, filling the seats in the stands. Still, she watched long enough to see the penalty kick, which she was glad she'd seen since the rest of the game had been a defensive battle, causing it to end with the one to zero score.

After cooling down and signing autographs, the Richey players began making their way towards the locker room tunnel. Randi, Carrie and Olivia were always the last ones to leave the field.

"Great game," Berkley said.

"Thanks," Carrie replied.

"Hey, we're going over to Lake Travis tomorrow. It's our day off," Randi said. "Do you want to join us?"

"You should come. It'll be fun. I'm sure Sasha will be there," Olivia said with a smile as she walked by.

"I'm on shift tomorrow night. Maybe I could go after the end of this shift, before I go to bed. What time are you going?"

"Probably like nine to maybe noon or one."

Berkley had planned to study as much as she could before her exam, but she'd been studying that material for several months. If she didn't know it by now, she shouldn't be taking the exam. "I can go for a little bit," she said, feeling like getting away might help clear her mind. "But I have to be back here by noon to go to bed," she added.

"Okay, sounds good. I'll text you in the morning to tell you where we are."

"Cool."

"Have a good night," Randi said. "Be safe," she added, looking into the eyes staring back at her.

"Always." Berkley smiled.

22

The night had been fairly quiet…until a white car sped through a stoplight, nearly colliding with Berkley. She quickly spun around and chased after it with her lights and sirens wailing.

"327—in pursuit of a 505; possible 502. Newer model, white, Toyota Camry. Texas: Kilo, Lima, Six, Two, Victor, Oscar," she radioed.

Suddenly, the car careened to the side, crashing over a curb and through a light pole before flipping on its side, where it finally came to a stop with the driver's side down.

"Holy shit!" she exclaimed, grabbing the mic.

"327—11-83. Start EMS to Longmire Plaza!" Berkley radioed as she jumped out of the car with her gun drawn. Thinking it was either someone hopped up on drugs, or really drunk, she took precaution as she moved towards the vehicle. A loud popping and fizzing sound was heard from the engine as smoke began to pour out. She quickly holstered her gun and rushed around, trying to see inside of the car, but it was dark and the windows were tinted.

"Damn it!" She ran back to her car and got her break stick, which was a long, skinny, metal baton used to bust windows. Finding it in the doorjamb where she kept it, she rushed back over, and began busting the back window out. "327—ETA on EMS…the vehicle is on fire."

"Three minutes out—327," dispatch radioed back.

"414—on scene," Garrett radioed as he jumped out of his car and raced over to help.

Berkley had already crawled into the car after smashing through the back glass window. The driver was still in his seatbelt and slumped against the door. She reached around, checking his pulse. It was weak and from what she could tell, and he was barely breathing. It was a kid, maybe eighteen or nineteen at most.

"Ward!" Garrett yelled, sticking his head through the open window.

"GT! Do you have an extinguisher?"

"No. EMS is two minutes out."

"I have to get him out! I think he's OD'd."

"The front of the engine compartment is on fire! You have to get out of there!" he yelled.

"Damn it, just hold on!" She pulled with everything she had, trying to get the seat to fold back. Finally, it broke and fell into her lap. She coughed a couple of times as smoke filled the car, but was able to get his seatbelt off.

When Garrett saw her dragging the man against her as she neared the smashed window, he tossed his flashlight to the side and quickly grabbed the young man, helping her slide out with him. Together, they carried him far enough away to be safe. Berkley glanced back at the wreckage. The interior of the car was completely filled with smoke and orange flames lit up the night from the engine compartment.

Garrett held his flashlight on the lifeless teen while she looked him over. His pupils were dilated and completely unfazed by the light and his pulse was so weak, she wasn't sure she felt it at all. Garrett watched her run to the back of her car and rush back with a small plunger of medication. She quickly shoved it against the young guy's arm and pushed the single dose of Narcan to reverse the effect of the overdose.

Sirens were heard in the distance as Berkley rubbed his chest and talked softly to him, telling him everything was going to be okay. Garrett watched the ambulance roll to a stop just as the man's eyes bugged out of his head and he inhaled a deep breath, almost like someone coming back from the dead. He began flailing around and Berkley held him down as best she could. Garrett rushed around to the other side to help keep him still.

"Calm down! You're okay."

"Let me go!" he yelled.

"Look!" she screamed, grabbing his face and turning him to see the fully engulfed car. "I just pulled your ass out of there. You're lucky you're alive! Now, calm the fuck down!"

"What do we have?" Dena said, rushing up to them.

"Overdose that led to that," Berkley said.

"She pulled him out just before it went completely up in flames," Garrett added.

"Oh, my God. How's your breathing? Did you get a lot of smoke?"

"I'm fine, D. Just look him over."

"What did you take?"

"Nothing," he mumbled.

"Alright, let's start with how old are you?"

"Nineteen."

"Great," Dena said, taking his blood pressure and checking his pulse. "Do you hurt anywhere?" she asked as the fire truck arrived and began putting out the fire.

"No."

"Officer Ward administered Narcan, and it brought you back to the living and breathing. Do you know what Narcan is?"

"Nope."

"It works against an opioid overdose. Therefore, you took something. Was it meth, heroin, what?"

"Dispatch said the car was reported stolen earlier this evening from North One District," Garrett said. "Did he say what he took?"

"No," Berkley sighed and shook her head. "What the hell is going on with this generation of kids?"

"No idea. Man, when I was nineteen, I was chasing tail, not my next high. I don't get it." Garrett shrugged.

"Me either."

"He admitted to doing an Eight Ball," Dena said, stepping over to them. "We're going to transport him to Richey General."

"I'll have a unit meet you there. He's under arrest for several charges as soon as he's cleared," Berkley said.

"Got it. You guys be safe out here," she said.

Berkley checked her watch. "I have just enough time for me to write up this report, then I'm out of here."

"You have a hot date?"

"As a matter of fact, I do," she replied with a grin. "The soccer team invited me to Lake Travis to hang out. I'll only be there a couple of hours, but I could use the time to clear my head."

"Uh-huh, that's a good excuse to hang out with a bunch of hotties in bikini's...one in particular."

"She's in a relationship."

"Keep telling yourself that. How's it working for you so far?"

"You're an ass," Berkley chided as she waved at Dena, who was climbing into the back of the rig with her patient. "327—10-16 at Richey General. EMS is en route with him now. Charges will be: 503; 505; and DUID."

"Copy—327. Transport en route."

"My night was boring as hell until this," Berkley said to Garrett as they walked to their cars. Two other officers who had arrived on scene behind the fire truck were staying to make sure everything was cleaned up. She checked her watch again as the sun began to peek through the night sky in the distance. Her shift was over in fifteen minutes, but it would take her at least thirty to write the report.

*

"I can't believe you invited Berkley," Sasha giggled like a schoolgirl with a crush as she sprayed suntan lotion onto her skin. They were in a secluded, more private section of the lake with a small white sand beach. About half of the team had come along for the few hours of relaxation.

"We should've left her at home," Randi mumbled, causing Carrie to laugh out loud.

"What?" Anna asked.

"Sasha is obsessed with Berkley and won't shut up about her," Carrie replied to her girlfriend. She was still surprised that she'd been able to join them. After all, it was her idea to begin with, but she'd been too busy to do much of anything lately.

"This is exactly what I needed," Olivia blurted as she stretched out and stuck her heels into the warm sand.

"I second that," Jorja added.

"Hey, Jorj, you want some of this?" Sasha called from the other end of the line of chairs. "You burnt everything but your ass the last time we were out here."

"Nope. I got it covered!" Jorja replied, holding up her own bottle of sunscreen.

*

Berkley swore she could still smell the smoke in her hair as she parked her truck in the lot, but she'd washed it three times. "Maybe it's just burned into my senses," she mumbled, getting out and grabbing her chair and small cooler from the back. It was a short walk down the path to the private area, and she quickly spotted the group of soccer players milling about a row of chairs and coolers.

"Look who made it," Randi said, noticing Berkley walking through the sand wearing a dark blue tank top, black board shorts that stopped above the knee, and flip flops. Her ever-present dark sunglasses covered her eyes. Randi had only seen her in t-shirts and her uniform top, so she was unaware that the half-sleeve tattoos that started at her elbows actually went up over her shoulders and across the top of her back, connecting as one whole piece of artwork. It was all done in grayscale and had various pieces that all joined together.

"I was busy saving a teen who stole a car, OD'd, and wrecked that car at high speed, causing it to flip over and catch fire," she said, nonchalantly. "But, hey, I made it!"

"Wow," Randi muttered.

"That's badass," Sasha said, happy that Berkley had placed her chair next to hers since she was on the end.

"We were just about to play football. You interested?" Olivia asked, tossing the pigskin into the air and catching it.

"Sure," Berkley said, kicking off her flip flops and removing her tank top, revealing the full tattoo, along with her muscled upper body. A black, sports bra style bathing suit top covered her breasts.

"Damn," Anna mumbled, taking in the sight in front of her. "She obviously does Crossfit or something. She's ripped as hell," she whispered to Carrie.

"Seriously, you think she's hot, too?" Carrie said as everyone gathered, picking teams.

"Hell yeah, but she's not my type. Doesn't mean she isn't nice to look at." Anna shrugged with a smile.

"Carr, you playing?" Sasha asked. "It's me, Berkley, and Jorja against you, Randi, Olivia, and Anna."

"Be right there!" she called. "You playing?"

"No. I'll keep score," Anna said. Sports weren't really her thing.

*

Berkley glanced around at the group. Olivia was in dark purple board shorts similar to hers, and a bikini top. The rest of the girls were in various bikini styles and colors, including Randi who was wearing a red string bikini that left little to the imagination. Berkley swallowed the lump in her throat and her chest tightened, threatening to squeeze the life out of her as her eyes raked over the gorgeous South American body. Randi's natural caramel coloring contrasted nicely with the brightly colored swimsuit, and her athletic frame had subtle curves in the right places. *This ought to be fun*, she thought, looking over at Olivia who was going over the rules.

"Okay, so we're playing 3V3, two-hand touch. There are flip flops marking both end zones, as well as out of bounds."

Carrie tossed a flip flop into the air. The bottom was tales and the straps were heads.

"Tales," Berkley said, calling it in the air. She grinned when it landed bottom up. "Come on," she said to her teammates, ushering them away from the other team. "I'll be quarterback. Sasha, you're my running back and my blocker. Jorja, you're my receiver. Are you good at catching?"

"Yep. We got this," she replied.

"Sweet," Berkley said.

The three of them went in close for a huddle to go over the play and Sasha casually put her arm over Berkley's shoulders.

Randi rolled her eyes and concentrated on Olivia going over their defensive play. She planned to go after the receiver because she was the tallest, and used to jumping in the air for balls. Carrie was fast, so she had her on the running back, leaving Randi to go after the quarterback.

As soon as they were ready, Sasha bent down with her ass in the air, giving Berkley a nice view as she prepared to hike the ball.

"We don't have to do a full hike. Just have the QB hold the ball and call the hike. You can stand behind your blocker though," Olivia said.

Randi was sure she saw Sasha pout as she stood up and handed Berkley the ball. *Seriously? Could you throw yourself at her anymore?*

"Shotgun, sixty-nine," Berkley called the play, then yelled, "hike!" She quickly rushed backward as Jorja took off running, then cut back in for a slant.

Sasha blocked Randi as she tossed the ball like a bullet through the air.

Olivia dove into the air, catching it before Jorja, but Jorja was able to get her hands on her to stop the play.

"Damn it," Jorja said as they got back into the huddle.

"It's alright. We've got this. Jorja, you're on Olivia; Sasha, you stay with Carrie. I've got Randi," Berkley said as they stepped up to the line.

Olivia called her play and dropped back similar to the way Berkley had, then launched the ball.

Berkley caught the ball, but Randi grabbed her from behind, stopping her progress.

Sasha slapped Berkley's ass as they went back into the huddle.

"This time, Sasha, when I call hike, you turn and run behind me. I'm going to hand it off to you and fake a throw."

"Got it," Sasha said.

"Jorja, you act like you're running out to catch it, but come back to block for her."

Berkley called hike and dropped back. She spun around and put the ball in Sasha's hands. Jorja returned to block for her after Olivia had taken off running to catch the ball. Randi and Carrie were confused as to who had the ball when both Jorja and Sasha took off running. Sasha crossed the goal line for a touchdown and Berkley and Jorja rushed up to her.

"That was awesome!" Berkley cheered, putting her arms around both women as they celebrated.

*

The game continued for several more plays, with Berkley's team up by one touchdown. Randi had just about had enough of Berkley and Sasha's flirting. She figured Sasha would be all over her, but she was surprised at Berkley for not only allowing it, but being playful right back.

"I'm going to change it up this time," Berkley said. "I'm going to call hike and run with it myself. Jorja, you fake for the pass and Sasha, you run to the opposite corner like you have the ball. If we score, we win. Otherwise, they get the ball for a chance to tie it."

"Let's go!" Olivia said to her team as they lined up.

Berkley called hike and faked a handoff to Sasha, who began running. Then, she faked a pass to Jorja before taking off towards the goal line with the ball in her hands. She had no idea Randi was right beside her until she slide-tackled her, sending them both tumbling in the sand at the goal line. Randi ended up on top of her and quickly rolled to her side.

"Did you score?" Jorja said.

Everyone began looking for the flip flops.

"Considering I was fouled, I'd say so," Berkley said.

"Oh, please," Randi huffed.

"You did tackle her," Carrie said.

"You definitely crossed the line," Olivia said.

"Yeah, but were Randi's hands on her before or after?" Jorja questioned.

"It's a touchdown!" Anna yelled. "Randi got her at the line. It's a score!"

"I have sand in places I really don't want sand," Berkley said as she headed down to the water.

"I'm going to rinse off," Randi said, turning towards the water as everyone else gathered the shoes and went back up to the chairs.

Berkley dunked her head and came up, spraying water around as she ran her hands through her short hair. Randi sunk down so that the warm water went up to her neck, washing the sand away.

"What's your deal?" Berkley asked, seeing her nearby.

"Me? What's your deal with Sasha? You look pretty chummy."

"Wait a second. Is that why you tackled me?"

"I was trying to stop you."

"Oh really?"

"Uh-huh."

"There's nothing between Sasha and I...just so you know. We were all just having fun," Berkley said. "But, even if there was, what's it to you? You have a girlfriend, or whatever you call your relationship that you casually hide and stoke the rumors on social media," she said as she walked out of the water.

"Is that story true?" Randi asked, catching up to her.

"What story?"

"When you got here. You said you saved a kid. That's why you were late."

"Yes."

"All of it?"

"Why would I lie?" Berkley questioned, stopping her pace. "I have nothing to prove to any of you."

Randi kept silent.

"We have to do this again," Sasha said as Berkley walked up to the group. Randi was a few yards behind her.

"Hey, we're having a party at our house for Jorja's birthday next weekend. We'd love it if you came and celebrated with us," Olivia said.

"Uh…sure. Yeah." Berkley smiled. "Can I bring someone?"

"Absolutely."

"Cool. I should probably get going. I need to go to sleep," Berkley said as she told everyone goodbye and collected her things.

"Did you just invite her to the party for Jorja?" Randi asked, coming in on the tail end of the conversation as she began to towel off.

"Yeah. Don't forget to give her our address."

Randi nodded as she watched her disappear into the path that led to the parking lot on the other side of the tree line.

23

As she went through the motions of a routine practice, Randi replayed her conversation with Berkley. *You have a girlfriend or whatever you call your relationship that you casually hide and stoke the rumors on social media.* She was right, but what bothered her the most was her own jealousy and how easily she'd acted on it. *Damn it. Why do I feel like I can't breathe?* She gasped, but no air was coming in. Carrie's voice was faint in the background behind the loud thoughts in her head.

"Randi!" Carrie yelled.

The coaching staff skidded to a stop, kneeling quickly next to the player who was laid out on the ground. "Randi…" Jason said as he rubbed his hand back and forth in the center of her chest. "Take a breath."

The thoughts clouding her brain began to fade into one word: *breathe.* The crushing feeling in her chest lifted and she sucked in a full breath, causing her to gasp and cough. Her eyes bounced around like marbles as they opened to the bright sunlight overhead. She was lying in the middle of the practice field with most of her teammates and the coaching staff surrounding her. *What the hell?*

"Back up, everyone. Give her some space. She just got the wind knocked out of her," Jason said, ushering the team away. "She'll be fine. Let's go run through the concussion protocol just to be sure you didn't hit your head when you fell."

"What happened?" she mumbled as he helped her to her feet.

"The ball hit you square in the chest. I don't think you saw it coming, then BAM! It laid you out right here."

Randi didn't remember any of it. One minute she was thinking about Berkley and the next, she was lying on the ground, unable to breathe.

One of the staff members handed her a cold bottle of water. She thanked him and took a few small sips. It was scorching hot, even at ten a.m., but like the rest of the team, she was used to it.

"I don't think you hit your head," Jason informed, finishing his assessment. "However, MJ said to take the rest of the day off anyway."

"I feel fine."

"Coaches orders, not mine. Although, I agree."

Randi rolled her eyes and began unlacing her cleats as he left the locker room. There was still two hours of practice left, so she wouldn't see Olivia for a while. She took out her phone and sent her a quick text, hoping she'd see it before she found out what happened. Then, she tossed her regular clothes into her gym bag with her cleats, slipped her flip flops on and left, still wearing her practice uniform.

As she got behind the wheel of her car, she plopped her bag into the passenger seat and pressed her forehead against the steering wheel. "You have to let her go," she sighed as she turned the key.

*

Berkley set her pencil down and checked her watch. Then, she took a deep breath. This was it. There was no reason to go over her answers. She'd taken the time to answer each question and mark her answers perfectly on the bubble sheet. Each of the essay questions had written answers, which she'd already spellchecked. She got up from the desk and walked over to the police academy instructor who was administering multiple tests at the same time for various departments.

"Good luck," he said as she turned in her testing materials.

"Thanks," she muttered, smiling thinly.

The afternoon sun was high in the sky. The seat on her motorcycle was burning hot when she climbed on and slid her hat on backward. She wanted to share her excitement, but her thoughts turned to Randi. *Why would I call her? We're not that close. She doesn't know about any of this. You have to let her go.* She chided herself for even thinking of her in that moment, then she started the bike and drove off with the thunderous roar.

*

Randi was freshly showered and asleep on the couch when Olivia walked in, waking her with a tap on the foot.

"What happened?" she asked, sitting on the adjacent chair.

Randi shook her head and sat up. "I have no idea. I must've lost the ball in the sun or something. The next thing I know, I couldn't breathe and opened my eyes to see everyone around me, staring at me like I was dead."

"Geesh. You weren't concussed, were you?"

"No. Jason checked me over. He probably would've cleared me to come back out, but MJ sent me home."

"Good for him. Getting the wind knocked out of you is no joke."

"I'm fine. How was your practice?"

"Same shit, different day," Olivia muttered, getting up to get something to snack on in the open kitchen. "Have you eaten?"

"No. I fell asleep," Randi replied, checking her phone. She had two texts and a missed call from Carrie, as well as texts from most of the team members, and MJ, checking on her. "You'd think I died and came back to life," she laughed and quickly sent a text to Carrie saying she was fine and would call her later.

"I rushed home to check on you, so I skipped out on the team lunch."

"We can order in, or go somewhere, if you want. I promise, I'm fine. It was a crazy, fluke thing. It's just never happened to me before."

"I'll order a cauliflower crust pizza from that place up the street. Do you want the usual toppings?" Olivia called as she walked down the hallway.

"Yeah, that's fine," Randi replied, staring out the window. She hated lying, and in hindsight, she hadn't exactly lied. What had happened to her had in fact never happened before. Her concentration on the field had never been broken, and she'd certainly never lost herself in her own head. She needed to talk about it, and Carrie was too close. She grabbed her phone and dialed her sister. "I'll be outside," she said.

*

"Ay dios mio! Miranda Francisca! You could've been killed!" Elisa growled.

"I'm fine," Randi stated.

"That's not like you to space out."

"You think?!"

"What's going on with this girl? Are you having an affair?"

"No! Nothing. That's just it. Nothing is happening. We're just friends."

"You kissed her."

"That was weeks ago."

"Uh-huh."

"Elisa, I'm serious."

"Then, why was she in your head today?"

"I don't know," Randi sighed.

"You want something to happen with her, don't you?"

"No...yes...Hell, I don't know."

"Where is Olivia?"

"She left to go pick up our pizza."

"Sis, you need to figure this shit out before you drive yourself crazy."

"I know, but I have no idea how. I've never been in this situation."

"Me either. I'm lucky to get one guy, much less two at the same time."

"I'm not with two people," Randi corrected.

"Maybe not physically."

"Olivia's back. I gotta go. Te quiero."

"Love you too," Elisa said just before Randi ended the call.

"How's the family?" Olivia asked.

"Good. Everyone says hi," she said, faking a smile.

*

Berkley pushed on the button for her garage door opener, which was in her front pocket, as she drove her street. The door was all the way up by the time she pulled into the driveway, riding through the wide space between her cruiser and truck. The bike rolled to a stop next to the trailer with her four-wheeler and ATV on it, and she killed the engine.

Walking into the house, she tossed her hat onto the kitchen counter and grabbed an ice-cold beer from the refrigerator. It was a bit too early to drink, but she was off with no plans to go anywhere, and she needed something to cool her down and clear her mind. An IPA sounded perfect.

24

Two days later, Berkley stood in the back of the roll call room, shifting her weight from one foot to the other as the lieutenant updated the oncoming shift before they went out on the road.

"What's wrong? You have to pee or something?" Garrett whispered.

"I'm supposed to go to the captain's office after this. I think my test results are in," she muttered.

"No shit?"

"What was that in the back? Tomayo, Ward? Either of you have anything to add?" the lieutenant asked.

Berkley shook her head.

"Alright. Be safe and have a good shift," he said to the group.

"I'll call you when I'm done here," she said to Garrett before turning and heading down the hall. She tapped her knuckles on the frosted glass before opening the door.

"Ward. Come in," the captain called, waving her inside. "I'll get straight to the point. You passed the SWAT exam."

Berkley stared at him, her eyes frozen.

"You look surprised. Did you expect to fail?"

"Uh…no, sir. I…"

"You only missed three questions. That's tied for the highest score ever, so you should be damn proud. Also, you're scheduled for the psych and PT exams in two weeks. If those go okay, which I think they will, you'll be going to SWAT training a week later. That's the next class opening."

"Okay. Great," she said, still in shock as she turned and left his office. *Holy shit.*

*

Randi pulled up in front of Carrie's townhouse and beeped the horn. She glanced at the rearview mirror. The girl looking back at her had a backward snapback covering her long wavy hair and Rayban sunglasses over her eyes.

Taylor Swift's song *Ready For It* was blaring through the open windows.

"It's game day, bitch," Carrie said, getting in and pulling her seatbelt on.

Randi grinned as she squealed the tires and drove off. Carrie's car was in the shop for routine maintenance, and they wound up running over the allotted time, so Randi had agreed to swing by and get her on the way to the stadium. It was a Saturday afternoon game, and Olivia had left earlier to do some media stuff for the front office.

"How are you feeling?" Carrie asked over the radio.

"Fine. Great," Randi answered, flipping on her blinker to change lanes.

"You scared the hell out of me. I've never seen you…"

"Lose concentration and make a rookie mistake?" Randi finished, turning her head to face her. "It won't happen again."

"It didn't have anything to do with Berkley and Sasha did it? They looked a little chummy at the beach."

166

"Nope."

Carrie nodded and reached over, turning the next song up louder as she began singing, "Look what you made me do."

Randi joined her, bobbing her head as she sang along.

One of the team's media crews was outside taking pictures and filming their arrivals for social media. They both waved as Randi pulled the white BMW into a parking space and pressed the button to roll up the dark tinted windows.

*

South Texas was hot at three in the afternoon. Way too hot for a soccer game. Once the warm-ups were finished, the Richey players headed into the locker room for much-needed hydration and air conditioning.

"We're going to melt out there," Jorja whined, wiping sweat from her forehead.

"Who the hell schedules games in the middle of the day?" Sasha grumbled.

"It's because it's being shown live on some new channel that is thinking of picking up all of the NWSL games for next season. Quit bitching and go out there and do your job, because if the league folds, you won't have one," Olivia snapped.

Carrie glanced at Randi, who raised a questioning brow.

"Everything okay?" Randi asked, stepping up next to her.

"Fine," Olivia sighed.

"What's wrong? Come on, it's me. We don't keep secrets," Randi said, feeling like a hypocrite.

"My contract is up at the end of the season. I'm not sure it's being renewed. I may get traded."

"What?" Randi's face scrunched. "That's ridiculous. You're the captain of the team and one of the best goalkeepers in the damn league. Besides, you're a federated player. They don't pay your salary. You cost them nothing."

"You don't think I know that?" Olivia growled. "I'm sorry," she sighed, looking at Randi's eyes.

"How do you know what's going on?"

"I overheard the owner talking on the phone when we were shooting the commercial this morning."

"Did he actually say your name?"

"No, but he said they are not renewing one of the federated players."

"Me, you, Carrie, and Mavis are the federated players. It could be any of us."

Olivia shrugged. "I may not make the national team next year. I'm getting older and younger keepers are nipping at my heels to take my place. If that happens, Richey will get rid of me. I'll have to go to another team…or back to Canada."

"I honestly don't see any of this happening. Go ask who he was talking about. If you won't, I will."

"Randi, we're about to play a game. Besides, I'm not marching into his office like a mad woman."

"Then, channel your anger and take it to the field. We need all the help we can get. It's hot as hell, and North Carolina has already beat us this year."

Olivia shook her head and laughed.

"Time to take the field, ladies," the assistant coach yelled outside the open door.

Most of the team was already in the tunnel. Randi and Olivia had gotten caught up in their conversation and missed them leaving the locker room. As she took her place next to Olivia, who was at the front of the line, Randi looked around for Berkley. She hadn't seen her at all and wondered where she was.

*

As soon as the ball moved off the centerline, Randi went into another gear. She was bound and determined to move on from her practice debacle, and scoring a quick goal would certainly help. She rushed after a midfielder who had the ball, chasing her all the way to the sideline before she won the ball, then bounced it off the other player so it would go out for a throw-in. This gave her team time to regroup as one of the midfielders ran over to take the throw. Randi cut between two North Carolina players in time to head the ball over their heads to Carrie, who was already on the run. Randi quickly overlapped her and Carrie sent her a beautiful pass. Randi trapped the ball and weaved around her defender. With one swift motion, she kicked the ball with the sweet spot on the inside of her foot, sliding it right past the keeper's gloved hands as she dove for it.

They were less than three minutes into the game and Richey had gone up one to nothing. Most of the team piled onto Randi with cheers and excitement before quickly reorganizing to start the ball once again. This time, a North Carolina player took off on a breakaway, easily slipping through the midfield and edging out Sasha. Olivia stretched as far as she could as she flew through the air like a superhero with no cape. The ball barely touched the tip of her longest finger on her right hand, but it was enough to push it slightly past the post. The replay on the big screen looked like it missed the goal by mere inches.

The Richey players quickly rushed into the box to help cover for the corner quick. North Carolina played a shallow ball, passing it back and forth between two players before sending it into the box. Jorja jumped up, heading the ball back out of the box, where Carrie kicked a long pass up to Randi who was on a breakaway with plenty of space in front of her.

The whistle blew when the offside flag flew up.

"Ref! No way!" Randi argued. "I wasn't offside!"

She ignored the protest and blew the whistle for the North Carolina player to take the indirect kick and restart play. Frustrated, Randi took off running to catch up to her mark.

*

By the time halftime rolled around, the score hadn't changed, but both sides were worn out from the intensity of play and extreme heat. Everyone rushed for water and sport drinks in the locker room.

"We have to slow the game down. If we keep at this pace, we'll have nothing left at the finish," Olivia said, sounding more like the captain they were used to hearing. "Push up and keep pressure on them. Don't let them get out into space. If they get on a breakaway, it's going to get harder and harder to run them down. I know they're as tired and as hot as we are, but this is a game of conditioning and ball control. We train in this smoldering heat day after day. They have an indoor facility. They're going to run out of gas, and when they do, we'll still be going with plenty left in the tank."

"I couldn't have said it better myself," MJ said, stepping into the middle of the room. He'd been their coach since the franchise began, and all of the women liked him and looked up to him. He was a retired national team player with many years under his belt. "Our midfield collapsed several times. That's how they're getting out on us. Stay tighter and work your triangles to overlap. When we win the ball, send it forward cleanly, but as fast as you can. Make sure they're the ones running up and down the field chasing the ball. Control…control…control. We control the ball; we control the score; we control the game." He glanced around the room, then nodded at Olivia.

"This is our house! We're not letting these bitches come at us!" Olivia yelled, putting her hand out. The other players gathered around her, putting their hands in. "What is this?"

"Our house!" everyone yelled.

"What?" she shouted.

"Our house!" they yelled again.

"You're damn right! This is our fucking house! Let's go!"

A few players slapped hands and some slapped asses as they lined up to take the field for the second half.

*

"Do you think taking Mags is a good idea?" Dena said, leaning her hip against the counter as she crossed her arms.

"You're busy, so…"

171

"She's your second choice? Given your history, and the fact that you know she still likes you…"

"I'm not into her. We're just friends. I told you it wasn't a date."

"And that makes it okay?" Dena huffed. "You sound like a guy."

"Hey, don't bring me into this," Garrett said, walking into the kitchen.

"Too late," Berkley uttered.

"Just because you have a penis, doesn't mean when I refer to the word guy, I mean you. Unless, of course you think it's okay to play a girl to get another girl," she said with a deadpan stare.

"What? No," he backtracked, wishing he could go back to their bedroom like he never entered the conversation. He loved Dena, but she was feisty and when she got on a roll, it was damn near impossible to stop her.

"Come on, D. You know I'm not doing that. I'm not *trying* to get anyone, much less someone who is with someone else. I've been down that road too many times. Those dangerous curves lead to a dead end. I simply asked Mags along as a friend because I didn't want to go alone. You know what it's like at a party when you know people, but don't quite fit in. I figured if I had someone with me, I wouldn't stand out like a sore thumb."

"Uh-huh," Dena muttered.

"Look, I said I was sorry I didn't tell you about SWAT."

"You think that's what this is about?" Dena shook her head. "You're both still in the doghouse with me on that one. I'm beyond pissed at you." She looked away, then back at the deep blue eyes staring at her. "But, I'm very

172

happy for you. You've talked about SWAT ever since you decided to leave me to go be a cop."

"Then, what's with the lecture?"

"Because I'm still pissed at you for one, and two, I think you're going to get yourself in trouble with this girl."

"I'm not. I promise," Berkley said, getting off the stool. "Can we hug it out? I need to get going."

"Yeah, we have a reservation, so…"

Dena spun around and looked at Garrett. "I'm not through with you," she grumbled before turning back and hugging her best friend. "I love you. I'm always going to have your back and call you on your shit. You know that."

"I know, and that's why I love you, too," Berkley said with a smile as she squeezed her.

25

"Oh shit," Carrie mumbled, pulling her drink to her mouth.

"What?" Jorja asked, turning around. Her lips quickly formed an 'O' when she saw the newest arrival to the party had brought a date with her. "Sasha's going to lose her shit," she uttered.

Carrie wasn't worried about Sasha's reaction; she immediately scanned the small crowd for Randi.

*

"Is it weird that I'm nervous?" Maggie asked.

"Their bark is worse than their bite," Berkley replied under her breath as a handful of people turned around, watching them walk out of the sliding glass door opening after having come through the house from the front door.

"Welcome to Jorja's birthday party," Olivia said, swigging a light beer.

"Thanks for the invite. This is my friend Maggie. Mags, this is Olivia. She's the team's goalkeeper."

"Cool," Maggie said, nodding her head.

"There's beer and water in the cooler and some kind of fruity rum punch in the container on the table. Various types of burgers will be coming off the grill in a minute.

Also, in case you missed it in the house, there are all sorts of appetizers and such, spread around the kitchen."

"I feel bad, we didn't bring anything," Berkley said.

"I didn't ask you to. This has been planned for weeks. It's no big deal." Olivia smiled. "I think you know most of the team. Make yourselves at home. We have cornhole and horseshoes. It'll cost you five bucks to get into any of the games. I'll warn you, these girls get pretty serious."

"I'm good, thanks," Berkley said before Olivia walked away to go deal with the grill.

*

"Hey," Olivia said, bumping into Randi in the kitchen when she brought the freshly cooked burgers inside. "With all of the excitement over the win, and getting ready for the party, I forgot to tell you I talked with the owner before I left."

"You did?" Randi stared at her with her eyebrows up, waiting to hear the news. "So…"

"It's Mavis. She's been plagued with injuries for the past two years, so it makes sense that she may not be a federated player next season, and they aren't going to pay her salary if she's not of use to them. He also told me I have a place on this team as long as I want to be here."

"Babe, that's great!" Randi exclaimed, kissing her on the cheek. They rarely ever showed affection in front of the team. That was their work environment, and they'd chosen to keep it that way.

"Got some other news too, your cop friend is here, and she brought a date." Olivia wiggled her eyebrows.

175

"She what?" Randi's face scrunched as she peered out through the sliding glass doors, trying to find her in the small crowd.

"She has a pretty blonde with her. Sasha's going to flip out," Olivia laughed.

"Yeah," she muttered.

Olivia went to work separating out all of the different burgers so the vegetarians, non-beef eaters, and regular people didn't get things mixed up, while Randi walked outside to the screened patio. A few players and friends were sitting and standing in there, and the rest of the group was out on the lawn, playing the games and standing around talking. Her jaw clenched when her eyes found their target. Berkley was standing near the cornhole game, wearing jeans and a tight black Polo that hugged her muscled frame. Her head shook involuntarily when her eyes scanned the blonde next to her. She was cute; dirty blonde hair pulled back in a ponytail, high cheekbones, and thin lips. She was in khaki shorts and a salmon-colored top.

"I see you staring at her like you want to choke the life out of her," Carrie whispered, sliding up next to her. "Pull it together before everyone else notices, too."

"I'm fine," Randi growled through her clenched jaw.

"No, you're not. What's going on with you?"

"Nothing." Randi shook her head and grabbed the beer from Carrie's hand, taking a long sip of it. "Your beer is warm," she mumbled, handing it back.

"If I can see right through you, so can Olivia. You really want that right now?"

"I kissed her," Randi whispered with a sigh. "It was a while ago, and a huge mistake."

"You think!" Carrie exclaimed.

Randi shot her a sideways look.

"Nothing else happened. She actually pushed me away because she knows Olivia and I are together."

"Well…" Carrie said, surprised. "I have a newfound respect for her."

"Yeah, she's a real saint," she grumbled, walking back into the house.

*

"Can you believe she brought a fucking date?" Sasha growled, plopping down on a stool in the kitchen.

"I honestly don't care," Randi said.

Sasha huffed and pouted as she made herself a plate of food and went out to the patio to eat.

"Did I do something?" Berkley asked, coming up behind Randi. With everyone outside eating, they were the only two people in the house.

"You weren't at the game today."

"I was off tonight, but it was an early game. I wouldn't have been working it anyway."

"You still could've come to actually watch it."

Berkley nodded. "That's not what's wrong with you, though. I saw you looking at me, then you came back in. If you didn't want me to come, you should've said something."

Randi got lost in the blue eyes staring at her when she spun around. "Who's the blonde?"

"Mags? She's Dena's riding partner. We've been friends for a few years. Does it bother you that she's with me?" Berkley asked, watching her expression.

Randi grabbed her hand and pulled her down the hallway, into the spare bedroom. The door was barely closed behind them before her lips met Berkley's in a ferocious kiss.

Berkley began to lose herself in the soft lips against hers as their tongues slid together. She put her hands on Randi's waist, and for a split second, she thought about sliding them up her back, pulling her closer, but she pushed her away instead, breaking the kiss.

"I'm not playing games," she said.

Randi bit her lower lip and sighed. "It's a long story, but I can't just dump Olivia to the curb. It's not like that."

"I'm still not getting involved with you," Berkley said. "She seems like a nice person."

"She is. She's great, but we're not great…anymore. Haven't been for a while."

Berkley pulled the door open and walked away without saying anything to her.

Randi watched from a distance as she and her friend said their goodbyes. *Miranda, what the hell are you doing?*

*

"I didn't mind staying longer," Maggie said as they got into Berkley's truck. "I still wished you would've picked me up on the motorcycle. You didn't have that back when we were dating. I think it's sexy as hell."

Berkley smiled and shook her head as she started the truck and drove away. It would be so easy to sleep with Maggie. She was more than willing, and single, but it wouldn't be the same. No amount of sex with someone else would get her mind off of Randi. "Maybe another time," she said, adding, "thank you for going with me. I had fun."

"Me too, but you suck at cornhole."

"I told you not to pay the money for me to play," Berkley laughed.

*

As soon as she was home, Berkley grabbed a beer and plopped down on the couch. She kept replaying the kiss and the conversation. "Damn you, Randi Rojas. What do you want from me?" she mumbled, twisting the top off the bottle. "Why play games? I'm too damn old for this shit. I've played every game in the book…from both sides. No one wins in the end." She tossed the metal cap towards the kitchen. It bounced off the wall and landed on the floor. *You have no idea what you do to me. I swore I wouldn't go down this road again.*

*

"I think it was a good party. Jorja certainly had fun," Olivia said, getting into bed.

"Yeah." Randi nodded.

"Berkley left early."

"She was tired. Tonight was her first night off in a few days," Randi lied. She squeezed her eyes closed and sighed inwardly. This wasn't her. Lying and sneaking around, kissing someone else. *What are you doing to me, Berkley Ward?*

26

Berkley's days off went by too fast. As she started her next work week, her mind was on two things…her psych exam and her PT exam, both of which were scheduled for a few days later.

After a particularly difficult call where she had to go with the Department of Children's Services to remove a child from an unfit home, she drove through Dunkin Donuts drive-thru. The horrible coffee and stale donut didn't matter. She wasn't even sure she tasted them. She'd just needed something to refocus her brain.

"South 5—11-80 reported at the corner of Nettles Road and Ranger Parkway," dispatch said over the radio. At the same time, the call came across the computer in Berkley's patrol car with a little more detail. It was a three-car accident with reported injuries. She grabbed the mic and pushed the button.

"327—responding, two minutes out," she said, pressing the gas pedal to the floor as she flipped the switch for the lights and sirens.

"415—responding, ETA four minutes," Garrett radioed behind her.

Berkley saw a small red car, a dark green SUV, and another vehicle that was so smashed, all she could tell was it was white. From the looks of it, the SUV had run the red light, plowing into the white vehicle, which hit the red car.

She skidded to a stop and keyed the radio. "327—10-98, request EMS." Then, she grabbed road flares out of her trunk and quickly popped a few to signal oncoming traffic even though there was ample light in the intersection, which was protocol for a multicar accident with major injuries.

"EMS is already en route—327," the dispatcher replied.

"Is anyone hurt?" she asked, going over to the red car, which was nearest to her.

"My neck is a little sore, but okay," the twenty-something young man said.

"Sit tight. EMS is on the way," she told him as she rushed to the mangled wreckage of the white vehicle. The driver, a middle-aged male, was slumped over the steering wheel, which was crushed into his chest, and his legs were pinned in an awkward position under the dash. She reached in through the broken window and checked for a pulse, but got nothing. She grabbed his arm, checking his wrist, then went back to his neck. Nothing.

"What do we have?" Garrett asked, rushing up to her. "EMS was right behind me, about two miles back."

"This one is DOA. Check the SUV. The guy in the red car is okay, but complaining of pain."

Dena and Maggie pulled up in the ambulance, with the fire truck coming in front of them. Both women rushed over to Berkley, who was standing next to the white vehicle.

"DOA?" Dena asked.

Berkley nodded.

"Damn, man. I hate those," she sighed as she went into the bag to get out a stethoscope to double-check. Sure enough, there were no breath sounds, no heart rhythm…no sounds of any kind at all.

Maggie had already gone to assess the guy in the red car, and the two people in the SUV were out, walking around.

Berkley stood aside, watching the firemen use the jaws of life to cut open the door so that they could retrieve the deceased man. As soon it popped open, they quickly cut the steering wheel off and pried the dash up before pulling him out and placing his limp body on the stretcher. Dena covered him with a white sheet.

"Guy in the red car has some neck pain but says he doesn't need to ride in the ambulance. His friend is on the way and will take him to the hospital. The people in the SUV are shook up, but otherwise fine," Maggie said.

"What a night," Berkley muttered as Dena and Maggie wheeled the stretcher into the ambulance. The stark white sheet with the outline of a human body lying under it made her sick to her stomach.

"Yeah, haven't seen one of these in a while," Dena said, closing the double doors.

"I had a DCF call right before this."

"Oh, no. Was it bad?"

"We removed a six-year-old."

"Aw. Berk, that sucks," Dena said, squeezing her forearm.

"Yep. Those are the saddest calls…next to having to go tell that man's family that he's not coming home tonight," she sighed. As the senior officer on the scene of a vehicular homicide, she needed to speak with everyone, so she walked away to start with the husband and wife in the dark green SUV.

"I don't think I've ever been to New Orleans," Carrie said as she boarded the plane for their national team friendly game against Mexico.

"Me either," Randi replied, opening a magazine.

"Have you been to the coffee shop this week?"

"If you're asking if I've seen Berkley, the answer is no. I haven't spoken to her since the party."

"I didn't see you talk to her at all."

"It was brief. She and her friend left right after," Randi said, watching the guy load their baggage through the window.

"Do you want to talk about the kiss you told me about?"

"Nope." Randi flipped the page in her magazine.

A few minutes later, the flight crew went through the safety procedures and the plane was pushed back from the gate.

"Here we go," Carrie said, mostly to herself, feeling the excited nerves she usually got when she flew.

*

The flight was quick, and as soon as they touched down, there was a chartered bus waiting to take Randi and Carrie to the hotel, along with a handful of other players who had flown in around the same time.

As usual, the two of them were assigned as roommates for the short trip. It was a weeknight game on Wednesday night, so they had plenty of time to get back to Richey for their away game on Sunday in Seattle.

Randi tossed her bag onto the bed nearest the window and flopped down beside it.

"We have a team meeting in two hours," Carrie said, mimicking her position. "Do you remember our first national team game together?"

"The game or the hotel?" Randi asked with a smile. "Man, that place was weird."

Carrie laughed. "Oh my God, I thought I was going to die when we accidentally ordered porn on the TV."

"Me too! You know what's crazy, we never got asked about it."

Carrie had tears rolling down her cheeks from laughing hysterically. "I bet they think we watched it!"

"It wasn't even in English."

"I bet the subtitles were hilarious!"

"How would you like to have *that* job?" Randi chuckled.

Just then, both of their phones beeped with a group text. The team meeting was starting in five minutes, then they were having a buffet dinner.

27

Berkley wasn't sure doing a psych exam right after the end of a shift was a good idea, but she had no choice. Her appointment was at nine o'clock in the morning. She'd gotten home just before seven, giving her enough time to grab a bite to eat and take a quick shower. She dressed in a pair of black slacks and a light gray button-down shirt with short sleeves. Then, she slipped on a pair of black oxford dress shoes and headed out the door.

"Geesh," she mumbled, riding through the parking lot of the office building, looking for an open space. Finally, after her third loop, someone pulled out. She quickly sped down the aisle from the other side as a yellow beetle turned the corner, obviously seeing the car leave. "Oh, no you don't bumblebee! I'll run your ass over," she said as she pulled up, blocking the beetle as she backed in. She grabbed the coffee she'd gotten from the Grind on the way, and got out of the truck.

"That was my spot asshole!" some young girl yelled out the open window of her car, flipping her middle finger at Berkley.

"Are there assigned spaces in this lot?" Berkley said, looking around for posted signs.

"Fuck you, bitch! I'll whip your ass!"

"Is that a threat?" Berkley asked. She wasn't worried, not in the least bit. She could put this girl over her shoulder with ease and give her the spanking she obviously never got at home as a child, all while holding her coffee cup.

"Bitch, I don't make threats; I make promises."

"Okay, so you promise to whip my ass? Is that correct?"

The girl threw her car in park and swung the door open. Berkley pulled her wallet from her back pocket and flipped it open, revealing her badge.

"I suggest you take your smartass mouth somewhere else. I don't know who raised you, but you certainly have no respect for anyone…including yourself," Berkley said, putting her wallet away. "If you threaten violence on me one more time, I'm not only going to arrest you for threatening an officer, but I'm going to give you the ass-whipping you deserve."

"You can't talk to me like that," the girl spat as she closed her door.

"I just did," Berkley stated, beginning to lose her patience with this kid. "Just so you know, three spots have opened in the two minutes you've been sitting here running your mouth."

The girl grumbled, then drove off.

Berkley shook her head and checked her watch. She had five minutes to get inside the building and up to the third floor. "Damn kid," she muttered.

*

Randi was running along the beach with a laughing smile on her face and the sun beating down on her face. The sand was warm on her bare feet. Suddenly, she tripped and fell.

"Wake up," Carrie whispered harshly when Randi startled awake.

The assistant coach was going over film for the team they were playing that night, when Randi looked towards the front of the room. The last thing she remembered was the head coach going over game strategy and talking about depth in every position, and cross-position players being valuable.

"How long was I asleep?"

"Long enough," Carrie mumbled.

"Is everything okay in the back?" the assistant coach asked. "I know we've been sitting in this dark room for two hours. Let's end it here and head over to the practice field to get our blood flowing."

Randi kept silent, and Carrie simply shook her head at her best friend.

"Is everything okay with you?" Carrie asked as they walked out of the conference center and headed up to their room to get ready for practice. "You seemed restless in your sleep last night."

"Yeah, I'm fine. I couldn't get comfortable."

Carrie didn't believe her. "Are you sure it's not some dilemma involving your girlfriend of five years and a certain good-looking cop?"

"No. I've told you, there's nothing going on with me and Berkley," Randi said harshly. "Maybe you should worry about your own relationship."

Carrie was taken aback. She looked like she'd just been slapped in the face. "Excuse me? What the hell is that supposed to mean?"

"Your conversations are a minute long, and when you're together, you barely talk to each other."

"At least I'm not trying to fuck someone behind her back!"

"Seriously!" Randi was about to go off on her, but she bit back her angry words. "Are we really going to do this?"

"You tell me," Carrie growled, ready to give her an earful.

"Come on, Care, you're my best friend. I don't want to argue with you." Randi sat on the edge of the bed. "I'm sorry," she sighed.

"Look, I know you're going through some shit, and clearly I am too, but snapping at each other isn't us."

"Hug it out?" Randi said, raising her eyes to meet Carrie's.

"Of course." She smiled, holding her arms out.

Randi stood up and stepped closer, hugging her best friend. "I really am sorry. If you need to talk, I'm here."

"I'm sorry, too, and I know. I'm just not ready."

"I understand."

"Come on," Carrie said, pulling away. "Let's go get all sweaty."

"You know we're not even playing tonight. This is a waste of time."

Carrie nodded in agreement as they left the room.

*

"Officer Ward…may I call you Berkley?"

"Sure," she said, looking at the doctor's beady eyes. He was probably in his mid-sixties and had a mixture of gray and brown hair on his head. However, his thin beard was nearly all gray. He was lean and lanky and reminded her of one of those large grasshoppers all folded up in his leather, wing-back chair with a yellow legal pad in his lap. She was directly across from him in a similar chair, with a cherry wood coffee table separating them. She'd never been to a psychologist's office. When she was going through everything to get accepted to the police academy, she'd gone through a psych evaluation, but it had been done at the academy, and by senior officers, not a real doctor.

"Tell me about your parents. Are they both still alive?" he asked.

"Yes. What does this have to do with SWAT?"

"Nothing. I'm just trying to get to know you a little bit."

Berkley nodded. "Let me speed this up a bit. I'm an only child. My parents met at the University of California, Berkley...hence my name. They moved to Texas when they were pregnant with me. They'd both just graduated and my father had a job offer. He's a mechanical engineer for Dyna Tech Oil, where he designs and builds oil rigs and other equipment. He's actually retiring next year. And my mother is retired from the school board. They live in Dallas, and I see them on the holidays. Before becoming a police officer, I was an EMT. When I finished school at the University of Texas, Richey Emergency Services was hiring EMTs and firefighters for two new stations. I applied. That's how I wound up here. I have nothing against Dallas, I was just looking for a place to start my life, and Richey seemed like a good one. After three years as an EMT, I was on a bad call one night where there was gunfire. We were staged a mile away while two people were bleeding to death. The police finally stopped the guy, and we rushed in to find that there was also a third gunshot victim. My riding partner and I did everything we could that night, but all three of them died. I realized I wanted to be the one protecting them, not just saving them. So, I went through the police academy a few months later. I am still EMT certified, and ride along with the fire station every quarter to keep my certification. I guess you could say I'm protecting *and* saving lives now. I'm single, by choice, and I love my job. I'm dedicated day in and day out to the people of Richey."

The doctor scratched his beard and set his pen down. "Well…that was a mouthful," he chuckled.

"I guess I'm nervous, and I have no idea what a psych evaluation for SWAT is," she said.

"Basically, I talk to you…or rather, listen to you." He smiled. "Then, I make an assessment based off our conversation. SWAT is like a beat cop on steroids, if you will. The department has to make sure the people they put there are mentally able to handle the job."

Berkley nodded. "So, me telling you my life story wasn't exactly needed."

"Correct, but it gave me some good insight. And, it's a good story." He smiled. "Listen, Berkley, I'm not here to derail your career path or anything like that. I've seen your file. You're an excellent officer. I'm actually surprised you haven't decided to move up in rank. Have you given any thought to taking the sergeant exam?"

"Sure, but I want to do more than ride a beat before that happens. I've wanted to be in SWAT ever since the academy. I've worked my ass…uh, butt off to get to this point, mentally and physically."

"How do you think you'll stack up with the other SWAT members?"

"The same way I do on the street. I'm a senior patrol officer, and I'm a woman. It takes guts, intelligence, integrity, and a hell of a lot of grit. Working with SWAT means the situation will change, but the variables are still the same. I'll still be a police officer working with other officers who put their life on the line every day, and who are sworn to protect the people of Richey."

He nodded and wrote a few notes. "It looks like our hour is up."

"Wow. That went by fast."

"Yeah, they usually do."

"Do I need to come back?"

"No, not unless you need to have a regular session with me."

"Nope. I'm good."

He held his hand out. "Good luck with everything."

"Did I pass?" she asked, shaking his hand.

"I have to turn in my report, but I don't see anything that would hold you back."

Berkley smiled and nodded before leaving his office. "Holy shit," she muttered as she got into the elevator. "Next up, Physical Fitness. If I can't pass this, I'm never working out again," she said to herself as she walked across the parking lot.

28

The United States was up three to zero with twenty minutes to go. Neither Carrie nor Randi had started the game, and both were still sitting on the bench.

"I told you she was only playing the rookies. She went on and on about position depth and so on," Randi said.

"Yep, put you right to sleep," Carrie laughed.

Randi shrugged.

"Here she comes," Carrie whispered. "One of us is going in."

"Doubt it. She's used most of her subs."

"Rojas, warm up!" the assistant coach said.

Randi gave her a thumbs up and got up. "Son of a bitch. She's really going to put me in with fifteen minutes left?"

"There will probably be some extra time," Carrie said.

"Yeah, two minutes," Randi huffed before jogging off to go through the rigorous routine to warm up her legs.

Carrie continued watching the game with the rest of the team on the bench, periodically glancing at Randi who was down near the other end of the stadium. When she finally jogged back by, she stood next to the assistant referee, who was holding up the board with the number for the player coming off the field lit up in red, and Randi's number lit up in green.

The worn-out player smacked Randi's hands, then she took off running out to her position. There were only ten minutes left in regular time, but with fresh legs, Randi was running all over the field. She quickly passed the ball wide to the midfielder who was running along the sideline with plenty of space. The Mexican defender caught up to her, but not before the midfielder got a cross off in front of the goal. Randi stretched her foot out, touching the ball enough to send it away from the keeper and into the back of the net. A few nearby players rushed over, hugging her before they regrouped to start play once more.

Mexican players worked together, passing the ball up the field, but The USA quickly won it back, sending a long ball forward as the assistant ref held up the sign indicating two minutes of stoppage time had been added.

Randi rushed up the middle but was called offside when a pass was sent to her. Mexico won the ball back, but another USA forward stole the ball and shot it quickly towards the goal. It bounced off the keeper's gloved hands and right over the net. The USA quickly set up for a corner. Randi was at the top of the box but made a run further in as the ball sailed closer. She dove into the air, turning her head as the ball bounced off her forehead. She fell back onto a Mexican player as the keeper jumped up, too late to stop the ball from going into the net.

Randi got up from the ground and ran out of the box with her fists pumping the air. Most of the USA players crashed into her in celebration.

"Hell yeah!" she yelled.

As soon as they lined up to restart play, the Mexican player kicked the ball and the ref blew the whistle, ending the game. The entire USA team rushed together to celebrate.

"Damn, girl!" Carrie said, hugging her best friend. "That header was crazy!"

"I know! I was all twisted around. I was sure it flew into the stands!" she laughed as they went over, shaking hands with the Mexican players and coaches.

"What a game!" the assistant coach said, hugging Randi. "What's that…forty goals for you now?"

"No, more like twenty-eight or maybe thirty," she replied, "but I think it was my thirtieth cap."

"You've got me beat," Carrie said as the assistant coach walked away to talk to another player. "I have nineteen goals and twenty-six caps."

"You know I don't care about the numbers. Give me the golden boot in the world cup," Randi said.

*

Berkley wiped sweat from her brow before it ran down into her eyes. The PT exam had consisted of a two-mile run, and a 150lb dummy pull or carry for fifteen feet. It finished with an obstacle course in full tactical gear, while also shooting at targets that popped out. She had no idea how she'd done, but she was exhausted.

"Your score is a tally of points from your run time, dummy time, and obstacle time. Plus, the number of targets you hit. Fifty is the highest score possible. Forty is the lowest score to pass," Sergeant Jones said. "How do you think you did?"

"Honestly, no idea."

"You got a forty-eight. That's damn impressive. I didn't even score that high," he said. "You beat me by a point. The average is forty-three."

"Wow," she uttered, slightly shocked that she'd done so well.

"We're all done here. I'll get this turned in, and depending on how your psych eval went, you'll hopefully be joining us soon."

"Looking forward to it," she said, shaking his hand. As soon as she was in her truck, she dialed Garrett on her phone.

"How'd it go?" he asked as he answered.

"Pretty damn good. I scored higher than Jones on the PT!"

"Get out...really? He's built like a brick shit house! But, so are you."

"And you," she said as she turned on the Bluetooth and pulled out of the parking lot.

"True."

"Anyway, I think he was smaller back then. He's been on SWAT for a while. I bet he'd get a perfect score if he took it right now though."

"Oh, I'm sure he would."

"Man, I'm exhausted...mentally and physically. I need to go to bed."

"I'll see you tonight," he said.

*

"Welcome back," MJ said, looking at Carrie and Randi. "You made it just in time for our last practice before we travel to Seattle. That was a hell of a header, by the way."

"Thanks." Randi smiled. Their return flight had been early in the morning, giving them enough time to regroup before meeting up with their club team for practice later that day.

"Today we're going to run through a tournament of small side games, starting with 3V3 and moving up to 6V6 with keepers. The players on the losing teams get dispersed and added to the winning teams each round. I've already assigned the first set of teams, so grab the color penny that you need and head out to the practice field. We'll go through our regular warm-up and get the ball rolling," he said.

"This already sounds like more fun," Randi said, picking a pink penny from the box.

"Right. And…I get to play too," Carrie agreed, grabbing a yellow one. "Ohhh…looks like we're enemies," she teased.

"May the best bitch win." Randi grinned.

Carrie laughed and pushed her in the direction of the doorway where everyone was exiting.

*

The first few games went by quickly because they ended when a team scored. After 3V3, they moved to 4v4, then 5V5. That's when Carrie and Randi wound up going head to head because both the pink and yellow teams hadn't lost a game. They were the final two teams in the 6V6 game. MJ blew the whistle to start play and Carrie kicked the ball wide to Jorja, who started up the field with it. A defender caught up to her and they battled until the ball went out. Jorja restarted play, throwing it in to Carrie who took a shot. The backup keeper jumped up, catching it easily, before sending it back down the field.

Sasha headed it in the middle of the small field, and the ball sailed up to Randi, but the defender went for the ball at the same time, connecting her knee with Randi's thigh instead. Randi immediately went to the ground, writhing in pain. Sasha began running towards her, but Olivia was much closer.

"What's wrong?" she asked, kneeling next to her.

"My quad feels like it's burning," Randi winced.

"Aw, man," the defender said. "I'm sorry, Randi. It didn't feel like that hard of a hit."

The entire team rushed over to them, along with the coaches and athletic training staff.

"Back up. Give her some room," MJ said. "Everyone, start cooling down."

"My quad hurts like hell," Randi said through clenched teeth.

Olivia reached out, putting her gloved hand on Randi's shoulder as the athletic trainer began checking out her injury.

"Looks like you bruised the muscle. We need to get some cold therapy on it now to prevent swelling. Can you walk on it?" Jason said after finishing his assessment.

Randi nodded and he and Olivia helped her to her feet. Her leg throbbed, but she got up and walked on her own.

"I'm going to go cool down. I'll catch up to you in a bit," Olivia said, squeezing her shoulder.

As soon as they entered the building, they bypassed the locker room where most of the team was and walked into the recovery room. Randi stripped her penny and practice jersey off and climbed onto a treatment table, sitting with her back against the wall. Jason pushed her foot to her butt, fully flexing her knee. Randi screamed out in pain.

"Damn, that hurts!" she cried.

"It'll help prevent a muscle spasm," Jason said, placing an ice bag on her thigh. "You know, I can't say I'm surprised. Your schedule over the past 72 or so hours has been a little hectic, and involved two flights."

"I've been hit like that a dozen times and never had an injury."

"It could've been lurking from your game in New Orleans, and the hit you just took made it worse."

"It's extremely hot out there. Are you sure it's not a cramp?" she said.

"Does it feel like a cramp?"

"No," she sighed.

"The good news is, it's a mild quad contusion, not a tear or strain. Cold therapy and rest should have you good as new in a few days, maybe a week."

"A week?!" she squeaked.

"Muscles don't heal overnight. You know that."

"He's right," MJ said, coming in to check on her after having a short meeting with the team. "You're not traveling with us tomorrow. Another flight, especially that far away, and back, will only make your recovery worse. The muscle will get tight and it could take even longer to heal."

"Son of a bitch," Randi uttered, feeling deflated. She hadn't had an injury in two or three years, at least not one significant enough to keep her completely out of a game. Her team needed her, and she was letting them down.

"I know it sucks," he said sympathetically as the team walked in to start their recovery.

"Let me tell them," she sighed.

Nodding, he turned and left the room.

"Once you've iced and stretched your quad, we'll move you to one of the ice baths to recover your body," Jason said.

"So, what's the verdict?" Sasha asked.

"No tear, but my quad is bruised. I won't be traveling to Seattle," Randi said, looking at her teammates.

"Oh, man. That sucks," Jorja said.

"Sorry," Carrie said, hugging her.

"I'm glad it's not worse," Olivia whispered, giving her a half hug.

"Thanks, guys. I'll be fine. I'll probably be back to new by the time you get home," she said as the team separated into two groups and got into the large, waist-deep ice bath pools.

"We're going to bring back three points for you!" Sasha yelled. "Good God, this is cold!"

"You'd think we'd be used to it," Carrie laughed.

Randi smiled. She loved this dysfunctional group of women.

*

After several minutes of the ice bath, the team left and began showering and going their separate ways. Randi had already moved to the ice bath. Olivia had come in to check on her after her shower and said she would come back to get her, but Carrie had said she'd take her home. She was running some errands close by, and there was no sense in Olivia driving all the way back.

"Are you doing electrical stimulation too? Doesn't that help muscles heal?" Randi asked, remembering she'd had it once before for an injury in college.

"Yes, stimulation does help in some cases, but with a bruise, the muscle is sore and aggravated, which is why we use ice to calm it and try to keep a hematoma from forming. If you hit it with a jolt of electricity, it's going to get pissed and tighten, possibly even cramp, making it much worse. I know RICE therapy is slow and old school, but with this type of injury, it's your only option," he replied.

Randi grabbed her phone and snapped a selfie for Instagram of her lying on her back on the massage table with an icepack on the leg. *Bruised quad. Out for this weekend's game in Seattle* ☹ Then, she put her headphones on and began listening to music.

Moments later, nearly a hundred people had liked her post and twenty had commented, saying they hoped she got better soon. One person said she was only going to the game to see her play.

Further down the line, her teammates began commenting, saying they were going to get the win and three points for her, and other things like get better soon, and we'll miss you. Olivia liked the picture and commented: *Won't be the same without you on the field.*♥

Some of her USA teammates also commented, hoping she got better soon.

Randi liked the first ten or so comments from fans and all the ones from her teammates. She replied to Olivia's comment with a smiley face.

A half-hour later, the athletic trainer tapped her shoulder, waking her. Randi pulled her headphones from her ears.

"Did I fall asleep?" she mumbled.

"Yep. Must be my healing touch," he laughed.

"Yeah, or the exhaustion from this week."

"You need to rest your body. Take it easy for the next two days. Continue ice and stretching every few hours and do it for thirty minutes at a time. Stay off of it as much as you can today and tomorrow, then on Sunday, take a short walk, maybe down your street and back every couple of hours. I'll see you back here on Monday morning, and we'll see how it's doing. You can take ibuprofen if it's hurting, or use some sport cream."

"Sounds like a fun weekend," she sighed. "Am I free to go?" she asked, realizing there was nothing on her leg.

"Yep. I texted Carrie a few minutes ago. She's on the way."

"What would we do without you?" She smiled, hugging him when she got up. "It doesn't hurt anymore."

"That's because it's calm and soothed like a baby with a fresh diaper and a belly full of milk."

Randi laughed. He and his wife had just had their first baby four months earlier, so his analogy must have been true. She went into the locker room and changed from her practice uniform to a pair of cutoff jean shorts and a white t-shirt. Then, she slipped her snapback on backward and walked out of the practice facility with her gym bag over her shoulder.

Carrie pulled through the parking lot, coming to a stop in front of her a second later. Randi opened the door and tossed her bag into the backseat before getting in and buckling up.

"That was quick," Randi said. "I literally just walked out. Thanks for coming to get me."

"No problem," Carrie replied, leaving the parking lot. "I was over at Anna's."

"How's she doing?"

"Good. Busy as usual. I rarely get to see her anymore."

"That sucks."

"Yeah. I thought about asking her to move in with me, but I'd really never see her. Out here, she's closer to the university and the library, which is where she spends all of her time."

"I can't believe she has two more years of law school."

"No kidding. Me either. I barely see her now as it is," Carrie sighed. "How's your leg?" she asked, changing the subject.

"Feels fine right now, but Jason has been working on it for two hours."

"I bruised my calf in a high school game. It hurt like hell. I can't imagine bruising my quad. That has to be worse."

"Oh, trust me, it hurt like a motherfucker when it happened," Randi said. "It was almost like I got stung by a bee, then someone slapped that spot with a big wooden paddle. The searing pain was insane."

"Ouch."

"I'd rather get hit with another full force ball to the tits."

Carrie laughed.

"That didn't hurt. I just couldn't breathe."

"Maybe there is something about you and practice." Carrie shrugged.

"I've never been hurt in practice, at least not until recently. I don't know what's going on."

"You have a lot going on…whether you want to admit it or not."

Randi didn't comment. She knew Carrie was referring to Berkley. In a way, she was right. Randi had let things get way out of hand, and it was starting to affect her game.

"Thanks for driving me," she said as Carrie pulled into the driveway. "Have fun in Seattle. Kick their asses for me."

"I'll do my best," Carrie said, hugging her across the console. "Take care of that leg," she called out the window.

"I will. I'm not doing anything but resting all weekend," Randi yelled back with a wave before walking inside.

"I was about to order Chinese. I know you like that when you don't feel good," Olivia said, meeting her at the door. She wrapped her arms around Randi, squeezing her tightly before kissing her briefly, and letting go. "You scared the crap out of me when you went down. I'm glad it's nothing too serious."

"Me too. I still hate missing a game."

"I know."

"Chinese is fine. Get my usual. I'm going to take a shower," Randi said as she walked down the hallway.

29

Berkley was happy to see six a.m. on her watch. It had been a long week with both of the evaluations in the middle of it. She was looking forward to three days off. After signing off her shift, she headed home, backing her police cruiser into the driveway.

"How's it going?" her neighbor asked when she walked down to check her mail.

"Not bad, you?"

"Same shit, different day," he laughed.

"No kidding." She smiled and waved as he got into his truck, obviously on his way to work. As she walked back up, she looked around at the yard and sighed. It was in dire need of attention. *I know what I'm doing this morning,* she thought as she went inside, setting her mail down on the counter on her way to her bedroom.

It took less than five minutes for her to remove her uniform, store her gun in the drawer next to her bed, and change into an old tank top, shorts, and sneakers. She rummaged through the refrigerator, grabbing the sugar-free strawberry jelly. Then, she opened the pantry and pulled out the peanut butter and bread. "Can't go wrong with a PB&J," she said as she began making herself a sandwich. She used only one piece of bread, and a little bit of jelly, then loaded it up with a few helpings of peanut butter, before squeezing it closed like a taco. Red jelly squirted out the backend, onto her hand when she took a Jaws sized bite.

She quickly licked it off and went in for another mouthful. By the time she made it outside, the sandwich was gone, along with half a bottle of water.

The sun hadn't been up long, but it was already hot enough for a bead of sweat to break out along her forehead and temples, and also run down her back. Luckily, her yard wasn't too large. After trimming the fence line and edging the drive and walkway, she traded the weed eater for the riding mower. Covered in sweat, she removed her tank top, using the least dirty section to wipe her face before tossing it aside. Then, she started the mower and went to work cutting the grass in her shorts and sports bra. She could care less who saw her. It wasn't like she was naked, and it was nearly a hundred degrees.

*

Randi lay on the couch, watching TV. She'd been up for a few hours and had already treated her leg with ice and light stretching for the required thirty minutes. It was a little sore when she'd first gotten out of bed, but was much better after the therapy. Her mind raced with a hundred things to do: from cleaning the house to heading over to Lake Travis for a day of sunshine and relaxation. After talking to her mother, who was more worried than she should be, she called her sister.

"What's going on with you?" Elisa asked. "You don't get distracted, and you don't get injured. I'm pretty sure they go hand in hand. Are you still messing with that cop?"

"No, and I never was *messing* with her. I'm fine. I wasn't injured when I got the wind knocked out of me, and this is a fluke thing that was probably caused by my crazy schedule this week. My body needed more rest than I gave it, and this was a way of warning me before I hurt myself worse."

"Uh-huh."

"Is she on my mind...sure. I'm not going to lie to you, but nothing else has happened."

"That doesn't mean you don't want it to," her sister chided.

"You want a million dollars. Doesn't mean you're going to get it," Randi bit back. "It's not a crime to desire things. People go their entire lives desiring things they never get close to obtaining."

"You're a hell of a lot closer to the thing you desire than most people."

"Elisa, I'm a big girl. I can handle myself."

"You're right."

"If you see mom, reassure her that I'm okay. She's acting like I broke my damn leg."

Elisa laughed. "You know how she is."

"Yep. I need to go put some sports cream on the muscle."

"Does it hurt badly?"

"Surprisingly, no. But, I've been off of it all morning. Anyway, I'll talk to you soon. Love you."

"Love you, too."

Randi ended the call and tossed the phone on the couch next to her. Then, she got up and lathered a thin layer of white cream on the front of her thigh that quickly turned clear as she rubbed it into the muscle. It smelled like menthol, but the scent didn't linger.

*

With the yard completed and nothing else pending on her chore list, Berkley showered and dressed in jeans and a slim-fitting, baby blue t-shirt that hugged her muscular frame. Then, she pulled on a pair of black Timberland hiking-style sneakers, and snatched her wallet and sunglasses off the dresser and walked into the garage.

As the door rose up, she got onto her motorcycle and started the engine, letting it warm up for a minute before taking off down the road. She was in the mood for a long ride and wished she could listen to music. That was the one thing she didn't like about riding the bike versus taking the truck. She was left with the thoughts in her head, which were anything but silent. Her mind flashed on Randi as she made her way to The Grind to get an iced coffee, and she was nearly taken aback when she backed into an open parking space next to a white BMW that looked a lot like Randi's.

Before she could even kill the engine, Randi stepped out of the coffee shop wearing a black tank top, jean shorts, and sneakers with socks that you couldn't see.

Berkley quickly pushed the button to quiet the bike as she walked over to her. "Hey, trouble. What's up?" She grinned.

"Trouble? I'm pretty sure that's you, not me," Randi laughed.

"Uh-huh. Aren't you supposed to be in Seattle or something?" Berkley said.

"I hurt my leg in practice and couldn't travel."

Berkley looked at the cutoff jean shorts sitting low on her hips, and cut high, revealing the tanned skin of her thighs as she examined her legs. *You are most definitely trouble.*

Randi's chest tightened. She swore she could feel Berkley's eyes on her, despite them being hidden behind the dark glasses. "It's fine...I'm fine," she mumbled, clearing her throat as her heartbeat thumped in her chest like a bass drum.

"Are you coming or going?" Berkley asked, nodding to the coffee shop.

"Just arrived, actually. I saw you pull up and came outside before I got to the counter to order."

"Hop on," Berkeley said, nodding towards the tiny seat behind her.

"I shouldn't," Randi said, biting her lower lip.

Berkeley shrugged and moved to get off the bike, but Randi pushed against her shoulder. Her jaw dropped in surprise as Randi put her foot on the peg and swung her leg over the tiny pad that was considered a passenger seat.

"Where are we going?" Randi asked.

"Where do you want to go?" Berkley muttered, clearing her throat of the huge lump that seemed to close it.

"Anywhere."

"You have to sit close and hold on tight...like you did on the four-wheeler. If you remember."

Like I'd ever forget that. "Uh, yeah," Randi said. Then, she slid forward until she was touching Berkley, but not completely against her, and wrapped her arms around her midsection.

"I'm sorry I don't have a helmet for you."

"You don't wear one."

"I've seen what happens when these things crash. There's almost no use, except to have an open casket, I guess."

Randi gripped her a little tighter.

"I didn't mean to scare you."

"You didn't," Randi said, her mouth inches from Berkley's ear, causing the blood to rush between her legs. "I trust you."

Berkley wanted to turn her head so bad, her chest actually ached. If she moved only a few inches, her lips would meet Randi's. *Damn it, pull it together! You're taking her for a ride on the bike, not fucking her in the middle of this parking lot!* "You ready?"

"Yep."

Berkley looked both ways, causing Randi's lips to graze her cheek, then she took a deep breath and started the bike.

*

The vibration of the machine between her legs was unlike anything Randi had ever felt before. The wind blowing on her face and through her hair was exhilarating as they rode down the street. *Why have I never done this before?* The sensation was like sex without the sex, and she loved it.

Berkley drove through town, then headed towards one of her favorite places, which was a national park that used to be an Indian territory just outside of the city limit, and in the opposite direction of her and Garrett's property.

The ride only took about twenty-five minutes, but Randi didn't care. She was enjoying every minute of being close enough to Berkley to smell her cologne and feel her muscles ripple under her fingers. The thrill of being on the back of her bike only added to Randi's excitement.

Berkley was happy to bring the bike to a stop a few feet off the road. Randi's steady breathing against her neck was driving her mad. "This used to be the home of a tribe of

Comanche Indians in the 1800s," she said, after cutting the engine. "It's now a national park."

Randi looked out at the rolling plain. There were trees scattered about, and open clearings here and there. She suddenly felt very calm, and her mind had cleared of all its thoughts. "It's peaceful," she said softly as she got off the bike to stretch her legs and get a better view.

"Yeah. I found this place right after I bought the bike. I wanted to take a ride and get out of the city traffic and stop lights, so I went in this direction. I love our property, but I like to think of this place as mine alone. You're actually the first person I've ever shared it with," Berkley said, walking up behind her.

"Really?"

"Yeah."

"How many girls have you taken to your property?"

"The only people who have ever been there are our emergency services friends, and those of us who own a piece of it."

"What about the girl who was with you at the party?"

"Mags? Yeah, she's been there a couple of times."

"Did you date her?"

Berkley nodded. "A few years ago, we dated for maybe a month. We are way better off as friends."

"She looked like she wanted more."

Berkley shrugged. "There's nothing I can do about that. I don't feel the same way about her."

"What about me?" Randi asked, turning around to face her. "How do you feel about me?"

"Randi…"

"Just answer me…please."

Berkley sighed inwardly. "I felt something shift inside of me the day we met, and it's never gone back to normal."

"I'm pretty sure I know that feeling. I look at you and all I think about is kissing you. I know it's wrong, but it feels so right. My life is such a mess right now. Not that is was perfect before I met you, but that revealed the flaws I never knew were there."

Berkley looked up to the sky when she felt a drop of water hit her face. A few large clouds were rolling in, but there was no lightning or thunder, and it hadn't gotten dark. Suddenly, the sky opened up and a summer rainstorm began spilling heavy drops, soaking them.

"Oh, my God," Randi squealed.

"Shit! Come on!" Berkley rushed back over to the bike and got on. Randi climbed on behind her as she started the engine. "Where do you want to go?" she asked.

Berkley turned to look at her. Rain poured down as Randi's lips closed the distance, landing on hers in a smoldering, wet kiss. Berkley didn't think about the consequences, or even what she was doing for that matter. She kissed Randi back...hard.

They were both soaked to the bone, but Randi didn't care. She ran her hands up and down Berkley's torso from behind, cupping her small breasts and feeling the hard muscles shivering under the shirt that clung to her like a second skin.

Berkley finally broke the kiss, panting slightly to catch her breath.

"Take me home," Randi said.

There was no one around, so Berkley started the bike and got back on the road easily. She pointed them in the direction of Richey and twisted the throttle. Drops of rain pelted her face, stinging her like tiny darts.

Randi tucked her face against the wet skin of Berkley's neck and held on tightly. Her clothes and her hair were completely drenched, as were her socks and shoes. The rain blasted her arms like needles as they rode down the highway.

As soon as they entered the city limit, Berkley took the back roads that led to her house. Within minutes, she was pulling into her driveway between her patrol cruiser and her truck, thankful the rain hadn't ruined the garage opener that was in her pocket as the door began to rise up.

*

Berkley walked into her semi-dark house with her heart pounding the walls of her chest so hard she wondered if that was what a heart attack felt like. Her mouth watered, dying to taste the mouth she'd become familiar with, and her gut wrenched in agony. She'd never wanted anyone so badly in her life, knowing it was wrong on so many levels.

Randi stepped inside and Berkley spun around, backing her up against the door, slamming it closed as their bodies came together. She brought one hand up, cupping Randi's cool, wet cheek as she bent slightly, claiming everything Randi was offering in a kiss unlike any other. Cool drops of water ran down Randi's face from her hair, creating a sultry mixture of rain and mint between their mouths. Soft, inviting lips opened to her as Berkley pressed for more. She pulled Randi's lower lip into her mouth, slowly running the tip of her tongue along the top of it before sliding it along the velvety surface of Randi's tongue once more.

Their sensual kissing continued for several long seconds that felt like minutes. Berkley pulled her mouth away breathlessly. Her deep blue eyes locked onto Randi's. Their bodies were still pressed together, and she could feel Randi taking quick, shallow breaths.

"We can't do this," she whispered.

Randi's eyes blinked closed as her shoulders dropped. "I know," she murmured, opening them to her.

Berkley ran her thumb over Randi's lips before removing it from her face as she took a step back, putting space between them. Randi's skin felt raw when the cool air hit the warmth Berkley's body had left behind.

"Come on, I'll drive you to get your car," Berkley said softly, grabbing her truck keys off the hook on the wall.

Randi simply nodded.

*

The short drive was silent except for the heavy drops of water pelting the windshield. Randi chanced a glance in Berkley's direction. Her eyes were trained on the wet road, and her chest rose and fell in a steady cadence under her skin tight, soaked shirt. She turned her head towards the window, watching the blur of buildings and streets go by until they rolled to a stop in a parking space next to her car.

Berkley put the truck in park and reached over the console, running her thumb over the back of her hand as she grabbed a hold of it. Randi squeezed her eyes shut and closed her hand around Berkley's.

"Thank you," she whispered as she let go and climbed out.

Berkley waited until she could tell the car was running before backing out and driving away. She let out a huge sigh and her shoulders sunk in dismay as she looked in the rearview mirror, watching the white car head off in the opposite direction.

*

Randi wiped a tear from her cheek as she drove. She had no idea how things had gotten so out of hand. It was as if she'd lost control of herself. Physically wanting Berkley, that she could handle. It was human nature to have sexual chemistry with different people. The growing intimacy between them was what scared her. She'd never had that kind of unbridled passion with anyone…including Olivia.

As she drove through the nearly empty streets, she thought about where she was in her life. For the past five years, she'd desired one person, loved that one person unconditionally, and gave her life to that person. In the matter of a couple of months, everything had been turned upside down. The fact that it had happened so easily, stunned the hell out of her.

*

Berkley pulled her truck into the driveway and rushed into the house, kicking her wet shoes off at the door before heading to her room to take a long, hot shower, hoping it would wash away the memory of Randi and the past couple of hours. In the back of her mind, she knew it wouldn't. *Did I do the right thing? Should I have played the game?*

"You're already in the game," she mumbled to herself as she stepped under the spray. "It began the moment you met. The question is, how is it going to play out?" She began lathering soap over her body as her tense muscles began to relax under the hot water. "You already know the answer to that. Everyone loses. But, for some goddamn reason, you keep playing anyway," she chided herself as she washed her hair. Then, she sighed as she rinsed the suds down the drain. *You've never met anyone like her. That's why.*

30

Randi sat around all day Sunday, replaying everything in her head. She was conflicted, wanted to get it off her chest, but there was no one to talk to. Her sister would give it to her straight like she always did, and Carrie…she had no idea how she'd react; she was teammates with Olivia, too, and the team was like family. She couldn't do that to her. It wouldn't be right to make her keep that heavy of a secret when she was already harboring so much.

Randi acted as if nothing had happened when Olivia returned later in the day with the team after a win in Seattle. She greeted her with a hug and simple kiss.

"Great game," Randi said. "I hated missing it."

"We damn near lost." Olivia shook her head. "If you go back and look at the tape, that was a foul in the box. They should've had a PK, but the ref made a bad call in our favor."

"That happens more often than not."

"I know. You'd think they would get better quality refs," Olivia sighed. "Anyway, how are you? How's the leg? I barely heard from you."

"It's fine. Doesn't hurt anymore or anything. I just laid around here and watched TV. There wasn't much going on besides ice and stretching therapy."

"Are you meeting Jason in the morning?"

"Yeah, he's going to re-evaluate everything and hopefully give me a return date for practice this week."

"Don't rush it. You'll be out the rest of the season if you tear it," Olivia said as she began walking down the hallway to unpack.

"I know," Randi sighed, watching her. She remembered a time when she would jump into her arms when she walked in the door from a trip away and they'd make love for hours. Five years wasn't that long; certainly not long enough to go through a lifetime of emotions, but Olivia had seemed fine with the way things had settled down. Truth be told, up until a few months ago, she had too. *When did we start just going through the motions, and why did we let that become our relationship?*

"You okay?" Olivia asked, walking back into the living room.

"Yeah…a little tired," she answered honestly. She'd hadn't slept much the night before.

"Why don't we order in? Is sushi okay, or do you want something else?"

Randi wrinkled her nose. "Let's cook dinner together like we used to do," Randi said, getting up off the couch.

"What? Cook? Who are you, and what have you done with my girlfriend?" Olivia laughed.

"I'm serious. Do you remember when we used to attempt to make all kinds of different cuisines?"

"Yeah, we burned or butchered most of them."

"We still had fun." Randi smiled.

"I'd rather order sushi or go to that new seafood house. I hear it's really good."

Deflated, Randi sighed inwardly. "The seafood house is fine. It'll do me good to get some fresh air anyway."

*

Berkley pulled her truck into an open parking space on the campus of the State of Texas Law Enforcement Academy, located in San Antonio. There were several buildings scattered around, as well as a dormitory, a cafeteria, an outdoor range, a driving training lot, a PT obstacle course, and two tactical courses. She grabbed her gear bag from the passenger seat and got out, pressing the lock button as she walked away. *Here we go.*

Once she was inside the main building, she found out there were two full-time, live-in police academy classes going on, as well as various training sessions like the one she was there for. The academy was only a couple hours away, but she'd opted for a hotel room a few miles away instead of staying on campus, which her department had paid for.

"You're all checked in, Officer Ward. Orientation for SWAT Training is in room D11. They should be starting in about twenty minutes," the administrator said, handing her an ID badge with her picture on it, along with her name, department, and training class.

Berkley remembered going through the academy there in what had felt like a lifetime ago as she stepped out of the office and headed off in the direction of building D. Not much had changed she noticed as she walked along the drab gray halls and dark blue floor. She checked her watch as she rounded the corner, finding the building she was looking for. Everything had come back to her like it was yesterday.

"Are you here for SWAT?" a man with a deep voice asked. He was dressed in full tactical gear and had two silver bars stitched on his collar to indicate he was a lieutenant.

"Yes, sir," she replied.

"We're meeting right in here. It should start within the next fifteen minutes. You must be Berkley Ward," he said, looking at her Richey PD t-shirt.

"Correct."

"You're the only female in this class. I had three last month."

Berkley nodded. She was used to it. There were only three other women at Richey PD, and she had been one of only four females in her academy class of thirty-five.

"Go find yourself a seat, Officer Ward. It's going to be a long day."

*

The rest of the day went by in a blur as Berkley was fitted with her tactical gear, then spent the next six hours watching videos, taking notes, and reading about SWAT specific procedures. The class was told there would be a test on the procedures at the end of the week. They needed to be able to tell right from wrong in several situations, as well as write out a description of what procedure to use, and how to use it step by step for multiple scenarios.

By the time she was leaving for the day, she was mentally exhausted. She knew the next day would be spent in the range and on the tactical course, which were more her thing. She'd never had issues with classroom work and taking tests; she just preferred to actually do the things herself, instead of reading or writing about them.

"Hey…Ward, right?" a male voice called from behind her as Berkley walked down the hall.

"Yeah," she replied, turning around. One of her classmates was standing a few feet away. He'd been sitting next to her all day.

"Heath Gore," he said, sticking his hand out.

Berkley sized him up as she returned the shake. He was the same height as her, which was short for a male, and skinny. Way too skinny to be on SWAT, in her opinion. He had mousy brown hair, cut short and neat, and brown eyes. She had a feeling he was a little younger than her as well.

"Want to grab a beer?" he asked.

Berkley hesitated, hoping he wasn't hitting on her. With her looks, she might as well be wearing a t-shirt that said the word: LESBIAN across the front of it, but some men were completely clueless.

"I promise I'm not trying to pick you up," he laughed. "I just make friends easily and figure it would be good to have a buddy. It sounds like this week is going to be tough as hell."

"Yeah, it sounded a little like boot camp when the instructor was going over everything."

"Did you serve?"

"No." She shook her head. "Wish I had though."

"Yeah, me too."

"Is the Blue Eagle still open?" she asked, referring to the hole in the wall cop bar she went to when she was in the academy.

"Yeah, that's where I'm headed."

"Sounds good. I'll meet you in like thirty."

"Cool," he said, walking away.

Berkley wasn't sure what building she'd be in, so her truck was parked in a completely different area. As she passed by the dorms, she ran into a couple of female academy cadets who gave her the once over, making her feel slightly uncomfortable. She smiled thinly and kept walking.

She reached her truck a minute later and headed over to the hotel to check in and put her stuff in her room. Then, she traded her Richey t-shirt for a slim-fitting, black one that hugged her ripped frame, before grabbing her keys and heading back out.

*

"I'm from Liberty PD," Heath said as the bartender set two light beers down in front of them. "What about you?"

"Richey," she answered.

"Where's that at?"

"Outside of Austin. Liberty is up by DFW, right?"

"Yeah. It's in the same circle," he said.

"I grew up in Dallas."

"Get out," he said, surprised. "How did you wind up in Richey?"

"I didn't want to stay in the DFW area. I actually drove down to Austin to check out the area and I found out Richey was hiring. I really liked the small city atmosphere."

"Cool." He nodded. "Are you staying in the dorms?"

"No. I'm in a hotel up the street."

"Me too. I'm too old to share a room with someone."

Berkley laughed, thinking he was probably five or six years younger than her, and more than likely hadn't been out of the academy that long.

"Plus," he continued, "I was just here three weeks ago for bomb squad training."

"Really?" she blurted, taken aback. She'd never known anyone who did both.

"Yeah. We're a small department, so a lot of us are cross-trained."

"I have a feeling this week should be easier than the last one," she said.

"Bomb squad was basically learning the techniques to defuse different types of devices, as well as manning the bomb robots. We did some tactical training, like clearing buildings and such, but most of it was about recognizing devices, seeing if you can defuse them, and clearing the device from the scene safely. This week will be a hell of a lot more physical," he said, peeling the label from the bottle before taking a swig. "I have a feeling I'm going to get my ass kicked."

She nodded in agreement. He certainly would never get accepted for SWAT in her department because of his small stature, but he was obviously a good cop if he was training for both specialties. Richey was a small city compared to the large metropolises in the state, but she knew Liberty was much smaller, which made sense that they would cross-train. "It won't be that bad," she said, taking a long sip of her beer.

"You must live in the gym," he said. "You'll get through fine."

Berkley chuckled. "Feels like it sometimes. Doesn't mean I'm not nervous, though. Brawn isn't the same as brains."

"You wouldn't be here if you didn't have both. I'm sure you come from a much bigger department."

"True," she said, finishing her beer. "I'm out of here. I need to get some dinner and go to bed. I work the dusk/dawn, six-to-six shift, so I feel like I haven't slept in twenty-four hours."

"Oh, this week is going to mess you up. By the time you get on regular time, you'll be going back to your shift."

"I know," she sighed. "It's going to play tricks on my brain for sure. I'll see you in the morning."

*

Randi lied on the massage table while the athletic trainer palpated her quad. Then, he put her leg through a few short stretches.

"It feels fine," she said.

"Stay off of it tomorrow. I'm clearing you for light fitness on Wednesday, which means an exercise bike and an elliptical. Nothing more until Friday. We'll re-evaluate then."

"Damn," she grumbled. "Am I going to miss another game?"

"Nah. I think you'll be good to get some minutes Saturday, but you won't start. By the middle of next week, you should be back to the full team practice but MJ has the final say."

"Okay," she said, getting up.

*

As Berkley got into her truck, her phone vibrated with a text message from Randi.

About yesterday…that can't happen again. I'm glad you stopped it.

I know. I agree, she messaged back. Then added, *I'm not going to have an affair with you.*

I never said I wanted an affair to begin with, Randi responded.

I'm glad we're on the same page, Berkley replied.

Me too. Be safe tonight.

I'm not working, but thanks, Berkley texted before tossing her phone into the cup holder. "She makes me crazy!" she growled as she started the truck and drove away.

31

The next couple of days went by in a blur for Berkley. She was a perfect shot every time they were in the range, and she performed well on the tactical course, despite wearing fifteen extra pounds of gear. It was the end of the week when her nerves kicked in; they were running through live drills using rubber bullets. They couldn't kill you, but they sure stung like hell. That was something she'd figured out right away after getting shot by a classmate during a drill when he missed her communication with the team and mistook her for the suspect. Instead of her vest, he'd hit her in the arm, which meant he wasn't a good shot either.

By the time the exam rolled around at the end of the week, she'd felt comfortable enough with the material, and had passed with one of the highest scores in the class.

"Ward…a word, if you don't mind," the instructor said once most of the class had received their certificates and left. A few stragglers hung around, talking to each other.

"Sure," she replied, stepping to the side with him.

"Heath Gore."

"What about him?" she asked, knowing he'd already left.

"You two became pretty chummy during the week."

Her feet felt welded to the floor as her shoulders squared. "What are you implying?"

"Nothing really, except he wouldn't have made it through training without you."

"Is there a problem with helping someone who needs it?"

"No. I've just never seen anyone do that before," he said. "At least, not the extent you went with him. I was just curious why."

"Did you know he's in an understaffed department with low funding? They offer the most money to the officers who cross-train. He was here a few weeks ago for bomb squad training as well. I figured if he was going to go back to his job doing SWAT work, he needed to be keen or he'd get himself killed. I just helped him read his surroundings a little better. That's all."

The instructor nodded. "He's a better cop because of you."

Berkley smiled, hoping he was right.

"You'd make a damn good FTO."

"One day, maybe," she replied. "I have to concentrate on SWAT at the moment."

Field Training Officers were completely in charge of training new hires who were fresh out of the academy. They were the ones who molded and shaped them into the officers they became. A bad FTO would more than likely have officers making mistakes down the road, or even get themselves shot because they had improper training. A great FTO would have officers who went up the ranks or went on to become detectives. She'd thought about it, but she'd need to become a sergeant first.

"Just so you know, I noted it in my report to your captain."

"Thanks," she said.

*

During her ride back to Richey, Berkley thought about what the instructor had said to her. She'd never known her department to have a female FTO, so she had her work cut out for her if and when she decided to pursue that promotion, which would only be available after becoming a sergeant. Right now, she was SWAT certified, the first-ever female for Richey, and heading home to show off how much her hard work on the job and in the gym had paid off.

*

By the time Berkley arrived home, it was late. She was tired, but she knew her friends were both working. She put them in a group text and sent them a snapshot of her certificate and captioned it: *Turning this in tomorrow!*

Garrett immediately called her.

"Way to go!" he exclaimed when she answered.

"Thanks. It wasn't easy."

"We need to celebrate."

"I need to make it official first," she laughed.

"You're back on tomorrow night, right?"

"Yeah. Let's hit the gym. Nine good for you?" she asked.

"That works for me. Shit, gotta go do a traffic assist," he replied hanging up.

Dena had texted while she was on the phone, so she clicked on the message.

Congratulations! I knew you could do it! Busy as hell tonight. Something is in the water around here! I'll swing by tomorrow!

And with that, Berkley unpacked her small suitcase and plopped down on the couch in front of the TV with a cup of coffee. She needed to stay up as late as possible to re-acclimate herself to being up all night.

*

Randi was happy to be back at practice mid-week, albeit, with minimal running and very few touches on the ball. The coach had made it clear for her to take it easy since it was her first session, which she found extremely difficult. Randi was a go hard or go home type of player.

She tossed her gym bag into the passenger seat of her car and looked around the parking lot. Olivia was already gone, but Carrie was walking towards her.

"Want to grab some lunch?" she asked.

Carrie shook her head. "I can't."

"Everything okay?"

"Yeah. All good," Carrie said, getting into her car. She waved as she drove off.

Randi got into her car and stared at the BMW logo on the steering wheel. She sighed, feeling the weight of what had happened with Berkley pressing heavily on her shoulders. She wished she'd told Carrie, or even her sister. But, she would've received a lecture, no doubt, and she was lecturing herself enough as it was.

*

The TV was blaring when Randi walked into the house from the garage. She walked through the kitchen, turning it down as she looked around for Olivia before heading to their room to put her gym bag away.

"Hey," Olivia said, smiling. "You looked good in practice today."

"You must have caught the only play I was allowed to participate in. MJ pulled me right after that," she said over her shoulder as she tossed her bag in the closet.

"He's just looking out for his star forward," Olivia said, placing her hands on Randi's shoulders. She began massaging circles with her thumbs.

"That feels good," Randi mumbled, feeling her tense muscles start to loosen up.

"You've been a little stressed lately," Olivia said, kissing her ear. "Injuries are an athlete's worst nightmare, I know that all too well."

Randi felt Olivia's hands slide down to her waist. Then, they moved around to her stomach as Olivia pressed against her backside, bringing their bodies together. She knew where this was going. She couldn't remember the last time they'd had sex, and a month ago, she would've been all over Olivia by now.

"I have a massive headache," she said, turning in Olivia's arms and kissing her softly before pulling away. It wasn't a lie. She was frustrated about practice, and the coaching staff babying her injury, but that certainly wasn't all that was plaguing her mind.

*

"I see your eating habits haven't changed," Dena chided. She was sitting on a barstool at the small island in

Berkley's kitchen, watching her scarf down a bowl of cereal. "No wonder you and Garrett get along so well. You're just alike."

Berkley laughed. "There's no added sugar in it though!"

Dena shook her head. "He told me SWAT training is like a boot camp for cops."

"Nah. It's nothing like that. We did some bookwork and watched a lot of videos of what to do and what not to do. Most of it was going through scenarios on the tactical course and using various weapons on the range. It was a long week, but I got through it. I made a few friends along the way, so that helped."

"Were you the only female?"

"Trainee, yes. But, the instructor's assistant was a woman."

"Was she cute?"

"Nope," Berkley mumbled, shoving another bite into her mouth.

"He also told me you're the first female in your department accepted to SWAT. That's a huge deal. Why is it I'm finding stuff out through Garrett these days? It seems like you and I never talk."

"I know," Berkley sighed, setting her empty bowl in the sink in front of Dena before she leaned back against the counter with her hands on either side of her, gripping the granite top.

"What's going on?" Dena asked, noticing the change in her disposition.

"Something happened with Randi a couple of weeks ago. I guess I've been avoiding you because I knew if I talked to you, I'd tell you, and I didn't want an earful."

"You slept with her," Dena uttered, staring at her best friend.

"No." Berkley shook her head. "It was headed in that direction, but I stopped it."

"How did it happen?"

"I took her for a ride on the bike. I think something clicked when we got stuck in the rain. We were soaking wet. I went to take her back to her car, but she told me to take her home. I brought her here." Berkley paused, reliving the moment in her head. "I've never wanted anyone so badly in my life. It took every ounce of self-control I have to pull away from her."

"Wow."

"I can't explain this thing between us. It's like we're magnets, pushing and pulling against each other."

"That's intense."

"No shit," she sighed. "I don't know if I'll be strong enough to stop myself next time."

"Do you think there will be a *next time*?"

"Honestly, yes."

"Is that what you want?"

Berkley shrugged. "If she wasn't with someone…"

"You've been down that road more than once. I don't have to tell you how it ends."

"I know."

"I'm not going to lecture you. You're a big girl."

"Thanks," she laughed softly.

"So, since we're talking about important shit, I think Garrett is a little sad about you joining SWAT."

"What? Why?"

"He said you're in the brotherhood now."

"Brotherhood?" Berkley shook her head.

"You guys are like Batman and Robin on the streets. Now, you've joined the Avengers."

Berkley laughed. "Okay, so first, Batman is not an Avenger. Second, Garrett is and always will be my first call. We have each other's back no matter what. Yes, I have other officers whom I work closely with, but that's only on SWAT calls. Everyone is scattered in different districts. It's not like I'll see them every day. We train together a few times a month and see each other on calls. He's my backup and I'm his, every single day. Nothing is going to change that."

"Maybe you should be telling *him* all of this."

"I had no idea he felt this way, or I would have."

"He hasn't come right out and said it, but I picked up on it and made my own assumptions," Dena said.

"We're going to the gym tomorrow after our shift; I'll talk to him."

Dena nodded. "Does he know about all of this with Randi?"

Berkley shook her head. "He and I have things we talk about, and you and I have things we talk about."

"That's probably a good thing," Dena chuckled.

"Yep. You know all boys talk about is tits and ass."

Dena rolled her eyes and shook her head, causing Berkley to laugh.

"Good luck tomorrow. I wish I could be there to see you get the official certification."

"Thanks. It's nothing major. The captain will award me my certificate and a new badge during shift change, and I'll hit the streets."

"It's still a big deal."

"I know it is. I honestly don't think it has sunk in yet that it has actually happened. It probably won't until I get my first call out."

Dena nodded. "I should get going. We've only seen each other in passing the last few days. I want to spend some time together before he has to go to bed."

"Or go to bed with him," Berkley teased.

"That's definitely an option." Dena smiled, hugging her best friend.

32

Berkley walked into the South District Station, fully dressed in her uniform and ready to start a new shift. Technically, she'd radioed in as soon as she'd left her house, which put her officially on duty. However, she still had to make an appearance for roll call before the start of every shift.

Everyone in the roll call room came to their feet when she walked in. The captain was standing at the front of the room with Sergeant Omar Jones, the South District SWAT Team leader. He was brown-skinned, and tall with broad shoulders, bulging muscles, and a black mustache and goatee. A sheen of sweat covered his bald head. Beside him was Lieutenant Mike 'Sully' Sullivan, the SWAT Team Commander. He was a veteran of Richey PD who still loved the thrill of riding the streets. His salt and pepper hair was turning mostly grey, but he was still stronger than most men in the department.

Berkley kept walking and took her place in the empty seat in the front row as her fellow officers sat back down.

"You all know of the honor, courage, and commitment it takes to be a police officer. Some men and women in blue go on to become detectives; some work their way up the ranks and wind up with desk jobs; some ride the streets their entire careers. Then, you have the ones who take it to the next level and join an elite team of police soldiers…if you will. The Special Weapons and Tactics Unit isn't for the faint of heart. It's certainly not for the weak. And, it most definitely isn't for the everyday police officer. However, it *is* for one special officer who not only passed the initial exam with one of the highest scores ever but blew away the training instructor at the academy. Tonight, it is my honor to promote Senior Patrol Officer Berkley Ward to SWAT, effective immediately," Captain Munroe said, waving her up. "I'd also like to note that she is the first-ever female SWAT officer for Richey Police Department," he added.

Berkley stood and walked up to him. He handed her the SWAT certificate and a shiny new silver badge that had SWAT on it in bold black letters. Then, he shook her hand.

Sergeant Jones smiled and shook her hand.

"Welcome to the show," he whispered.

She grinned and moved to Lieutenant Sullivan.

"Welcome to SWAT," he said, shaking her hand before pinning the metal SWAT insignia onto her shirt, which was a solid silver bar made of the four letters. He placed it next to the EMT insignia that was stitched above her name.

"Thank you," she replied.

As soon as she sat back down, the two SWAT members left, along with the captain, and the station lieutenant went on with the shift change meeting.

*

"Are you shitting your pants yet?" Garrett teased.

"Nope." Berkley grinned as they left the roll call room to start their shift.

"Ward…" the lieutenant called.

"I have your new uniform shirts on my desk. I ordered six. If you need more, let me know," he said.

"Wow, that was quick. Thanks."

"This new company we are using has a forty-eight-hour turn around, and they're local, so easy delivery," he said.

"Let's meet up for dinner," Berkley said, talking to Garrett.

"Sure." He nodded, holding his fist out.

She bumped it with her own and said, "Ride or die."

"Ride or die." He smiled, walking in the opposite direction.

Berkley quickly changed into one of the new shirts, noticing the SWAT insignia was now next to the EMT insignia above her name. The badge on the opposite side matched the new metal one she'd received from the captain, with SWAT on it as well. She loved the fact that everything was stitched onto their shirts. She didn't have to worry about anything getting hung up or ripped off in an altercation. She stepped into the restroom to check the mirror and make sure everything was correct, then she grabbed the remaining shirts and headed out to her patrol car.

"SWAT is broken up into two teams of five," Sergeant Jones said, walking over to her. "I'm the Team Leader for the Alpha Team, which you've been assigned to. The city is divided into two sections. We go to all of the callouts for our section and Team Beta goes to everything in the other section. Depending on the severity of the situation, both teams are called out. Anyway, we train together twice a month. I'll get the schedule sent to you. We go to the range one of the days and use an old warehouse for tactical training on the other day. We try to get our schedules lined up. You'll either be with me or Officer Connor McGill until you get your feet wet, so to speak."

"Sounds good. I know Connor. He's on day shift out of West Four, right?" she said, placing her new shirts on the front passenger seat before shutting the door.

"Yeah." He nodded.

"Great. I'm looking forward to it." She shook his hand again, and he walked away, heading towards his patrol car.

*

The game was in full swing by the time Berkley arrived at the soccer stadium. The score was one to zero with Richey ahead of Utah; the second half had only been going for three minutes. She quickly radioed the other officers and took her post on the sideline near the tunnel. She eyed the players, surprised when she didn't see Randi on the field. They hadn't talked since their ride on the motorcycle, except for a couple of texts to say what had happened between them wasn't happening again. That was a week ago.

She scanned the crowd, looking for anything she needed to be concerned about. When she noticed Randi sitting in the players' box on the sideline, it took an extra second for her to pull her eyes away. Thoughts flooded her mind of their soaking wet, passionate kiss in her house, sending her blood flowing south. She shook her head, forcing herself to concentrate on the fans and the job she was there to do…until the place went crazy. She didn't have to look towards the sideline. She knew who was coming into the game.

*

With thirty minutes to go, the coach yelled for Randi to warm up. She stood and removed her penny before going through the motions of their stretching routine. By the time she actually entered the game, causing the crowd to roar, there were only twenty minutes left. She immediately got on the ball, but passed it off when she had two defenders close in her on.

Sasha won the ball back and sent it to Jorja, who worked through the traffic in the midfield with her fancy footwork. Then, she passed it wide to Carrie, who crossed it with one touch in front of the box. Randi got part of her foot on it but shot it directly into the Utah keeper's hands. She sent it all the way to the circle with a powerful kick. Jorja rushed to head it down, but a Utah player beat her to it. Sasha ran backward, anticipating a one on one battle as the player ran down the sideline.

The fans on that side of the stadium were on their feet, screaming and cheering. Sasha watched the ball as the player tried tricking her with fancy footwork, pushing her all the way to the corner flag. Sasha went for the ball and the Utah player accidentally kicked it out, giving it back to Richey for a throw-in.

With only five minutes left, Richey was in defense mode, doing everything they could to hold onto their only goal, and the three points that came with the win. Randi, Carrie, and a few other players went back and forth with a game of keep away until the clock finally ran down and one minute of stoppage was added on. Jorja sent a long ball forward, which Randi chested down right outside of the box. Three Utah defenders were all over her. With no other choice, she kicked the ball back Jorja. Then, the ref blew the whistle, ending the game.

Surprised they'd won another one, and against the team leading the points, the entire team dove on top of each other, celebrating in the middle of the field. The thunderous sound of the sold-out crowd was louder than ever before.

"Holy shit!" Sasha yelled.

"We did it!" Jorja cheered.

"I played!" Randi laughed.

"Way to go, ladies! This is our house!" Olivia exclaimed when they huddled in a circle.

Once she finished the captain's post-game speech, they stretched out a little bit, then walked around the stadium waving at the fans. Some of the players went to the locker room, but most stayed out, signing autographs and taking selfies for half an hour.

"I'm exhausted," Carrie said, bumping into Randi.

"Not me. I only played long enough to get sweaty."

"How's the leg?"

"Fine. If one more person asks me, I'm liable to rip it off and beat them to death with it," she grumbled.

"Guess who's here," Sasha squealed, running up to them.

"Mickey Mouse!" Carrie blurted.

"Huh?" Sasha rolled her eyes and shook her head, causing Randi and Carrie to both laugh hysterically.

"Let me guess, Berkley?" Randi said.

"Yep." Sasha turned and headed towards the tunnel like a giddy teenager.

"Maybe they should go out," Carrie muttered as they started walking across the field.

"Berkley's not interested in her."

"Because she wants you?" Carrie questioned.

"What? No. I just meant if Berkley liked her, she would've gone out with her by now."

Carrie nodded. When they neared the tunnel, she said hello to Berkley, then went inside towards the locker room.

"You look different," Randi said, softly meeting the blue eyes staring back at her.

Berkley shrugged. "I'm on the SWAT team now. Maybe that's it."

"SWAT? Isn't that dangerous?" Randi questioned, noticing the new insignia sewn on her uniform shirt.

"Being a cop is dangerous in general. This is just another element to the job. It's a huge promotion that I worked my ass off to get. I'm also the first female on SWAT for Richey PD, so it's a pretty big deal."

"Wow," Randi said in surprise. "That's great. I'm happy for you." Her chest began to tighten and her stomach started fluttering with butterflies the longer she stared into the deep pools of blue looking back at her. She felt herself inching closer as the tip of Berkley's tongue snaked out, moistening her lips.

Berkley fought the urge to reach out and touch her silky, smooth skin. She was sure Randi had moved closer. If she took a step…

"Be safe out there," Randi whispered before turning and walking away.

Berkley watched her until she disappeared around the corner. Then, she kicked her steel-toed boot against the base of the wall. "She makes me crazy," she mumbled.

*

The rest of the night was quiet in Berkley's area of town, until she got a call around midnight for a drunken person outside of Dunkin Donuts, demanding they open the door for him. When she arrived, she saw the young male in a white t-shirt, jeans, and sneakers, pacing outside, smacking his hand on the glass doors periodically.

"327—on scene," she radioed as she got out of the car. "Hey, buddy!" she yelled to get his attention.

"Oh, man. Come on," he slurred when he turned around and saw her a few feet away. "I just want some fucking donuts. That's not illegal!"

"It is if you're beating on the door, acting like a fool. What's your name?"

"Joe."

"Alright, Joe. You have some ID on you?"

"Nope."

Berkley sighed in frustration. "You have a last name, Joe?"

"Dirt."

"Okay, Joe Dirt," she said, moving a little closer. She could smell the alcohol permeating off of him. "How much have you had to drink tonight?"

"I don't know," he slurred again, banging the glass door once more. "I want some donuts!" he yelled.

"If you touch that door one more time, you're going to have a lot more problems than just wanting a donut!" she growled. "Put your hands behind your back."

"You're not arresting me!"

"Public intoxication *is* against the law, but I never said you were under arrest. I need to cuff you so I can pat you down."

"You're not touching me!"

"So, now you're refusing to cooperate with me."

"Get the fuck away from me," he mumbled as he turned to bang on the glass again.

Berkley lunged, smashing him against the glass as she fought for his hands. "I tried to do this the easy way, but you obviously want the hard way," she said as she wrestled him to the ground. "Give me your damn hands!"

He struggled, wiggling around, but he was a skinny young punk who had no match for her strength. Berkley got one handcuffed, then put her knee in the center of his back, squeezing his lungs as she applied her weight until he relinquished his other hand. Once she had the cuffs secured, she got up and left him lying on the ground screaming obscenities at her.

"327—10-15," she radioed, letting dispatch know she had someone in custody. "10-16," she added, asking them to send another officer to take him down to the jail. "You don't have anything in your pockets that's going to stick me, do you? No needles or anything like that?"

"Stick your hand in there and find out," he growled, still lying face down on the sidewalk outside of Dunkin Donuts.

Berkley shook her head in his direction and pulled a pair of gloves from her back pocket. She noticed the blood on her right knuckles from where they'd scraped the pavement when she was trying to apprehend the drunken man. "Damn," she said to herself.

"Looks like you've been having fun without me," Garrett said, pulling up and getting out of his car.

"Yep. Loads of fun," she replied dryly. "You want to check his pockets for me? Joe Dirt won't tell me if he has any needles."

"Looks like you're already bleeding."

"Scratched my hand on the sidewalk. It's nothing."

"Wait…did you say Joe Dirt?"

"Yep. That's the name he gave me," she said, walking over to check his back pockets for a wallet, which she found. "Stanley Marvin Brewster," she laughed. "I see why you go by Joe Dirt."

"Let's go. Up on your feet," Garrett said, placing his hands under the young guy's armpits and pulling him up off the ground.

Berkley called in his ID to see if he had warrants while Garrett went through his pockets.

"No warrants," she said.

"Nothing but a lighter and a pack of smashed cigarettes in his pockets."

"You're getting a resisting arrest charge and you weren't even trying to hide something." She shook her head. "All of this really was for donuts."

"He's drunk, and he's hungry."

"Well, he's going to jail. Here comes your ride," she said, seeing the transport car pull into the parking lot.

Garrett stuffed the drunk into the back of the car. "If you piss in here, Officer Mickler's not going to be happy," he said, nodding towards the officer who had gotten out of the car.

"Congratulations on making SWAT."

"Thanks," Berkley replied, shaking his hand. "He's ready to go. I put his information and charges into the computer."

"Sounds good," the other officer said as he got back into his car.

"After all of that, now *I* want a fucking donut," Garrett laughed.

"I thought you cut out sugar?"

"I did."

Berkley shrugged and checked her watch. "Want to break for lunch?"

"Sure, but I'm getting a donut first. You want one?"

"Nope."

"How do you have so much willpower?"

"I've been asking myself that a lot lately," she muttered as she headed over to her car.

*

Berkley stared at the stars in the sky as she ate her sandwich. "I took Randi for a ride on the bike before I left for SWAT training."

"Oh yeah, how'd that go?"

"We got soaking wet and nearly slept together."

"No shit?"

She nodded.

"I thought you weren't playing those games anymore."

"I wasn't…I'm not. I stopped it."

"Did you tell Dena?"

"Yeah. She was pissed. She thinks I'm making a huge mistake just being friends with her. Maybe she's right. I mean we clearly can't just be friends."

"You're a big girl. You can make your own decisions. Although, I don't want to see you get hurt."

"Thanks." She wadded up her trash and put it back in her lunch cooler as Garrett tore into his donut bag.

"You want half?" he asked, holding up a frosted blueberry donut.

"Give it here," she said.

"I knew it!" he laughed, handing her the whole donut. "I got two!"

Berkley shook her head and smiled. "I guess my resolve isn't as strong as I thought," she mumbled, taking a bite.

"Nope."

"Listen, there's something else," she started, finishing her donut in two more bites. "You're my best friend on and off the job, and you're my first call, always. SWAT isn't going to change any of that."

"Did Dena say something to you?"

"Yeah, but she didn't have to. I've been so busy with going through the process, we haven't had much time to talk at all. I was waiting to catch you in person."

"It's going to take some getting used to. I won't lie. We've been each other's backup from the beginning, but now you have a whole brotherhood behind you."

"Yeah, but they won't be there day in and day out. They'll never replace my best friend. You're like the brother I never had."

He nodded.

"Don't start crying or I'm going to have to tell Dena," she teased, hoping to cut the seriousness.

"I'm not." He grinned.

"Great, we have an assault call," she said, grabbing the mic next to the computer in her car. "327—10-8. Responding 240. ETA five minutes," she radioed, letting dispatch know she was back in service and headed to that call.

"Why do people drink too much every damn Saturday night and want to fight?" he muttered, grabbing the mic and mimicking her call to dispatch.

33

"All packed up?" Randi said, plopping down on the bed.

"Just about," Olivia answered, walking out of the closet with the last bit of clothing for her suitcase. She smiled at Randi as she zipped it closed.

"It's going to be quiet around here without you for a few days."

"Are you saying I'm loud?" Olivia questioned with a raised brow.

"No. I meant I won't have anyone to talk to, so it's going to be quiet." Randi grinned.

"I thought you said you were going to see your family."

"I don't know. Maybe." She shrugged, following her into the living room. "Five hours is a long drive...alone. Especially when you have to turn around and come right back."

"Yeah," Olivia agreed, grabbing a banana from the counter.

"Are you ready to go?"

"Might as well. My flight leaves in three hours."

Randi nodded and grabbed her keys from the counter. Then, she turned and pulled Olivia into a hug, trying to remember what it felt like to be held by her, but the contact was brief. Olivia kissed her lips quickly and pulled away.

*

The drive to the airport hadn't taken more than twenty minutes since there was a lot less traffic mid-morning. Once she'd dropped Olivia at the terminal, Randi headed to The Grind for a cup of coffee. She checked the strip of parking spaces, looking for any signs of Berkley. The last thing she needed was to run into her. She wasn't quite sure how they'd left things when they spoke briefly after the game, and that was two days ago. She felt like a runaway train, trying to get back on the right track…but wondering where the new track was headed to at the same time.

She pulled into an open parking space when she didn't see the motorcycle or Berkley's truck and headed inside. She contemplated the idea of traveling to see her family while she waited for Paul to make her order. She missed her parents and her sister, but the thought of spending ten hours in a car by herself within 72 hours wasn't appealing at all. "I'll just stay here," she mumbled to herself.

"What was that?" Paul asked, handing her an iced double-shot mocha. "I have two chocolate chip muffins left."

"Not today." She smiled. There was no one at home to take it to. She took a sip of her coffee and glanced around the small area where half a dozen empty tables and chairs sat.

"She hasn't been in lately," he said.

Randi nodded and held her cup up in a gesture of thank you, before walking out the door.

Berkley backed her patrol car into her driveway and turned the key. She'd already radioed the dispatcher that she was home and off shift when she turned into her neighborhood. Looking forward to three days off, she yawned and grabbed her lunch cooler from the passenger seat.

"Morning," her neighbor across the road said with a wave as he got into his truck.

She waved as she walked around the car and entered her house through the front door. She set the cooler on the counter and headed to her room to strip out of her uniform. She'd promised to meet Garrett at the gym later in the day, but contemplated canceling on him. It had been a few days since her commendation for making SWAT. She hadn't had any call outs, but the team was getting together in a week to do some tactical training. She thought about Randi briefly, before her phone lit up with Dena's picture.

"My savior," Berkley said, answering.

"I'm not sure if that is a good thing or a bad thing," Dena laughed.

"Let's go with neither. What's up?"

"We all just got off shift, and if you're anything like this beast sitting next to me, you're starving to death."

Berkley laughed. "I'm fine. I'm actually about to go do my yard work. If I don't get it done today, it won't get done with the nasty weather headed this way from tropical depression what's his name."

"That storm's not coming anywhere near here," Garrett yelled in the background. "If it was, they would've put us on standby."

Berkley knew he was right, but they were still going to get some rain.

"Are you sure we can't entice you to come out with us? We were thinking pizza."

"Nah. I'm not interested in doing extra cardio," she chuckled.

"I heard you guys ate donuts the other night," Dena stated. "A couple slices of pizza won't kill you."

"The donuts were your boyfriend's idea, and that was a call from hell."

"That guy pissed in Mickler's cruiser, by the way," Garrett yelled.

"Ew, gross!" Dena exclaimed.

"It happens more often than not. I hate dealing with the drunk ones," Berkley said. "I'm glad I don't have a cage anymore. Someone else can deal with that mess."

"We were called out last night for a homeless man with hypertension. He smelled like week-old shit. I thought Mags was going to puke. She had to ride in the back with him."

"Damn," Berkley mumbled.

"It took us two hours to get the smell out of the rig. I swear we wiped down everything five times!"

"On that note," Berkley laughed, "I'm going to mow my grass. Enjoy your pizza. Garrett, you better be ready to burn that shit off later!"

*

At nine p.m. the tropical depression passed right over Richey, bringing a ton of howling wind and heavy rain with it. Randi was sitting in the living room in a tank top and a thin pair of cotton shorts with nothing under them, and her hair up in a messy bun watching the news report of the storm…until the power went out. She searched the house for candles and found two small ones, both of which put out tiny flames when lit.

"Son of a bitch," she said, finding a flashlight with dead batteries. She searched for anything else to light up the dark house, but found nothing.

She thought about just going to bed, but the house was eerily quiet, and nearly pitch black, causing her heart rate to increase and the hair on the back of her neck to stand up. The wind continued to blow, causing tree limbs to fall on fences and cars, and pelting rain battered the roof and windows.

A shrill scream came from her mouth when she heard a loud banging noise right outside. She grabbed her phone, scrolling her contacts for Olivia's number.

"Hey, babe," she said, answering.

"I should've gone to see my family," Randi said.

Noticing the difference in her voice, Olivia sat up straighter and turned down the TV in her hotel room. "Is everything okay?"

"No." Randi tried to keep it together. "There's a nasty storm. A tropical something or other. The power is out. I can't find any fucking candles. It's dark and I just heard a loud bang."

"Call Carrie. Maybe she and Anna can come spend the night."

"Her brother is in San Antonio for business this week. She drove down to see him. Besides, I'm sure no one is on the streets right now."

"The cops probably are. Why don't you call Berkley to come check everything out?"

"I'm sure she's busy."

"Okay…" Olivia sounded frustrated. "You're sitting there alone in the dark, hearing noises. You sound scared. I'm just trying to find someone who can come check on you. A cop is your best choice."

"Alright," Randi sighed, knowing she was right. "Love you."

"Love you, too," Olivia said, hanging up.

Randi bit her lower lip, staring at Berkley's name in her phone. A flash of lightning lit up her backyard, followed by a loud crack of thunder that caused her to jump a foot off the couch. She quickly pressed the call button.

*

Berkley spread the blinds with her fingers, looking out at the trees swaying in the pouring rain, thankful she was off and hadn't been called in. Still, she kept her phone close just in case she was needed. Suddenly, it vibrated in her hand, then began ringing. She glanced at Randi's name on the screen and raised a brow.

"Hello?" she answered.

"Berkley?"

"Yeah. Hey."

"Are you working right now?"

"No. Why? What's up?" she asked, walking away from the window. Two large battery-powered lanterns had her living room lit up almost as brightly as a light bulb.

"My power is out. It's dark as hell because our candles suck, and I keep hearing banging noises. I was going to see if you'd stop by for a minute and check things out. Olivia is in Canada, so I'm alone and a little freaked out."

251

"I'll be there in about ten minutes…maybe fifteen if the roads are bad," Berkley replied, already rushing around to gather up her candles to take over to her.

"You don't have to come over. I thought maybe if you were working—"

"It's fine. This storm isn't letting up anytime soon, so your power is bound to be out the rest of the night. The least I do is bring you some decent candles and maybe figure out what the banging noise is." Berkley tried not to think about the worst-case scenario as she tossed the candles into a box. Then, she slipped her gun into a small carry case, and shoved her wallet with her badge inside, into the back pocket of her comfortable jogger pants, zipping it closed. She knew power outages made nicer neighborhoods easy targets for thieves and robbers because they didn't have an alarm system to contend with.

"The roads are probably really bad. You shouldn't be on them," Randi said.

"If I were working, I'd be on them. It's okay. Stay on the phone with me. That way you'll know everything is okay." *And I won't worry about you.*

"Alright," Randi agreed.

"Leaving now," Berkley said, grabbing the keys to her truck, thinking if the roads were flooded, she had a better chance of getting through since it was higher up.

34

Berkley walked around the exterior of the house with her flashlight, searching for any sign someone had been trying to get in. Heavy rain still fell, and periodic gusts of wind bent the trees over.

"The patio door latch is broken," she said, removing her raincoat as she came inside. "I need some string or something to tie it closed."

Randi began searching through the kitchen drawers. Finding nothing, she went out into the garage, holding one of the candles with an oven mitt. She tripped over something and nearly crashed to the ground. Luckily, she had good balance and hadn't dropped the glass jar. "Damn it," she growled.

"Are you okay?" Berkley asked from the doorway.

"Yeah. I tripped over an old shoe, I think."

"Does it have laces?"

"Hold on…" Randi said, bending down carefully with the candle. *Why didn't I take her flashlight?*

Berkley went back into the kitchen to retrieve her flashlight when Randi came out with the shoe in her hand.

"Will this do?"

"Perfect." Berkley pulled the lace out of the shoe and walked through the house to the sliding patio door.

Randi tried to watch through the blinds, but it was pitch black. All she saw was the light from Berkley's flashlight bouncing around. A minute later, Berkley returned to the door and Randi slid it open for her.

"I tied it to the grill. At least it won't slap back and forth anymore."

"Thank you," Randi said. "You didn't have to do all of this."

"I couldn't leave you here in the dark."

Randi looked at the candles burning on the kitchen island, setting the open room in a soft glow. "I understand if you need to go," she said softly.

"It's fine. I'll hang out for a bit," Berkley muttered, looking through the blinds to make sure the string was holding. "This thing should be passed us in a couple of hours."

Randi bit her lower lip and nodded.

"You can go to bed if you want. I'm used to being up all night."

"I don't think I could sleep through this if I wanted to," Randi said, sitting on the couch.

Berkley nodded. She had never been able to sleep through bad storms either. She checked her phone, making sure the station hadn't tried to contact her. Then, she sat down on the couch, leaving a good amount of space between them.

"I remember dealing with hurricanes when I still lived at home. My family is in Galveston."

"I've never experienced a hurricane. I'm from the DFW area."

"My mom would make a bunch of food and we'd have a family hurricane party."

Berkley smiled. "Do you have a big family?"

"Yes and no. Our family is quite large, but they are all in South America. My parents immigrated from Chile.

My sister and I were born in Texas. It's just the four of us here."

"Wow. Do you go back and visit?"

"When we were little we went once a year, but I haven't been there in three years." Sadness filled her voice.

"It's just me and my parents. The rest of our family is scattered around. I saw my grandparents when I was younger, but all I have left is one grandmother. She's in a nursing home."

"What made you become a cop?" Randi asked.

Berkley gave her a sideways look. "That's not a very interesting subject change," she chuckled.

Randi smiled and waited for her to answer.

"You know I was an EMT first. I had a bad call one night and I realized I could've done more for the people who wound up dying if I'd been a cop, not just an EMT." She shrugged. "What about you? How did you become this soccer star?"

Randi laughed. "I'd hardly call myself a star."

"Have you been to your games?" Berkley questioned with a smirk. "I'm pretty sure you have more fans than Tom Brady."

"Nah."

"How many followers do you have on social media?"

"I don't know. A couple hundred thousand, maybe."

"Holy shit." Berkley shook her head.

Randi laughed.

"How much is your autograph worth? I have a few things I'd like to pay off," Berkley teased.

Randi rolled her eyes and chuckled.

"Seriously though, how did you wind up playing soccer for a living?"

"It's all my dad's fault. He grew up poor, playing soccer in the streets like the rest of the kids with half-deflated balls and no shoes most of the time. When my sister and I were little, he put us in soccer. I loved it, and continued playing for the local club, working my way up to the premier and elite teams. My sister wasn't interested. She cheered in high school for a year, then tried drama, and the debate team. Anyway, I got a scholarship to play for the University of Texas and was drafted by Atlanta into the NWSL. When the organization folded, I went overseas to play in France for a year, but it wasn't for me. I came back to the NWSL and my rights had been traded to Richey, which was where I had wanted to play in the first place, and here I am." She smiled. "Did you play sports in school?"

"Softball for two years. Then, they started girls' flag football. I switched to that and became the captain. I played my last two years."

"No wonder you were so good at the lake! You're a ringer!" Randi playfully smacked her on the arm.

"I never said I didn't know how to play," Berkley replied, grabbing her wrist in a swift move that left Randi stunned. Feeling her pulse quicken, Berkley let go and stood up.

Randi noticed the instant change in her demeanor and got up, following her over to the blinds where Berkley was looking out, watching the rain pour down. The trees in the backyard were still whipping back and forth occasionally from gusts of wind.

"What are we doing?" Berkley mumbled, feeling Randi's presence behind her. She squeezed her eyes closed and slowed her breathing to calm her racing heart.

"I don't know," Randi said softly. "I've tried to make myself not want you."

Berkley turned around, facing her. The flames of the candles flickered on the walls in the background. She tried focusing on the shadows they were causing, anything to keep herself in check. She was so tired of the game they were playing, and damn tired of walking away from what she wanted…what they obviously both wanted.

"Look at me," Randi whispered.

Berkley exhaled slowly as she lowered her eyes. Her nerves were on fire with the urge to kiss Randi's slightly parted lips, causing her chest to burn. Unable to fight herself any longer, Berkley bent her head, laying claim to Randi's mouth with a deliberately slow, and delicately soft kiss.

Randi ran her hands up Berkley's arms to her shoulders. She linked her hands behind her head and pulled her closer for a much deeper kiss as her tongue snaked out, tasting the hint of mint on Berkley's lips from the gum she'd been chewing when she'd arrived.

Berkley put her hands around Randi's waist, pressing their bodies together as she slid her hands up her back, then down to cup her ass. In one swift motion, she lifted Randi off the ground. Randi wrapped her legs around Berkley's waist, clinging to her without interrupting their passionate kissing as Berkley walked over to the couch, laying her down on her back. Her body followed, settling her weight between Randi's legs.

Berkley knew in the back of her mind she shouldn't be doing this, but when Randi slid her hands down Berkley's back and began pulling her t-shirt up, she adjusted her position and allowed her to remove it completely, revealing the hard body that had teased Randi's thoughts since that day at the lake. Before Berkley could return to her original position, Randi unclasped her sports bra and dragged it up over her head, adding it to the shirt on the floor. Her hands moved from Berkley's back around to her chest, kneading her small breasts softly and tweaking the nipples between her thumb and fingers.

Berkley moaned into her mouth as their lips found their way back to each other. She held her position, allowing Randi's hands free-rein of her upper body, until they moved lower, teasing the waistband of her pants. Berkley pulled back, breaking the kiss as she hovered over her.

Randi's eyes found Berkley's in the dim candlelight as she ran her hand up the center of her chest, all the way to her cheek. "Touch me," she whispered.

Berkley closed her eyes, feeling the words sink to her core. When she opened them again, Randi was looking back at her with the same hunger in her eyes. She pushed herself back further and pulled Randi into a seated position so she could remove her shirt and bra. Then, she claimed her mouth in another searing kiss as she laid her back down.

Randi gasped as Berkley's lips left her mouth, sliding down to find an erect nipple. She swirled her tongue around the outside before sucking it into her mouth. Randi grabbed a handful of her short hair with one hand while the other ran up and down the rigid muscles of her back. Berkley dragged her tongue away, making swirls around the center of Randi's chest as she moved to her other breast, then kissed her way down her taut stomach. She didn't care that she was wadded up, nearly into a ball on the other end of the couch as she eased Randi's shorts and panties off her hips and over her thighs, tossing them to the floor. Before she could move from her position, Randi sat up and ran her hand over the ripples of her stomach and tugged on the waistband of her cotton joggers. Berkley unraveled herself and stood next to the couch, allowing Randi to slide them down, along with her black boyshorts.

Randi's eyes ran up and down, taking in every inch of the striking body in front of her. She felt warm wetness and a dull ache between her legs as her heart pounded in her chest. Throwing caution to the wind, she leaned forward, pressing her mouth between Berkley's legs, licking up and down in delicate strokes.

Berkley spread her legs further, grabbing the arm of the couch for support while giving her more access as Randi sucked her clit into her mouth. Then she released it and swirled her flattened tongue through the folds in a move that drove Berkley crazy. It had been so long and she was right there. She grabbed Randi's head, holding her in place as she rubbed herself against the mouth assuaging her every need.

Randi cupped her ass with both hands and teased her opening with the tip of her tongue, then continued licking the edges of her clit before suckling it over and over.

Berkley let out a guttural moan from somewhere deep inside as the climax hit her like a ton of bricks. She held on, allowing her body to receive all of the pleasure being given to her until she was too sensitive for Randi's mouth. She took a step back on wobbly legs and pushed Randi softly back down onto the couch. She followed, lying on top of her once more. The heady scent of Randi's wetness made her mouth water as she moved down, tracing a lazy path with her tongue from Randi's chest to the top of her thigh. Randi's hips rose up, urging her further, but Berkley took her time, running her tongue from one hip and thigh to the other, carefully skirting the sensitive flesh beckoning her in between them.

Randi's nerves fired in all directions, almost causing her body to spasm when Berkley's tongue finally passed over her warm, wet center, spreading the folds to graze her clit with a velvety touch. Her head sunk into the cushion under her and her back arched, pushing herself further into Berkley's mouth. A soft moan escaped her lips as her chest heaved.

Sensing how close she was, Berkley slipped her tongue inside before swirling it around her clit once more in a move she repeated a few times. Then, she pulled her mouth away, replacing it with her fingers, causing Randi to whimper as she slid back up her body.

Their lips met in a breathtaking kiss. Tasting herself on Berkley's mouth as her fingers slid in and out of her, was enough to send Randi over the edge. She held onto her strong shoulders tightly, riding the waves of orgasm as Berkley's fingers moved inside of her, dragging out every single crest.

Breathless and panting, Randi pulled away from the kiss as her rigid body began to go limp. Cool air tinged her heated skin as Berkley moved to her side. She couldn't remember ever feeling so sated as she drifted off.

Berkley watched her chest rise and fall to the sound of rain pelting the windows and roof until her eyes slammed shut a couple minutes later.

35

Randi stretched and opened her eyes; she was lying on the couch with only a throw blanket covering the lower half of her nude body. The sun was shining through the open blinds and the light over the kitchen island was on. She looked around the room, remembering the storm from the night before…just before a replay of everything else rolled through her head. *Shit.* She got up, finding her shirt and shorts on the floor near her feet, she quickly pulled them on and walked around the house.

"Well…fuck," she sighed, flopping back down on the couch. Her phone was blinking on the table with text messages and missed calls. When had she turned it on silent? She couldn't remember. Picking it up, she quickly texted Olivia to let her know she was fine since she had sent several messages and called three times. Then, she had a missed call from her sister, obviously checking on her with the storm, and a message from Carrie who had been doing the same.

She scrolled through her contacts and pressed *call* next to her sister's name. She ignored her growling stomach and pinched the bridge of her nose as she leaned her head back against the cushions. The line rang enough times to go to voicemail before a groggy voice answered.

"I guess you made it through the storm," Elisa mumbled.

"Yeah."

"You call me at seven in the morning, and that's all you have to say? Is there any damage? Did you lose power? The news said there were power outages and flooding. Mom and dad were freaked out. I told them you've been through hurricanes in Galveston, so a tropical depression should be a cakewalk."

A hundred things were going through Randi's mind, including all of the answers to her sister's questions. *I don't know if there is damage. I haven't been outside. Yes, the power was out all night.* But, she blurted, "I slept with Berkley," instead.

"Excuse me?"

Randi sighed.

"Miranda Francisca?!"

"Do I have to say it again?" Randi uttered.

"How did this happen? What the hell were you thinking? More importantly, where the hell was Olivia?"

"She's in Canada."

"Okay…so how did you wind up in Berkley's bed? Wait, was this last night?"

"Yes, it was last night, and I wasn't in her bed."

"Wherever you were doesn't matter…does it?"

"Calm down."

"I *am* calm."

"You sound like mom."

"Girl, she'd beat you with a wooden spoon through the damn phone if she knew about this!"

"I know," Randi chuckled.

"Seriously, what happened?"

"I don't know. Maybe I do. Hell, I'm so confused."

"Were you drunk?"

"What? No."

"She's had you twisted around since you met," Elisa muttered.

"It's not her fault."

"Isn't she the single one?"

"I initiated things between us…more than once. If anything, I went after her."

"I had a feeling this might happen the first time you told me about her," Elisa sighed. "What I don't understand is why. You're with Olivia. You guys have been together forever."

"It's not perfect."

"Life isn't perfect, Randi. You don't just go sleep with someone else."

"I didn't intend to sleep with her."

"You need to figure out what you want. Olivia doesn't deserve this."

"I know," she replied, wiping a tear from her cheek.

"Listen, no one else knows. You have one chance to clean this up before it gets any worse. Tell Berkley you made a mistake and you will never do that again. Tell her you love Olivia and that's where you want to be."

"Elisa…what if it's not?"

"You can't live your life on *what if's*."

"I know," Randi whispered. "I'll call you later," she added, ending the call. She stared at the dark screen for nearly a minute before scrolling through her contacts and calling another number.

Hi, you've reached Berkley Ward. Leave a message and I'll get back to you. Thanks.

Randi ended the call just before it beeped. "What would I have said if she'd answered?" she chastised herself, having no idea, but one thing she was sure of, they needed to talk.

*

Berkley dressed in an old pair of jeans, waterproof boots, and a t-shirt. She avoided looking at herself in the mirror for fear her eyes would give away the grief she was carrying around in an *I told you so* way. She threw on a ball cap backward, grabbed her phone and keys and headed out into the garage.

Memories of the night flickered through her mind like an old 8MM film as she gassed up her quad and set up the ramps to drive it up into the back of her truck. She was meeting Garrett at their property to check for storm damage, specifically downed trees and flooding that would destroy their trails. Neither of them had been called into work. However, Dena had been called in the middle of the night and still wasn't home, so she wasn't accompanying them.

Berkley was in the process of strapping down the quad when she heard a car door. Popping her head up over the cab of the truck, she saw a white BMW sitting in her driveway in front of her patrol car.

"I tried to call you," Randi said, stepping up next to the truck.

"I've been a little busy. I'm meeting Garrett to go check on the property."

Randi nodded. "Can we talk?"

"What's there to say? *It was a mistake. We can't do this again.* I know that road by heart."

"I think there's a little more to it than that…don't you?"

Berkley shrugged and jumped out of the truck. She slid the ramps in next to the quad and tied them down as well.

"Do you want some company?"

"Garrett is going."

"I meant me."

"I know," Berkley said, closing the garage. She looked back at Randi standing by the truck in a t-shirt, jeans with rips across the thighs, and Vann shoes with no socks. Her hair was up in a messy bun. Just looking at her tugged at Berkley's chest. She should've said no, but reluctantly nodded for her to get into the passenger side instead.

*

"I hope those are old clothes and shoes," Berkley said as she drove along the washed-out road on the other side of the gate. She didn't have far to go to reach the clearing where they usually parked, but she'd already had to put the truck in four-wheel-drive.

"Does it matter at this point?" Randi answered, looking around at all of the mud.

"What are you really doing here?" Berkley asked, pulling to a stop next to the concrete pad. She turned the truck off, unbuckled her seatbelt, and half-turned to face Randi.

"Last night..." Randi paused, biting her lower lip.

"It was a mistake. I'll say it for you."

"I don't know what it was. I just know, I can't let it go." Randi brought her eyes to Berkley's. "I can't let *you* go."

"Randi," Berkley let out a deep breath and closed her eyes. Garrett picked that moment to pull up next to them, blowing the horn like a little kid.

"You ready to get muddy," he laughed through the open window.

"Apparently, not as ready as you," Berkley replied.

He took his sunglasses off, peering over Berkley's shoulder at her passenger. "Hey, Randi," he said. The surprise was evident in his voice.

Berkley grabbed her phone and texted him.

I'll explain later.

"I brought some help," Berkley said, getting out of the truck.

Randi watched as they unloaded the quads, waiting to assist if needed, but they'd obviously done this on more than one occasion.

"I didn't bring any helmets," Berkley said, walking past her.

"I'm sure we'll be fine. Just getting on that thing is against our liability policy with the team, so it doesn't matter."

"I figured we could check out the pass first and work our way through the gulch, over to the camp area. Hopefully, the creek hasn't flooded too bad," Garrett said, strapping a chainsaw and rope to the rack on the back of his quad.

"I was thinking the same thing. It's best if we stay together," Berkley replied, adding a small toolbox to hers that contained folding shovels and handsaws, along with a cooler full of bottled water and sandwiches.

"Ready when you are," he said, climbing onto the seat and starting the engine to warm up the machine.

"Ready?" Berkley asked, looking at Randi. "You can stay here in the truck if you want."

"I'll be fine."

"Alright." Berkley started her quad and motioned for Randi to get on behind her.

Randi moved up close to her, wrapping her arms around Berkley's midsection, just as she'd done the last time they'd ridden together, but this time she remembered the feeling of Berkley's body on top of her as soon as her hands came in contact with her. *What the hell was I thinking coming along?*

*

The property only had one tree down, which Berkley and Garrett cut up, and the flooding had already subsided. All of the trails were full of thick mud that slung all over them, no matter how slowly they rode.

Berkley tried not to think about Randi's hands on her, but that feeling was already burned into her memory from their night together. She couldn't take it back. It happened, and she needed to deal with the aftermath of her actions. *You shouldn't have brought her,* she thought as Randi held on a little tighter through a rough section that bounced the quad around a little bit.

When they finally pulled up behind the trucks, the quads were full of mud, and they all had mud on them from the waist down. Randi was thankful it hadn't gotten in her hair. Berkley had taken extra caution not to sling mud all over them because she was with her. Otherwise, she wouldn't have cared much since she'd brought a change of clothes with her.

"Thanks for lunch," Garrett said, climbing off his quad. "You make a pretty mean PB and J."

Berkley laughed. "It beats some of the crap you eat."

"What's wrong with cold leftovers?"

Berkley shook her head.

"I'm glad there wasn't much damage. It could've been worse."

"Yeah, I was thinking the same thing," Berkley said, checking to make sure her ramps were secure on the truck so she could drive the quad up into the back of it.

"Why are you two cleaner than I am?" he muttered, looking at them as she walked by.

"You ride like a bat out of hell through the mud. That's why you were behind us the entire time."

"I figured we'd wash off in the creek like usual," he said.

"You get just as muddy riding back afterward. That's why I didn't," Berkley replied, knowing the real reason was because she had Randi with her and doubted she had a bathing suit on under her clothes.

"Hey, where's Dena? I figured she'd be here," Randi asked as Berkley put her quad in the back of the truck.

"Work. Oh, I just got a text. She's home. She was called in at one this morning."

"She's going to be fun to be around today," Berkley laughed.

"No shit," he agreed. "That's okay. I need to wash the quad and I'm sure I can find a ton of other things to do. What time are we meeting at the gym?"

"I don't know. I'll text you," she replied as she strapped the quad and ramps in place. Garrett finished right behind her. "I'll lead the way out of here so you don't fling mud all over my truck!" she yelled as she got into her truck.

He laughed and waved for her to go on.

36

Berkley backed the truck into her driveway and killed the engine. The air in the cab was thick and heavy, like clear fog. The entire ride back to her house had been in silence. She removed her sunglasses and turned her head. Her eyes locked onto Randi's. It would've been so easy to take her into the house and make love to her all over again, but she knew that couldn't happen.

"For months we've been stealing these tiny moments, and all the while, I'm reminded that you're not mine, you're someone else's. I've been there more times than I care to count. I've been the one cheated on, and I've been the one having the affair. It's not fun in any situation." She straightened her head, pulling her eyes to the front of the truck. "As much as it pains me, I know I have to be the one to let you go. I never meant for anything to go this far, but I'm not sorry."

"I know," Randi whispered, wiping a tear from her cheek. "I should go," she murmured, feeling more tears welling up in her eyes.

Berkley nodded softly. She held her breath as she watched Randi get out of the truck and walk over to her car, all the while wiping tears from her face. "Damn it!" she yelled, smacking her hand on the steering wheel as the white BMW drove away. "It's for the best," she tried telling herself as she got out and began unloading the quad.

Randi was sitting in the chair, staring at the couch when her phone rang. A half-empty bottle of beer was on the table in front of her. A photo of Carrie making a goofy face lit up the screen on her phone. Reluctantly, she answered with a drab hello.

"Hey. Did you get through the storm okay? I tried calling you last night."

"Yeah," Randi mumbled. "I was with Berkley."

"What…wait. You didn't sleep with her, did you?"

"It doesn't matter."

"You need to get your shit together, Randi and stop playing games."

"It's over. All of it," she sighed.

"You sound like you've been crying. I'm coming over."

"You don't need to do that. I'm fine."

"No, you're not."

"Okay, you want the truth? I'm completely torn, Carrie. I feel like my heart is being squeezed in a vice. I've never felt like this. Olivia has been my safe haven for what seems like forever. But, Berkley…God, everything is so different with her. When she pushed me away, it was unlike any pain I've ever known."

"She was right to end it. I'm pretty sure you've been lost for some time now. You need to find yourself, Hun. You can't work on your relationship, or start a new one, if you don't know where *you* are underneath everything. At the end of the day, it's *your* life, no one else's," Carrie said seriously. "I'm sorry."

"Don't be. This is my mess. And, you're right. I don't know who I am anymore," Randi sighed. *The problem is, I don't know when I lost myself. Where do I go from here?*

"Are you sure you don't want me to come over?"

"Nah, I'm fine."

"Alright. I'm going to start dinner. Anna is coming over in a little bit. You're welcome to join us."

"I'm good. Have fun," Randi said, getting off the phone.

*

Berkley opened a beer and flopped down on the couch with the TV remote. Nothing looked appealing as she scrolled through the channels. Although, she wasn't paying much attention to the show titles passing by on the screen. She couldn't get the heartbroken look on Randi's face out of her mind.

When her phone vibrated on the table, then began to ring, she knew who it was without looking at the screen.

"You slept with her, didn't you?" Dena stated as soon as she'd answered.

"Well…hello to you too, princess," Berkley replied, sipping her beer.

"She's going to break your heart."

"Too late. I did it for her, and it hurt like hell."

"You ended it?"

"Uh-huh," she replied, taking another long swallow.

"I'm sorry, babe."

"It's going to take some time to get over her. I should've never let it go that far, but I couldn't help it. One kiss and I was gone."

"Are you in love with her?"

"It wouldn't matter if I were. She's with someone else," she sighed. "But, damn, D. This one hurts."

"I knew the first moment I saw you two together that this wasn't going to end well," Dena said. "I wish I knew how to turn back time."

"I wouldn't do it."

"Really? Not even to stop yourself from sleeping with her?"

"No."

Dena sighed. "You're in deep, my friend."

"I know. I'll be alright."

"Want me to come over? I just got home, but—"

"Nah, I'm good. I know you were called in."

"Yeah. What a crazy night. Why do women always go into labor during storms?"

"I heard it's something to do with the pressure in the air or something like that."

"We nearly delivered one of two women we transported, on the side of the road. Other than that, it was a lot of calls for elderly patients needing oxygen and so on because their power was out."

"I would've been better off getting called in," Berkley uttered.

"Oh…so, it just happened last night?"

"Yep."

"And you ended it today?"

"Yeah. We both got what we wanted. Why prolong it?"

"When did you decide, before or after you slept with her?"

"I knew when I woke up in her house this morning that it had to end."

"You did it at her house?! Holy shit. Where was her girlfriend?"

"Out of the country."

"At least there was no chance of getting caught…this time."

"No kidding. Getting chased down the street, half-dressed with no shoes, by an angry husband, wasn't exactly good times."

Dena laughed. "I was sure you'd learned your lesson, too."

"Funny."

"It seems like that was forever ago," Dena said.

"A lifetime ago for me. I was still working with you at the Fire Department."

"I know. I remember."

"Thankfully, that hasn't happened again," Berkley muttered. "I swore I was done playing these games the last time I snuck out of someone's bed before the sun came up."

"I'm pretty sure this time was a little different," Dena said sympathetically.

"Yeah," Berkley sighed.

Dena hated hearing the sadness in her best friend's voice. "I was serious about hanging out," she said.

"I know. You're my best friend and I love you to death, but I need to get through this on my own."

"Okay. I'm going to take a shower and go to bed. Get those tits up, or I *will* come over there."

"I will," Berkley laughed hysterically.

37

Randi tossed and turned restlessly all night as her mind raced. By the time the sun rose, filling her room with an orange glow, she'd given up on sleep and moved to the kitchen to make coffee. She'd thought about going to The Grind, but the memory it invoked was still too raw. Sitting on a stool at the island, sipping from her mug and staring at the couch across the room wasn't helping matters either. She was certain she would never be able to get that night out of her head, but she wasn't interested in trying either.

Her stomach growled, bringing her back to reality, despite not having much of an appetite. Her nerves felt like the ends were frayed. She couldn't remember ever feeling so helpless. Carrie was absolutely right. She *was* lost and had been for far too long.

*

By the time Olivia arrived home later in the day, Randi had taken a jog, did the laundry, and watched two movies, neither of which she actually remembered.

"Hey," she said, walking inside with her suitcase in tow.

Randi smiled and hugged her. "How was your flight?"

"Great until I changed planes and had to deal with screaming babies," Olivia replied, heading down the hallway to empty her suitcase. "How were things here?"

"Fine," Randi said, leaning against the doorway.

"What's wrong?"

"Nothing."

Olivia kicked her shoes off and pushed the suitcase aside. Then, she sat on the side of the bed and patted the spot next to her. Randi walked over and sat down.

"What's going on?" she asked.

"What are we doing, Liv?"

"Us?"

"Yes. Do you feel like we're going through the motions?"

"I don't know. Where is this coming from?"

Randi shrugged. "I've been so lost lately. I wondered if you felt the same way."

"No."

"Seriously?" Randi shook her head. "You just came home from being away nearly a week and we barely hugged each other. That's okay to you?"

"What's going on with you?" Olivia questioned.

"We used to struggle to keep our hands off each other, scared our teammates would realize we were a lot more than friends or roommates. I feel like that's all we are anymore."

"I think people grow apart a little once a relationship settles down. There's nothing wrong with that."

"How many times have we made love this year?"

"I don't know. I don't keep count."

"Can you count to four? It's August and we've had sex four times. That doesn't sound odd to you?"

"Where are you going with this, Randi?"

"I'm trying to figure out why you're comfortable with this...with all of it." Randi wiped a tear from her cheek. "We've been living together as friends with benefits, and the benefits aren't even happening anymore. I don't know when all of this happened. I've tried to pinpoint a time when our relationship shifted. You can't say you haven't felt it, too."

Olivia shrugged. "I guess, maybe."

"Maybe?"

"Okay, fine. Yes."

"Why haven't you said anything to me?"

"I don't know, Randi," she growled. "What we have is comfortable. I guess."

"Not for me."

"What are you saying?"

"I'm saying we need to see this relationship for what it is. We're friends, Liv, not lovers. Not anymore. It hurts and it's sad because for the last five years, we've been *us*. But, somewhere along the line, *us* turned into *friends*. Neither of us is happy, not if you're being honest with yourself."

"You're right. Being content isn't a relationship." She reached over, grabbing Randi's hand. "We've both changed so much," she sighed.

"We grew up, and we grew apart."

"Yeah." Olivia nodded, wiping a tear from her cheek. "I feel sad, but I can't be angry or upset. We've been avoiding this for a while. I'm glad we finally talked."

"Me too."

"Where does this leave things?"

"I'll move into the spare room," Randi said.

"There's no reason we can't live together as roommates. We're obviously good at it."

Randi laughed. "You're right. Why not give it a try?"

"We already split the bills, so that won't change."

Randi nodded.

"It's a little scary how easy this was," Olivia said.

"I agree, but an amicable split is much better than a nasty fight. Besides, we've never been nasty fight people anyway."

"True," Olivia agreed, pulling her into a side hug.

38

Berkley drove past The Grind, taking a slightly altered route on her way to the gym before the start of her shift. She knew Randi wouldn't be there, but she felt her presence nonetheless. It had been the better part of a week since she'd ended things, and it still stung like a freshly opened wound. "She was never yours," she whispered to herself as she pressed the gas pedal and drove away.

*

"I'm not Dena, so I don't know how to do girl talk and all of that, but…I'm here if you want to talk," Garrett said. He was next to Berkley, doing dumbbell curls alongside her.

"Like man to man?" She grinned.

"Something like that," he laughed. "The best way to get over a girl is to get under another one."

Berkley grinned and shook her head. "I used to play that game…pretty well, actually."

"I remember."

"Not this time, though." She changed weights and continued. "I won't tell Dena your advice. She's liable to smack you over the head."

He shrugged and laughed. "What did she say?"

"She told me to get my tits up."

"What?" he exclaimed, nearly dropping the weights in his hands.

"You've never heard the expression 'get your tits up'?" she laughed.

"Uh…nope. Is that something girls say to each other?"

"It's like 'get back on the horse' or 'put your big girl pants on'. It's an expression. We got it from a movie we saw together, and we say it to each other when we need encouragement. It's a girl joke," she chuckled. "But, feel free to get your tits up if you need to."

"Funny," he replied, setting the weights back on the rack.

"If you don't start doing flies to work your pecks, you'll need to get those tits up."

"Fuck you," he said with a grin while shaking his head.

"Come on, grab those forties since you're a weenie, and I'll spot you for flies."

Reluctantly, he grabbed the heavy dumbbells and walked over to the bench.

"Thank you for reaching out. It means a lot, and I know I can talk to you, too. It doesn't always have to be her."

He nodded and lied back, ready to start lifting the weights.

"Are these thirties?" she laughed. "No wonder you're growing tits," she teased, feeling much happier than when she'd arrived an hour earlier. Most of her thoughts of Randi had vanished.

*

Randi lied on the spare room bed, staring at the ceiling. It was her fifth time waking up in there, and it still didn't feel like her bed or her room. She and Olivia had kept their split a secret the entire week at training. She'd wanted to tell Carrie, but hadn't found the right time. It felt like a dream. A really confusing, bad dream. During the day she went through the motions, mentally separating her life and Olivia's. They'd already split their possessions, but living in the same house kept them intertwined.

At night, Berkley filled her thoughts, making it difficult for her to sleep. As much as she wanted to reach out to her, it was clear Berkley wasn't interested after both of her calls went unanswered.

Randi grabbed her phone from the nightstand and scrolled through her contacts.

"Are you up?" she asked when her sister groggily answered the phone.

"I am now. What's up? Why are you whispering?"

"I'm not. I'm just trying to be quiet. I'm not sure if Olivia is still sleeping."

"Okay?" Elisa sat up, putting her pillow behind her against the headboard. The deflated sound of her sister's voice was like alarm bells going off in her head. "What's going on?" she asked softly.

"It's over," Randi sighed.

"What's over? The thing with Berkley? You and Olivia? What?"

"All of the above."

"Wait. What? You and Olivia?"

"It's been over for a while. Neither of us wanted to admit it. Berkley helped me see it."

"Wow. I'm sorry."

"Don't be. It's fine."

"You were together for five years. It can't just be fine, Miranda."

"I meant we're in a good place. It ended easily…which is still a little crazy to me. It's weird. I won't lie. This roommates thing is going to take some getting used to."

"You're still living with her?"

"Yeah. What was I supposed to do? Go to a hotel? I couldn't just move out."

"That's nuts."

"We've been living like roommates for a while now, we're just not sleeping in the same room anymore. Not much else has changed, really. That's a pretty big sign that we did the right thing."

"I'd say so," Elisa exhaled deeply. "I can't say that I'm completely surprised. After our last conversation, I had a feeling you were heading down this road. What about Berkley? Where are things with her?"

"Over too."

"Really?"

"Yeah. She ended it before all of this. She has no idea. She won't return my calls."

"I'm sorry."

"Thanks."

"It's probably best right now anyway. You just got out of a long relationship and technically, you're still in it to some degree since you're living under the same roof."

"Yeah."

"Do you want me to tell mom and dad?"

"No. I'll do it. It's been five days and I'm just now telling you. It feels like it hasn't sunk in yet."

"Give it some time, and give yourselves some space. I'm sure Olivia feels the same way."

"It's funny you're talking about Olivia and I'm thinking about Berkley. I can't get her off my mind. Not seeing her hurts so much worse than ending things with Olivia. That's shitty in a way. I never meant to step out on her. I couldn't help being drawn to Berkley like a moth to a flame. I've never felt chemistry like that with anyone else, and I probably never will again."

"Randi, you're in love with her, whether or not you want to admit it," her sister said sympathetically.

"I have a feeling it's a little too late for all of that."

"Work on you. That's most important. When the time is right, if it's meant to be, you'll be brought back together."

"When did you become so philosophical?" Randi laughed quietly.

"I spend too much time with mom and dad."

Randi laughed again. "Maybe I should come home and do some Yoga with mom."

Elisa chuckled. "It might help clear your chakra or cleanse your palate…or something like that."

"On that note, I'm getting out of bed. Thanks for talking to me. I miss you."

"I miss you, too. Good luck at the game tonight."

*

Berkley stood in the back of the roll call room with her hands resting on her utility belt, listening intently as the longwinded lieutenant went on and on.

"Someone stuff a sock in his mouth," Garrett whispered.

Berkley bumped shoulders with him.

"One final note, welcome back Senior Patrol Officer Crawford. It looks like you're all healed up. I don't suppose you'll be jumping on your kid's trampoline any time soon," the lieutenant said with a big grin.

"Nope," he replied.

"Alright, everyone. Be safe."

All of the officers began to disperse when he walked from the front of the room with his thin notebook. "Ward," he called, catching up to her.

"Oh hell," Garrett said. "I'm out of here. Catch me on the radio when you're rolling."

"Yes, sir," Berkley said, turning to face the lieutenant as Garrett disappeared.

"You are relieved of duty at the soccer stadium since Crawford is back. Thank you for filling in."

"Sure. No problem," she replied.

As she walked away, heading towards her patrol car, Berkley felt a dull ache in her chest. Randi had called her twice during the week, both of which she'd sent to voicemail, but no message was left. She knew if she heard her voice or saw her face, they would be right back where they were a week ago, too tangled in each other to care about the consequences. The sadness of knowing she wasn't going to purposely see Randi anymore, cut her deeper than she thought it would, but the idea of not being forced to see her, was almost like a weight lifting off of her shoulders. No matter how she looked at it, it was a double-edged sword.

As soon as she got into her patrol car, Berkley noticed a message on the computer screen.

What did he want now?

She laughed and typed: *No more soccer stadium duty since Crawford is back.*

That's great. Now, you won't have to see Randi and you can do real police work. It's a win/win.

Something like that, she replied. *Leaving HQ. I'll call you later.* As she closed the messenger box, she pushed the thoughts of Randi from her mind and went into work mode.

39

Randi sat on the bench in the locker room, lacing up her cleats. She ignored the conversations going on around her, and the thoughts racing through her head. She had a job to do, and the team needed her focused.

"Hey, Rojas," Sasha called. "Where's Berkley? The dude she replaced is back."

Randi shrugged and said, "No idea."

"Why do I feel like you just lied?" Carrie mumbled.

"Not now," Randi mouthed.

"Let's go, girls. We have work to do!" Olivia yelled, bringing everyone in for her captain's speech. "We only have three games left in the regular season. Richey FC is sitting in third place. We need to stay in the top four if we want to play in the postseason games for the championship. Who is with me?"

Everyone started cheering.

"Let's go kick some ass!" Olivia shouted, leading them into the tunnel to line up with New Jersey for the traditional walk out onto the field.

The nearly sold-out crowd thundered with cheers for their favorite players as they were introduced. Once the national anthem ended, the players headed out to their positions and waited for the referee to blow her whistle, starting the game.

Randi's heart rate skyrocketed from the burst of adrenaline. She was itching to go hard and let go of everything. She'd planned to leave it all on the field…hoping for those ninety minutes she forgot about everything going on in her life.

At the sound of the whistle, Carrie kicked the ball back to Randi and play began.

*

"South 5—245 in progress at Ol' Red's Bar, 1021 Maple Street," the dispatcher radioed, indicating an assault with a deadly weapon.

Berkley was only five miles away. She flipped the lights and sirens on in her car and cut a u-turn in the middle of the intersection. "327—responding," she said into the mic attached to her computer as she navigated the traffic at a high rate of speed.

"414—responding," Garrett radioed as well.

Berkley sped into the parking lot and slammed her car into park. She checked the computer screen for updated information and found out a woman had hit a man with a pool cue, busted a beer bottle on the table and was threatening to cut anyone who came close to her.

"Damn idiot," she muttered, getting out of her car. She drew her gun as she moved towards the door. There was no metal detector, so she had no proof that no one inside was carrying a gun. She took a few deep breathes to even out her heart rate. Seeing Garrett's car pull in behind hers helped calm her nerves.

"The hillbillies are at it again," he said, stepping up next to her.

"Right." She grinned. "I'll lead. You pull the door and come behind me on my left side."

"10-4," he said, grabbing the door.

*

Jorja passed the ball up to Randi, who dribbled around her defender and crossed it to Carrie. The defender on her side of the field came out of nowhere, stealing the ball and sending it to the opposite side of the field to a midfielder who took off with it up the middle. Randi's lungs burned as she sprinted, chasing after her. She couldn't quite get to the ball, but she slid anyhow, tackling the player and sending her tumbling to the ground.

"Fuck you!" the girl said, getting in Randi's face when she got up.

The ref had blown the whistle, calling a foul on Randi.

"You've been coming at me all night!" Randi growled back at her.

"If you weren't so slow, I wouldn't be stealing the ball from you," the player taunted.

"Bring it on, bitch!"

"If I hear either of you cussing at the other one more time, I'm going to yellow card the both of you!" the ref yelled.

Randi rolled her eyes and backed up for the player to take her direct kick, which Olivia caught easily. Everyone repositioned as Olivia drop-kicked the ball to midfield. Jorja jumped up, heading it even further. Randi ran through the box and stretched out as far as she could, catching the tip of her cleat on the ball as it came down. It felt like slow motion as she watched the ball sail past the keeper and into the back of the net as her body slammed hard into the ground. The crowd roared with cheers and the team ran over to celebrate with Randi, who was still lying on the ground.

"I'm fine," she said, taking an extra second to get up.

"Listen, we have twenty minutes left. We're up one to nothing. We just need to hold them off," Jorja said.

"No, we need to get another goal!" Randi yelled. "This is our house!"

Everyone cheered as they went back to their positions to restart play.

*

"Richey PD!" Berkley yelled, rushing in through the open door. "Hands in the air!"

Garrett ran in behind her and flanked her left side. Together, they scanned the crowd of twenty or so people sitting at various tables, on barstools, and standing around the pool table. That's where she spotted the woman with the broken bottle.

"Put the bottle down!" Berkley yelled, concentrating on her while Garrett watched for any movement from the rest of the patrons.

"Get out of here!" the woman slurred.

"I'm not going to ask nicely again. Put it down!"

She waved the bottle around, howling like a wild animal as she stumbled.

"What the hell is she on?" Garrett said.

"Nothing. She's drunk out of her mind and trying to kill me!" one guy replied.

"You screwed that whore in our bed! You're damn right I'm going to kill you!" the woman screamed, lunging towards him.

Berkley had already holstered her handgun once Garrett had the rest of the patrons safely behind them. She quickly fired a shot with her taser gun, catching the wild woman in her side. She flopped on the ground, screaming and writhing in pain. Berkley rushed over and kicked the broken bottle out of arms reach. The woman bucked around, trying to get her hands on Berkley, as she fought to get her hands in the cuffs.

Garrett dove on her, grabbing her flailing arms.

"That bitch shot me!" the woman screamed. "Get off of me!"

As soon as she was secure in the cuffs, Berkley searched her, and then pulled her back to sit on her butt. "Don't move. You're under arrest for assault."

"I didn't assault no one!" she screamed. "You shot me! I'm dying!"

"That was a taser lead, not a bullet. You're not dying." Berkley shook her head, grabbing her radio. "327— one in custody, request EMS." She needed EMS to remove the taser leads that were stuck in her skin. She could do it, but she preferred for the fire department to do it in case they needed to transport the person.

"Copy—327. EMS en route."

"Are you okay?" Garrett asked the guy whom she'd hit with the pool cue. He was apparently the same guy she was trying to cut with the bottle.

"Yeah, man." He shook his head. "She's my old lady. I don't want to press charges."

"You don't have to. The state is doing it for you."

"Damn it, Trisha! See what you did? You're probably going to jail for a while this time," he growled at her.

"You did this! I told you to stay away from Pam!"

"I didn't do anything with her!"

"Listen, it's best if you step outside with me. I'll take your statement. There's no need to instigate this any further. She's under arrest and will be going to jail once EMS removes the taser leads."

"Man, she's my wife. I hate seeing this."

"Here's an idea, stop drinking."

"I've only had one. I came out after work with my buddy. She showed up here already drunk and acting crazy. She thinks I'm having an affair with a chick in our trailer park. I swear I'm not."

"It's none of my business whether you are or not," Garrett replied as the ambulance pulled up.

Dena got out with her medical bag and walked over to the two of them. "What's up?" she asked.

"He has a small cut on the side of his head, but the woman inside needs her taser leads removed. Berkley has her."

"Mags, he needs a gauze pad. I'll go deal with the taser leads," she said, heading into the bar.

Most of the patrons had left, leaving the place wide open. The smell of stale beer and cigarettes stung her nose as Dena walked inside. Berkley was in the back near the pool tables. Tiny shards of glass were on the floor a few feet away from where an angry redhead sat with her hands cuffed behind her back.

"How are you?" Dena asked.

"Wonderful," Berkley laughed. "This is Trisha and she has two taser leads in her left side," she added, pulling the woman to her feet.

"That bitch shot me! I'm dying!"

"First of all, you're not dying. It's an electrical current and it's long gone. Second, that bitch is my best friend, so let's be a little nicer," Dena said as she began assessing the situation.

"Go to hell!"

Dena looked at Berkley and rolled her eyes. "Looks like they're in there pretty good," she said, grabbing a pair of medical pliers. "This might sting a little," she added, plucking the leads out.

"Ouch! You're hurting me, bitch!" the woman screamed.

"All done. You want us to transport her?"

"If her vitals are fine, she's going down to central booking."

Dena nodded and checked the woman's blood pressure and pulse rate. "She's good to go."

"Wonderful," Berkley said, grabbing the mic clipped to her shoulder. "327—10-16," she radioed, requesting a prisoner pick up.

"Copy—327."

"Let's go," Berkley said, grabbing the woman by the arm, leading her out of the bar. "Your ride will be here shortly."

"How are you, really?" Dena asked once Berkley had the woman sitting on the curb near Garrett. Her husband had already left.

"I'm fine. Life goes on, right?"

"Uh-huh. Have you seen her?"

"Nope. I'm not working the soccer stadium anymore, as of tonight, and I've avoided The Grind all week."

"Have you thought about talking to her?"

"No. There's nothing more to say. Besides, I checked her social media account. She and Olivia are still sharing pictures and cute comments."

"I'm sorry, babe."

"No sorry needed. Life goes on." Berkley said with a shrug. "Here's your ride!" she called to the woman on the curb.

"How's it going?" Maggie asked, walking over.

"Good. You?"

"Same shit, different day," Maggie laughed. "It's good to see you."

"Yeah, you too."

"We're out of here," Dena said. "Call me when you get off shift. Let's get breakfast or something. I know you guys are headed to the gym, but maybe before."

"Sounds good," Berkley replied.

"I second that. I'm down for breakfast," Maggie agreed.

Garrett walked over after stuffing the angry woman into the back of the patrol car that had just arrived. "What are we doing?" he asked as the ambulance drove away.

"Apparently, going to breakfast," Berkley said.

"Sweet."

*

Randi dribbled the ball past the midfielder she'd been tangling with all night, avoiding her slide tackle with a spin move that sent her in the opposite direction as the girl slid out of bounds. Then, she kicked the ball towards the box, putting just enough bend on it for Carrie to get to it. She took a shot with one touch and the ball went right through the keeper's hands for another goal.

The team rushed to Carrie, fist-pumping and cheering. They were already a minute into their two minutes of stoppage. Everyone lined back up to restart play.

The ref blew the whistle, ending the game as soon as Randi kicked it back to Jorja.

"Yes!" Randi shouted, as the entire team gathered in a circle.

"Hell yeah, ladies!" Olivia said, hugging everyone. "Great game," she said to Randi, avoiding hugging her.

"Thanks, you, too." Randi smiled.

"Three more points in the house!" Carrie exclaimed.

The cheering fans gathered along the first row, waiting for autographs as the team began their cool-down stretches. Once they were finished, they walked around, signing jersey's and taking selfies.

"This is what it's all about," Randi said to Carrie, who was walking around with her. Olivia had started in the other direction with Sasha and Jorja. A few other team members were also going around, greeting fans.

"What got into you? You were a badass tonight. I was sure you and Andrea Wilson were going to throw down at midfield."

Randi laughed. "I would've kicked her ass."

"No doubt." Carrie smiled.

"She kept pulling my jersey and tripping me. I'd finally had enough, so I sent her ass to the ground."

Carrie chuckled. "You should've been carded for that."

"She backed off, didn't she?"

Carrie grinned and shook her head.

As they made their way towards the tunnel, Randi glanced around, looking for the person she knew wasn't there.

"Why wasn't she here?" Carrie asked, watching her line of sight.

Randi shrugged. "I'm hungry. You want to split a pizza or something?"

"Sure. My house or yours?"

"Yours," Randi said as they entered the tunnel. "I'll be over as soon as I leave here."

"Okay…" Carrie raised a brow. She'd expected Olivia to come with her, and went to ask why she wasn't coming along, but Randi had already joined in the team celebration in the locker room.

*

Carrie pulled open the door to her townhouse as soon as Randi rang the bell. The pizza hadn't arrived yet.

"Why do I feel like this is going to be a long night?"

"What do you have to drink?" Randi asked, walking in and setting her keys and phone on the table.

"Water and tea I brewed earlier. There's also a bottle of wine, and maybe a beer or two. There might be some liquor in the freezer. What kind of drink are you looking for?"

"One that says Olivia and I split up. We're currently living together as roommates."

"Oh, my God. Are you serious?"

"Yep."

"She found out about Berkley, didn't she?"

"No. She has no idea. I realized we were already living like that and pointed it out to her. She agreed. It was actually really easy, which is still a little weird. I didn't say anything about Berkley. There's no need to hurt her. Especially when that's over anyway."

"I take it you haven't seen her."

"Nope. She wouldn't take my calls."

"Do you blame her? You were in a relationship when the two of you slept together."

"Well, I'm not now…not that it matters."

Carrie shook her head and leaned against the kitchen counter. "You'd never know you guys had split. Nothing has changed between you…at least as far as the team is concerned. When did all of this happen?"

"A week ago tomorrow, and that's just it. Nothing has changed period, except we're sleeping in different rooms." Randi pulled a stool out and sat down. "You were right," she sighed. "We were both lost in a complacent relationship that was nothing but a deep-rooted friendship in the end."

"What happens now?"

"Get over all of this and get back to being me, I guess," Randi said, crossing her arms.

"Isn't there a saying, 'To get over a woman, get under another one?' That's my brother's motto, anyway."

"I'm pretty sure I did that already."

"Yeah…oops." Carrie scrunched her face. "Well, you played a great game tonight, so there's that."

Randi laughed.

"Can I ask you something?"

"This must be serious."

"Not really. I just wondered what it was about Berkley that drew you to her. I mean, I've seen her. She's not my type, but she's attractive, I won't deny that."

Randi uncrossed her arms and clasped her hands together on top of the counter. "At first, it was flirty fun with a hot chic. But, the more time I spent with her, the more I realized how different she was. Do you know we've never once talked about soccer or police work? I've never hung around anyone outside of soccer, except my family. And I've always dated soccer players."

"I think that's what drew me to Anna. She's my life outside of soccer. It's nice to have that."

"I agree."

"Open that bottle of wine," Carrie said, seeing her phone light up with the doorbell camera. "The pizza is here."

"Pizza and wine, just like the old college days," Randi chuckled.

"At least it's not boxed wine," Carrie replied.

"Or Boone's Farm!" they said together, laughing hysterically.

40

Berkley got on her motorcycle and flipped the ignition switch on before pressing the button to start the engine, which came to life with a throaty growl. She twisted the throttle to rev it a couple of times, then waved to her friends before putting it in gear and driving off with a belly full of waffles and bacon from their breakfast.

A mile away, she rolled to a stop at the red light and a young blonde in a convertible Mustang with the top down, pulled up beside her. She smiled and licked her lips seductively in Berkley's direction as she revved her engine.

I can't tell if you want to fuck or race, Berkley thought, watching her intently before shaking her head. The girl gave her a pouty look before smiling once more. When the light turned green, she lit up the tires, squealing them several feet as she took off down the road, but not before Berkley got a good look at her license plate.

"I'll see you again," she muttered as she drove off, doing the speed limit. She nearly turned down the side road that would take her to The Grind, but changed her mind and continued home.

*

"Hey, stranger," Paul said when Randi walked into his coffee shop. "You want the usual with a muffin?"

She thought for a second. Would Olivia want a muffin? Was she even home? Randi had no idea. She'd spent the night at Carrie's after consuming too much wine and had decided to stop for coffee on her way home the next morning. *You're not together anymore. You're not obligated to bring her breakfast.* "Just the coffee today, and make it a triple," she finally answered.

"Long night?" he teased.

"Something like that." She smiled, turning to look out at the parking lot.

"She hasn't been in here in a couple of weeks," he said somberly, sliding her cup across the counter to her. "I read in the paper she recently became Richey's first-ever female SWAT officer. I guess she's been pretty busy."

"Yeah," she muttered, swiping her card on the machine. "Thanks, Paul."

"Have a good one," he replied as she left.

Randi started the car and switched the radio through several stations, bypassing commercials and love songs. "The hell with it," she grumbled, turning it off before backing out of her parking space. She didn't want to be alone with her thoughts all the way home, so she rolled the windows down and let the hot Texas air fill the car.

*

Olivia's SUV was in the garage when Randi opened the door and pulled in next to it. She wondered if she should feel something different, maybe even sadness for the love they'd once shared.

"Did you stay out all night?" Olivia asked when Randi walked in through the kitchen. She was sitting on a barstool at the island, eating a piece of toast with a mountain of jam on it.

Randi nodded as she set her keys and phone down. "Are we going to do this?"

"Do what?"

"Question each other."

"I didn't mean anything by it. I just noticed you weren't here when you walked in." She pushed her empty plate aside. "Randi, you can come and go as you please. We're just roommates now, remember?"

"I guess I'm still getting used to that…this," she sighed, pulling out a stool and sitting next to her. "I was at Carrie's, by the way. We drank too much wine."

"I figured," Olivia laughed.

"You didn't think I was out with another woman?"

Olivia shook her head. "Why? Is there someone else?"

Randi wasn't sure how to answer that. She thought about it for a second, then said, "No."

"There was though. I can hear it in your voice."

"I'm sorry," Randi said, looking at her chocolate brown eyes.

"Don't be. We needed to come to an end. How we got there doesn't really matter at this point," Olivia said. "I won't say it doesn't sting a little, but that's only temporary. We had some pretty good years together."

"Yeah, we did," Randi agreed.

*

Berkley checked her watch as she pulled off the road to catch up on some paperwork for speeding tickets she'd written near the start of her shift. It was barely eleven p.m. and she still had eight hours to go in her shift.

"South 5—Code 11, Sherman Oaks Mobile Home Park. REPEAT: Code 11, Sherman Oaks Mobile Home Park," the dispatcher said across the radio.

The tiny hairs on the back of Berkley's neck stood up. A Code 11 was a call for all SWAT team members. She tossed her paperwork into the passenger seat and grabbed the mic on the side of the computer as she scanned the map on the screen that had a bright red dot blinking.

"327—responding, Code 11," she radioed as she threw the car in gear and sped away with her lights flashing and sirens wailing. The call was on the other side of town, and nowhere near her district. Her heart thumped against her chest, pumping adrenaline-fueled blood through her body with every beat.

Most cars pulled over and came to a stop, others just changed lanes, allowing her to pass by. Once she was clear of intersection traffic, she increased her speed once more, racing down the side roads until she came upon the neighborhood she was looking for. She turned her lights and sirens off as she turned in, following the main road around to the back where four police cruisers were parked. She pulled up behind them and threw the car in park.

"327—on scene," she radioed before getting out and walking around to the trunk of her car.

"There's a sixty-year-old male threatening to kill himself in the fourth trailer down on the left. The one with the red truck in the driveway," Sergeant Jones said, walking up to her.

"Is he alone?" she asked as she removed her uniform shirt and bulletproof vest, trading them for the

SWAT tactical vest that went over the black dri-fit shirt she always wore under her uniform.

"We aren't sure. All we know is he has several guns, including high powered hunting rifles. Right now, our job is to clear all of the trailers around his. A bullet could easily travel through the walls of one and into another one, or possibly more. I want you and McGill to clear the trailer directly across from his, and the one just on the opposite side of that one. Send anyone you find to the next street over. We have a patrol officer shuttling everyone to the front of the park. There is a staging area up there."

"10-4," she said, switching her radio to the channel they were using as she looked around for Connor McGill. She'd met him before, so she knew she was looking for a young, blonde-haired, blue-eyed officer with a muscular build. The other SWAT members had nicknamed him: Pretty Boy because he was always well groomed with perfect hair and perfect teeth, and he still had a babyface.

It was near midnight, so it was fairly dark outside, despite the street lights illuminating various areas. She found him at his patrol car, loading his rifle.

"You ready to do this?" she asked, stepping up next to him.

"Yeah, you?"

"I'm good. Let's go," she said.

He closed his trunk and fell in step next to her. "If you want to do the knocking, I'll back you up," he said, putting his rifle strap over his shoulder.

"That's fine," she replied, as they backtracked and cut across to the next street over. She counted in her head as they walked along the street. "This is the first location."

Connor gave her the signal and stood back with his rifle ready as she put her hand on her Glock and knocked on the door. A few seconds later, a young woman opened the door with a small child clinging to her leg.

"Ma'am, we're with Richey Police Department. We need you to come with us, now."

"What's going on? Why are there cops everywhere?" she said.

"There's a situation with one of your neighbors. Are you the only two occupants of the home?"

"Yes."

"I need you to come with us right now." Berkley waited a split second, then moved closer to the woman. "Listen to me, it's for your own safety."

"Janie, get your blanket and your cup. We have to go with these nice officers. Okay, baby?" the woman said to the little girl.

"Send the car down," Berkley radioed.

A police cruiser began backing down the road with the lights completely off while Berkley and Connor shielded the woman and her child. When the car stopped, Berkley opened the door and ushered them inside.

"Drive up a hundred yards and hangout a second. We're going to the residence next door," Connor said to the officer behind the wheel. Then, he looked at Berkley and gave the hand signal to move on to the next location.

Together, they moved stealthily through the dark, avoiding the streetlights and any noise that would give them away. When they arrived at the back door, Berkley knocked softly. She stepped back and waited, but nothing happened.

Connor signaled to knock again, which she did, a little harder this time. Suddenly, what looked like every single light in the trailer came on.

"Shit," Connor whispered.

The door swung open and Berkley heard the distinct pop, pop, pop of gunfire. She grabbed the old man at the door, flinging him to the ground with her body on top of his as Connor took a position behind the nearest tree with his rifle positioned on the trailer across the street.

"Shots fired! Everyone, hold your positions!" Lieutenant Sullivan, the SWAT team commander radioed.

"Where did it come from?" Connor radioed to Berkley as the patrol car sped off with the woman and young child.

Berkley felt around. The man with her didn't have anything in his hands. "Has to be across the road," she replied.

"Cover me. I'm coming to you," he said.

Berkley slid to the side and backed up against the wall with her gun drawn. She could see the trailer across the road. It was too dark to see movement in the windows.

Connor dove inside the trailer and stayed down low. "We need to get these damn lights off," he said, crouching down and moving around the room to unplug the lights.

The older gentleman began to get up off the floor.

"Sir, you have to stay on your belly, okay?"

"Who the hell are you people?" he asked.

"We're with Richey Police Department. One of your neighbors is shooting a gun."

"Don't tell me it's that crazy son of a bitch across the road," he muttered. "I heard he was getting evicted. It's about damn time."

"Does he live alone?" Berkley asked.

"Yeah, but his on and off girlfriend Wilma or Wanda or some shit like that, is there from time to time."

"Is she there now?"

"How the hell would I know? I was sound asleep until you were banging on my door. My hearing isn't too good anymore."

"Does she have a car or anything?"

"Yeah. She drives an old green Pontiac. She's not there during the week. She works at the titty bar as a bartender."

Berkley got on her radio, giving the new information to the lieutenant.

"I didn't see a car," Connor said.

"Me either."

"Walter Hicks, you need to put your guns down and come outside with your hands up," Sergeant Jones called over the megaphone.

Everyone waited in position, but nothing happened for several minutes. Another SWAT officer continued calling the man's phone, but it just rang and went to voicemail. Sergeant Jones made another call over the megaphone that went unanswered.

Berkley checked her watch. It was nearly one a.m. "Do you think he took himself out?" she said, looking at Connor.

"I don't know. Could be he's waiting for us to make a move. Or…he's dead as a doornail and we're wasting our time. You know the SWAT motto: Hurry up and wait."

"Yeah."

"We're popping smoke. Everyone, hold your positions. Team one, move in on my count. Team two, hold your positions, but be ready to back them up."

"10-4," everyone radioed back.

One of the SWAT officers tossed a flashbang through the window. It exploded with an ear-piercing sound. Nothing happened inside.

"Breach!" the lieutenant radioed.

Two officers kicked in the front door and rushed inside, while two more went in the backdoor.

"One deceased male in the living room, gunshot wound to the right temple. The rest of the residence is clear," one of the officers radioed.

Berkley and Connor got up off the floor.

"They found him," she said to the older man.

"He shot himself, didn't he?"

"I can't give any details. Sorry. The scene is safe. That's all we know," she replied before following Connor out the door. They quickly caught up with the rest of the team.

"It's a mess in there," Sergeant Jones stated, shaking his head.

Berkley shook her head. She'd been to a couple of homicide scenes and a handful of car accidents with instant deaths. They never got any easier.

"All of team two is being dismissed. You guys head home, or back to your districts if you're on shift," he said.

"Until next time, Ward," Connor held his hand out.

"Yep," she replied, shaking it. Then, she headed back to her cruiser to remove her tactical gear and get her regular vest and uniform shirt back on.

41

Randi spent most of the week going to practice as if nothing had changed. In truth, she went through her usual routine. She and Olivia had different media schedules, and their practices were quite different. It wasn't unusual for them to take separate cars.

"Have you ever been somewhere, but wanted to be somewhere else?" Carrie muttered as she laced up her cleats.

"Tons of times. Where do you want to be right now?" Randi replied, sipping her sports drink.

"On a beach in Hawaii."

"Oh…I'm with you there." Randi smiled.

"Hey, I heard Olivia signed a deal with Adidas."

"Where did you hear that?"

"Saw it on her Instagram."

"That must've been her meeting this morning. She mentioned something on her way out. That's great," Randi said.

"Are things weird between you guys?"

"No, not really. She knows there was someone else, but not who it was. She asked and I was honest. I have no reason to lie to her. We're not together anymore."

"That still had to be hard."

Randi nodded. "So, what's going on with you? Why are we escaping to Hawaii?"

"I could use a break from life for a hot minute," Carrie said.

"We all could," Randi replied, giving her shoulders a squeeze in a side hug. "Come on, we have some calories to burn off."

Carrie laughed and followed her out onto the practice field.

*

The SWAT call was still fresh on Berkley's mind long after her shift had ended. She'd gone straight to bed when she got home, something she never did. Then met up with Garrett later in the day since it was the start of their three days off. He was sympathetic, he'd been to suicide calls before, but that wasn't where she wanted to be, or who she'd wanted to be with.

She needed to find a way to clear her head. She was working a pre-planned special assignment with SWAT that evening and needed to be as focused as she was rested.

Leaving the gym, she took the long way home, trying to clear her head as she rode her motorcycle. She hadn't intended on going to The Grind, but a late decision as she'd passed by caused her to turn around and go back. She backed the bike into a parking space and went inside.

"Hey, stranger," Paul said with a smile.

"How's business?"

"Pretty steady. What can I get for you?"

"The usual is fine…if you remember." She smiled.

"Of course. One iced cinnamon and unsweetened almond milk latte coming up."

Berkley leaned against the counter as she waited. A few patrons were sitting at tables, and another person had come in behind her. She was happy to see local businesses making it despite the large chains popping up on every corner.

When her coffee was ready, she retreated to a table and picked up the newspaper lying in the chair. She scanned the front page as she sipped her drink, looking for any storyline about the SWAT call.

*

Randi was about to pull out of the Target parking lot when she saw a familiar face walking up to her car.

"What are you up to?" Carrie said, popping her head in the open passenger window.

"Not much. I needed to pick up a couple of things. I'm about to go grab a coffee. You want to go?"

"Nah. I have domestic chores I've been neglecting."

Randi laughed. "Don't wear yourself out."

Carrie laughed. "I'll see you at the game," she said, backing away.

Randi waved and pulled out of her parking space, blasting the radio as she headed down the road.

The traffic was light so it hadn't taken her long to cross town. When she turned into the strip center where The Grind was located, she nearly rear-ended the car in front of her. Her heart thumped so hard, it felt like it was going to rip right out of her chest at any moment, and it wasn't because of the near-collision. She pulled into an empty space and got out of her car. She glanced at the motorcycle sitting a few spaces down before walking inside.

*

A grinning smile spread across Randi's face when her eyes landed on Berkley. She knew it was her behind the newspaper. Everyone else was on an electronic device, but not the hardnosed cop. She was old school, and Randi loved that about her.

"I see you're still keeping the local post in business," she said, pulling out the chair across from Berkley.

"Old habits die hard I guess," Berkley replied, lowering the paper. She wasn't prepared for how hard it would hit her seeing Randi again. She felt like someone had swung a bat at the center of her chest. It had only been about three weeks, but it might as well have been three months.

Randi stared at the deep blue eyes looking back at her, searching for any kind of sign that Berkley missed her too. "You've been missed around the soccer stadium. Sasha has pretty much begged for your number."

Berkley folded the newspaper correctly and set it aside. "Is that why you sat down at my table? To tell me Sasha is still interested in me?"

Randi shook her head. "I tried calling you."

"I've been busy."

"Olivia and I split a couple of weeks ago."

Berkley nodded.

"We're roommates currently. Although, that's about all we've been for longer than I can remember. It should've happened a while ago. You helped me see that."

Berkley sipped her coffee and leaned back in her chair. "I'm not social media savvy, but I'm pretty sure your followers seem to think you two are going to get married and have soccer star babies any time now."

"Those are just fans. They don't know anything about me. Olivia and I haven't told the team yet, so we're sort of keeping up appearances."

"That doesn't make much sense."

"There are only a couple of games left in the regular season. If we win or at least tie in them, we'll go to the playoffs for the first time. We're trying not to upset the mojo with the team."

"So, you're broken up, but still living together…and no one knows. Am I right?"

"Carrie knows, and my sister as well."

Berkley nodded.

"I miss you." Randi bit the side of her lower lip. "I miss *us*."

Berkley wanted to believe her. More than that, she wanted to pull her close and kiss her like she'd never tasted her lips before. She put her hand on the small table, inches from where Randi's sat. She knew if they touched, it would be over. She'd be too weak to stop herself from claiming the lips that were beckoning her. But, at the last second, just when Randi's hand moved, she backed away, crossing her arms.

"It sounds like you're still playing games."

"Games? With who?"

"Anyone who will play them."

Randi shook her head. "I'm not—"

"Look, I want to believe you. I know you're not a liar. I guess I don't understand how you would break up but still live together, and then keep the breakup a secret. It doesn't add up, Randi." Berkley stood and took the last sip of her coffee. "I have to go. I had a rough shift last night, and I have to go in today on my day off. It was good seeing you," she said before tossing her cup in the trash on her way out.

"Damn it," Randi mumbled under her breath as she watched her mount the bike and drive off. Then, she stood up and walked out the door, having never ordered the coffee she'd come to get.

*

Randi was unusually quiet as she dressed for the game in the locker room. She heard the conversations going on around, but wasn't listening to what anyone was saying, including her ex-girlfriend, the captain of the team.

The only words tumbling around in her mind were: *You're still playing games*. The idea that Berkley thought she was lying to keep having an affair cut her deep. She could sit around and replay their conversation a hundred times in her head, but it was only making her angry, and she had a game to play. She finished lacing her cleats and followed the team into the tunnel.

*

"Are you ready for this?" Connor said as he adjusted the straps on his tactical vest.

Berkley looked at the reflection of herself in the window of her patrol cruiser. She looked like a soldier ready for battle, except she was wearing all black instead of drab green or tan, and her tactical vest had SWAT written in white across the front and back of it. "Yeah. You?"

"I live for this shit." He grinned. "This is why I joined SWAT."

They were doing a drug raid on a house a block away. The plan was to go on foot from two different directions, so the full SWAT team was broken up into two teams, Alpha and Bravo. Sergeant Jones, Connor, and Berkley were the Bravo team. Their orders were to come in from the back of the house while the Alpha team went through the front door with the search warrant.

"Bravo—move into position," Lieutenant Sullivan radioed. "We're fifty paces out. Breach in one minute."

"Copy," Sergeant Jones replied, setting his watch for one minute so he'd know when to breach the back door. He gave quick hand signals to his team to climb the fence and stay behind the shed.

Berkley scaled the wooden privacy fence and backed up against the dilapidated shed. Connor followed and wound up near the opposite corner. Both officers looked at Sergeant Jones, waiting for the 'go' signal while he watched the timer count down. He flashed three fingers and a closed fist for thirty seconds.

Suddenly, Berkley caught sight of something out of the corner of her eye. A white male in jeans and a red t-shirt had burst out the back door and was climbing over the fence. She took off after him, scaling the fence like a cat. The brightly colored shirt gave away his position twenty-five yards ahead of her as he cut through another yard. She had no time to listen to the commands on the radio, she was running full out, trying to catch the guy before he got away.

Finally, after he jumped the fence into the third yard, she caught up and grabbed him off the fence. Together, they fell to the ground. He began swinging his arms like a madman, but she was able to get away from him before getting hit hard enough to leave a mark.

"Stand still! You're under arrest!" she yelled, pulling her Glock out of the holster on her waist and pointing it at him. She'd left her AK-47 rifle behind the shed when she took off running, but her handgun was always on her side.

Before she could say anything else, he put his hand in his pocket and pulled out a knife.

"Drop it!" she yelled.

He continued jumping all around like an unhinged animal, but never let go of the knife. She had no idea if he was going to lunge at her or not.

"Drop the knife!" she shouted. *Don't make me shoot you*, she thought as her adrenaline spiked, causing her blood pressure to skyrocket. Her heart was beating so hard, she feared she might pass out.

The way he was moving all around reminded her of a cartoon character. He was most definitely on some serious drugs. His eyes looked twice as large as normal and his nostrils flared.

Berkley was barely ten feet from him. A hundred different scenarios went through her head while several calls came over the radio. Her team was looking for her and she could do nothing but stand there and stare him down. She knew she was in the row of houses behind the suspect house and roughly three houses north.

"Put the damn knife down, now!" she yelled.

A loud thump sound got the man's attention. His hand dropped loosely to his side as he turned slightly to see what the noise was. Berkley lunged at him, knocking him to the ground and fighting to get the knife from his hand at the same time. She won the battle and tossed it back behind her, out of reach.

"Are you okay?" Connor said, jumping over the fence.

"Yeah," she replied, sitting on top of the man.

Connor got on the ground and helped her wrestle him into handcuffs. Once they'd finished, the man was lying on his stomach with his hands behind his back. However, he was still flailing all around and saying all kinds of incoherent words.

"What the hell is he on?" she said, shaking her head as she put on a pair of gloves and began searching his pockets.

"Meth more than likely. They had a meth lab in that house. LT found several pounds of meth, and all of the ingredients to make more. Plus, a ton of paraphernalia, cash, and guns."

"Yep," she said, pulling a skinny glass cylinder from his pocket and a small baggie with white powder in it.

"Get up!" Connor growled, grabbing the guy's arms.

Berkley opened the gate for the fence, and they walked out onto the street where a patrol car was waiting. She opened the door and Connor shoved him inside.

"Drive him back around. We'll hop the fence," he said to the officer. When the car drove away, he turned back to Berkley. "You okay?"

"I nearly shot him."

"I saw you. I'm sorry it took me so long to catch up."

She nodded.

"You know…we were supposed to have the easy job on these last two calls."

"Someone should redefine easy for the brass," she laughed.

"No shit. Come on, let's go help them tally up everything since we've done the grunt work for them."

"I'm getting too old for this shit," she mumbled as they climbed over the fence to get into the yard behind the one they were standing in and went through the gate to walk the rest of the way down the street.

*

Richey was up by a goal over Portland when they stepped out of the locker room after halftime. Olivia had given her pep talk, and the coach had discussed areas to improve for the second half. Jorja and Sasha were on yellow cards. Portland was playing dirty and getting away with it in front of the referee. Randi was already on edge from her conversation with Berkley and getting shoved around on the field only pissed her off more.

"They think they can come into our house and push us around, bitches please!" she yelled in the huddle before they took the field. "We need a win here, or the championship is out the window. Now, let's go!"

"Hell yeah!" Sasha yelled, followed by Jorja and Carrie as they put their hands in.

"Kick some ass on three," Randi shouted. "One, two, three…"

Everyone yelled, "Kick some ass," before running out onto the field.

The ref blew the whistle and Carrie passed the ball back to Randi, who lobbed it forward back to her. Then, Randi ran up the side, anticipating a wide pass. She didn't bother looking for the defender near her as she watched the ball coming straight to her. It wasn't until she was hit from behind and flew to the ground that she realized the defender had been right on her.

It took an extra second for Randi to catch her breath before she got to her feet. The ref never blew the whistle and the ball had continued in play. She threw her hands up at the ref and shook her head.

"What the fuck was that?" she growled as she ran past her.

"Language!" the ref yelled.

Randi ignored her as she got back into play. Sasha quickly sent a long ball forward. Randi dove into the air, heading it down. The same defender who had body-checked her, wound up with the ball. Randi cut her off at the sideline. They fought for the ball, back and forth, tugging jersey's and elbowing each other in the ribs until Randi finally hip-checked her and she fell to the ground.

The ref quickly blew the whistle for a foul and awarded Portland the ball.

"Are you fucking kidding me?!" Randi yelled at the ref.

"That's your first warning. The next time it's a yellow," the ref said.

"Oh, for fuck's sake!" Randi spat. "That's a bullshit call and you know it!" she added, walking away.

Everyone got back into position for the indirect kick. As soon as the girl kicked it, Randi ran towards the center circle to cut her off when she went around Carrie and took off on a breakaway. Randi caught up to her, but she'd already sent it in to the box to a teammate who took a quick one-touch shot.

Olivia dove through the air, punching the ball up and over the back off the goal, giving Portland a corner quick. Randi went into the box, leaving Carrie as the only forward, with one midfielder with her near the circle.

The Portland player lobbed the ball right into the middle of the box. Everyone went into the air to head the ball. Randi and a Portland player crashed into each other's shoulders and the person behind them wound up getting her head on the ball. It bounced to the ground and was kicked back and forth by players on both teams as they fought for it. Randi wound up with it and tried to clear it from the box, but the player she'd tangled with shoved her from behind. Randi landed on the ground and quickly jumped up in the girl's face.

"What the fuck is your problem?" Randi yelled.

"Get out of my way, bitch!" the girl shouted, shoving her back.

"I've had enough of your shit!" Randi countered, pushing her equally as hard.

Play had kept going and most of the players were near the other end of the field as the two of them continued yelling and pushing each other. The sideline ref finally got the center ref's attention and she turned to see Randi and the Portland player tussling at the edge of the box, literally about to start swinging fists. Olivia ran out from the goal line, doing the ref's job for her as she got between them, quickly wrapping Randi in a bear hug and walking her backward, just as the ref blew the whistle and raced up the field towards them.

"I could red card you both!" the ref yelled as she showed them the yellow.

"Come at me again," Randi growled to the Portland player.

"Calm down, Randi!" Olivia said.

"You better get your girl," the Portland player sneered at her.

Both players caught back up to everyone else and play restarted. It didn't take long for Randi to find the ball once more. A different Portland player shoulder-checked her and won the ball. Having had enough, Randi took off at full sprint, slide-tackling the Portland player and kicking the ball away a split second before the player tumbled to the ground. The ref quickly pulled the yellow and the red card from her pocket, showing them to Randi.

"You are the worst ref I've ever seen! Are you fucking blind?" Randi yelled, shaking her head.

The ref ignored her as she waited for her to clear the field.

"This game is out of control," Carrie said as she and Jorja watched Randi leave the game to a standing ovation and boos by the crowd.

There were only five minutes left in regular time when Randi stepped off the field. The assistant coach handed her a penny to put on over her jersey, but she just threw it over her shoulder and sat down in one of the bench chairs.

*

Randi was in the locker room, removing her cleats when the coach walked in. They'd won the game by the skin of their teeth.

He shrugged and moved to the front of the room to address the team. "We came out on top tonight, but it was sloppy. They were aggressive and we matched their style of play instead of playing our game. If they're being overly hostile, it will force mistakes. If we play with finesse, we will be able to take advantage of those mistakes, but if we're playing their game, we're only being destructive. Was the ref making bad calls? Absolutely. Is there anything we can do about that? No. We got lucky, especially going down to ten players with five minutes plus another five in stoppage time." He crossed his arms. "The only thing that came out of our win tonight is three points that moved us up to second place. Next week is the final game of the season, so even with a loss, we're still in the playoffs."

Everyone cheered.

He held his hand up. "That doesn't mean that next week's game is a wash. We need to regroup this week and come in playing *our* game. Orlando needs a win to get into the playoffs. They will be coming at us hard. We cannot do what we did tonight." He ended and stepped over to Randi.

"What got into you tonight?" he asked.

"That ref was an idiot."

"Yeah, but you were out there fighting and playing just as aggressive. She was looking for a scapegoat to show she had control and you let it be you."

I wish this damn day was over already, she thought.

"Next week will be hard enough, now we have to do it without you," he added before leaving the room.

Randi changed clothes and grabbed her backpack.

"Everything okay?" Carrie asked.

"Yeah," Randi mumbled, before walking out of the building without showering.

42

Berkley lied on the couch, staring up at the ceiling fan spinning around. The adrenaline coursing through her veins had long worn off. The reality of what could've happened earlier that night filled her conscience, hitting her at full speed. She was a cop, she was bound to be in hairy situations from time to time, but she'd never had to make the decision on whether or not to take someone's life. All the while, wondering if they were about to take hers instead. She couldn't remember thinking of anything in the moment, but several thoughts had crossed her mind since, like her last conversation with Randi. The more she replayed it, the more it bothered her. She'd basically called Randi a liar, something she knew she wasn't, which made her feel bad. She should've stayed and talked more, but nothing Randi said made sense to her.

"Who breaks up with their girlfriend, yet continues to live with her?" she mumbled to herself. "I knew I'd see her again, but that was definitely not the way I thought things would go."

She shook her head and pursed her lips. Hearing Randi say she'd missed her…had missed them together, tugged at the tear in her heart that had opened when she'd said goodbye to her. "Do I really want to go down this road again?" she sighed.

I don't think you have a choice, her thoughts answered.

*

Randi cracked her eyes open when she heard her phone vibrating on the nightstand. Rays of sun were filling the room with streaks of light. She reached out blindly, grabbing it just before whoever was calling, hung up on her voicemail.

"Hello?"

"Are you still sleeping?" Elisa asked.

"I was. What time is it?"

"Ten."

"Ugh," Randi groaned. No wonder her stomach was growling. She'd skipped dinner after taking a quick shower and spent the rest of the evening in her room. Olivia had tried to coax her out, but talking about the game was the last thing she'd wanted to do. And she certainly couldn't talk to her about Berkley.

"So…what happened last night?"

"Let me guess, you saw the game?"

"Uh, yeah. Along with mom and dad and some of mom's yoggies."

"What the hell is a yoggi?"

"Her yoga buddies," Elisa chuckled.

"Oh, for crying out loud."

"You were clearly having a bad night."

"You think?" Randi muttered, sitting up and pulling a t-shirt over her head to cover her naked chest.

"Want to talk about it?"

"Not really."

"Ay dios mio! Miranda Francisca, fighting on the field…no bueno."

"You sound like mom."

"Exactly. She'll be calling you next. You might as well talk to me so I can run interference."

"Ohhhhh. You play a good game, Elisa Sofia," Randi laughed, feeling like they were kids again, keeping secrets from their parents for each other. "I saw Berkley yesterday," she finally said with a sigh.

"I take it things didn't go so well."

"Nope. She thinks I'm playing games with her."

"Weren't you? At first, I mean."

"I don't know. Maybe. It was flirty fun…until I kissed her."

"Then, you kept on until you slept with her."

"You make it sound like I seduced her. She came onto me just as hard."

"Yeah, but you had a girlfriend whom you were living with the entire time. That's playing games, sis."

"I fell for her somewhere along the way. It was no longer a game at that point."

"She doesn't know that. All she knows is you're supposedly single, but still playing house with your ex. Think about that for a minute. If it were reversed, would you have anything to do with her?"

"I doubt it."

"Exactly. Who wants to get mixed up in that mess? It's an unhealthy situation, even if you *are* best friends."

Randi sighed.

"You need to figure out what you want and where you want to be and make it happen. This is obviously a lot deeper than you realize if you let it affect your game."

"Yeah."

"Do you love Olivia?"

"What?"

"Are you in love with her? Do you see things working out with her?"

"No. That's over."

"Then why are you still living in her house?"

Randi brought her knees to her chest and wrapped her free arm around her legs. "I don't know."

"That's your starting point."

"Are you sure you're not a psychologist?"

Elisa laughed. "If I am, you owe me $500."

"What?" Randi chuckled. "That's a bit steep, don't you think?"

"You owe me for at least five sessions. Not to mention your teenage years."

"Uh-huh. On that note, I'm getting off the phone."

"I'll deal with mom, but you owe me."

"Put it on my bill," Randi laughed as she hung up. She set the phone down and laid her head on the top of her knees. Her sister had given her a different perspective. She definitely wouldn't have given Berkley the time of day if she had been dating someone, much less living with them.

"You okay?" Olivia asked, rapping her knuckles on the door.

"Yeah."

"I'm leaving for my recovery massage."

"Okay," Randi answered. They were off for the next two days but required to do some form of recovery the day after a game, and a form of exercise on their other day off. She'd planned to go to the pool for a long, relaxing swim, but at the moment she had other ideas. Grabbing her phone, she scrolled through her important contacts and waited until she heard the garage door going back down, before hitting the call button.

"I was just about to call you," Carrie answered.

"Are you busy?"

"No."

"Anna isn't with you?"

"No. She missed the game and didn't come over last night."

"Bummer. Law school is a bitch."

"Yep. What's up? You sound like you're in a better mood," Carrie said.

"Something like that," Randi replied, getting out of the bed.

"Want to do something together for recovery?"

"Nope. We're going apartment hunting. I'll be there in thirty," Randi stated before ending the call.

*

The echo of Berkley's motorcycle sounded like thunder as she rolled up next to the open fire station bay. She killed the engine and got off, locking the frame with her key so that it couldn't be stolen, before walking inside with her backpack slung over one shoulder.

"Hola, Chica!" Dena yelled from the top of the staircase leading to the second floor, where the living quarters were located.

Berkley smiled. "Where's Captain Sanders?"

"Right here," he said, removing his glasses and wiping them on his shirt as he walked out of his office. "Good to see you, Ward. I heard you made the SWAT team."

"Yes, sir," she replied with a nod.

"Good for you. I take it you're here to join us for a rotation?"

"Correct. Gotta keep that certification up to date. I scheduled it with the lieutenant a couple of weeks ago."

"He's out on paternity leave. His wife went into labor a month early, but their baby girl is doing fine."

"That's good."

"Anyhow, no need to go over formalities. You know your way around. You can double up in the rig with Hernandez. I'll put Grace on the truck."

"Okay."

"It's always good to have you back…even if it *is* only for twenty-four hours."

"It's nice to have a change of pace," she replied honestly.

"Everything good?" Dena asked, sliding up next to her.

"Yeah." She smiled. "Looks like I'm riding with you."

"Oh, shit! The dynamic duo is back together," Dena giggled.

Berkley chuckled. The last time she'd done a rotation, Dena and Maggie were off, so she'd ridden on the truck as a backup EMT.

"Sometimes I hate being a firefighter/EMT," Maggie pretended to pout.

"Girl, please. You talk about how much you love it all the time," Dena chided.

"Yeah…until she comes to play with us." Maggie grinned.

"I'm going to go get settled in," Berkley said, shaking her head and laughing as she walked away.

43

Cher's cover of *Gimme! Gimme! Gimme!* by ABBA was blaring on the radio when Carrie opened the passenger door to Randi's BMW and slid into the bucket seat.

"Gimme! Gimme! Gimme! A woman after midnight!" Randi sang as she drove off.

Carrie laughed. She couldn't help feeling like she was in a gay club with the techno tune playing. She quickly joined in. "Take me through the darkness to the break of day!"

When the song ended, Randi turned the volume down.

"Are you really moving out of Olivia's house?" Carrie asked.

"Yep."

"You know, I have plenty of room."

"Thanks, but I need to do this on my own. I've never lived alone. It's time I put my big girl panties on and see what adulting is all about."

Carrie nodded.

"Any suggestions on where to look first? I found a couple of places online. I'm looking for a studio or one-bedroom apartment. Nothing big."

"I hear Pinewood is nice."

"What's the one Anna lived in before she moved on campus?"

"Laredo. They're nice inside, but she dealt with a slew of issues."

"Figures." Randi shook her head. "What's she up to today?"

"No idea," Carrie said, turning her head to look through the window. "We broke up last night."

"What?!" Randi hit the brakes a little too hard coming to the red light, causing the car behind her to honk the horn. Randi held her right hand up, shooting the person a bird despite knowing her tint was too dark for him or her to see it. "Are you serious?" she questioned, looking at her best friend.

"Yeah. We'd been heading in that direction for weeks. I knew it was time to call it."

"You broke up with her?"

Carrie nodded.

The car behind them honked again because the light had turned green.

"I'm going to bitch slap this asshole if he honks one more time!" Randi growled, shaking her head. "What is wrong with people?"

Carrie chuckled. "Sounds like you're still fired up from last night."

"Maybe a little," Randi laughed.

"I was pretty sure you were about to give that girl a beat down right there in the box."

"I was ready to go a few rounds with that damn ref, for sure. I still can't believe she red-carded me." Randi pulled into the Pinewood Apartment Homes parking lot. "Nice change of subject, by the way. You still owe me some details."

Carrie released her seatbelt and got out without saying anything.

*

"South 5—Rescue 21. Overturned vehicle on Longhorn Boulevard. Engine 21 is on scene. Please respond," the dispatcher radioed.

Dena and Berkley had just finished a call with a man who had fallen off a ladder and hurt his ankle. He didn't want to be transported and said he'd get his wife to take him if the swelling got worse.

"Rescue 21—en route. ETA two minutes," Berkley replied using the mic in the cab of the ambulance as Dena switched on the lights and sirens and sped through a red light.

"Have you spoken to Randi…you know, since everything ended?" Dena asked.

"How can you have a conversation and drive like a maniac through traffic at the same time?" Berkley questioned, watching the road in all directions.

"The same way you chase people at over a hundred miles an hour while radioing other officers and watching the computer screen. We're gold medalists when it comes to multitasking. You have to be to do what we do. Now, spill it. You've seen her, haven't you?"

"We're almost on scene," Berkley said.

"Look at the screen. Minor injuries reported. It's not life or death. And, the engine is already there."

Berkley shook her head. "Yes. Fine. I saw her…once. It was yesterday, actually. And it didn't go well. I pretty much called her a liar. I feel bad about it. Now, can we go do our jobs?" she huffed as they pulled up to a small group of people standing near a blue, two-door sedan that was on its roof.

*

"What do you think?" the rental clerk asked as they got onto the golf cart to ride back to the front of the complex.

"It's spacious and I like the floors, but the wait time is longer than I was looking for," Randi replied.

"Our single units don't last long. Sometimes, we have a waitlist. In fact, that one has been rented, but the person isn't moving in for a few more days. Otherwise, I wouldn't have anything open to show you."

"Wow," Carrie uttered.

"Thanks," Randi said as they stopped near her car. "I'll let you know today, if I want to move forward."

The clerk waved as she went back inside the office.

"Where to now?" Carrie asked as they got into the car.

"I'm going to take you home. I feel bad for dragging you with me. You should've said something."

"Randi, I'm fine. If I didn't want to go, I wouldn't be with you. Now, let's check out Oxford Villas. I heard they were really nice."

"Aren't those luxury apartments?" Randi asked, backing out of the parking space.

"So was this place."

"Really?"

Carrie nodded. "They're right down the road. It won't hurt to look."

Randi pulled out of the complex and drove towards the next place. She hadn't bothered turning the radio back on since they weren't going far. *How did I not know what was going on with my best friend? I've been so caught up in my own shit.* She shook her head. "I'm sorry," she muttered.

"What?" Carrie looked over at her.

"I've been a horrible friend lately."

"No, you haven't," Carrie replied as they pulled into the parking lot for Oxford Villas.

"I had no idea what was going on in your life."

"I didn't either. At least, not until I talked to you about your own mess. It made me see what was right in front of me...or more importantly, what wasn't. It's fine. I'm fine. We went our separate ways in a five-minute conversation. It's not like we were together for several years and lived together and so on. It was two years of an almost nonexistent relationship. Now, come on. Let's go find you a new place to live, or you're moving in with me."

Randi laughed and got out of the car.

"Good morning, ladies. Are you in the market for a lovely new place to call home?" a bubbly man said with a big smile. He was already outside of the office, waiting for them to get out of the car. His perfectly manicured hair, pressed suit, and shiny shoes made Randi think she was looking at a place in Beverly Hills.

"She is," Carrie said, pointing at Randi.

"Wonderful," he said, extending his hand. "I'm Derrick."

"Randi," she replied. "This is my best friend, Carrie."

"Excellent. So, Randi...are you familiar with the Oxford property?"

"No, not really."

"Oxford is a one-hundred-acre property with an eighteen-hole golf course. Oxford Estates is the lavish neighborhood that surrounds the course. Oxford Hollow, on the other end of the property, is a group of high-end townhomes, and Oxford Villas is a luxury apartment community. Our residents have the option to use the golf course amenities. Of course, if you're not into golf, they wouldn't be included in your rent."

Randi nodded.

"What are you in the market for? We have one to three-bedroom units. As well as lofts."

"Ohhhh, definitely a loft," Carrie cooed.

Randi chuckled.

"We have a nice furnished unit that just came available. Let me grab the keys and we can go take a look. It's on the backside of the property, so it has a view of the golf course."

"This is a bit much, don't you think?" Randi said when he walked away.

Carrie shrugged. "He'll probably show you the place of your dreams and then hit you with a rent price that's triple everywhere else."

"Here we go, ladies. We'll take the golf cart," Derrick said, walking over to the dark green cart with a white top. *Oxford Villas* was written on the side in white.

Randi got in next to him and Carrie sat in the back. As soon as they were settled, he drove through the gate to get into the actual complex, and headed over to the gym and the pool, showing off the amenities.

"Each unit comes with a washer and dryer, so we don't have a laundry facility," he said as he headed over to the golf course. "Do either of you play golf?"

"No," they laughed.

"Soccer keeps us busy enough," Carrie said.

Derrick snapped his fingers. "I knew I'd seen you somewhere. You play for Richey FC, don't you?"

"Yes," Randi replied.

"I've been to a couple of games. Your picture is plastered around."

Randi pursed her lips and nodded. She was one of the faces of the team, so she was used quite a bit in their advertising.

"Here we are," he said, pulling up to one of the structures. "The buildings in the back are only two units high, but the ones in the front are three units, with the top unit having a much better view over the top of these back buildings, so they're a little higher priced. The open unit here is on the second floor, but the view is the same, so it doesn't affect the price."

"Speaking of price," Carrie said.

Derrick led them up the stairs and unlocked the door.

Randi walked in first, noticing the white and gray granite counter top in the kitchen and stainless appliances. It had light, bamboo colored wood floors and crème colored furniture with dark accents. The small kitchen had an island that opened up into the dining/living room area. A half bath was off to the right, and across from the living room were the sliding glass doors that went out to the balcony, where a small iron patio set was located. The iron spiral staircase was on the left side of the room, which led up to the loft bedroom with a queen bed and bathroom with a glass shower and single sink next to the toilet. There was plenty of space for one person in the apartment, and it would still be comfortable if she had company over. She tried not to look excited, but she'd never lived on her own, and this place felt perfect.

"What do you think?" he asked.

"How much is it?" Carrie questioned.

"It's nice. I could see myself living here," Randi said. "But, yeah…what's the rent?"

"Well, if you want the full package, access to the gym, the pool, and the golf course…this unit is $1900 per month."

"Holy shit," Carrie spat. "My mortgage isn't that much."

"I'm definitely not interested in playing golf, and I have access to the team gym seven days a week, so I don't need that either. I wouldn't mind access to the pool though. What would that be?" Randi said.

"Without the golf and gym amenities, this unit would be $1300. The deposit is equal to one month's rent, as well."

"That's still steep," Carrie said.

"What's your price range?" he asked, looking at Randi.

"I haven't thought much about it. I agree though, thirteen is a bit high."

"We do have a special, if you pay first and last month's rent upfront, we take $100 off, so you'd be looking at $1200. This includes utilities. I don't think I mentioned that."

"That makes more sense," Randi said. "When is it available?"

"Right now. You fill out the application and pay the three-hundred-dollar deposit. Then, we run your background check and credit report. That takes about five minutes. After that, you sign the lease." He checked his watch. "If everything clears, you'd have the keys with enough time to move in today."

"Wow," Randi mumbled. "Is the lease for a year, or can I do something shorter?"

"We do offer a nine-month lease with terms. Otherwise, all of our leases are a year."

"What are the terms?" Randi asked.

"You pay first and last month's rent, plus a deposit equal to a month's rent."

She bit her lower lip and looked at Carrie. "I'll do nine months," she said as a big smile spread across her face.

"Wonderful," he said and grinned. "Let's go get your paperwork started."

44

"Can you believe this happened because she swerved to miss a squirrel?" Dena shook her head.

"Yeah," Berkley muttered, watching as Maggie and the other firefighters cut the door off the side of the overturned car. The elderly lady inside was stable and complaining of pain in her ankle, but they had to take full precaution to prevent a spinal injury.

"When she comes out, we're going to have to move quickly. She's been suspended upside down for close to fifteen minutes. Her circulatory system is being severely stressed," Dena said.

Berkley nodded in agreement and unstrapped the backboard that was lying on top of the stretcher. When the door popped off, opening the entire driver's side of the car, she and Dena rushed over.

"Okay, Hilda. Now, we're going to slide you onto this hardboard as we pull you out, okay?" Dena said.

"Alright," the elderly woman replied.

Berkley got under her, using her strength to hold her steady while Dena slowly pulled her free. Maggie helped out, holding the backboard in place. Once they had her free, they strapped her down with the backboard lying on the ground. Then, they secured the board to the stretcher and wheeled her to the back of the ambulance.

Dena started the intravenous line while Berkley began collecting her vitals.

"Everything looks good so far," Dena said.

"I can't see anything but the bright lights and I know this isn't the ride to the pearly gates."

Berkley laughed and leaned over so she could see her. "Hi."

"Well…hello," Hilda said. "I'd flip my car more often if handsome ladies like you came to my rescue every time."

"You'd probably see me, I'm actually an officer with Richey PD. However, I don't recommend swerving for squirrels anymore. Or intentionally rolling your car."

"What are you doing in here if you're a cop? I like their uniforms better, by the way," she said with a wink.

"I'm EMT certified, so a couple times a year I work with fire rescue to keep my certification up to date."

"I see. A Jill of all trades. I bet you have a beautiful young lady at home."

"Nope," Berkley muttered as she finished writing down all of the vitals.

"Surely the ladies love you. Back in my prime, we certainly didn't see anyone like you walking around. We probably would've torn each other's beehive hair out to get to you."

"Don't let her fool you, she's in love," Dena laughed. "Miss Hilda, how's your pain level?"

"I'm a tough ol' bird. How's my ankle?"

It's pretty swollen. I splinted it as best I could. The doctors will know more after an x-ray," she said. "I'm going to head up front and get us on the road. The hospital is about five minutes away."

"Great," she replied, looking around until Berkley appeared over her again. "Now, does this girl love you back? If not, tell that broad driving us to swing by her house so I can smack some sense into her."

Berkley smiled. "It's a little more complicated than that."

"That's the problem with you kids these days. Old fashioned romance and love are gone. It's all about Tweetbooking and Snipping pictures on your phone." She shook her head. "Take her on a proper date. Hold her door, and push her chair in. Order only one glass of wine, if she does first. Make her laugh because her smile should light up the room. Otherwise, why are you with her? Casually hold her hand when you walk. When you drop her off, walk her to the door and kiss her cheek. And for God's sake, leave your phone at home!"

Berkley chuckled. "Yes, ma'am."

"We're here," Dena called from the front of the rig as they rolled to a stop in the emergency room bay.

Berkley unhooked everything from the machines as Dena opened the double backdoors. Together, they wheeled the elderly woman into the hospital and handed her off to the waiting staff.

"She was something else," Dena laughed as they filled out the paperwork and headed back to the rig. "I'm pretty sure she had a crush on you."

"You think everyone wants me." Berkley shook her head.

"That's because they do."

"Uh-huh." Berkley rolled her eyes as she got into the passenger seat.

"Sounds like she gave you some sound advice."

"Yeah, maybe I'll use it next time a hot girl falls into my lap."

Dena shook her head and laughed.

"You know, I've never been called handsome before now. Would you use that word to describe me?"

"I'd say you were good-looking. I don't use the word handsome. It's old-fashioned, I guess. So, anyway, why did you call Randi a liar?"

"We're back to that?"

"Yes," Dena replied as she pulled out of the hospital parking lot. "Why don't you start at the beginning?"

Berkley checked her watch and sighed.

Dena smiled. "Yep. You're stuck with me for a while. You might as well spill it."

"She and her girlfriend broke up, but they're still living together."

"What?"

"I accused her of trying to play games and keep me around."

"What did she say?"

"I left."

"Berkley!"

"What was I supposed to do?"

"Hear her out."

"I heard enough."

"Sometimes, I want to check to make sure you don't have a penis because you act like an asshole male," Dena chided and shook her head.

"That's nice," Berkley muttered.

"Well, it's the truth."

"I should've just had an affair from the very beginning, keeping is solely physical like I always do."

"You said you were done playing games...especially with taken women."

"It looks like I'm the liar."

"No. It looks like you fell in love with Randi and don't know what to do about it."

"It's not that simple."

"What if it is?"

"She's still living with her ex, and they literally just broke up."

"Has it occurred to you that they probably broke up because of you? She's obviously in love with you, too."

"Thank you for analyzing everything, Dr. Phil."

"Fuck off," Dena chuckled.

Berkley was about to say something when the radio went off with another call. She grabbed the mic. "Rescue 22—en route. ETA three minutes."

*

"I can't believe I'm doing this," Randi said as she began pulling her clothes out of the closet. "Am I crazy?"

"To move out of your ex-girlfriend's house or move into your own place?" Carrie asked. She was already home and Randi had her on speakerphone.

"When you put it like that…"

"It's the right decision."

"I need a drink," Randi said, tossing her shoes into an empty box.

"Are you sure you don't want me to come help you?"

"There's not much to pack, honestly. We've already split our stuff up. I'm not going through the house and nitpicking everything like an angry divorced couple. This is her house. My apartment is furnished. The only things I need are personal belongings."

"It still sucks to do it alone."

"I'll be fine. I have my big girl panties on," Randi laughed.

"You're a mess. Call me when you get settled later."

"I will," Randi said before ending the call. She looked around the room. Everything she owned was in six brown boxes and her clothes were in piles covering the bed. With nothing else to pack, she began taking everything out to her car.

It was like a real-life game of Tetris trying to make everything fit, but she finally got it all. The spare room looked just like it had before she'd taken it over two weeks earlier. A tear slid down her cheek as she took the house key off her key ring. She wasn't sad about the breakup, but leaving behind the life she'd known for the last five years choked her up. She quickly pulled it together when she heard the garage door.

"Hey," Olivia said, walking up a minute later.

"Hey," Randi replied, stepping away from the counter. "Can we talk?"

"Sure. What's up?" Olivia pulled out a stool and sat down at the island.

Randi slid the key over, and Olivia looked at her with a raised brow.

"I'm moving out…technically, I've already done it."

"What? Where did this come from?"

"We're not together anymore. It's the right thing to do."

Olivia nodded. "You could've stayed."

"I needed to be on my own. You'll always have a place in my heart, but living together isn't the best idea."

"I know. You're still one of my best friends. I think that's what sucks the most about this."

"Yeah," Randi agreed.

"Do you want any of the furniture? Half of all of this is yours."

"No. I told you before, keep it. I'm good with what I have. Besides, my place is furnished."

"If you change your mind, let me know."

"I will. I should probably go. I'll see you at practice on Tuesday. We can tell the team then if you want. Or wait until after the game Saturday."

"Whatever you want to do is fine with me."

Randi nodded and gave her a quick hug before leaving.

45

Berkley was beat from the 24-hour shift with fire rescue, and planned to spend the last of her time off on the couch, catching up on some much-needed rest...until a knock on the door woke her up. She yawned as she got up and padded across the house. She was dressed in an old t-shirt and gym shorts, with no bra, but she didn't care. If someone was at her door, they knew her and they were there for a reason.

"I hate that you know where I live," she said, answering the door to Dena's smiling face.

"You love me and you know it."

"Do I smell coffee and donuts?"

"I thought you didn't want me here," Dena replied, pretending to turn and go.

"Get your ass in here and hand me that bag of donuts," Berkley mumbled, opening it as she walked away.

Dena waited for her to get some coffee and sugar in her system.

"I figured you might be tired. That was a pretty busy shift."

"It's been a long week to begin with, and it starts all over tonight," Berkley uttered between bites of pumpkin donut. "I can't believe they have these out already. It's barely September."

"I know. The stores are practically putting Christmas shit on the same aisle as Halloween. I guess

Thanksgiving doesn't exist anymore." Dena shook her head. "Anyway, that's not why I'm here."

"I figured. You don't just show up. What's going on? Is everything okay with you and GT?"

"Yeah. We're fine. Still having sex like rabbits," she laughed.

"I didn't need to hear that." Berkley rolled her eyes.

Dena shrugged. "No, I couldn't sleep when I got home this morning. I kept thinking about your situation with Randi."

Berkley nodded as she chewed her donut.

"I think you're scared."

"Scared?!" she blurted, causing donut chunks to fly out of her mouth.

"You're in love with her, and you haven't let yourself feel like this…ever."

Berkley chugged some coffee to wash the pastry down before she choked. "She has a girlfriend or ex-girlfriend or whatever the fuck it is and they live together. That's a complicated mess that I don't want to be involved in."

"You're already involved, Chica."

"I should've just slept with her and moved on weeks ago," she muttered, shaking her head.

"You mean like with all of the others?" Dena chided. "This has been a pattern with you for as long as I've known you. I thought you said you were finished with games? Yet, you played the game one more time. The only difference is, you fell in love this time." Berkley opened her mouth to speak, but Dena held her hand up. "If she's broken up with this girl, then she probably feels the same way about you. Have you thought about that?"

Berkley grabbed her phone and searched for Randi's Instagram account. She scrolled through the most recent posts, showing Dena pictures of her and Olivia together. "They don't look broken up to me."

Dena shrugged. "I guess I don't understand why you're not fighting for her."

"Because I've been down this road," she sighed. "Her name was Selena. We dated all through college, even lived together our senior year…until I found out she was cheating on me with a guy in one of her classes. I was going to ask her to marry me, so I was shocked and completely heartbroken. I nearly failed two of my classes. It took months for me to pull myself together. After that, I knew I wanted to be on the other side of the equation. I wasn't getting cheated on again, so I played the game, and I played it hard. Hell, you know that. Married women threw themselves at me. It was easy to get what I wanted and move on. I got tired of the game and decided I was done. Then, out of the blue, this beautiful girl spits coffee all over me. She took me completely by surprise, and I was instantly attracted to her. I thought maybe I'd give it a shot, lightning rarely strikes twice."

"Then, you found out she had a girlfriend."

"Yep. I tried to back away, but I couldn't. She pursued me as much as I did her. We both got what we wanted in the end."

"I'm sorry. I never knew. I just figured you were scared of being in a relationship."

"I am…in a way. I guess. It's safer to play the game. There are no strings attached. I can't get hurt."

"Can't you see this is different? Don't throw her or this away, Berk. She's not Selena."

"I know she's not, but how can I believe her when I see this?" she said, holding up her phone.

"You need to give her a chance to explain everything. You talked to her for all of two minutes and wrote her off."

"I called her a liar. She probably hates me."

"You love her, don't you?"

"Love has nothing to do with it."

"It has everything to do with it," Dena stated. "It's the reason you've pushed her away." She shook her head. "Just talk to her, Hun. That's all I'm saying."

Berkley sighed. "It may be the only way I can get her out of my head." She took the last sip of her coffee and set the cup back down. "I think her last regular-season game is tonight. I'll ride over during my shift right before the game ends and catch her before she leaves."

"Good idea. Now, give me that last donut. If I go home without any, Garrett will be pissed."

"I thought he wasn't feeling well? Didn't he eat some bad food or something?"

"Yeah. He went to Rooney's last night for dinner and it messed him up pretty good."

"He can't eat it anyway, so blame me," Berkley said, shoving it in her mouth.

"Damn you," Dena laughed. "The two of you are like little kids. I don't know how I put up with either of you."

"You love us."

"Yeah, like a damn mother hen," she growled.

Berkley laughed as she walked her to the door. "Thanks," she said seriously as she hugged her.

*

Randi turned the volume louder on her iPod, blasting the Beatles through the Bluetooth speaker as she shopped on Amazon on her phone for a few items to make her new place feel a little more homey. So far, she'd felt like she was in a fancy hotel the entire week. She was getting more comfortable, but something was missing.

"Ohhh, I like this," she said aloud, clicking on a painting of Galveston Bay at sunrise. "It reminds me of home," she muttered, adding it to her shopping cart. After a few more essential items like scented plugins, pot holders, a few Tervis cups with her favorite things on them because the ones in the cabinet were glass, and a shower caddy for her bathroom. "I work all day, to get you money, to buy you things," she sang along to *Hard Day's Night.*

She hated that it was the last regular game of the season and she was sitting out on a red card, which was why she was online shopping. She'd needed something to do to keep her mind off everything before she went stir crazy. She'd practiced with the team all week as usual, except she and Olivia had broken the news to everyone on Tuesday. Carrie had already known, but everyone else was genuinely surprised. However, they'd respected their privacy and hadn't bombarded them with questions. The rest of the week went by in a blur, almost as if nothing had happened, which was what they'd been hoping for.

As soon as she closed the Amazon app, her phone lit up with Carrie's picture. She swiped her finger across the front to answer the call.

"Hey," Carrie said. "How was your day?"

"I went shopping on Amazon. I'm pretty sure my wallet is going to bitch slap me next week," Randi replied.

Carrie laughed. "I was calling to see if you wanted to ride together."

"Nah. I'm going to grab some dinner on the way."

"Okay. Just checking. I'll see you there."

"Yep," Randi said before ending the call.

46

"That's all I have for tonight," the lieutenant said from the front of the room. "Oh, Garrett Tomayo is out sick, so Curt Mickler is covering his area."

Berkley adjusted the utility belt resting on her hips.

"Hopefully, it'll be a quiet night," Curt said, walking over to her as they headed out to their cars.

"Yeah." She nodded.

"What happened to Tomayo?"

"He got food poisoning last night. I talked to him earlier. He feels better, but he's pretty weak and tired from puking and shitting for twenty-four hours."

"Damn. I don't blame him. I would've bowed out, too."

"Men," she laughed.

"What's that supposed to mean?"

"Nothing." She shook her head. "Call me if you need backup. I'm going to take an early break around ten."

"Sounds good," he replied as she got into her patrol car.

*

Randi sat in the locker room, leaning back on a chair against the wall as her teammates prepared for the game. She knew her role. She was there to motivate the team and help lift the players she knew would falter without her on the field. It still struck a nerve knowing she wouldn't be taking the field alongside them when the whistle blew.

"I know how much you're hating this," Carrie said, sitting down next to her as she tied the strings of her cleats.

"Yeah," Randi sighed.

"We've got this. Win or lose, we're going to the playoffs."

"Yeah, but a win means home-field advantage."

"I know."

"Listen up, everyone!" the assistant coach yelled, gathering the group's attention as the head coach, athletic trainer, and team owner walked in behind him.

"I'm going to make this short and sweet," MJ said. "If we win, we're playing here in front of our sold-out crowd full of rowdy fans. If we lose, we're traveling up north or across the country to play on someone else's turf and in front of people who won't be cheering for us. We owe it to these diehard fans of ours to play at home. Rojas won't be on the field tonight, but each of you knows your role. Go out there and do your job." He turned to look at the owner who was standing with Jason, the athletic trainer.

"I have a short housekeeping announcement. Our beloved athletic trainer has decided to leave us after four great years to move back to Colorado to raise his new baby closer to family," she said. "Jason, you've been a gift to this organization and we will surely miss you. We wish you and your family nothing but happiness."

Several of the players spoke up, saying they would miss him and so on before she continued. "With that being said, he will continue with us until our season ends, hopefully after a championship win. His replacement is coming to us from Seattle, where she's been for the past five years, working with the Storm WNBA team. She's also finishing up her current season, as the Storm has made it to the playoffs. She will join us for the start of our pre-season next spring. She is a former collegiate softball player who was highly recommended. I believe you will all get along nicely with her."

"What's her name?" one of the players asked.

"Dashtin Oliver," the owner replied.

"Cool," Jorja said as Sasha immediately grabbed her phone and began to search for her on social media.

"That's all I have, other than go out there and kick some ass!" the owner yelled, rousing up the team before they headed out to take the field.

*

Randi had forgotten all about the news of Jason leaving as she watched the start of the game. She couldn't help looking down towards the corner of the field, searching for the person she knew wouldn't be there. She nearly missed seeing a tackle by Sasha that sent the ball forward to Carrie, who took a quick shot. It was a couple of feet wide, but it still had the sold-out crowd on their feet, screaming and cheering. Her excitement was short-lived when she saw the male officer appear at the tunnel entrance. *I wish it were as easy to let her go as it was to fall for her,* she sighed inwardly, knowing deep down that wasn't true.

Turning her focus back to the game, she yelled, "Let's go, Richey!" as her team battled in the box on a corner kick, which connected perfectly with Carrie's head and landed in the back of the net for a goal. Randi threw both fists in the air above her head and jumped up out of her seat, screaming and yelling with the fans around her. She was in the team's box seats, but there were fans all around. Some of which she'd signed autographs for and had taken photos with before the game.

She hated not being on the field. Sitting in the stands on a red card was like sitting in the timeout chair while all of your friends got to play in the sandbox. But, as much as she hated it, she had to make the best of it. She was there and it was the last game of the season. They were headed to the playoffs in a couple of weeks.

*

"I stopped you because you rolled through the stop sign, not because you have barely enough weed in this bag to make a decent joint," Berkley said, shaking her head. "If I came down hard on every stop I made where less than an ounce of marijuana was involved, I'd do nothing but waste my time writing tickets." She handed his license to him after the check came back clear. Everything was valid and there were no warrants in his name.

"South 5—273D in progress; 651 Egret's Landing. Multiple units in the area, please respond," the dispatcher radioed, calling for two to three officers to head over to a domestic disturbance involving a husband and wife.

"459—responding; ETA two minutes," Curt radioed.

"You're free to go. If I stop you again with weed, you're going to jail," Berkley said, walking away from the man she had stopped on the side of the road. "327—responding," she radioed as she got into her car and raced off to go back him up. As soon as she'd heard the address, she knew it was Garrett's area and Curt would be taking the call. She drove as fast as she could with the lights and sirens wailing. Domestic calls could be as simple as an argument or as bad as husband beating the snot out of his wife. She'd seen them both more times than she cared to count.

Curt was already on scene when she pulled up behind him. "What do we have?" she asked, getting out with her hand resting on her gun.

"She says its nothing, but the neighbor witnessed her husband slap her across the face when they got out of his truck," he replied, nodding towards a blonde woman standing a few feet away.

"Where is he now?"

"She says he isn't home."

"Did you check the residence?"

"No. She came outside as soon as I pulled up."

"327—clear channel," she radioed. "Ma'am, where is your husband?" Berkley asked walking over to her.

"I swear he isn't here," she urged. "Please, just leave."

"Are you sure? Someone saw him arrive home with you," Berkley said. "Maybe he's inside and you're afraid of him. We're not going to let him hurt you."

"He's not in there."

"Good, then you won't have an issue with me looking around inside," Berkley said as she began to walk away from her.

Suddenly, the front door swung open and a loud pop from a gunshot echoed. "Get off my property!" an angry man snarled as the woman screamed.

Curt dove behind the man's truck and pulled his gun, firing over the bed of it and hitting him square in the chest. "Ward!" he yelled, looking around for her as he ran back around the truck.

"Oh, my God! Oh, my God!" the woman was screaming.

Berkley was lying on the ground nearby with a hole in the front of her uniform. Curt ran to her side. "Can you hear me?" he said as he ran his hand around to see if she was bleeding. She'd been wearing her vest, which had stopped the bullet, but not before it had caused enough pain for her to blackout. "459—11-99!" he yelled into the mic on his shoulder. "Officer down! I repeat, officer down. Ward has been shot! Suspect is deceased."

"Copy—459. EMS has been dispatched to your location," Dispatch radioed.

"601—459, I'm en route," Lieutenant Cooper radioed.

Curt cuffed the woman and put her in the back of his car, then went back to Berkley, who was still lying unconscious on her back. The man who had shot her was lying half in the house and half on the stairs with a huge red dot in the center of his shirt and blood seeping out from underneath him.

"Berkley? Rescue is on the way. Can you hear me?" He knew she was breathing, but it was shallow, raspy breaths, almost like she was struggling to get air.

Several of the neighbors had come outside in time to see the ambulance come skidding to a stop. Two male paramedics jumped out and rushed up the driveway with equipment bags and the stretcher. One of them unzipped her uniform shirt, revealing her vest. A silver circle showed the location of the bullet and what was left of it after impacting the material. He quickly opened the straps on the sides and folded it up over her head while the other medic started an IV line in her arm.

"Her lung is collapsed," the first guy said after listening to her chest. "We need to get moving."

"Does he need assistance?" one of them asked, looking up at the man in the doorway of the house as he grabbed the backboard off the stretcher and held it to the side so they could roll her onto it.

"He's dead," Curt said as he helped them remove her vest completely.

Then, they strapped her down and wheeled her to the waiting ambulance. It took all of one minute for them to get settled and head down the road with the lights and sirens wailing, just as the lieutenant pulled up.

*

Randi met the team in the locker room after the game ended. "Great win, ladies!" she said, high-fiving everyone. "Now, it's on to the playoffs!"

"We missed you out there," Carrie said.

"Trust me, sitting in the stands nearly drove me crazy. I don't plan on doing that again," Randi replied before turning to Olivia. "That save was unbelievable."

"Thanks," she said.

"Save of the week for sure," Sasha added.

"Hey, anyone else have breaking news on their phone?" one of the other players asked as she went over to the TV.

"I left mine in the car," Randi said. "I wasn't carrying my cleat bag and I usually put it in there."

"Oh, my God!" Sasha yelled.

Randi turned towards the TV to see the words scrolling across the bottom. *Female SWAT Officer with Richey Police Department shot while on duty. Currently in critical condition at Richey General. No further details at this time.*

"No," she whispered, shaking her head.

"She needs you," Olivia said softly, placing her hand on Randi's back.

Randi turned her head, looking at her.

Olivia simply nodded in understanding.

Randi wiped a tear from her cheek as she ran out of the locker room.

*

"When can we see her?" Garrett asked the desk clerk.

"Right now, it's only family members," she replied, looking out at the multiple police officers crowding the waiting room.

"I'm sure they will let us know something soon," Dena said, squeezing his hand.

"If I had been there–"

"Babe, you don't know what happened. Don't do this to yourself. She wouldn't want that."

"I know. I'm just pissed. I should've been with her."

"You were sick."

"She's right, Tomayo," Lieutenant Cooper said, walking by with a cup of coffee in his hand.

Garrett nodded, then jumped up when he saw Randi rushing into the room.

*

Cops littered the waiting area for the emergency room as Randi walked briskly inside. "Can you give me an update on Berkley Ward?"

"We're only allowing family members at this time," the woman said, sounding like a broken record.

"That's her fiancée," Garrett said, walking over.

"Huh?" Randi gave him an odd look.

He winked at her.

"Oh, right. Yes, I'm her fiancée. I play for the Richey FC soccer team. Our game just ended. I ran out so fast, I forgot my ring," she said.

"Alright," the woman replied, getting her name for the computer. Then, she gave her a sticker to put on her shirt as her pass to get into the room. "Go through the double doors and take a left. She's in room two."

Randi turned around and looked at Garrett.

He nodded.

The entire room watched in confusion as she went through the open double doors and disappeared when they closed behind her.

*

"Hi, I'm Doctor Yuri. She's stable. The bullet was stopped by her vest, but the force of the impact broke two ribs and collapsed her right lung. She'll need to stay overnight so we can make sure the lung doesn't go down again. I believe she'll go home sometime tomorrow."

"Um…okay," she mumbled nervously. "Can I see her?"

"Sure. She's right through there," he pointed. "Don't worry, she's fine."

"Can you please tell them what you just said to me?" she pointed down the hall to the double doors. "Her entire department is pacing the waiting room."

"Yes, ma'am. We were waiting for her family to arrive. I'll go speak with them right now."

Randi opened the door and stepped into the brightly lit room. Berkley was lying on the bed, still in the lower half of her uniform. Her uniform top was completely gone and her black, drift undershirt was cut in half, but pulled somewhat closed, revealing her black sports bra through the opening. An IV line came out of her right arm and an oxygen tube was in her nose. She appeared to be sleeping until her lids fluttered and bright blue eyes zeroed in on Randi as she stepped up next to the bed, grabbing her left hand.

"Hey, you," Berkley said softly as her mouth formed a thin smile.

"I'm so sorry," Randi whispered.

"Why? You didn't shoot me."

"I should've called you. I picked the phone up so many times."

"I was about to come see you at the game on my lunch break until all of this happened. I should be the one saying I'm sorry. Our last conversation…"

"I moved into an apartment last weekend," Randi said, cutting her off. "It's my first time living alone, but so far, it's not bad."

"That's great."

"I know I haven't said anything on social media about the breakup, but that's because I wasn't ready to deal with tens of thousands of questions and comments from my followers. I guess I needed some time to find myself."

"Randi, I'm sorry if I made you feel like you needed to do all of this."

"You may have made me think about it, but I pushed myself. I plan on taking some time off…away from soccer after the playoffs and championship, if we get that far."

"So, when is the big day?" the nurse asked, walking into the room to check Berkley's vitals, specifically her oxygen level.

"Huh?" Berkley muttered.

"We haven't set the date yet, but we're thinking this winter," Randi answered.

"Oh, I love winter white weddings. They're so pretty. Congratulations. Anyway, your numbers look great. I'll update Dr. Yuri."

When the nurse left the room, Berkley raised a brow and stared at Randi.

"I had to tell them I was your fiancée to get in here."

"Oh, really?" Berkley grinned.

"Garrett actually told them. I just went along with it."

"I see."

"I probably looked like a scared animal when I came running in. I had no idea how bad it was. All I knew was you'd been shot." Randi wiped a tear from her cheek. "I've never been so scared in my life. I thought I…" She paused when her voice cracked. "I thought I was going to lose you before I could tell you I love you."

Berkley squeezed her hand.

"I know things have been a mess with us—"

"I love you, too," Berkley said.

"Really?"

"More than anything."

Randi smiled and bent her head to kiss her. Berkley's lips parted hers, allowing their tongues to collide in a sensual kiss that left them both wanting more.

"Uh oh, none of that. At least until your lung function is back to normal," Dr. Yuri chided with a smile. "You'll be discharged in the morning. I'm going to keep an eye on you tonight, but I think you'll be fine. Besides, you have this beautiful woman to take care of you when you get home."

"I'm going to do that, you know," Randi said as he left the room. "Take care of you," she added.

"Promise?" Berkley teased.

"Oh, yeah," Randi smiled.

"Good, now tell me again how much you love me."

Randi bent her head. "I'm...madly...in...love...with...you...Berkley...Ward," she said, kissing Berkley's lips playfully between each word.

About the Author

Graysen Morgen is the bestselling author of several bestselling lesfic titles. She was born and raised in North Florida with winding rivers and waterways at her back door, as well as, the white sandy beach. She has spent most of her lifetime in the sun and on the water. She enjoys reading, writing, fishing, coaching and watching soccer, and spending as much time as possible with her wife and their daughter.

You can contact Graysen at graysenmorgen@aol.com; like her fan page on Facebook.com/graysenmorgen; follow her on Twitter: @graysenmorgen and Instagram: @graysenmorgen

Other Titles Available From Triplicity Publishing

Rebel Sweetheart by Sydney Canyon. When a headstrong, country music superstar starts getting threatening letters while on tour, her manager has no other choice but to hire someone to investigate the threats, and keep her safe. Haley Nielsen is as stubborn as it gets. She does things her way, and her way only. The last thing she needs or wants is a babysitter following her every move and controlling everything she does. Shane Crowley isn't your typical private investigator, or bodyguard, for that matter. She's a former U.S. Deputy Marshal with a lot of experience, and an all or nothing attitude. Tempers flare and the energy burns red hot between the two women as they spend weeks together cooped up on Haley's tour bus, traveling the country. Will they stop resisting each other long enough to see eye to eye? Or will the letter writer make good on his threats?

A tale of Spiders and Canned Soup by Kathy L. Salt. Living on your own can be hard, but even more so when you're dealing with haphephobia; the death of a twin sister; and a crush on your teacher. Mika is still in contact with her foster family who homes the loves of her life, three young children she would do anything for, when she begins attending University of Aberdeen and meets Pauline, an Australian that teaches Viking history. Neither woman is used to breaking the rules, and their way to each other is a hard one, especially when Mika vows to get custody of the children, whether she is ready to be a parent or not. *A story about growing up. A story about dealing with grief. A story about Mika and Pauline.*

A Night Claimed by Domina Alexandra. Bonnie Collins had plans. And being a werewolf wasn't one of them. Attacked by a rogue who was out to claim her, and facing what she now has no choice of becoming, Bonnie can't let go of her human life as a Paramedic. The last thing Bonnie needs is more challenges. However, Rikki, the Alpha of Mill City will be just that. Finding her to be possessive and ruling, Bonnie begins challenging the Alpha's every breath. Finding out her attack was no accident only makes her more angry at the situation. A group of rogues are out to get her. With no clue why, Bonnie has no choice but to seek help from the alluring Alpha and her pack, accepting the new world she was forced into.

Stunted by Breanna Hughes. Professional stuntwoman Jessie Knight takes her job very seriously and although she works in the entertainment industry, she has zero desire for fame or notoriety. She also has a very strict no-dating policy when it comes to coworkers. That is, until, she meets famous actress Elliot Chase on the set of her new film. The adrenaline rush of the stunts is nothing compared to the sparks that fly between them. After a passionate night together, a sex tape is leaked that sends Jessie and Elliot's private and professional lives into a spiral. Will the fallout be too much for them to last? Or will they find a way out of the mess together?

Mission Compromised by Graysen Morgen. Natalia Moreno is thrilled when she arrives in Fiji for a relaxing vacation. However, she soon discovers the overwater bungalow she's staying in has been double booked for the entire stay, and the resort is full. Annoyed and frustrated, she has no other choice but to share her hut with a stranger. Christian Garnier is sent to Fiji for what she refers to as a working vacation, until she finds out she has an ornery roommate for the next two weeks who is dead set on making her job twice as hard. Soon, all hell breaks loose and the two women are sent around the world on a wild goose chase.

Stargazing by Kathy L. Salt. Lissa stared open-mouthed at the GIF that played over and over on the screen in front of her. Heat flushed to her face, igniting her skin. Her heart started pounding in her chest. *Stupid internet, it should really come with a warning label.* She's never been interested in relationships or sex and as the years have gone by she has retreated more and more into her work. Everything changes when she meets Star, a porn actress with a heart of gold and a troubled childhood. *They say that opposites attract, but how much of that is true? What chance do they have when one of them is a virgin and the other one star in pornography?*

I Belong with Her by Domina Alexandra. Tajel Pierce loves the thrill of being a paramedic. Every call she goes on gives her a rush. She makes no time for a personal life. No one can ruin her love for her career. Then there is Arianna Castaldi, who just transferred to her new paramedic position in a whole new state. All she needs is a new start without any distractions. Arianna and Tajel's relationship doesn't start off perfect. Embarrassed of the one night stand Arianna believes she had with Tajel, she wants to pretend they never met and make their relationship strictly business. The only choice they have to keep from strangling each other is to go from denying their feelings to accepting them as they work through intense 911 calls.

Awakened by Fate by Lynn Lawler. Jackie is a woman living life according to her own rules. She's married, but it's the unspoken, open kind. She can have as many female lovers as she likes; she just can't talk about them. After a bizarre encounter turns her world upside down, things slowly begin to change. She finds herself in desperation as she searches for answers. What she discovers is nothing is delivered in a neatly wrapped box. Now that everything has been brought out into the open, she finds she can't run away from her truth anymore. With her new life, comes new responsibilities and a different outcome than what she was expecting. Jackie isn't alone in the story. She meets several new people who help her along her journey.

Nautical Delights by S. L. Gape. Lady Elizabeth Barrington has spent her entire life trying to please her family; constantly opting for a quiet life, she utilises her profession as a doctor to keep out of her families' clutches; bar the annual two-week Caribbean private cruise, where there is simply no budge. Confined to two weeks on board the Iconica super yacht, she intends on keeping her head down and enjoying as much of the holiday as she can, whilst keeping her family at arm's length. Until a crew member catches her eye.

Worlds Apart by S.L. Gape. Hollywood A-lister Heidi Spencer-Brady is everything you'd expect of an Idol. Loved by all, the British Beauty is graceful, talented, humble and so far removed from the 'typical' LA scene. When her husband's infidelity with his new 'leading lady' is leaked, Dawn, Heidi's best friend and manager, goes all out to protect her. She arranges for Heidi to go back to the UK and stay on her cousins farm they had visited as children, much to the disappointment of the animal fearing Heidi.

Castor Valley (Law & Order Series Book 2) by Graysen Morgen. Jessie Henry is torn when she reads about the capture of the Doyle brothers, two young men who were part of her old gang. Unable to let them hang for a crime she's sure they didn't commit, Jessie leaves her wife and the Town of Boone Creek behind, and sets out on a journey back to the one place she thought she'd never see again, *Castor Valley*. Ellie Henry watches the love of her life leave, not knowing if she will ever return. When she gets an odd telegram, nearly a week later, she fears Jessie is in trouble. With no other choice, she goes to the one person who can help her.

Fight to the Top by S. L. Gape. Georgia is a forty year old, single, Area Director from Manchester, UK who is all work and definitely no play. Having no time to socialise or spend time with her family she prides herself on being fit and well-polished. Erika is an Area Director for the same company, but in the United States. Whilst she is concentrating so heavily on the promotion she has been fighting for, she's starting to feel like her life outside of work is falling apart. The two women are exceptionally different, and worlds apart. Both of their lives are turned upside down when their jobs are snatched from under their noses, and they are suddenly faced with being thrown together by their bosses for one last major project...in Texas.

Boone Creek (Law & Order Series book 1) by Graysen Morgen. Jessie Henry is looking for a new life. She's unknown in the town of Boone Creek when she arrives, and wants to keep it that way. When she's offered the job of Town Marshal, she takes it, believing that protecting others and upholding the law is the penance for her past. Ellie Fray is a widowed, shopkeeper. She generally keeps to herself, but the mysterious new Town Marshal both intrigues and infuriates her. She believes the last thing the town needs is someone stirring up trouble with the outlaws who have taken over.

Witness by Joan L. Anderson. Becca and Kate have lived together for eight years, and have always spent their vacation in a tropical paradise, lying on a beach. This year, Becca wanted to try something different: a seven day, 65-mile hike in the beautiful Cascade Mountains of Washington state. Their peaceful vacation turns to horror when they stumble upon a brutal murder taking place in the back country.

Too Soon by S.L. Gape. Brooke is a twenty-nine year old detective from Oxford, who has her life pretty much planned out until her boss and partner of nine years, Maria, tells her their relationship is over. When Brooke finds out the truth, that Maria cheated on her with their best friend Paula, she decides to get her life back on track by getting away for six weeks in Anglesey, North Wales. Chloe, a thirty three year old artist and art director, owns a log cabin on Anglesey where she spends each weekend painting and surfing. After returning from a surf, she stumbles upon the somewhat uptight and enigmatic Brooke.

Never Quit (Never Series book 2) by Graysen Morgen. Two years after stepping away from the action as a Coast Guard Rescue Swimmer to become an instructor, Finley finds herself in charge of the most difficult class of cadets she's ever faced, while also juggling the taxing demands of having a home life with her partner Nicole, and their fifteen year old daughter. Jordy Ross gave up everything, dropping out of college, and leaving her family behind, to join the Coast Guard and become a rescue swimmer cadet. The extreme training tests her fitness level, pushing her mentally and physically further than she's ever been in her life, but it's the aggressive competition between her and another female cadet that proves to be the most challenging.

Never Let Go (Never Series book 1) by Graysen Morgen. For Coast Guard Rescue Swimmer, Finley Morris, life is good. She loves her job, is well respected by her peers, and has been given an opportunity to take her career to the next level. The only thing missing is the love of her life, who walked out, taking their daughter with her, seven years earlier. When Finley gets a call from her ex, saying their teenage daughter is coming to spend the summer with her, she's floored. While spending more time with her daughter, whom she doesn't get to see often, and learning to be a full-time parent, Finley quickly realizes she has not, and will never, let go of what is important.

Pursuit by Joan L. Anderson. Claire is a workaholic attorney who flies to Paris to lick her wounds after being dumped by her girlfriend of seventeen years. On the plane she chats with the young woman sitting next to her, and when they land the woman is inexplicably detained in Customs. Claire is surprised when she later runs into the woman in the city. They agree to meet for breakfast the next morning, but when the woman doesn't show up Claire goes to her hotel and makes a horrifying discovery. She soon finds herself ensnared in a web of intrigue and international terrorism, becoming the target of a high stakes game of cat and mouse through the streets of Paris.

Wrecked by Sydney Canyon. To most people, the *Duchess* is a myth formed by old pirates tales, but to Reid Cavanaugh, a Caribbean island bum and one of the best divers and treasure hunters in the world, it's a real, seventeenth century pirate ship—the holy grail of underwater treasure hunting. Reid uses the same cunning tactics she always has before setting out to find the lost ship. However, she is forced to bring her business partner's daughter along as collateral this time because he doesn't trust her. Neither woman is thrilled, but being cooped up on a small dive boat for days, forces them to get know each other quickly.

Arson by Austen Thorne. Madison Drake is a detective for the Stetson Beach Police Department. The last thing she wants to do is show a new detective the ropes, especially when a fire investigation becomes arson to cover up a murder. Madison butts heads with Tara, her trainee, deals with sarcasm from Nic, her ex-girlfriend who is a patrol officer, and finds calm in the chaos of police work with Jamie, her best friend who is the county medical examiner. Arson is the first of many in a series of novella episodes surrounding the fictional Stetson Beach Police Department and Detective Madison Drake.

***Mommies (Bridal Series book 3)* by Graysen Morgen.** Britton and her wife Daphne have been married for a year and a half and are happy with their life, until Britton's mother hounds her to find out why her sister Bridget hasn't decided to have children yet. This prompts Daphne to bring up the big subject of having kids of their own with Britton. Britton hadn't really thought much about having kids, but her love for Daphne makes her see life and their future together in a whole new way when they decide to become mommies.

***Rapture & Rogue* by Sydney Canyon.** Taren Rauley is happy and in a good relationship, until the one person she thought she'd never see again comes back into her life. She struggles to keep the past from colliding with the present as old feelings she thought were dead and gone, begin to haunt her. In college, Gianna Revisi was a mastermind, ring-leading, crime boss. Now, she has a great life and spends her time running Rapture and Rogue, the two establishments she built from the ground up. The last person she ever expects to see walk into one of them, is the girl who walked out on her, breaking her heart five years ago.

***Second Chance* by Sydney Canyon.** After an attack on her convoy, Marine Corps Staff Sergeant, Darien Hollister, must learn to live without her sight. When an experimental procedure allows her to see again, Darien is torn, knowing someone had to die in order for this to happen. She embarks on a journey to personally thank the donor's family, but is too stunned to tell them the truth. Mixed emotions stir inside of her as she slowly gets to the know the people that feel like so much more than strangers to her. When the truth finally comes out, Darien walks away, taking the second chance that she's been given to go back to the only life she's ever known, but she's not the only one with a second chance at life.

Meant to Be by Graysen Morgen. Brandt is about to walk down the aisle with her girlfriend, when an unexpected chain of events turns her world upside down, causing her to question the last three years of her life. A chance encounter sparks a mix of rage and excitement that she has never felt before. Summer is living life and following her dreams, all the while, harboring a huge secret that could ruin her career. She believes that some things are better kept in the dark, until she has her third run-in with a woman she had hoped to never see again, and gives into temptation. Brandt and Summer start believing everything happens for a reason as they learn the true meaning of meant to be.

Coming Home by Graysen Morgen. After tragedy derails TJ Abernathy's life, she packs up her three year old son and heads back to Pennsylvania to live with her grandmother on the family farm. TJ picks back up where she left off eight years earlier, tending to the fruit and nut tree orchard, while learning her grandmother's secret trade. Soon, TJ's high school sweetheart and the same girl who broke her heart, comes back into her life, threatening to steal it away once again. As the weeks turn into months and tragedy strikes again, TJ realizes coming home was the best thing she could've ever done.

Special Assignment by Austen Thorne. Secret Service Agent Parker Meeks has her hands full when she gets her new assignment, protecting a Congressman's teenage daughter, who has had threats made on her life and been whisked away to a Christian boarding school under an alias to finish out her senior year. Parker is fine with the assignment, until she finds out she has to go undercover as a Canon Priest. The last thing Parker expects to find is a beautiful, art history teacher, who is intrigued by her in more ways than one.

Miracle at Christmas by Sydney Canyon. A Modern Twist on the Classic Scrooge Story. Dylan is a power-hungry lawyer who pushed away everything good in her life to become the best defense attorney in the, often winning the worst cases and keeping anyone with enough money out of jail. She's visited on Christmas Eve by her deceased law partner, who threatens her with a life in hell like his own, if she doesn't change her path. During the course of the night, she is taken on a journey through her past, present, and future with three very different spirits.

Bella Vita by Sydney Canyon. Brady is the First Officer of the crew on the Bella Vita, a luxury charter yacht in the Caribbean. She enjoys the laidback island lifestyle, and is accustomed to high profile guests, but when a U.S. Senator charters the yacht as a gift to his beautiful twin daughters who have just graduated from college and a few of their friends, she literally has her hands full.

Brides (Bridal Series book 2) by Graysen Morgen. Britton Prescott is dating the love of her life, Daphne Attwood, after a few tumultuous events that happened to unravel at her sister's wedding reception, seven months earlier. She's happy with the way things are, but immense pressure from her family and friends to take the next step, nearly sends her back to the single life. The idea of a long engagement and simple wedding are thrown out the window, as both families take over, rushing Britton and Daphne to the altar in a matter of weeks.

Cypress Lake by Graysen Morgen. The small town of Cypress Lake is rocked when one murder after another happens. Dani Ricketts, the Chief Deputy for the Cypress Lake Sheriff's Office, realizes the murders are linked. She's surprised when the girl that broke her heart in high school has not only returned home, but she's also Dani's only suspect. Kristen Malone has come back to Cypress Lake to put the past behind her so that she can move on with her life. Seeing Dani Ricketts again throws her off-guard, nearly derailing her plans to finally rid herself and her family of Cypress Lake.

Crashing Waves by Graysen Morgen. After a tragic accident, Pro Surfer, Rory Eden, spends her days hiding in the surf and snowboard manufacturing company that she built from the ground up, while living her life as a shell of the person that she once was. Rory's world is turned upside when a young surfer pursues her, asking for the one thing she can't do. Adler Troy and Dr. Cason Macauley from Graysen Morgen's bestselling novel: *Falling Snow*, make an appearance in this romantic adventure about life, love, and letting go.

Bridesmaid of Honor (Bridal Series book 1) by Graysen Morgen. Britton Prescott's best friend is getting married and she's the maid of honor. As if that isn't enough to deal with, Britton's sister announces she's getting married in the same month and her maid of honor is her best friend Daphne, the same woman who has tormented Britton for years. Britton has to suck it up and play nice, instead of scratching her eyes out, because she and Daphne are in both weddings. Everyone is counting on them to behave like adults.

Falling Snow by Graysen Morgen. Dr. Cason Macauley, a high-speed trauma surgeon from Denver meets Adler Troy, a professional snowboarder and sparks fly. The last thing Cason wants is a relationship and Adler doesn't realize what's right in front of her until it's gone, but will it be too late?

Fate vs. Destiny by Graysen Morgen. Logan Greer devotes her life to investigating plane crashes for the National Transportation Safety Board. Brooke McCabe is an investigator with the Federal Aviation Association who literally flies by the seat of her pants. When Logan gets tangled in head games with both women will she choose fate or destiny?

Just Me by Graysen Morgen. Wild child Ian Wiley has to grow up and take the reins of the hundred year old family business when tragedy strikes. Cassidy Harland is a little surprised that she came within an inch of picking up a gorgeous stranger in a bar and is shocked to find out that stranger is the new head of her company.

Love Loss Revenge by Graysen Morgen. Rian Casey is an FBI Agent working the biggest case of her career and madly in love with her girlfriend. Her world is turned upside when tragedy strikes. Heartbroken, she tries to rebuild her life. When she discovers the truth behind what really happened that awful night she decides justice isn't good enough, and vows revenge on everyone involved.

Natural Instinct by Graysen Morgen. Chandler Scott is a Marine Biologist who keeps her private life private. Corey Joslen is intrigued by Chandler from the moment she meets her. Chandler is forced to finally open her life up to Corey. It backfires in Corey's face and sends her running. Will either woman learn to trust her natural instinct?

Secluded Heart by Graysen Morgen. Chase Leery is an overworked cardiac surgeon with a group of best friends that have an opinion and a reason for everything. When she meets a new artist named Remy Sheridan at her best friend's art gallery she is captivated by the reclusive woman. When Chase finds out why Remy is so sheltered will she put her career on the line to help her or is it too difficult to love someone with a secluded heart?

In Love, at War by Graysen Morgen. Charley Hayes is in the Army Air Force and stationed at Ford Island in Pearl Harbor. She is the commanding officer of her own female-only service squadron and doing the one thing she loves most, repairing airplanes. Life is good for Charley, until the day she finds herself falling in love while fighting for her life as her country is thrown haphazardly into World War II. Can she survive being in love and at war?

Fast Pitch by Graysen Morgen. Graham Cahill is a senior in college and the catcher and captain of the softball team. Despite being an all-star pitcher, Bailey Michaels is young and arrogant. Graham and Bailey are forced to get to know each other off the field in order to learn to work together on the field. Will the extra time pay off or will it drive a nail through the team?

Submerged by Graysen Morgen. Assistant District Attorney Layne Carmichael had no idea that the sexy woman she took home from a local bar for a one night stand would turn out to be someone she would be prosecuting months later. Scooter is a Naval Officer on a submarine who changes women like she changes uniforms. When she is accused of a heinous crime she is shocked to see her latest conquest sitting across from her as the prosecuting attorney.

Vow of Solitude by Austen Thorne. Detective Jordan Denali is in a fight for her life against the ghosts from her past and a Serial Killer taunting her with his every move. She lives a life of solitude and plans to keep it that way. When Callie Marceau, a curious Medical Examiner, decides she wants in on the biggest case of her career, as well as, Jordan's life, Jordan is powerless to stop her.

Igniting Temptation by Sydney Canyon. Mackenzie Trotter is the Head of Pediatrics at the local hospital. Her life takes a rather unexpected turn when she meets a flirtatious, beautiful fire fighter. Both women soon discover it doesn't take much to ignite temptation.

One Night by Sydney Canyon. While on a business trip, Caylen Jarrett spends an amazing night with a beautiful stripper. Months later, she is shocked and confused when that same woman re-enters her life. The fact that this stranger could destroy her career doesn't bother her. C.J. is more terrified of the feelings this woman stirs in her. Could she have fallen in love in one night and not even known it?

Fine by Sydney Canyon. Collin Anderson hides behind a façade, pretending everything is fine. Her workaholic wife and best friend are both oblivious as she goes on an emotional journey, battling a potentially hereditary disease that her mother has been diagnosed with. The only person who knows what is really going on, is Collin's doctor. The same doctor, who is an acquaintance that she's always been attracted to, and who has a partner of her own.

Shadow's Eyes by Sydney Canyon. Tyler McCain is the owner of a large ranch that breeds and sells different types of horses. She isn't exactly thrilled when a Hollywood movie producer shows up wanting to film his latest movie on her property. Reegan Delsol is an up and coming actress who has everything going for her when she lands the lead role in a new film, but there one small problem that could blow the entire picture.

Light Reading: A Collection of Novellas by Sydney Canyon. Four of Sydney Canyon's novellas together in one book, including the bestsellers Shadow's Eyes and One Night.

Visit us at www.tri-pub.com